Perfect
Secrets

Perfect Secrets

BRENDA JOYCE
KATHLEEN KANE
JUDITH O'BRIEN
DELIA PARR

St. Martin's Paperbacks

PERFECT SECRETS

"When Dreams Won't Die" copyright © 1999 by Brenda Joyce Dreams Unlimited, Inc.
"The Return of Travis Dean" copyright © 1999 by Kathleen Kane.
"Across a Crowded Room" copyright © 1999 by Judith O'Brien.
"Redemption" copyright © 1999 by Mary Lechleidner.
Excerpt from *The Third Heiress* copyright © 1999 by Brenda Joyce Dreams Unlimited, Inc.

ISBN: 0-312-97029-3

Printed in the United States of America

St. Martin's Paperbacks edition/August 1999

10 9 8 7 6 5 4 3 2 1

Contents

When Dreams Won't Die

BRENDA JOYCE

This novella is dedicated to Daniele Pereira for her kindness, compassion, and loyalty. With love, always.

Prologue

*T*here it was. The house on the hill.

Blair slowed, coasting to a stop on her shiny red bicycle, wisps of hair escaping from her two thick braids to stick like glue to her dampened face. It was a warm, early-spring day, and all around her, the trees were as green and lush as the fields and pastures, with wildflowers sprouting up everywhere. And suddenly, Blair was afraid.

What had she been thinking of, to ride her bike all the way out there just so she could see Rick's house?

If her grandmother found out, she would probably be grounded for an entire week.

Blair stared up the hill, unable to look away, her heart racing, wishing she were inside that house, which to her seemed as imposing and remote as a storybook castle. There was a dirt driveway in front of her, winding up to the house through a series of fenced-in pastures. Behind Blair, most of the land was wooded, although Grandma said Rick owned the land as far as an eyeball could see. Ahead and to Blair's right a couple of old, swaybacked horses grazed. Blair didn't notice them. She stood with the April sunshine bathing her back and bare arms, wondering what it must be like to live there, wishing desperately that Rick had married her mother so that the three of them could be living up there on that hill together.

And the truth was, the last time she had seen the house, it had been from the road, passing by in Grandma's 1965

Ford pickup with the souped-up 360 V8 engine, with Dana at the wheel, complaining about the car and the summer heat. Dana liked to drive fast, and they'd sped by so quickly that Blair had hardly glimpsed the huge stone ranch house sitting on top of the hill, lording it over the surrounding fields and pastures like a king over his subjects. But then, Dana was always moving, her life an endless series of motions—everything she did was fast, fast, and faster still.

Blair didn't want to think about her mother now. She wanted to imagine what it was like to live in that house with Rick. She bit her lip as she gazed at the house shimmering white and bright in the sun, but as hard as she tried, she just couldn't imagine coming home from school every day to the ranch. She couldn't imagine being on that front porch when Rick's helicopter settled down on the landing pad behind the house as he returned from his office in Dallas.

Blair was so immersed in her thoughts that she didn't hear the school bus until it was too late to jump on her bike and ride away. Suddenly the big yellow bus appeared on the road beside her, blocking her path. Blair was frozen, gripping the handlebars of her shiny new bike, which Rick had given her on her last birthday. Her hands were clammy.

The door had opened; a blond girl came down the steps in a beautiful short white sundress and red sandals, her hair tied back with a red ribbon. Four years older than Blair, she carried an armful of books—and she stopped dead in her tracks when she saw her.

Blair stared back.

The bus door closed and the school bus pulled back onto the road and drove off. "What are you doing here?" the blond girl asked rather curtly. Her eyes were blue—bluer even than the Texas sky that day.

Blair bit her lip, a bad habit Grandma was always trying to correct. "I was taking my new bike for a ride," she half-lied.

The girl stared. "I don't believe you," she said. She turned her back on Blair, went to the open gates that closed over the drive, and picked up a bike Blair had not noticed until then. It was a vivid pink, and as shiny as Blair's. But unlike Blair's, it was a slim, sleek English bike with gears and handbrakes; Blair's American-made bike suddenly seemed stout and babyish in comparison. Blair watched her sister get on the bike and pedal up the drive without even glancing back over her shoulder.

Suddenly a sadness Blair couldn't identify came over her. It was so heavy, like a big old wool comforter that just couldn't be kicked off in the middle of the night. She slowly picked up her bike, wondering why Faith and her mother lived with Rick up there on the hill, wondering why she and Dana lived with Grandma down in town. Confusion overcame her, not for the first time. It just made no sense. How come Rick had never married Dana? How could Rick have two daughters, but one wife? Didn't a man and a lady have to be married to have children in the first place? That was what Grandma always said.

Blair began the trip home, riding far more slowly than she had when she'd begun her journey, still sad and even sorry that she had come. Worse, she had misjudged the distance to Rick's, because by the time she was at the halfway point on the highway at old man Potter's garage, she realized by looking at the sun in the sky that it was already suppertime—which was five-thirty—and she was going to be late. Grandma would be so angry that Blair couldn't even imagine it.

When Blair finally turned into her street, the first thing she saw was a blue station wagon with the words "Ron's Limousine Service" on its doors sitting in the drive of her grandma's house. Blair suddenly slowed pedaling, her heart beginning to pound in her chest. As she turned into the drive and slipped off the bike, she saw two beat-up suitcases on the front porch and a Samsonite vanity case. Her heart careened, flipping wildly, and Blair froze.

The screen door swung open and Grandma rushed out. "Blair! Where have you been!" she cried, hurrying down the steps. "Oh, God, Richie said he saw you riding your bike on Cedar Avenue. Where did you go? I've been driving all over town looking for you.''

Blair hung her head, as her grandma paused before her, gripping her shoulders and then crushing her in an embrace. She was a tall, lean, gray-haired woman in a housedress. ''I'm sorry,'' Blair mumbled against her grandmother's chest. ''I went to see Rick's house.''

Blair felt Grandma stiffen, and as she released her, Blair looked up. ''Now, why on earth did you ever do such a thing?'' Grandma asked, no longer shouting and no longer scolding, her gaze direct but warm and questioning.

''I don't know,'' Blair whispered as the screen door swung open and shut again.

Blair and her grandma both turned as the most beautiful woman in the world stepped onto the porch. She had waist-length pitch-black hair and a perfect, slim body with just enough curves; but it was her face that was so arresting. Her cheekbones were high, her skin tawny, her eyes dark, her brows black and slashing. Dana was wearing skin-tight jeans, red lizard cowboy boots, and a very small white halter top. Her long dark hair was parted arrow-straight down the middle. She carried a fringed buckskin jacket over one arm and wasn't wearing a stitch of makeup. She didn't have to. ''I'm going to miss my flight,'' she cried, rushing down the steps.

She saw Blair and stopped. ''Blair!'' she said, surprised. ''I thought you were out.''

Blair's heart was pounding so hard now that it hurt. She wanted to nod, but she couldn't seem to move her head.

''Well, at least we get to say good-bye.'' But even as Dana was talking to her daughter, she was looking at the cab as the tall, lanky bearded driver got out. It was impossible to miss the way he eyed Dana, but then, men always looked at her that way. And Dana was already asking him to get her bags, making sure he understood that all three of them were going with her to the county airport.

Blair couldn't even swallow, because there was this huge lump in her chest or throat or somewhere that felt as if it were choking her. She didn't feel as if she were breathing, either, and all in all, she felt sick.

"My flight leaves at seven, damn," Dana said. And then she snapped, "Oh, Mom, stop looking at me that way!"

Blair glanced from her gorgeous mother to her grandmother and saw that Grandma's face was pinched with disapproval and anger. "Have a pleasant trip," Grandma said, clearly not meaning it. She stepped closer to Blair, putting her arm around her.

"The two of you make me crazy!" Dana said with exasperation. "All that stone-faced disapproval. Loosen up! Blair, I'll call you soon and you can come visit. Would you like that?"

The pounding of her heart was deafening. Blair wanted to speak. She desperately wanted to say yes, because there was nothing she wanted more than to visit Dana in Los Angeles, but she couldn't get the words out, she was frozen, unable even to move.

Dana patted her head and rushed to the cab, jumping in. "As fast as you can," she told the driver. As the pale blue wagon drove away, Dana waved once. Her eyes were bright with excitement.

Blair watched it turn left on Cedar Avenue, and stared after it until she could no longer see it.

"Blair," Grandma said with false cheer, "I've made your very favorite supper for tonight. Fried chicken, my dear, with fried bananas—and I thought we'd go to Dairy Queen afterward for a big hot fudge sundae. What do you think?"

Blair faced her grandmother. "I'm not really hungry," she said.

Grandma's smile vanished. She looked close to tears. "Oh, dear." She bent over, brushing hair off Blair's forehead, stroking her cheek. "We have to talk, Blair. Come, let's go out back and sit down on the swing for a bit."

Blair couldn't even form a smile. "It's okay. I know she's not coming back."

Grandma did not move.

"I'm going to put my bike away now," Blair said, and she picked up the bike, which had somehow fallen over, and walked it slowly around the house to the shed that was out back.

Chapter One

*O*nce, Blair had sworn that she would never return home. It had been far more than a simple vow, for the pledge had been filled with guilt, despair and anger.

Blair felt all of eighteen again. Eighteen and lonely and vulnerable and afraid. And no matter how she reminded herself that she was a grown woman—and a successful one at that—those unwelcome feelings would not fade. She gripped the steering wheel of the rental car, hardly hearing her daughter, who was chattering away beside her. The sun beat down on the windshield of the Honda, making it hard to see the highway ahead, in spite of the dark glasses she wore, in spite of the fact that she should know this road by heart. But maybe the glare wasn't why she couldn't really see; maybe it was the tears that kept threatening to flood her eyes. Oh, God. Harmony, Texas, was just around the bend. But it wouldn't be the same. Charlotte's house had been sold five years ago when she passed on, Faith and Jake were married now, and Rick was dead.

Rick was dead. Her father, a king among mere men, the man she had always worshiped and admired more than anyone, was dead. Blair still didn't believe it. She couldn't believe it. Her father had been immortal, hadn't he? Bigger than life itself. When he had entered a room, he'd always dwarfed everyone present, and he hadn't even been particularly tall. When he spoke, not only had everyone listened, there had always been absolute silence in the wake of his words. There had been no one more in control of his destiny than Rick Hewitt. Or so she had always believed.

But Rick was dead.

If only Charlotte were alive to hold her and comfort her now.

"Mom, there's a town ahead. This is where you grew up? This place is way cool!" Lyndsay cried from the front seat beside Blair.

Blair realized that not only did she have a death grip on the steering wheel, she was sweating buckets—not just because of the midsummer humidity but her own sudden claustrophobia and the ceaseless fear. Rick was dead. Somehow, fate had caught up with him after all, but the concept remained incomprehensible. Blair knew she was in shock—and shock could only be her enemy now. Blair was afraid that fate was about to catch up to her and her daughter, as well.

"Mom! Is this Harmony?" Lyndsay demanded.

"Yes, this is where I grew up with your Grandma Charlotte," Blair said, forcing a lightness into her tone that belied the panic and heaviness inside her. Impulsively, she reached out to squeeze her daughter's hand. The one thing Lyndsay had always received in abundance from Blair was warmth, attention, and love.

"This place looks like a western movie," Lyndsay cried excitedly. "Can we drive by the house where you and Grandma grew up?"

Blair glanced at her daughter as they drove down Main Street. There was nothing and no one Blair loved more than her daughter, and even now, with tears trying to blur her vision, she smiled at the sight of Lyndsay in her trendy black flared pants, her chunky-heeled sandals, and her tiny T-shirt with the faces of the Spice Girls imprinted on its front and back. Lyndsay's short, blunt fingernails were painted a metallic blue, and they sparkled in the Texas sunlight. Lyndsay looked every bit the way hip, too cool, and too grown-up New York kid that she was.

"Honey, let's get up to the house. We can go by

Grandma's tomorrow.'' A little voice inside of Blair's head reminded her that tomorrow was the funeral. But Blair knew she could not handle seeing her old home now.

A siren sounded briefly somewhere behind them. Vaguely Blair heard it, but did not pay attention.

''How big is this place, anyway, Mom?'' Lyndsay asked, beaming, her short hair swinging around her face. ''I mean, look at this little town. It's probably smaller than Central Park!''

The siren shrieked again. Two loud, brief noises.

Blair froze, glanced in her rearview mirror, and saw the black-and-white car behind her. She could not believe her eyes.

''Are we getting a speeding ticket?'' Lyndsay asked just as Blair glanced down at her speedometer and saw she had been doing forty in a twenty-five-mile-an-hour zone.

''Apparently so.'' Blair pulled over, trying not to lose the little composure she had left, but this felt like the very last straw—she was about to burst into tears. The town's small public library, a two-story brick building located next to the sheriff's and mayor's offices with their western-style, false-front façades, was in front of them. Most of Main Street consisted of small shops with friendly signs hanging out front. Anyone who wanted to do some serious shopping would drive out Highway 82 to the mall.

''Oh, my God, he looks so mean,'' Lyndsay breathed.

Blair twisted to watch an officer from the sheriff's department slamming closed the door to his vehicle, a tall, broad-shouldered figure in his tan uniform, wearing a shoulder holster in plain sight. He strode over to them as Blair rolled down her window, a blast of hundred-degree heat hitting her in the face. He was wearing reflective sunglasses and Blair felt as if she were in a really lousy seventies movie. His expression was impossible to read.

''Officer, I'm sorry,'' she said before he could speak, removing her own sunglasses. She dug frantically into her purse for her driver's license.

''Ma'am, this is a twenty-five-mile-an-hour zone.''

Blair couldn't find her license and she dumped her purse out on the seat between her and Lyndsay. "I know," she said breathlessly. "I'm sorry. I'm so distracted—"

"Blair?"

Blair froze.

"Blair Anderson?"

Blair looked up at the officer as he removed his sunglasses, revealing very blue, very keen eyes. Then she looked at his face. He was sun-tanned, with high cheekbones, a Roman nose, and slashing black eyebrows. His jaw was square. He was tall, broad-shouldered, muscular. Did she know him? Then she met his gaze, and something tried to click somewhere in the depths of her mind.

He smiled. "Blair, I guess I shouldn't expect you to recognize me, it's been some time. Matt Ramsey."

Blair's eyes widened, as she tried to make the connection between this broad-shouldered, solidly built man and the gangling boy who had once tried to torture her as best he could. "Not the Matt Ramsey who slipped a live toad down my dress in church on Easter Sunday?"

He laughed. "Sorry, but that was me." His smile faded as he looked carefully at her.

Blair tensed. The look was frank. Like herself, he was trying to connect the past with the present, she knew. But she didn't want that connection made. She hadn't come home by choice.

Blair stepped out of the car. "I'm sorry about the speeding," she said, meaning it. He seemed taller than he'd been the last time she had seen him—the summer after her senior year in high school, when he'd been home for a visit and to attend the wedding.

He was staring at her knee-length beige jersey skirt. Or at her kitten-heeled slingbacks. It was hard to say. "You've changed," he remarked, taking in her white stretch tee, the muted coral lipstick. "The kid I knew wouldn't be caught dead out of jeans or overalls."

Blair folded her arms across her breasts. "I've been liv-

ing in New York these past years. A city will do tu
you."

His gaze met hers. "I heard. And I've seen you. You're
a television reporter." It wasn't a question. But his gaze had
now slid to Lyndsay.

"*Eyewitness News.*" The panic returned and escalated.

"You've done well for yourself, and I'm not surprised,"
Matt said. He looked at Lyndsay again.

Blair felt sick. "This is my daughter, Lyndsay. Lynn, I
grew up with Matt. We went to school together."

"Hi," Lyndsay said, smiling. "I hope you're not going
to give my mom a ticket. She didn't mean to speed. She's
really upset."

Matt just stared. Blair could feel his mind racing. She
knew, damn it, that he was doing some real fast math. So
Blair said, "I thought you went off to Yale, Matt, for a law
degree."

He smiled at Blair. "I did. Believe it or not, I was prac-
ticing in the Big Apple for about four years. Last year I took
down all those fancy plaques, packed my books and bags,
and came home. Got elected town sheriff last fall."

The irony of the situation was not lost on Blair.

"New York's a big town," he said, as if reading her
thoughts.

"It certainly is," Blair said.

"I'm sorry about your father."

Blair stiffened.

"Real sorry, Blair. He was a good man, well liked, well
respected. The whole town's feeling his loss."

Blair nodded. She couldn't speak. She was going to cry,
and she didn't want to, not in front of anyone, but especially
not in front of her daughter. Lyndsay had to be protected at
all costs.

"Are they expecting you?" Matt's baritone interrupted
her thoughts.

Blair met his gaze. "I think so." She knew he was referring to her half sister and Jake. "Rick's lawyer called last
night. Matt, I don't understand. I can't get over this. I mean,

ppen? Rick was born on a horse.''

ipped to her arm, the gesture simple and

ntly, Blair pulled away. He seemed to

g an autopsy,'' he said.

For one moment, Blair stared back at him, trying very hard to understand. ''An autopsy? The lawyer, he said something about a bobcat and Rick falling off his horse, hitting his head. It was an accident.''

''Like you said, Rick was born on a horse.''

Blair looked at him, and finally said, ''What are you saying?''

''Not much. Not now. Only that I'd like to do an autopsy.'' His glance held hers.

It was too much for Blair to digest. She slid back into the car; Matt closed her door. ''Slow down, okay?''

Blair nodded.

He leaned on it before she could drive away. ''It's good to have you back, Blair. I just wish it were under different circumstances.''

Blair bit her lip. What could she say? She hated being back, and the circumstances were tragic, unfair, horrendous. ''People change,'' she finally said, forcing a smile. ''Sometimes there's no coming back, no coming home.''

Matt stepped back from the car, unsmiling. And he looked at Lyndsay again, the question right there in his eyes.

Blair drove away.

The driveway had been paved. As Blair turned onto it, she wondered what else had changed.

''This is like *Dallas*,'' Lyndsay whispered, as the stone ranch house appeared at the top of the hill, a vast and sprawling structure surrounded by whitewashed stables and corrals and green lawns.

Blair knew she was referring to the television show that had been a hit in the late seventies and early eighties. Charlotte had adored it. ''You were too young to watch *Dallas*,'' Blair managed, very dry now, her heart racing in her chest. She dreaded the next few minutes, hours, days. She was afraid, more so now than ever. Soon, very soon, she must face Faith . . . and Jake.

There was a mantra inside her mind, one she kept repeating . . . No one would know, no one would guess. Not Faith, not Jake. Her secret was safe.

But now Matt Ramsey was on her mind, too, a man she hadn't thought about in years. He didn't know, he couldn't know, could he? But she kept recalling the way he had looked first at her and then at Lyndsay. She kept remembering how damn smart Matt had always been—smart enough to get into Yale on an "early decision" basis—and now she thought she remembered someone remarking that he'd gone to Georgetown Law, as well. Rick or Charlotte, it didn't matter who. Matt might guess—if he put his mind to it.

Blair was going to have to distract him, somehow.

"Rick was really rich," Lyndsay commented as Blair halted her car right in front of the house, beside a red convertible Mercedes. She assumed the flashy sports car belonged to Faith, but then, Jake had favored motorcycles as a boy, so who knew? She did not move, sat there staring at the front door of the house, willing herself to be calm, cool, composed—the new Blair, the New York professional, the Blair in the chic yet casual outfit, the Blair she hoped no one would recognize at first. Now was not the time to regress to being insecure, confused, a kid again.

"I can't believe I even have an aunt," Lyndsay said, wrinkling up her tiny nose. "I mean, don't you think you might have mentioned this to me before last night?"

"It didn't seem to matter." Blair tried to breathe normally. She tried to recall the lines she had rehearsed. "Hello, Faith, this is so terrible, I'm so sorry." And "Hello, Jake. It's good to see you again." Just like that, casual, indifferent, polite, as if they were mere acquaintances.

"But Mom, she's your sister," Lyndsay was saying. "Are we going inside?"

Blair couldn't find a response. The moment of reckoning was at hand. Lyndsay was already pushing open her door and jumping out. Blair followed slowly, her mouth terribly dry, her pulse sky high.

"Mom, you're as white as a ghost. Are you okay?" Lyndsay asked as they climbed the three front steps of the porch.

Blair inhaled. "This is so hard for me, Lyndsay." That much was the truth, and Blair just couldn't say any more.

"Mom, I loved him, too," Lyndsay said, assuming Blair was focused solely on Rick's death. "I'm so glad he came to see us in New York the way that he did. I just wish you'd let me visit him here, the way he always asked."

Blair felt the sweat dripping down her temples, pooling between her breasts. It was not a good idea to perspire in nylon and jersey. She could not form any reasonable reply, because Lyndsay didn't know the truth—and never would. But there had been no way in hell that Blair would ever let her daughter spend a summer vacation up at the Triple H. Never.

"I can't believe we're going to stay here," Lyndsay said, glancing around excitedly. "Maybe I'll even learn to *ride*."

Rick had been killed riding a horse. Blair shook herself free of Matt's odd statement about his wanting an autopsy. "We may have to stay at the hotel in town," she reminded her daughter. She hadn't spoken to Faith or Jake, and Faith's mother, Elizabeth, was out of the picture because she had Alzheimer's. She barely remembered the conversation she'd had with the lawyer, but undoubtedly he had conveyed to Faith that Blair was on her way. Yesterday remained a big blur.

A housemaid in a pale blue dress and white apron let them into the spacious, stone-floored foyer. Although the house had originally been decorated in a rustic and western style, as befitted a man who played at ranching as Rick had done—the family's wealth came from oil, and Rick had augmented it with another fortune based on computer chips—someone had redone it. Gone were the wood beams and Navajo rugs. Copper pillars held up the high ceilings in the foyer and living room, and modern furniture in textured fabrics and slick leathers had replaced the more mundane furnishings Blair recalled seeing when she was a child. As Blair glanced into the living room from the foyer where she stood, she suspected Faith had been the one who had redecorated. Once, the house had been warm and cozy. Now it was a dramatic showcase.

"Mom, this place is so cool," Lyndsay said in a hushed tone, walking over to a bronze sculpture of a nude woman that was twice her size.

The living room was to their right, stairs were to the left. A sound from the staircase made Blair turn, but not before her heart dropped like a rock.

Faith stood poised there, one hand on the iron banister, her eyes wide and shocked.

Blair began to breathe again, because, for one horrid moment, she had expected to see Jake.

"Blair?" Faith's wide blue gaze went from Blair to Lyndsay and back to Blair again.

Then the relief vanished. She had to stare, just as Faith was doing. Faith looked even better than she had the day of her wedding. She was tall and curved, a perfect size six, with her blond hair perhaps a shade lighter than it had once been. In a knee-length designer suit that matched her blue eyes exactly and a pair of high-heeled pumps, a huge diamond ring on her left hand, she was beautiful, elegant, stunning. She had not become fat and matronly at all.

"Hello, Faith," Blair said, as Lyndsay came back over to her. Blair resisted the urge to pull her daughter tightly to herself.

"Blair?" Faith came downstairs. Her expression changed, becoming stiff and set. "I almost didn't recognize you. You cut your hair."

Blair's hair was short, layered, with long pieces she tucked behind her ears. The cut had cost her a hundred dollars and was worth every penny. Her appearance was a part of her job. Millions of viewers in New York saw her every night on the five and six o'clock local news. "It's been a while," Blair said, thinking of Faith not as she now was, but as she'd been on her wedding day, radiant in a long, slim Caroline Herrera wedding dress, Jake never leaving her side, not once that entire day. The memory was still overpowering; it still made her ill.

"I didn't know you were coming," Faith said abruptly.

Blair blinked. "A lawyer called me last night. Williams, I think. We came as soon as we could."

Faith stared. "Tad Williams, Daddy's lawyer. I hadn't realized that he'd called you."

Blair's eyes widened. Did Faith mean that she'd had no intention of telling Blair that Rick was dead? That had to be impossible.

"We weren't expecting you," Faith said firmly, making it clear that Blair wasn't welcome.

Blair knew she must not allow the tears to come now. "I would never miss his funeral," she said.

Faith folded her arms, her eyes misting over. "The funeral was this morning."

Blair knew she had misheard. "What?"

"We buried him this morning."

Her heart began to thud. It felt like a huge drum beating painfully inside of her breast. And Matt hadn't said a thing. "How could you?" she whispered. "I needed to say goodbye, too."

"I told you, I didn't know you were coming," Faith said, with anger. "You left here eleven years ago. I haven't seen you since. It's not like we've been in touch. How the hell would I know that you were coming?" she cried. "This is a complete shock!" And she glanced directly at Lyndsay.

Distressed, Lyndsay stepped closer to Blair. Blair was so stunned and bewildered that she could not speak, or even think about what this confrontation might be costing her daughter.

The sound of a powerful engine being cut outside washed over them all.

Instinctively, Blair knew who that was, and she stiffened. She pulled Lyndsay close, hugging her hard, and turned to gaze out of the window.

A black Chevrolet Blazer was now parked beside her rental car. The windows were tinted, and Blair could only see the silhouette of the man inside, until the door swung open and the denim-clad driver stepped down from the cab.

Her heart slammed harder. There was no mistaking who it was.

Like Faith, he had not changed, not at all.

Jake Cutter strode up the front steps of the porch, disappearing for a split second from view, before entering the house. His gaze went right to Blair, where it riveted on her face. Unlike Faith, his eyes did not widen with surprise—he knew damn well who she was. He tipped up the Stetson he wore. "Blair. Good to see you." He smiled, a flash of white teeth in his naturally dark and sun-bronzed skin, and came right over to kiss her cheek, as if they were old friends.

But they had never been friends.

"I didn't know she was coming," Faith interrupted. "Did you?"

Jake turned. "Tad called her. It was my suggestion."

Faith stared at her husband. "You could have said something."

"Maybe I did. I don't remember." He was harsh. "It's been a helluva long night."

"You should have told me. I'm not prepared for this." Faith paced, her strides long and tense.

Jake turned away from her.

Blair's own tension increased. Was there trouble in their marriage, or was the shock of Rick's death the cause of their tension? She realized she'd been staring at Jake, and she tore her gaze away. "We'll go back to town and take lodging in the hotel." She spoke to Faith. "It'll be best for everyone. But I will go to the grave."

"You can stay here," Jake said flatly. Their gazes met. "We have plenty of room." His eyes strayed to Lyndsay.

Faith stared at Jake as if he'd lost his mind. "The guest rooms aren't ready," she said quickly, her eyes filling with tears. "Oh, God." She walked quickly away, to sit down in a huge leather chair in the living room, with her back to the foyer and everyone present there.

Jake did not go to her to comfort her.

Blair tried to feel sorry for Faith, but she couldn't. How could she? Faith had grown up with everything: this house, a real mother, Rick, and finally, Jake. Blair had nothing but her Grandma. And Blair recalled every single time she and Faith had passed one another in the halls at school, as children and teenagers, or in town. And it was easy to recall every moment, because they'd always been the same. With Faith pretending that she didn't know Blair, that Blair wasn't her half sister, that she didn't exist.

Blair couldn't find compassion for her. "We'll stay in town." Blair was firm. She told herself to stop glancing at Jake. To be cool, calm, casual. But it was easier said than done.

"You look like hell. At least stay here tonight. If you want to go to town in the morning, I'll take you myself." Jake's gaze locked with hers. "I would have picked you up at the airport if I'd known you were coming."

Blair found it even more difficult to breathe. Was there a hidden meaning behind his words? "I told Williams."

He shook his head. "Actually, you didn't. I asked Tad; he said you hung up on him. Shock's a funny thing." And suddenly he looked right at Lyndsay, just the way Matt had done. "Is this your daughter?" he asked.

Blair nodded, almost choking with panic now. "This is Lyndsay."

Lyndsay just nodded, wide-eyed and perhaps now as tense and ill at ease as her mother. Jake continued to study her, his expression inscrutable.

"I had no idea that you had a daughter," Faith said, clearly stunned.

Blair shrugged. "As you said, it's not like we've been in touch." Her heart continued to drum inside of her chest.

Faith glanced at her left hand. "You're divorced?"

Blair looked at Lyndsay, who had flushed. She hugged her close. "I never married."

Faith stared, and Blair could read her thoughts—like mother, like daughter. Two peas in a pod. The curse of the Anderson clan. Illegitimacy—never being loved or wanted enough by a man.

Jake stepped forward. "So you live in New York City," he said to Lyndsay with a smile.

Lyndsay nodded.

"I've been to New York once or twice. Awfully big place. Got lost both times." He continued to smile. Jake could charm a snake if he wanted to, and Blair knew it for a fact.

The memory almost swamped her, coming out of nowhere—and she had thought it long since forgotten. The moon and the stars, the heat and the humidity, the whispering night. And Jake. Abruptly, Blair shut off her thoughts, appalled.

And she was also shaken. She hadn't thought about that night in eleven years. How could the memory have arisen like that, so vivid, so poignant, so haunting?

And Lyndsay smiled. "Actually, it's an easy city," she said. "I could teach you how to get around if you ever come back." She seemed eager now to help.

"I'd like that," Jake said. "I might be up in New York next fall. We could make a trade. You take me around the city, I'll show you the ropes out here."

"That would be great," Lyndsay exclaimed.

Blair could not believe their conversation. "We're exhausted," she cut in. "Could we go to our rooms now?"

Jake straightened, but addressed Lyndsay. "Guess your mom doesn't want me visiting you in New York," he said. "How old are you?"

"Ten," Lyndsay's reply was prompt.

Blair seized her arm. "Let's get our bags." Her T-shirt was sticking to her skin now.

Jake looked from Lyndsay's shyly smiling face to Blair's. "She looks just like you."

Blair didn't know what to say. She didn't know what he really meant, or what he was really thinking.

"I think she looks like Dana," Faith said, coming to stand beside Jake.

"Blair looks like her mother, too," Jake said, unruffled. "I've always thought so." He smiled at Blair and Lyndsay. "I'll go get your bags." He strode out.

"Mom? Can I help Jake?"

Blair looked at her daughter speechlessly, sensing that everything she had striven for in the past ten years was already spiraling dangerously out of control. Before she could reply, Lyndsay took her silence for an affirmation and dashed outside after Jake.

Blair wanted to cry. Or run away and hide.

"You've finally got your wish, haven't you?"

Blair flinched, slowly facing Faith. "Excuse me?"

"You've always wanted to be inside this house. And now, here you are." Suddenly Faith's eyes filled with tears again.

Faith was her sister, but they weren't friends. Blair reminded herself of that. She reminded herself of the antagonism and condescension before saying, coolly, "Yes, I've always wanted to be inside this house. Thank you for your hospitality."

"I want you going to a hotel tomorrow," Faith said. "No matter what Jake says."

"I intend to go. I want to be here as much as you want me to be here."

"I doubt that." Faith's fists were clenched by her sides. "I can't imagine why Jake had Williams call you. He's reading the will tomorrow. Knowing Rick, I'm sure he left you something. I expect you to leave afterward."

"I'm not here because of Rick's will," Blair said. "I came here to bury him, I came here to say good-bye." She hadn't even thought of an inheritance, for God's sake.

"I don't believe you." Faith shrugged, tears slipping down her face.

Lyndsay's laughter sounded from outside, the free, unfettered laughter of a happy child. It startled them both. And a moment later Jake Cutter laughed, too, the sound rich and warm, a sound that was rare—or used to be rare, Blair thought. She realized she was gripping her own hands so tightly she was hurting herself, and she made an effort to relax. But it was futile. She did not want them to be friends. But a friendship seemed to be unfolding before her very eyes.

Faith had moved to stand before the window, watching them both. Now she confronted Blair. "How old did you say she was?" she asked, her tone high.

Blair hesitated. "Ten."

"Ten. And you left here eleven years ago—the day after my wedding." Faith's gaze bored into Blair's.

And Blair looked away.

Faith stepped over to her. "Were you pregnant when you left here, Blair?"

Blair jerked. "That's none of your business," she said.

"I think it is my business." Faith looked out the window again. Jake and Lyndsay were strolling toward a corral where two young horses stood, having left the luggage by the Honda. Clearly they were completely sidetracked.

"Who is the father?" Faith demanded, flushing.

Blair's pulse rioted. "No one you know," she lied.

"Is it Jake?" Faith asked.

And Blair felt the color draining from her face.

Chapter Two

*B*lair lay on her back in bed, staring up at the ceiling, her hands clasped under her head. The events of the day kept replaying through her mind, especially her arrival at the ranch. It was close to midnight, but Blair couldn't sleep.

She had hoped to guard her secret about the identity of Lyndsay's father, and already Faith suspected the truth. How long would it take Jake to figure it out, and more importantly, then what would he do?

Lyndsay meant everything to Blair. Faith and Jake were childless. Blair's deepest fear was that Jake would try to take her daughter away from her.

Blair squeezed her eyes shut against a sudden onslaught of hot tears. She was never this emotional, but the toll of Rick's death and returning home was huge.

And little scenes kept trying to filter through the careful screen she had long ago placed upon her memories. Jake as a sullen boy of eleven or twelve, being dragged off to detention for some unmemorable crime, Blair watching and feeling so sorry for him, understanding him the way no one else could. Like Blair, he'd had only one parent—but his father was an alcoholic with a huge temper, a rotten job, and two huge, meaty fists. Jake was always in trouble. Half the time he failed to show up at school, and he'd done it all, from fistfights to petty larceny, and once, he'd even stolen a car. He'd been suspended more times than anyone could count. The only reason he hadn't wound up in a juvenile detention center was because the town was so small, everyone knew everyone, and Matt's father, a minister, had continually and actively lobbied on Jake's behalf. When

Jake was sixteen, he was kicked out of school. That was no easy task, because the school was public, but Rick had stepped into the breach, offering Jake a job at the Triple H. Blair was quite certain that Frank Ramsey had arranged it. Jake had gone to work for Rick that summer and had never left.

Blair hated where her thoughts were leading and she flopped over on her stomach, but the memories wouldn't quit. Jake and Faith were the same age. Faith had always been the most popular girl in school, but until that summer, she'd never given Jake the time of day. Blair didn't really know what had happened that summer, but by the time Faith returned to school as a senior, she and Jake were a not-very-secret item. Rick must have been livid, Blair thought, or maybe not, as the security of the Triple H had indeed re-formed Jake as much as he could be reformed. Five years later Faith and Jake were married right there on the big house's front lawn, in front of the entire town.

Blair flopped over again. Her temples throbbed excruciatingly now. What did the past matter? What mattered was getting through the next few days in one piece—both she and Lyndsay. What mattered was the future, which for them was New York City. Tomorrow she would go visit Rick's grave. Maybe they'd even go home the day after that.

Home. Her three-bedroom apartment in Park Slope, Brooklyn, had been home for almost six years. But now the word felt empty, and even though Blair had never been in this room before, there was something far more compelling about it than her noisy city apartment. The bedroom smelled of cedar, a scent Blair had grown up with. Outside, the crickets made a lullaby, which was also all too familiar. Blair thought she could smell fresh-cut grass, and she kept expecting to see Rick walking through her door at any moment, smiling in greeting, because every inch of the house felt like him. Blair didn't want it to be this way, and she was angry.

She tried to listen to the night, because the sound of crickets and the occasional settling wooden beam was so soothing, but her anger continued to simmer inside her. Her home was New York; she had turned her back on Harmony, Texas, a long time ago.

There was a knock on her bedroom door.

Blair shot up like a rocket. Lyndsay had fallen asleep at nine o'clock, exhausted from the trip. And Lyndsay slept like a rock; nothing ever woke her up in the middle of the night. Blair could only stare at the door in horror, imagining who stood on the other side.

She assured herself that it was Faith—one of the last people she wished to see. But she knew it was Jake.

"Blair? You awake?" Jake's voice sounded from the other side.

Oh, God, Blair thought, folding her arms across her chest.

"Blair?"

Undoubtedly he saw her lights; still, she could refuse to answer and pretend she had fallen asleep. She hadn't locked her door—but he wouldn't dare just walk in.

And the memory flooded her: his hands, his mouth; the half-moon and winking stars, the hard, hard ground. Soft cries, low moans, and his rich, warm laughter. Words. Words that had been empty promises, even deliberate lies. Words she had chosen to believe—for the space of one endless, enchanted evening.

Blair clutched her pillow to her chest. She wasn't going to answer that door. If she did, she didn't trust herself—not in any shape or form.

He thrust open the door and their gazes instantly met.

Blair jumped to her feet. She was wearing a simple yellow silk chemise that barely covered her thighs, but she did not give a damn. "Get out."

"Whoa. We need to talk." He took a look at her legs.

"We do?" Her hands fisted on her hips. "You have a helluva lot of nerve. But how could I have forgotten that?"

He smiled at her. "I take that as a compliment."

"You're a moron."

"So now we start name-calling?" His brows lifted. "That's real constructive."

"What about Faith? I don't think she'd like this very much."

His smile faded. His gaze was direct. "Faith's out for the night. Sleeping pills. Doctor's orders. I want to talk to you. Put on some clothes and meet me in the kitchen." He turned and left—not closing her door.

Blair stared after him in disbelief, anger, and dismay. She didn't want to talk to him. She didn't want to be alone with him. Not now, not ever. It was the worst of ideas.

Because she'd never forgotten that single night, and she never would.

Because she had fallen in love with him when she was a child, and nothing had changed.

Blair turned and put on a Gap T-shirt and jeans and went downstairs to the kitchen.

The kitchen had also, clearly, been redone. It was a huge room, with two refrigerators, a freezer, an oven, and four sinks all in stainless steel. The counters were black granite, the floors gray and white tile. Jake was standing with his hip against the center island, which was also black granite, a bottle of Kentucky bourbon beside him, a full glass in hand. He was also wearing jeans, but with a red T-shirt. His feet were bare.

He lifted an empty glass. "Drink? You look like you could use one."

Blair shook her head. "No, thanks. I'm not much of a drinker." The moment she spoke, she wished she hadn't.

He said, slowly, "Yeah." And she knew he was remembering, too.

Blair ducked her head. This was too painful.

"Blair, is she mine?" His words cut right through her.

Blair stared. "No. She's mine. I carried her inside me for nine months, I brought her into the world, I held down two jobs and went to school in order to better myself so I could give her a decent life. I raised her, I love her, Lyndsay's my daughter."

He swigged. "Faith and I started to try having kids a

couple of years ago. So far, zip." His hazel eyes held hers. "I guess I'm wondering whose fault it is."

Blair wet her lips. "Have you seen a doctor?"

"Been putting it off. And now . . ." He sighed. "Maybe it's been a blessing in disguise that we haven't had kids."

Blair was almost afraid to ask what that meant. "What do you mean?"

He looked her in the eye. "Oh, come on. We were kids when we married. We had nothing in common. We still have nothing in common—except for this ranch and our love for Rick."

"I don't want to hear about your problems," Blair said, walking over to a refrigerator and opening it. She wasn't hungry and she wasn't thirsty but she saw a pitcher of iced something and she pulled it out, found a glass, and poured what turned out to be apple juice. She kept her back to Jake, trying not to think the single refrain, over and over, "trouble in paradise."

When he spoke, he was right behind her, his breath on her neck. "I told Tad Williams to call you. I knew Faith wouldn't even think of it. She has no idea that all these years Rick was in touch with you, that he went up north to see you. Rick didn't tell me, but I figured it out. But the truth is, my motives weren't pure. I've thought about you, Blair, these past years."

Blair was so tense she thought she might snap in half. She turned, saw they were chest to chest and knee to knee, and backed up against the counter. "You're crowding me."

"I know." His smile was faint. Nothing fazed Jake Cutter. He did what he wanted, when he wanted; it had always been that way. Blair knew she should despise him. But she couldn't because she'd been inside the shack that had been his home when they were kids, because she'd seen him with black and blue eyes, trying not to cry, because she knew his swagger was all façade. She told herself that he wasn't a boy anymore, he was a grown man. Secure, successful, with a wife who just happened to be her half sister. But he was also the father of her daughter, and he'd been her first love, and the first man she'd ever allowed to make love to her.

Unfortunately, that seemed to count for more than a lot—it seemed to count for everything.

"What do you want, Jake?" Blair asked, not moving. She tried not to look at his mouth. Blair had had two affairs in the past ten years. They were with men she'd worked with, genuinely cared about, and had tried very hard to fall in love with. But love hadn't happened. Not the way it had happened for her with Jake.

"I'm not sure." His honesty startled her. "Maybe I want another chance with you. Maybe I want the truth about Lyndsay."

Blair's heart had turned over at his first statement; his second made her blurt, "She's not yours. I was heartbroken when I got to New York. I was easy prey, Jake, and I got involved right away with someone I was working with."

He studied her, his gaze opaque, hard to decipher. Blair kept a straight face. She wasn't going to allow Jake back into her life.

"Okay." He smiled a bit. "I'll buy that—for now. How long will you stay, Blair?"

She was startled. "Not long. I have a job to get back to."

"Lyndsay likes it here. It's her heritage, too. Don't you think you should give her a chance to get know her family, and this kind of life?"

Blair assumed he was referring to Faith. "My sister isn't thrilled to have us here."

"I don't think that's what stopping you now," Jake said softly.

Blair slipped away from him, sidling down the counter. "You're right. It's you. I'm not happy to see you again—and can you blame me?"

His eyes darkened and he came toward her. "It takes two to tango. Don't go putting all the blame on me. You wanted that night as much as I did."

"I was just eighteen, and I was drunk—on beer you provided!"

"How the hell was I to know you'd never had a brew before? You came on to me," he said heatedly. "I wasn't looking for company. Hell, I wanted to be alone."

"I did not come on to you," Blair whispered furiously. "You looked so lonely sitting there on the porch of your daddy's, I knew you were upset. I was only trying to be a friend."

"You were wearing the shortest pair of shorts I ever saw," he returned flatly.

Blair blinked. "It was a hundred degrees out, and humid as all hell! We were in the middle of the monsoon season!"

"You'd been making eyes at me all summer—or should I say, all of my life?"

His tone was caustic, cutting; his words hurt. Because they were the truth. "I won't deny I had a crush on you, Jake. But you were four years older than me, and you were engaged to Faith. Your wedding was four days later."

He just looked at her. Finally he said, "I'll admit it. You did something to me then, just like you do now. And I'm a man, Blair, not a saint." He turned his back on her, walked to the island, grabbed his drink and slammed it down. Only then did he face her.

Blair had not wanted to hear this last revelation. She said, "No one ever mistook you for a saint, Jake." And she hurried from the room.

Blair sat on the front porch, barefoot, sipping a mug of black coffee that had gone cold. It was perhaps six-thirty in the morning, far too early to be up and about, but she'd been unable to sleep after her late-night encounter with Jake. She was about to take a sip of the coffee when she saw a black-and-white cruiser rolling up the drive. Her eyes widened as the police car with the words "Sheriff's Department" emblazoned on the doors came to a stop before the house. She watched Matt get out of the car.

He smiled at her as he approached, slipping off his sunglasses. "Good morning."

Blair stood. Her mind was racing. Was Matt here because of Rick's death? "Hi. Is everything okay?"

His gaze slid to her unpainted toes. "I'm on my way to work. I thought I'd stop by—on the chance that you were already up. Louie's Diner still makes the best omelet in town. Care to join me?"

Blair blinked. "You're inviting me for breakfast?"

"Yeah. I am."

Blair was tired and she sank back down on the porch steps. "I'll take a rain check, Matt, but thanks."

"I figured you'd say something like that." He smiled at her again. "You look real tired, Blair. Rough night?"

Blair met his intent blue gaze and nodded. "Everything's happened so quickly. I still can't believe Rick is dead."

He nodded and sat down beside her, surprising her. "Do you mind?"

For a moment, Blair just looked at him. It was the old Matt, yet he had changed so much, perhaps as much as she had. Maturity had wrought such calm and self-assurance. In a way, she found his presence soothing. "No. I don't mind."

"Want to talk about it?"

Blair felt a bubble of panic. "Talk about what?"

"Oh, I don't know—what's bothering you." His gaze was probing.

"It's just Rick," she said firmly.

His black brows rose. "And being under the same roof with Jake Cutter has nothing to do with it."

Blair's heart sped up and she stood. "What are you talking about?"

He stared at her. "Blair, this is me, Matt. I know you about as well as anyone. We grew up together, remember?"

She had folded her arms tightly beneath her breasts. "You don't know me, Matt. No one here does. Not anymore."

He stretched out his long legs, as if he intended to stay for a while. "Well, that would be a shame. Because the tough little kid I knew was cute as all hell, and I'd hate to think she's completely disappeared."

Blair grimaced. "Well, she has."

He eyed her. It was a moment before he spoke. "You know, Blair, I think the jeans and bare feet suit you a lot more than the makeup and the sexy outfit."

She felt her eyes widen. "What?"

"You belong here. New York's not for you."

"I'm having a lot of trouble with this conversation," Blair said, after a pause. She could feel her annoyance rising.

"I know you are. Because the truth can hurt. Don't we all know it?"

She had had enough. "What the hell would you know about painful truths?" she flung at him. And she stormed away, barefoot, toward one of the corrals.

She knew he followed her. She was leaning on the fence, thinking about Matt's family, when he paused beside her. His father had been far more than the town's minister, he'd been the town's father—with everyone knowing him and liking him and going to him with their problems. Matt's mother had been a lot like Charlotte, kind and simple, always involved in church socials and fund-raisers and with the town's neediest families. Matt didn't have a clue what it was like to grow up illegitimate and poor.

"We've all been hurt," Matt said quietly, beside her. "You don't have a monopoly on grief."

"You're way off base." Blair refused to look at him.

"I'm divorced," he said.

Shocked, Blair twisted to stare. "I never even knew you were married."

His smile was slight—and crooked. "Right out of law school. She's still in New York. Still a high-powered lawyer, driving a Mercedes, the owner of a Fifth Avenue co-op and two closets of designer clothes. Her life is wining and dining clients at the Four Seasons, chairing the most fashionable charities, screwing the opposition. Not literally. In fact, I heard she remarried recently."

"I'm sorry, Matt." He was trying to hide his feelings, but Blair could see that he'd been betrayed and deeply hurt.

"I was a fool." He shrugged. "I assumed she shared my values. Real old-fashioned ones. You know, loyalty, family, integrity." He smiled again.

Blair touched his arm. It was as hard as a rock, and she didn't know why that surprised her, but it did. "She didn't deserve you. Is that why you quit? Came home?"

"There was a lot of soul-searching. I thought I wanted what she wanted—the power, the position, the six- or seven-figure income. But I'm not too fond of swimming with sharks, Blair. I didn't like the man I was becoming."

"Good for you," Blair said quietly.

They lapsed into silence, watching two young Thoroughbreds prance about the corral. The front door of the house closing sounded behind them. Blair turned, as did Matt. Instantly she stiffened. Jake was coming down the steps. He saw them and hesitated.

Blair recalled their exchange in the kitchen, her pulse speeding, her cheeks heating. Jake seemed to make up his mind and he strode toward them, a lean figure in his jeans and scuffed boots, a western-style sports coat over a button-down with a string tie, and a Stetson with a turquoise and silver hatband. "Morning."

Blair nodded very curtly.

"Going into Dallas?" Matt inquired casually.

Jake nodded. "There's business that can't be avoided, and Faith isn't up to it."

"Convenient," Matt said.

Jake stared, his eyes becoming as hard as diamonds. "What the hell does that mean, Matt?"

"Oh, I don't know. Rick fired you three months ago and now you're back in the driver's seat."

"You got something to say, come right on out and say it."

Blair looked in shock from Jake to Matt and back again. Jake was furious, Matt was completely unruffled.

"I'll have the results of that autopsy soon."

Jake stared. "If you think I had something to do with Rick's death, then you are wrong. He was a father to me." Jake spun on booted heel and strode away.

Blair stared after him, watching him opening the six-car garage with an electronic device. The vehicle of his choice today was a silver Porsche. As he backed out of the garage, she faced Matt. "You're crazy. Rick had an accident, and even if he didn't, Jake would never hurt Rick—much less murder him."

"Money corrupts," Matt said. "So does greed and the lust for power."

The Porsche roared down the driveway, spitting dust and gravel in its wake.

"You don't like Jake. You never did." Blair stared after the sports car.

"And you're still as much in love with him as ever, aren't you?" Matt said flatly.

Blair froze. "I was never in love with him."

Matt shook his head. "Blair, the whole town watched you trail after him like a puppy dog, right up until he went to work for Rick. Is Lyndsay his daughter?"

Blair almost choked. First Faith, then Jake, and now Matt. "No."

His sad smile told her he didn't believe her. "You were the most miserable person I ever saw at the wedding. I felt so sorry for you. And I wasn't the only one to notice that you left town the next day—never to come back. Until now."

Suddenly tears came to her eyes. "I don't want your pity."

He was sharp. "You don't have it. You're tough and smart and stubborn—you've done well for yourself. I just hate seeing you mooning over him still."

Blair opened her mouth to protest, but Matt cut her off. "It's written all over your face. Every time you look at him. Don't try to deny it."

"You know what?" she finally managed, at once angered

and horrified by his perceptions. "How I feel isn't your business."

He stared. "I care. I'm your friend. So it is my business."

Blair shook her head in negation.

"Well, a word of warning. Jake hasn't changed. He'll never change."

Blair didn't want to know what he meant, and she didn't want to believe him. "Now what charges are you going to sling against him?"

"Christ! You'll defend him to your dying breath, won't you? You figure it out." Matt stalked away.

Blair hugged herself, watching him slide into the front seat of his cruiser. She was shaken. This was terrible. Matt knew how she felt, and seemed to believe that the whole town did, too. Did Jake know? Did Faith? Was everyone in town assuming that Lyndsay was Jake's daughter?

Matt turned on the ignition and the cruiser came to life.

Suddenly Blair ran over to the car, before he could drive away. "Matt. I don't want to fight. Not with you."

His expression remained tense. "Neither do I, Blair, but I wish you'd wake up."

"Jake isn't as bad as you think. You just don't understand him the way I do."

He shook his head, grim and resigned. "You're going to get hurt all over again," he said. He had slipped on his reflective sunglasses, but suddenly he seemed to be staring right at her. "How much do you want to bet that those autopsy results will be interesting?"

She stared at her reflection in his glasses. "Do you want to pin Rick's murder on Jake?" She regretted the words the moment they were out of her mouth.

"If Rick's death was a murder, then I intend to find out who did it, and frankly, Jake would be at the top of my list of suspects."

Blair realized she was trembling like a leaf. "Did you have any other reason to have an autopsy done besides the fact that Rick rode a horse like he was part of one?"

He removed his glasses. "Actually, I do. I was up at the site with one of my deputies. I found two spent casings on the scene. Rick wasn't armed when he left the ranch that day. I already checked."

Blair felt a ripple of shock go through her. "Oh, God," she heard herself whisper.

He nodded, slipping his glasses back on. "One more thing. The reason I wanted to take you to breakfast in the first place."

Blair looked at his set mouth and felt herself tense even more. "What?"

"I thought you should know. Dana's in town."

Chapter Three

"I'd like to wait another few minutes before we begin, if you don't mind," Tad Williams said. His demeanor was somber, as befitted the occasion. Blair sat with Faith and Jake in Rick's study; she was the sole occupant of the sofa. Faith and Jake had chosen to sit in front of Rick's very neatly organized desk, side by side in two huge chairs with carved backs. Tad Williams, a tall, balding lawyer from Dallas, stood behind it, a sheaf of papers in hand, preparing to read the will or do whatever it was that estate lawyers did at such a time.

"Why are we waiting? We all seem to be present," Faith said tersely, recrossing her legs, which were adorned with sheer stockings. She was wearing a knee-length black sheath. She looked more like a New Yorker than a Texan. Blair knew Faith was not happy that she was present. She had made her feelings abundantly clear the moment Blair had appeared in the study. But Williams had requested that she be present for the reading of the will, and Blair had suddenly realized that Rick had left her and Lyndsay something. Until this moment, she hadn't given his will any real thought.

She was still reeling from Matt's revelation earlier that day. Dana was in town.

Blair's stomach tightened to impossible dimensions at the mere thought. Blair did not know how she felt. She remained stunned, bewildered, confused. She hadn't seen her mother in twenty-one years. The postcards, one or two a year, didn't count. When Blair turned thirteen, she had started tearing them up, unread. As far as Blair was concerned, she did not have a mother. As far as Blair was concerned, her mother was dead.

"Am I interrupting?"

Blair jerked at the sound of Matt's voice coming from the threshold of the room.

Faith and Jake twisted to look at him, as well. Jake's face tightened.

"Come in, Matt, come in." Williams smiled.

Matt glanced briefly at Blair, and their eyes met. He went and stood by the window, leaning one slim hip against the sill. He was wearing his uniform, but not his hat. Unlike everyone else in the room, he seemed casual, unconcerned, relaxed.

"Excuse me," Faith said abruptly. "Why is Matt here?"

"I've asked him to be present, and if you will let me begin, the reason will become clear." Williams cleared his throat. "Rick was intending to make a trip to New York just before he died." He gazed at Blair.

Blair had no comment to make. She shifted uneasily in her seat, very aware of Matt standing a few feet from her, and the sudden tension that his presence had generated for Jake. The two men had not been rivals as boys. They hadn't been friends either, and Blair wasn't quite sure what to make of the animosity between them now.

Tad continued. "He wanted to brief you on the trusts he has set up. Blair, along with Faith and myself, you are an executor of his estate."

Blair was overcome with shock. "What?"

Tad Williams repeated what he had just said. Before he could continue, Faith was on her feet. "Daddy named Blair an executor of his estate?" She was incredulous.

As was Blair. She looked at Faith, then glimpsed Jake's set expression. Surely he had not been excluded. Her heart went out to him.

"Yes, he did. And Matt was named the fourth executor of the estate."

Even more surprised, Blair looked at Matt, who did not seem surprised at all.

Faith twisted to look at Matt. "I don't believe this. First Blair, now Matt." She reached out to hold Jake's hand, but he shook her off.

Jake commented, "Guess he didn't trust you to run things by yourself."

Faith stared at him. "Well, at least he included me."

Jake was already flushed. He stood up abruptly, almost causing his chair to overturn. "He tell you why he left me out? I've worked my ass off for him since I was sixteen."

Williams was unruffled. "No, he did not. I'd like to get to the will."

Jake sat back down. Blair knew he was more than angry. She couldn't believe Rick had excluded him this way. Rick had been crazy about him. Hadn't he?

"The will is quite straightforward," Williams said. "Hewitt Enterprises was divided up between the two sisters, with Faith receiving two-thirds and Blair a third. In the event that Blair decides to stay in Texas and become an operating executive of the company, that changes to fifty–fifty. You would draw a salary commensurate with the degree of involvement in the company that you choose. Should you return to New York, your trust allows you an annual income of about two hundred thousand a year."

Williams had paused; Blair could barely assimilate what she had heard. Two-thirds, one-third, but if she stayed, fifty–fifty? Of course she wasn't staying in Harmony! Her home was New York now. Her life was New York. There was nothing for her here but bad memories. Wasn't there?

"Well, well," Matt was drawling, "Rick was full of surprises."

Blair glanced at him. He was smiling, as if pleased. And he smiled at her.

Blair quickly glanced away.

"All of Rick's personal effects are left to his first daughter, Faith. That includes his extensive art collection, the wine cellars, the cars, the Learjet, the condos in Dallas, Palm Beach, and Aspen. There is one exception: this house."

Faith was staring at Williams as if he spoke gibberish. "This house?" she breathed.

"This house was left to Blair."

Blair almost fell off the sofa.

Jake was on his feet. "That old bastard! Are you done yet?" He was seething.

"Not quite. A trust was also set up for Lyndsay. The only funds that can be removed from it are for her schooling and medical costs. Blair, you have enough in that trust to send her to the finest schools, the best Ivy League college. When she's twenty-five, the money's hers." He smiled at Blair and looked at Faith and Jake. "In the event that you have children, similar trusts have been set up. In the event that there are no children, those trusts revert back to the estate."

Blair slumped against the sofa, reeling, when Jake said, "That's it?" And she looked at his sullen face and saw not the man but the outcast boy with the black and blue eyes, the torn jeans, the hidden tears. Compassion filled her.

"I'm afraid so."

Jake strode out of the room, a blur of angry motion.

Faith was on her feet and shaking like a leaf. "I won't stand for this. He leaves Jake nothing. He leaves her"—and she pointed a trembling finger at Blair—"one third of the company if she goes back to New York, fifty percent if she stays? And the house? The house is mine!"

"Not according to the terms of this will," Williams said quietly.

Faith was crying. "How could he do this to us? When we loved him so?"

No one answered her.

Blair still didn't know what to think—except that she was acutely aware of Jake having left the room, of his being hurt and angry, and of her own urgent impulse to go after him. He hadn't deserved this. She was angry with Rick when she should be thrilled. Her temples throbbed. What had Rick been thinking?

Dear God, he had left her the house!

"A very interesting will." Matt's drawl cut into her thoughts.

"I intend to fight it in court," Faith cried.

"Not a good idea. You'd have to prove Rick was out of his mind—or unduly influenced—when he wrote it," Matt said.

Faith burst into tears.

Matt reached out to pat her shoulder once. "Faith. Maybe this will work out for the best." His tone was kind.

She shook her head but she did look at him; clearly she was listening.

It was also clear to Blair that on some level, Faith and Matt were friends, that she trusted and respected him. That disturbed Blair, but she could not dwell on that now. Instead, Blair took the opportunity to slip from the room, knowing she should have thanked Williams, but helpless to stop herself. She was in her jeans and wore a pair of loafers with lug soles; she broke into a run. Through the windows in the foyer she saw Jake pacing outside, smoking a cigarette, bathed in brilliant sunshine. She hurried out the door and down the front steps.

He saw her, halted in the act of inhaling, then exhaled angrily and threw the cigarette down. He ground it out with the heel of his worn lizard boots.

She paused in front of him, out of breath.

His gaze searched hers, and as it did, some of the anger softened.

"I'm sorry," she said when she could speak. She touched his bicep, let her hand linger there. "I'm really sorry. I don't understand any of this."

He glanced up at the sky, as if it were heaven. "Neither do I." Then he met her gaze. "I thought I was like a son to him. Shit."

"You were like a son to him." Blair wet her lips. "But you are married to Faith. Half of what's hers is yours. That must have been what he was thinking."

"Maybe," Jake said. "He sure was thinking a lot about you."

Blair flushed. "I'm in shock. I haven't digested this at all."

"I'll bet."

Behind them, the front door slammed and Blair jerked, almost guiltily. She turned to see Matt walking toward them. He didn't seem to be in a hurry, and he also didn't seem to be inclined to mind his own business. His gaze was directed at her and Jake, and Blair knew what he was thinking. His cruiser was parked by the corral. She stiffened when he paused beside them.

He didn't glance at Jake. The look in his eyes was one of pity. "Congratulations, Blair," he said.

Blair watched him slide into his cruiser. Her confusion grew, and she did not understand it. There was no reason for her to feel guilty; she had done nothing wrong. As a friend, she had every right to comfort Jake.

The cruiser drove off.

Watching it, Jake said, "Guess he's still got the hots for you."

Blair was taken aback. "That was crude—and untrue. Matt's not like that."

"Oh, come on. I'm a man. I know how men think." His gaze pierced through hers.

Blair drew away. "I doubt there's a generic way all men think."

He smiled. "For a TV reporter, you're still the same naïve little Blair."

"I'm not naïve." Blair didn't move. Their gazes had locked. Once, she had been very naïve—where Jake was concerned.

He just smiled again. "But that makes you real sweet. Thanks for caring, Blair."

Blair stared, trembling, suddenly hoping for—yearning for—the impossible.

Jake touched her cheek. The gesture was brief, but Blair was certain that if they weren't standing in broad daylight right in front of the house, he would have kissed her, full on the mouth—tenderly.

Jake walked away.

And Blair wondered, desperately, what was wrong with her, to still be nutty over the man who had wronged her so terribly ten years ago and who was now her sister's husband.

"Mom!" Lyndsay burst into Blair's bedroom, where Blair had been trying to take a nap, without any success. All she could think about was Rick's shocking will, Jake and Faith, and Matt. She knew she had to leave Texas, the sooner the better, before she did something terrible—like allowing Jake to seduce her only to lose her heart all over again. But this time, she would be betraying her sister in the process.

Not that she owed Faith very much.

Blair sat up slowly. Lyndsay was wide-eyed and flushed, and still appearing every bit the New York brat in a miniskirt and platform sneakers. "House on fire?" Blair asked.

"Mom! Dana's downstairs," Lyndsay cried.

Blair's heart slammed to a painful stop.

"Did you hear me?" Lyndsay was practically jumping up and down. "After all these years—she wants to see you!"

Blair didn't move. Her mind raced—twisted and gyrated. She could hardly think with any degree of coherence. But finally, one thought crystallized. She did not have to go downstairs.

"Mom?"

Blair became aware of the terrible pounding of her heart. Huge, thick bursts that felt unnatural, uncomfortable, frightening. Blair was on her feet. Her mother was downstairs. The woman who had walked out on her twenty-one years ago, without ever looking back. Not a visit, not a phone call, just those damn postcards from LA, Honolulu, Seattle. And now she was here, in Harmony. *She was actually downstairs.*

"Let's go," Lyndsay said eagerly, grabbing Blair's hand.

"You stay here," Blair heard herself say. And she realized she was going to go down those stairs anyway—against her better judgment, against her will.

Lyndsay was incredulous. "Mom, she's my grand-mother—"

"You don't have a grandmother," Blair snapped.

Lyndsay's face fell.

"I'm sorry," Blair cried, suddenly focusing on her daughter. Her anxiety, her anger—her terror—were no excuse for either lashing out at Lyndsay or failing to have compassion for how she must be feeling now. Blair hugged her briefly. "Wait here, please. Let me talk to Dana first. This is important, Lynn. Okay?"

Lyndsay nodded, but tears had formed in her hazel eyes.

Blair kissed her and left the room, her heart booming, her palms wet on the smooth wooden banister. She saw Dana standing on the landing below, shifting with a rest-lessness Blair remembered all too well. Something stabbed through her. Dana saw her and started, finally becoming motionless.

Two pairs of dark eyes met.

"Blair!" Dana cried, smiling widely, arms outstretched. "If this isn't the end-all, can you believe it? After all of these years, the two of us in the same town at the same time—Harmony, no less?"

Blair paused at the bottom of the stairs, shoving her hands into the pockets of her jeans. Her mother was forty-six. She had been seventeen when she'd gotten pregnant with Blair. She had aged very well. Blair was shocked, because her mother was every bit as beautiful as she had been when Blair had last seen her. The few lines around her eyes only seemed to heighten her attractiveness, and she had cut her waist-length hair. The classic bob was even more flattering to her perfectly classic features. Even more confusing was the fact that she was wearing a beautiful suit. The white skirt was short, the jacket fitted, the lapels and cuffs exquisitely embroidered, and it screamed *designer* all over it. Blair realized the handbag her mother carried was alligator. The shoes were strappy Gucci sandals; Blair recognized the silver clasps immediately.

Dana had done well for herself, Blair thought with a

surge of bitterness. Her heart seemed to sink even more. She had abandoned Blair to become an actress, and apparently she had succeeded in some way or another. "Hello, Dana."

Dana was not put off by Blair's tone or stance. She hugged and kissed her, then stepped back to study her. "My! All grown-up and gorgeous! God, Blair, we can't tell anyone the truth—we'll have to say we're sisters."

Blair felt like crying—Dana's first thought, as always, was about herself—but she refused to do so. Her mother wasn't worth her tears. "We don't have to say anything at all," Blair said coldly.

Dana finally ceased smiling, looking closely at her. "You're angry with me," she said with some puzzlement. "I'm excited to death to see you, but you're as mad as a hornet."

"Why would I be angry with you?"

"You have no right to be angry with me, none," Dana flared. Then she smiled again. "Honey, it's been so long. I still can't believe this. I hear you're now a famous television reporter. And you have a daughter! We have to catch up. I want to know everything," Dana cried.

"What's the point?" Blair asked, when a sound behind her made her turn. She stiffened at the sight of Lyndsay coming slowly down the stairs. Her daughter had flagrantly disobeyed her.

Lyndsay only glanced at Blair once, then she stared wide-eyed at Dana.

"Oh, my. She looks just like you. Are you my grand-daughter?" Dana smiled, taking in her miniskirt, her platforms, and her blue nail polish.

Lyndsay nodded, not smiling yet.

"Come here, let me look at you! What a beautiful child," Dana exclaimed. "I like your outfit, darling. Très hip."

Lyndsay came forward, smiling a little now. Blair grew colder inside herself. She had forgotten how charming her mother could be when she wanted something. She had to want something now. But what?

It could not be money. She was clearly wealthy, and besides, Blair didn't have any money. On the other hand, she was about to inherit a huge number of assets from Rick. Blair did not like this last thought.

"How come you've never visited us until now?" Lyndsay asked.

Blair folded her arms, looking at Dana, with no intention of coming to her rescue.

Dana hugged Lyndsay and straightened. "Honey, my life's been a wild one. A real roller coaster, lots of ups and downs. I'm just getting through a very nasty divorce. My fourth husband, I'm afraid." She laughed somewhat apologetically and glanced at Blair. Then she grimaced. "You look just like Charlotte, standing there with your mouth all turned down and your nose all pinched up."

Blair stiffened. "Should I approve? And if so, of what? Divorce number four? Or your sudden cooing interest in me and my daughter? You left twenty-one years ago!"

Dana stared. "I was a child when I had you, Blair. I was immature, wild, reckless—completely unready for motherhood. My mother did a fine job by you, if appearances mean anything. If I had raised you, you'd be a mess." Dana was angry. Her eyes snapped. "My first husband was a would-be actor with a heroin habit. I didn't divorce him—one day I came home and found him dead in the bathroom. Imagine if that had been you finding him like that?"

Blair was taken aback. "Well, I'm glad it wasn't," she said.

"You're going to punish me, aren't you, for wanting a life? I was too young to be a mother! Surely, Blair, you can understand that?" Dana said plaintively.

"Not really. Because I was nineteen when I had Lyndsay. And from the day I realized I was pregnant, I knew my daughter would be my first priority, that I would do anything to give her the home and the love she deserved."

Dana stared at Blair, Blair stared back. She jerked when she felt Lyndsay tugging on her hand, and then she looked down and saw her daughter's tearful face.

"Mom, please don't fight with her. We might not see her again. Ever," Lyndsay whispered.

Blair realized how selfish she was being, fighting with Dana in front of Lyndsay, distressing her daughter with her own very personal issues. "You're right, honey." She smiled at Lyndsay, then looked coldly at her mother. "Well, you've had your little moment of reunion, so why don't we call it a day?"

Dana hesitated, her gaze on Blair. "I was hoping we might have dinner together. The three of us." She smiled, but slightly. She seemed hesitant now—when Dana had never been hesitant a moment in her life. "For old times' sake."

"There are no old times," Blair said.

Dana's mouth pursed.

Blair suddenly felt like a hateful, ugly person. Her mother seemed upset. As if Blair had actually hurt her.

But that was impossible. Dana cared only about herself. She had thick skin. Blair would have to hit her over the head with a two-by-four to do any real damage.

Dana finally nodded. "Maybe tomorrow, then," she said, gripping her beige alligator bag tightly.

"I don't think so," Blair said, ignoring Lyndsay's yank on her hand.

Dana's face turned into a mask that revealed nothing. She turned and walked gracefully from the house. Watching her from behind, Blair thought she could still be mistaken for twenty-one. Behind her, the door closed. And Blair stared at it as if she might see through it.

She heard the roar of a car starting outside.

A piece of her heart felt as if it were shredding apart.

"Will we ever see her again?" Lyndsay whispered, choking back tears.

Blair suddenly sat down on the second step of the stairs. That very question was emblazoning itself on her mind.

"Mom?" Lyndsay sat down beside her.

Blair turned, pulling her daughter into her arms, and she wept.

*   *   *

The sun was setting, casting a shimmering pink glow over the foothills that framed the back side of town. Blair closed the door to the Honda as she and Lyndsay stood on the curb of Cooper Street, which bisected Main Street and housed some of the town's most popular restaurants. A few cars were driving by, pedestrians were strolling down the block. Blair was aware of receiving the occasional glance from a passerby, and she did not think it was due to her turquoise chiffon skirt and sky-blue jersey T-shirt. She had no doubt she had been recognized. Harmony was a small town. Everyone in it had to know she had come home and that Rick had made her an heiress.

"Mom, I know Mrs. Guerrera recommended Smoky Joe's for dinner, but that diner looks cool," Lyndsay said, fidgeting and gazing at a large restaurant with huge windows across the street.

Blair followed Lyndsay's gaze. Cooper Street hadn't been built up like this ten years ago, with trendy cafés and modern diners. Back then it had housed one family-style restaurant and a couple of rather decrepit bars. "I guess the diner would be fine," Blair said. She could see why Lyndsay wanted to go. Because it was all glassed in, she could see inside. Half the diner seemed to be filled with teenagers. Lyndsay, on the other hand, was only ten.

They were about to cross the street when Blair saw a familiar silver Porsche, and she froze. She watched Jake park it expertly in one of the few spots left on the street. A moment later he emerged from the car, a tall, lean figure in tight jeans and a pale blue chambray button-down shirt. As usual, he was wearing his ancient lizard boots and a belt with a huge silver buckle.

He was on the opposite side of the street, facing them; he saw them in that moment. And he smiled.

Blair gripped Lyndsay's hand as Jake crossed the street with long, casual strides, pausing before them. He grinned at Lyndsay first. "Let me guess. You're going to drag your mom off to The Pegasus for a burger and fries?"

Lyndsay nodded eagerly. "It looks like a fun place."

He patted her shoulder. "A big hangout for the kids in this town. Hey, Lynn. How about we make a deal?" He winked at her, still not looking at Blair. "I'll buy you dinner, but you let me take your mom into Sunset's for a drink." He straightened and finally locked gazes with Blair.

"I think I'll go with Lyndsay," Blair said hastily, telling herself that she must not have a drink with Jake. She still didn't trust herself with him.

"Mom! That would be great! I'd love to go over to The Pegasus by myself. Please? There's a whole bunch of kids in there my own age."

Blair couldn't tear her gaze from Jake's. His eyes were hazel, like Lyndsay's. Thick-lashed, just as hers were. Tonight, though, they were vividly green. Blue colors did that to Lyndsay's eyes, too.

"You look like you could use a drink," Jake said, taking her arm. "And after today, I sure as hell could use a couple myself."

The events of that day flashed through Blair's mind. She was hurting—there was no denying it, not to herself. And so was he. Blair softened. Jake must be feeling devastated by the terms of Rick's will, now that some of the shock had worn off. And she didn't blame him. "Lynn, one hour. Then I'll be over to get you and we'll go back to the house."

"Mom, you're the best!" Lyndsay waved at them both, checked to make sure there was no oncoming traffic, and ran across the street. Blair watched her daughter disappear into the diner.

"She's a great kid," Jake said softly, still holding her arm. His hand was warm and possessive. "You did a great job with her."

Blair turned slowly, to look into his eyes. "She is a wonderful child. Smart, but kind. And she's very caring."

"She's like you," Jake said.

Blair pulled her arm free. "No. She's not like me." Blair was thinking of the difference between her childhood and

Lyndsay's, she was thinking of Dana. If only her mother had not reappeared in her life.

Jake gestured and they turned and walked into the bar, which was behind them. Inside, it was crowded, noisy, and smoky. Whoever had designed the bar had done so eons ago; the oak floors were scuffed and worn, the booths boasted vinyl seats, and on the walls, antlers, stuffed bear heads, and other hunting trophies vied for the patrons' attention with poorly done oils depicting scenes of the Wild West. Jake led the way to the bar, where he found two stools. As they sat down, he said, his thigh against hers, "Heard Dana was out to the house today."

Blair tried to put some space between them, but that only pushed her up against a heavy woman on her other side who was smoking up a storm. She gave up and settled against Jake, her back to the smoker. "Yes."

"You okay?"

"I'm fine." Blair kept her eyes on the bar.

The bartender paused before them, a pretty blonde in a short spandex dress who smiled at Jake. Blair ordered a white wine, he ordered a bourbon, straight up. If the bartender impressed him, he gave no sign.

Blair recalled now that in junior high and high school, the girls had always gossiped and speculated about Jake behind his back. She recalled how he'd walk down the hall, with her friends always following him with their eyes. In fact, now she was remembering that he'd had a string of girls back then, until Faith. She couldn't remember any names, but every single one of them had been fast and easy. Blair sighed.

Jake had drained half his drink and now he turned to study her. "What are you going to do?"

Blair tensed. "About?"

"You give any thought to the will?"

"It's all I can think about," Blair said.

He eyed her. "Really?" First her mouth, then her breasts, outlined by the thin blue top she wore.

Blair couldn't help it, her body tightened, at once comfortably and uncomfortably. She pushed at her short, wavy hair. A couple of silver bangles danced on her wrist.

When she didn't speak, he said, "I was hoping you might be thinking a bit about me."

She met his gaze, then silently admonished herself for doing so. He had the kind of eyes that grabbed you and never let go. And tonight they were so damn green . . . "I don't understand why Rick did what he did. I don't like the way he treated you," Blair said, meaning it.

Jake's face softened. He reached up; Blair tensed. And he pushed her hair back behind her ear for her. "I like your hair short. And I'm a long-hair kind of guy. You look like that actress, except she's blond and older than you. Sharon Stone."

Blair shook her head, denying it—denying what was happening. "I hardly look like Sharon Stone."

"Should we fight about it?" Jake asked, signaling the blond bartender for another drink.

As he did so, Blair noticed a woman sitting on the other side of the horseshoe-shaped bar, staring at them. She was also blond, with "big" hair, wearing the tightest T-shirt Blair had ever seen. She looked away when she realized Blair was watching her. "I don't want to fight," Blair said, toying with her wineglass. "Not about anything."

"Good. Neither do I. I make you nervous?"

Blair jerked.

He smiled. "You are so easy to read," he said. "You were always an open book, and nothing's changed."

"Well, then I hope you've changed," Blair said, straightening. "And maybe this time you won't take advantage of my confusion and my feelings for you."

He stared. Then, "Maybe it won't be taking advantage, Blair, maybe it'll be more like opportunity knocks, once, twice, and sometimes, if you don't seize the moment, there's no third time."

Blair studied her drink. Her cheeks were hot. She was hot. Drinks were a mistake. But the chemistry between them hadn't changed. Not at all; she'd been hoping that it had.

"Hey." He touched her shoulder. "I don't bite. Not unless asked."

She knew his eyes would be twinkling, so she didn't look up. "What did Rick hope to gain by that will?"

"Well," Jake took a swig of his bourbon, "obviously he wants you to stick around, get involved in the company. God. Faith's a wreck. He left you the *house*."

Blair wished she could tell Jake that she didn't want it, but she didn't know what to say. Because she did want the house. And maybe that was all she wanted: Rick's house— the place that she'd never been able to call home.

"Faith's hoping you'll sell to her. The house, the shares in the company, everything." He spoke flatly, but there was a question in his eyes.

"I don't know." Blair glanced up. "I'll think about it."

Jake nodded. And now he stared at his drink.

"What is it?" Blair asked.

He sighed, and when he looked at her, he was grim. "Faith and I have a lot of problems. Rick leaving her everything, that's his way of protecting her if we divorce."

Divorce. Blair sat up straight, her heart thundering. "Is that what the two of you are thinking of doing?"

"We haven't talked about it, but I've pretty much had it. Now, though . . ." He trailed off.

"Now, what?"

"He left her everything." Jake stared. "We get divorced, there's no way I'm coming out as well off as where I am now." And he cursed.

Blair stared. "So you would stay in a rotten marriage for the money?"

He looked at her with a self-deprecating smile. "You forget who I am? Who my old man was? I have to tell you, Blair, I've gotten used to cashmere in the winter, private jets year round. I even like champagne—the good stuff. What should I do? Walk away from all of this so I can be a foreman at some ranch around here, making fifty grand a year?"

"I remember who you are and how you grew up," Blair said slowly. That was more than the truth. "But by now you must have connections. Do you mean to say you couldn't walk into any one of a dozen first-rate companies in Dallas and not get an executive position?"

Jake formed his fingers into a bridge over his nose. "You know what?" he finally said. "I'd make less than what that trust would pay you annually if you decide to leave."

Blair studied the highly polished but scarred wooden bar.

"Don't judge me," Jake warned.

Blair shook her head. A terrible sadness overcame her and she felt her eyes moisten. She laid her hand on Jake's arm. "I've never judged you, Jake. Not even when I ran away from here, the day after your wedding."

He stared.

Blake felt her mouth quivering. "In a way," she said, "we're kindred souls. Two lost and lonely outcasts."

"Yeah," he said. His hand cupped her cheek. His thumb stroked over her skin. "You've always understood me, better than anyone, I guess."

Blair didn't pull away. Her heart beat slow and steady, with inevitability. The same kind of inevitability that had begun the moment she had returned to Harmony. Or was it from the moment Jake had taken her under the moon and stars, eleven years ago?

Jake stood. "Be right back," he said.

Blair watched him stroll with his masculine swagger to the men's room. Then she turned, to find herself the recipient of a hostile glare. It was the big-haired blonde across the bar in the too-tight T-shirt.

Blair drank her wine, thinking that it would always be this way, with other women chasing Jake and throwing themselves at his feet. She waved the bartender over. "Do you know that woman?"

The bartender turned briefly. "She's a regular. Cindy Lee. Why?"

"I think she'd like to poison my drink," Blair said.

The bartender hesitated. She had a pretty, open face, and

her blue eyes mirrored some concern. Then she said, "Maybe you should ask Jake about Cindy Lee." She smiled at Blair and walked away.

Blair drummed her fingers on the table, not liking the bartender's innuendo, when Jake reappeared. Simultaneously, they smiled at one another.

Then Blair thought about Lyndsay. She glanced at her watch. "We've only been gone a half hour," she said, relieved.

"If you're done, I'll walk you over anyway and we can check up on her," Jake said, tossing some bills onto the bar.

The bartender called out a thank-you to him.

They squeezed their way through the crowd and wound up outside. It was dark now, and a few stars were shining brightly overhead in an otherwise blue-black sky. They paused beside someone's oversized pickup truck, Jake still holding Blair's arm. "She seems to be having a good time," he said. "Maybe we shouldn't interrupt her."

Blair glanced across the street and through the huge windows of the diner. Lyndsay was sitting at a table with five other girls, and they were giggling up a storm. Blair smiled.

While Jake turned her around, pulled her into his arms, and kissed her.

He had taken her completely by surprise and Blair's response was to stiffen. But Jake did not let her go.

Instead, he deepened the kiss, pressing her lips open with his own.

What was happening suddenly hit Blair. She was pressed fully against him, and his body was strong, warm, hard. In fact, she could feel the tendons in his back beneath her hands. His mouth was doing terrible things, rampaging against her at will, pulling, sucking on her lips, until Blair was pulling and sucking back. Her buttocks found the side of the truck. Jake pushed his stiff groin urgently against her and their tongues met.

Blair's mind had gone blank. He was grinding his mouth on hers, his teeth were grating the corners there. Blair's hands slid lower, to his hips. Suddenly he was sucking her lower lip into his mouth, and it almost hurt. An instant later his tongue was inside her, thrusting violently against her palate. His groin felt hot and huge against her belly; Blair felt as though she might faint.

One of his hands moved up her side, then covered her breast. His other hand slid down over her buttock, pulling her even closer to his heat.

And finally, in unison, they tore apart, coming up for air.

Blair was panting as if she'd run a marathon. And the look in Jake's eyes was one she recognized—because she'd seen it once before.

Blair wiped saliva from her mouth, dazed, and vaguely noticed a fleck of blood on her hand.

"Gee, I hate to break this up, but you own a twenty-two Winchester, Jake?"

At the sound of Matt's cutting voice, Blair froze, as brutal reality struck her with the force of a lightning bolt.

She shifted, to see Matt standing a step behind Jake, his face rigidly set in what had to be anger or distaste—or a combination of both. He wasn't looking at her, only at Jake, as if he didn't even see her standing there.

Blair wanted to run away, to hide. She had just been caught making out like a frantic, foolish teenager with her sister's husband—on a public street. And suddenly the worst possible scenario struck her. Blair whirled, but thankfully, Lyndsay was still seated with her new friends in the diner. Relieved, Blair slumped against the truck. She was shaking now like a leaf.

For one moment, she had lost all control, for one moment, she had almost done the unthinkable.

"Beg your pardon?" Jake drawled, facing Matt, eyes cooling.

"You own a twenty-two Winchester?"

"Why?" Jake challenged.

Blair suddenly stiffened. What was going on?

"As sheriff of this town, I'm asking you a question. Not that I don't already know the answer." Matt smiled coldly.

Jake's jaw flexed. "Actually, I do."

"Good. Now, we can go together and you can turn over the gun, or not. But"—Matt produced a piece of paper from his shirt pocket—"I got a search warrant here that entitles me to a look at your place. I want the rifle, Cutter."

Blair stared at Matt in shock. Surely he didn't think that Jake was involved in Rick's accident? Unthinkingly, she blurted, "Matt! What's going on?"

He ignored her. "Do I have to go and get the rifle by myself, or are you going to hand it over to me?"

Jake stared.

Matt no longer seemed to be himself. He was like a stranger, a cold, frightening law-enforcement agent capable of hurting the man she still loved. Blair wet her lips. "Matt, you're making a mistake."

He finally looked at her, so coldly that something sickened inside of Blair and she drew back, away from him. Then he returned his hard gaze to Jake.

"You can search the house all you want," Jake finally said, sullen now. "But you won't find the rifle."

"No? And why is that?"

"Because I don't have it. You charging me with something?"

"No one's being charged with anything right now. Where is the gun?"

"I don't know. It disappeared. A couple of days ago."

Matt nodded knowingly.

Blair hugged herself. "Matt, if this is about Rick's death—"

He cut her off. "Where were you on the twenty-third, Jake, between twelve noon and three P.M.?"

Jake stared. "I don't remember," he finally said. "You're way off base, Matt."

Matt ignored that. "You sure you don't remember where you were?" Matt pressed.

Blair stared at both men in growing horror as Jake shook his head.

Suddenly the big-haired blonde stepped forward. Until then, Blair hadn't even realized she was present. "I know where he was," she said, her gaze on Jake, her red mouth pursed.

Jake stared back at her, not a flicker in his eyes.

Matt looked annoyed as he turned to her. "Yeah, Cindy Lee? Let me guess. He was over at your place."

She smiled, this time at Blair. "Over at my place, in my bed, over me." She was triumphant.

Blair looked at Jake, something inside of her giving way and crumbling, a little, bit by bit.

Jake looked at the ground, cursing.

"You swear to that in a court of law?" Matt asked Cindy Lee.

"You know it, Sheriff. Jake didn't kill Rick Hewitt. He couldn't, he was with me." She smiled at Blair again.

Matt nodded but Cindy Lee made no move to leave.

Blair told herself it was stupid to allow the other woman to upset her, but she felt sick. She licked her lips, managed to find her voice. "Matt."

He finally looked at her. His blue eyes remained as cold as ice.

Blair hated the way he was regarding her. She trembled, and shoved her hands behind her back to hide their trembling. "Does this mean you got the autopsy report?"

His gaze locked with hers. Blue steel. "I did. Rick didn't hit his head when he fell off his horse. He was struck with a heavy metal object, and it was that blow that killed him."

"Oh, my God," Blair whispered.

"You are not to leave town," Matt said to Jake. And then he looked at Blair. "And that goes for you, too."

Chapter Four

*T*he shadows of night around the house had taken on a menacing character.

Blair walked up the front steps, one hand protectively on Lyndsay's shoulder. The trees around the house seemed to loom larger than ever; they seemed to bend and twist. There was no wind. Blair felt like glancing over her shoulder, and she finally succumbed. No one was lurking about.

Her mind raced. It refused to quit. And she was no longer thinking about Jake and the kiss they should have never shared.

Rick had been murdered.

Someone had hit him on the head with a heavy metal object. Someone had deliberately ended his life.

Blair could not seem to comprehend it.

"I really had fun tonight, Mom," Lyndsay said as they walked into the house. The foyer was brightly lit, the rest of the downstairs was in darkness. "Can I go visit Mary tomorrow afternoon? We want to go to the mall. Her mom will drive us."

Absently, Blair agreed. "Lynn, get ready for bed, okay? I'll be up in a moment."

For once, Lyndsay didn't protest. Blair watched her race upstairs, then she turned and stared out of the window at the dark, almost starless night.

Who would kill Rick? And why?

She shivered. Matt was after Jake. Was his suspicion professional—or was it personal?

Blair knew he was wrong. Jake was not a murderer. Jake

had looked up to Rick, more than most people did to their own fathers. Jake had worshiped the man.

Blair saw several pairs of headlights coming up the drive and she tensed. That would be Jake, and Matt with his damn search warrant. She bit her lip, the hungry kiss she'd shared with Jake flashing through her mind. She was more than ashamed, she felt terribly guilty, but she was confused, too—he wanted to divorce his wife. But he wasn't divorced yet. And his wife—her half sister—was upstairs at that exact moment.

Blair felt she had no choice. She wanted to warn Faith about what was happening; it was the humane thing to do even if she was guilty of trespassing with her husband. She hurried upstairs, going directly to the master bedroom at the end of the hall, vowing not to go near Jake again—not until he was a truly free man, and maybe not even then. Inhaling for courage, she knocked.

There was no answer and she knocked again, certain she heard the television from the other side of the door. When that did not bring any response, she pounded twice on the door.

Suddenly the door swung open and Faith stood there in a bare and very expensive ivory negligee and robe. Blair felt a moment of absurd envy—she didn't have Faith's curves and she didn't have Jake. Faith looked beautiful, elegant, sensual. "Can we talk?"

Faith stared at her as if she didn't understand. "You want to come in?"

Blair nodded and Faith stepped aside.

Something was wrong, but Blair wasn't sure what, and she eyed her sister as she moved past her. Faith did not shut the door. "This is a surprise. A visit from my little sister," Faith said, her speech somewhat odd.

"Did you take a sleeping pill?" Blair asked suddenly.

"No. To what do I owe this honor?"

Blair thought Faith's speech was more than odd. If she didn't miss her guess, she'd say it was slightly slurred. "Something's happened," Blair said, glancing around the room. She didn't have to look very far. On the bedstand beside the king-sized master bed was a glass that contained an inch or so of what was either bourbon or scotch. Then Blair saw the bottle of Dewar's on the bureau. It was almost empty.

Faith had followed her gaze. "I'm not allowed to have a drink before bed?" She walked over to the bedstand and lifted her glass. "Care to join me?"

"No, thanks," Blair said, wondering just how inebriated she was. If someone did not know her, they might not even notice that her speech was off. But Blair had also seen her lose her balance slightly as she reached for her scotch. "Maybe you've had enough," she tried.

Faith whirled, this time stumbling noticeably. "Don't you ever tell me what to do!" she cried. "This is my home, my house, and—" She stopped, her face crumbling. "No matter what that damn will says!"

Blair folded her arms tightly across her breasts. "Faith, it *is* your house. Rick made a mistake," Blair said, wanting to defuse the situation. She heard male voices downstairs and she winced. "Faith, there's—"

But Faith cut her off, having heard the voices, too. "Who's that? Is Jake home?" She glanced at the crystal clock on the mantel. "It's only nine. Jake's never home this early." She flew past Blair, leaving her drink behind.

Blair hesitated, dismayed. Her first impression was that Faith was glad that Jake was home—as if she'd missed him, as if she loved him. Blair tried to shake herself free of the heavy feeling of dread settling over her. Jake had implied that Faith was as dissatisfied with the marriage as he was, and besides, Faith was drunk and still reeling from Rick's death and the reading of the will.

Blair caught Faith in the hall. "Stop. Please." She moved around her, blocking her way. "Jake is downstairs with Matt."

"Matt?" Faith's expression was puzzled, then it softened. "That's odd."

"Are you and Matt friends?" Blair asked, because it was

obvious to her that Faith had fond feelings for him.

Faith smiled. "We grew up together, Blair. We went to school together. I've known him my whole life. If there's one good person in this world, it's Matt."

"Are you in love with him?" Blair asked abruptly, hearing how tight and sharp her tone sounded.

Faith's brows lifted. "With Matt?" She laughed. "He's like a big brother, Blair." Then, like a child, "I wish he really was my brother. I can talk to him about almost anything."

Blair felt a relief she didn't understand, but she also felt a sense of jealousy. She shook her head to clear the confusion from it. "Faith, there's something I have to tell you—"

"Ladies," Matt said, coming up the stairs and interrupting Blair.

"Hello, Matt." Faith smiled, going to him and kissing his cheek as she tightened the belt on her robe—not that the thin silk outer garment did very much to cover her body. Blair watched them. If Matt noticed Faith's charms, he gave no sign.

"Honey, I'm afraid this isn't a social call." Matt's tone was kind, but as if he sensed Blair's scrutiny, he glanced her way and their eyes locked. Then he looked away. "Let's go downstairs. We have to talk."

"This is so strange," Faith said, as Matt let her precede him down the stairs. He continued to treat Blair as if she did not exist—and she trailed after the two of them, growing angry.

He was letting her know just how he felt about her display in the street with Jake. He was judging her and condemning her all at once, and it wasn't fair. Everything had happened so quickly; if she could erase those few minutes, she would. She knew that what she'd done was wrong. On the other hand, she hadn't asked to come home; she hadn't been the one to start things up all over again with Jake.

Blair hesitated when she saw Jake pacing in the living room. In that instant, her certainty about keeping her distance from Jake vanished. She didn't know why she felt a connection to him still, after all these years, but it was undeniable.

He glanced at Blair, then at Faith. Then he said, "Oh, Christ."

Faith, now worried, went to him. "Jake? What's wrong? You're so upset." She stroked his shoulder.

He shook her off. "Ask your buddy Matt."

Matt took Faith's arm and guided her to the tan leather sofa. "How much have you had to drink, Faith?" he asked quietly, sitting in a chair close to her.

"Just a drink," she said, eyes wide, blue and innocent.

"More like four or five," Jake interjected harshly. "She was having a scotch when I left here at seven, two hours ago." His disgust was obvious.

Faith stiffened, staring with a set face at her lap. Jake didn't seem to notice, or care, that he'd hurt her feelings.

Matt took her hands in his, regaining her attention. "Your father didn't have an accident, Faith. He was murdered."

Faith's eyes narrowed and she drew in her breath sharply. "What?"

Matt repeated what he had said. "We performed an autopsy. Rick was hit on the head with a metal object. I don't want to jump to conclusions, but it looks like someone was firing a twenty-two-caliber rifle at him, which caused him to lose control of his horse, to finally fall off. And whoever that person was, he came down from the rocks above the trail to finish the job. We found traces of powder and resin there. You okay?"

"I can't believe this," Faith whispered, and then, again, "I can't believe this." She shot a glance at Jake. It was plaintive; he was motionless, grim. "Why would anyone want to kill Daddy?"

"He's made a few enemies in his time," Matt said quietly. "And we're working on that angle. Tomorrow I'd like to sit down with you and go over the idea that someone really harbored a grudge against him in the business world. Maybe a deal gone sour, who knows? But in the meantime, I wouldn't be doing my duty if I didn't explore every possibility."

"Your duty," Jake said, low and terse. It was almost a sneer. But he'd walked over to Faith and now he stood behind her chair.

Matt ignored him. "I happen to know that Jake owns a twenty-two Winchester, which he claims is missing. I have a search warrant, and I'm afraid my men are going to have to search the house and the premises."

Faith stared at him as if he'd spoken Chinese.

Blair, who felt helplessly caught up in the swirling tides of tension in the room, finally said, "Matt? Can't this wait until the morning? Everyone is shocked and tired. Surely you can see that."

Almost lazily, he stood up, to his full height. He was a good two inches over six feet tall. "Sorry, Blair. The trail's already too cold for comfort—that autopsy should have been performed three days ago." His gaze locked with hers.

Blair couldn't help feeling that, in that moment, he was thinking not about the missing rifle but about the scene he'd witnessed on Cooper Street, and that his revulsion was clear in his eyes, for her and everyone to see. He made her want to explain, to defend herself. But she didn't owe him a damn thing. "May I put Lyndsay to bed?" she asked.

"After we search her room."

He refused to let her put Lyndsay to bed. Blair could not believe it.

"For the next few hours, I'd like everybody to remain here in this room," Matt said. Then he went to the front door and let his deputies in.

Blair's bedroom had its own bathroom. She had just finished brushing her teeth and washing her face, thinking about the fact that last night Matt and his men had not found the rifle, when she heard a movement in her bedroom. It was only a quarter to seven, and Blair couldn't imagine what had awakened Lyndsay at this hour. Her daughter would sleep half the morning if she wasn't awakened, and the entire household had been kept up until one in the morning because of the damned search.

Blair stepped into the room and froze at the sight of Jake standing in the doorway, barefoot, clad in Levi's, his shirt hanging out and completely open. A wide slab of his flat chest and torso was revealed. "What are you doing?" Blair gasped.

He smiled at her. "I could hear you were up." He closed her door by reaching behind him, without turning around.

Instantly, Blair became uneasy. "Jake! You shouldn't be in here." She didn't know what he wanted, but whatever it was, it could wait.

"Guess not. But you're awake, I'm awake, and last night was the night from hell." His glaze slid over her tiny, sheer tank top and cotton boys' boxers. "Nice pajamas," he said.

Blair wet her lips, her heart slamming. "If Faith walks in—"

"She can't get up before eight. The booze," he said, moving forward. "She got plastered last night. Today she'll probably sleep till nine or ten."

Blair backed up even as she absorbed the extent of Faith's drinking problem. "If you want to talk, let me get dressed. I'll meet you in the kitchen."

"Why? Why are you running scared now?" His gaze was probing.

She felt her eyes widen. "Because Faith is right down the hall and this is wrong, all wrong. Last night was wrong."

"Was it wrong? To me, it felt damned right." His hazel eyes held hers.

She noticed the dark circles beneath them then. "I won't deny that we have some kind of crazy chemistry—"

He cut her off. "We have a lot more than that."

Blair froze, but only for an instant. It was hard to remain firm—especially because of the way he was regarding her. "I'll meet you downstairs." Without giving him a chance to respond, she fled into the bathroom, slamming the door behind her.

Once there, she gripped the vanity, breathing hard, staring unseeingly at herself in the mirror. Her mind had become curiously blank. She couldn't seem to think straight, or hang on to her resolve. She kept seeing Jake standing in her room with his shirt open, in his tight, faded jeans. Abruptly Blair turned on the cold water, let it run, then began splashing her face.

And her first thought was, if they had more than chemistry, why hadn't he tried to get in touch with her in the past eleven years?

She felt him first. A pair of hard hands, closing over her hips.

Blair froze, automatically turned off the water, and looked up. She met Jake's eyes in the mirror, amazement overwhelming her, making her speechless. And he pressed his body against her from behind.

Her heart stopped.

She could not seem to move.

His grip on her hips tightened; he bent, nuzzled her neck. His lips moved there. "You smell great. You are sexy as all hell in the morning. I couldn't sleep last night, Blair. Not a wink," he murmured in a whiskey-smooth voice.

Her heart resumed its function, but with heavy, slow beats. She was filled with both desire and dread. "I hope you couldn't sleep because of all that Matt said," Blair managed. She couldn't seem to breathe, and she could feel his erection against her buttocks.

"I was thinking about you, about us," he said, kissing her neck and wedging himself firmly between her cheeks.

For one moment, Blair could not even speak. "There is no us. There's only Faith and you," Blair said, trying to twist around to face him and break the contact between their bodies. But he wouldn't let her turn. His hands held her solidly in place.

"Don't move, not yet," he whispered. "Maybe I am out

of my mind." He moved against her. His breathing was harsh, loud.

"Don't," Blair said, eyes closing.

In response, his hands slid around to her stomach and paused. Blair froze. One hand slid low, right over her pubis. Through the cotton boxers, he rubbed her.

"Stop," Blair said, thinking about Faith and Lyndsay and even Matt, panicking as shock waves of pleasure began to radiate out from the wake of his fingertips.

His face was against her neck; she felt him smile. And he slid his hand between the opening of the shorts, between the folds of her flesh. "I want you, Blair."

In that moment, the building urgency vanished as Blair imagined Faith barging into the bathroom. She twisted around, only to find herself in Jake's arms. He started to kiss her, reaching for her low again; she ducked away. "I want you out!"

"Bullshit. We both want this. You look like you slept about as much as I did, and no one will know. Relax."

"Relax? Are you serious?" She pushed at his shoulders. "Faith is down the hall. Lyndsay's next door. What's wrong with you?" she cried.

"You're what's wrong with me," he said, no longer trying to kiss her. "And you're going to be what's wrong with me until we finish something that should have been finished a long time ago."

Blair didn't move. She hadn't realized it until now, but tears were slipping down her cheeks.

Jake, angry now, dropped his hands and stepped back from her. "Why are you looking at me that way? What's wrong with my wanting you like this? Didn't you say we were two of a kind?"

Blair couldn't speak. She just shook her head wordlessly.

"Blair. We're not through. Not by a long shot." His tone softened and he reached out to touch her face.

She found her voice. It was supremely difficult. "Please leave my room. If you want to talk to me, I'll be downstairs in twenty minutes."

He studied her briefly. "All right, in the kitchen in twenty minutes." He turned and strode from the room.

Blair sank down on the edge of the bathtub, where she slumped in relief, wiping the errant tears from her face. An hour later she finally went downstairs—having finally seen Jake drive away in his Chevy Blazer.

Blair tipped the bellboy of the Menger Hotel, watching as he put her and Lyndsay's bags onto a luggage cart. Beside her, Lyndsay was scowling and making no effort to hide her extreme displeasure over the fact that they had packed up and moved to Harmony's only hotel.

Blair ignored her, walking swiftly to the registration desk. Within minutes, she and Lyndsay were checked into a single room with double beds.

"I really liked it out at the ranch," Lyndsay grumbled as they left the desk, room keys in hand. "This hotel is old and ugly, Mom."

Blair didn't respond. What could she say? But there was no way she could remain at the house, under the same roof with Jake. Not after that stunt he had pulled that morning. The more Blair thought about it, the more appalled she was.

Had he really intended to make love to her in the bathroom—with Faith right down the hall? Blair wanted to believe that he had been acting impulsively, that he would have returned to his senses before anything happened. But no matter how determined she was to think the best of him, she was sick inside.

They left the dark lobby with its wood beams and pillars behind, and paused in the full glare of the midday Texas sun. Suddenly Lyndsay was jumping up and down. "It's Mary and her mom," she cried.

"I see that," Blair said, trying to rearrange her expression before meeting Mary's mother. But she had never been a good actress, and she had no doubt that her distress was all too evident to anyone who cared to see.

Five minutes later, Lyndsay was driving off with Mary and her mother for an afternoon at the mall. Blair was relieved. She needed some time to think. Everything had happened far too quickly since she had learned of Rick's death. She felt as if she were in a whirlwind, swept off the ground. She needed to regain her balance, but right now it didn't seem to be possible.

Blair was confused. Rick had been murdered, and she couldn't even begin to analyze who might be responsible, or why it had happened. This morning, Jake had acted like slime. Faith appeared to have a serious drinking problem, and for some reason, she couldn't stop recalling the way Matt had treated her last night. As if she were the slimy one.

Blair wasn't a drinker, but right now, a beer or two seemed like a temporary solution—or at least an escape. Either that or she could go talk with Matt, try to arrive at some kind of truce, and pick his brains. He'd said something about finding powder and resin on rocks above the trail where Rick had fallen from his horse and died. What else had he found? What else did he know that he wasn't telling anyone?

"Blair."

Blair froze at the sound of Dana's voice. Reluctantly, she turned, to see her mother walking briskly toward her, clad in a short red linen dress and beige sandals. She was wearing tortoise sunglasses, carrying a red bag that looked like a classic Hermès, and she had a red print scarf over her hair, Jackie O–style. Blair was grim. She didn't want to spar with Dana today, or at any time, actually. To make matters worse, her mother looked like a movie star or a socialite. Heads were turning as she walked past other pedestrians.

"Hello, Blair," Dana said with a brief smile, pausing before Blair.

"I was just about to hail a cab," Blair lied, looking up and down Main Street, anywhere but at her mother. Just being next to her was making her shake—and feel all of seven years old again.

Dana did not take the hint. She removed her sunglasses. "Did you just check into the hotel?" she asked, with some confusion evident in her eyes.

Blair faced her angrily. "If I did, it's really nobody's business but my own." Her head was now throbbing.

Dana stared. "I'm concerned. The whole town is talking about the autopsy."

"Well, that's nice to know. Anyone have any theories about who did it?" Blair could hear how cutting and caustic her own voice was.

"Well . . ." Dana was cautious. "I guess everyone's wondering if Jake really did it."

"That's ridiculous," Blair snapped. "Jake was a wild kid, but he grew up years ago." The minute she'd spoken, the ugliest comprehension raced through her mind—that Jake hadn't grown up at all.

Blair regretted ever having the thought. She told herself it wasn't true. Jake was thirty-three, and about as self-made as a man could be.

But something inside of her hurt.

Dana was studying her with what seemed to be compassion—and maybe pity. "Is it? Rick kicked him out of Hewitt Enterprises, demoting him to a mere ranch foreman. You still care about him, don't you?"

Blair looked at her, having no intention of answering her. "How do you know that, Dana?"

She seemed uncomfortable. "Everyone knows, Blair. Harmony hasn't changed. You hang out your undies and the whole town knows you favor pink."

Blair stared at her mother. "I have to go," she finally said. "I'm late." She turned.

Dana gripped her arm from behind. "Please wait."

And Blair whirled. "Now you ask me to wait?" She was incredulous. "Did I ask you to wait when you walked out on me and Grandma twenty-one years ago?" The words popped out of their own accord. But Blair was glad they had, and she faced her mother furiously.

"Don't you think there have been times when I've regretted my choice?" Dana asked. "You have no idea what my life has been like."

"I know that I don't have a mother. My mother died

when I was eight,'' Blair said, knowing she was going for the jugular and deriving an immense satisfaction from it.

Dana froze. Blair expected her to turn on her high heels and leave. Instead, she said, "You are so high-and-mighty. Is everything always black-and-white in your world, Blair?"

Of course it wasn't. But Blair said, "This is one of those rare occasions."

"You'll never forgive me?"

"Is that why you're here? To gain forgiveness—absolution?" Blair was incredulous.

"I'm here because I care about my daughter and her child," Dana said quietly—and with surprising dignity. "And now, now I'm afraid you'll make the very same mistake you did eleven years ago. Blair, Jake will hurt you."

"Oh, really!" Blair lost all control. Rage made her actually see red. "This is strange, don't you think? Twenty-one years go by with nothing but a few lousy postcards, and now you tell me you care? And how dare you interfere in my personal life!"

"I've asked you repeatedly to meet me when I was in New York," Dana cried. "But you never bothered to respond. You could have at least called and said no."

Blair said, "What?" Surely she had misheard.

Dana was taking a tissue from her two-thousand-dollar bag and wiping her eyes with it.

Blair gripped her wrist, hard. "What did you just say? That you asked me to meet you in New York?"

"Yes, that's what I said. After my mother died, I begged you to meet me, time and again." Dana's eyes filled abruptly with more tears. They seemed to be real. "There was no point in my trying to see you while Charlotte was alive."

Blair was frozen. She couldn't seem to think. "I threw out every single card once I turned thirteen—without even looking at them," she finally said slowly.

Dana just stared.

Blair tried to recover. But all she could think about now was the fact that Charlotte had disowned Dana from the day she had left Harmony when Blair was seven years old. "Well, you sure didn't try to meet up with me before I was thirteen—I read all of those cards." Blair felt a moment of hard satisfaction as she spoke.

"Your grandmother made it very clear to me that I was not welcome—that I would never be welcome. I called so many times. She never let me speak to you. She actually threatened me, Blair. My own mother." Dana shook her head. "Mostly, though, she just hung up on me. As if I were calling the wrong number. As if I were a tiresome stranger."

Blair began to tremble. She was in shock. She reminded herself that Dana had abandoned her, that there was no excuse for that. And then she told herself that Dana wanted something now—at the least, she wanted forgiveness, and maybe she was lying about the phone calls and the postcards.

"Oh, Blair. Can't you try to understand? Yes, I ran off, leaving you behind, a young and wild girl chasing her dreams. But children grow up. Life teaches us strange lessons. I've so much wanted to find you, Blair. Talk to you, laugh with you, trade stories. Can't we let bygones be bygones?" she pleaded.

"No, we cannot," Blair said, folding her arms beneath her chest, finding her resolve once more. "I don't give a damn that you saw the light a few years ago and tried to get in touch with me. I buried you a long time ago, and the dead cannot be resurrected."

Dana turned blindingly white. So much so that Blair thought she might faint.

And Blair didn't wait to see what happened. Savagely, she turned on heel, and ran smack into Matt.

Chapter Five

*J*ake rapped impatiently on the door. He was standing on the second floor of a three-story apartment building on the outskirts of town. Below, in the parking lot, was his silver Porsche. A two-lane highway ran past this building and half a dozen others similar to it. The number on the gray door read 2 D. He knocked again.

It finally opened. "Hello, Jake," Cindy Lee said. She was wearing an extremely short denim miniskirt, a white tank top, and four-inch silver mules. "I was wondering how long it would take you to come calling." She smiled at him with bubble-gum-pink lips.

His gaze slid over her, his expression annoyed. Without a word of greeting, he walked past her into the living area of her small but pleasantly furnished one-bedroom apartment. Then he faced her, hands on his slim, denim-clad hips.

Cindy Lee closed the door and leaned against it, watching him carefully. A long, silent moment passed.

"If you think I'm gonna get down on my knees and thank you, you're wrong," Jake said.

She laughed. "Oh, I think you'll get down on your knees all right, but not to thank me."

His gaze slid to her long, bare legs.

"You owe me, Jake Cutter," she said, still smiling, but her pulse was rocketing now. "And I aim to collect."

He folded his arms, unsmiling, gaze hooded. But Jake was always that way. Inscrutable, impossible to read. And the sexiest man Cindy Lee had ever met. "I owe you," he drawled. "But I didn't ask you to tell Matt that I was with you when Rick died."

"You mean when he was murdered," Cindy Lee corrected calmly. She wondered what Faith would think—and do—when she learned about Jake's alibi. Cindy felt an immense satisfaction—hopefully Faith would divorce Jake without thinking twice about it.

Jake didn't even blink at her choice of words. "Yeah, I mean when he was murdered." He glanced at her legs again.

She knew what he was thinking. She knew her power over him. Her pulse, already high, accelerated. Her sex was warm and wet beneath the skirt, and very bare. Cindy Lee didn't think much of underwear, except for an occasional garter belt or G-string. "I'd lie for you anytime, Jake. Anytime, anyplace, to anybody." She meant it.

He strolled toward her, in no rush, with that swaggering stride of his which was one of the first things Cindy Lee had noticed about him—that, and his long-lashed, perpetually hungry, hazel eyes. "In court? To a judge? In front of a jury?" he breathed.

Her breathing was coming more rapidly now as he paused in front of her. She felt a wetness trickling down her thighs. "In a court, in front of a judge and jury," she murmured.

"Is that so?" he drawled, sliding his hand up her inner thigh. Without preamble, he palmed her, hard.

Cindy Lee thought she might come, then and there. She reached for his shoulders, straining forward, wanting to kiss him, hard.

"No," he said, avoiding her lips. "Turn around and bend over."

Cindy Lee obeyed.

Matt was the second-to-last person that she wished to see. Blair took one angry look at him and tried to barrel past him. But he caught her arm in a hard grip, detaining her immediately. "Blair?"

Vaguely, Blair heard how kind his tone was. It had no effect upon her. "Am I under arrest? Maybe I'm a suspect in my father's murder," she flung with open bitterness.

"Damn it," Matt cursed. But he didn't release her. "Hello, Dana," he said.

"Matt." Dana's lips were tightly pursed and glaringly red in her white face. She glanced at Blair, who immediately gazed past her as if she did not exist. "I guess I've outstayed my welcome," she said, her tone hoarse. She turned and left, her high heels clicking on the sidewalk.

When she had crossed the street, Blair felt some of the tension draining out of her body, but she caught herself before she slumped against Matt. He had released her. They both watched Dana get into a dark green Jaguar and drive away.

"Nice car," was all Blair could think of saying. But now the tension had renewed itself. She did not want a confrontation with Matt. Before, she'd thought of pumping him for information, picking his brains. Now she only wanted to escape. Preferably to the peace and privacy of her hotel room.

But he moved his body in front of hers, while sliding off his reflective sunglasses. "A nice car," he agreed, his blue gaze steady upon her. "But it's not hers. Apparently she borrowed it from a friend."

Blair blinked. "What?"

He shrugged. "I ran a make on the plates. How you holding up, Blair?"

Blair's eyes had widened—she could feel it. "I don't understand."

"How about a cup of coffee?" Matt asked casually—as if his disgust of the other night had never existed.

Blair was trying to comprehend what his running her mother's license plates meant as he guided her back into the hotel, one hand cupping her elbow firmly. "Why would you do such a thing?" Blair asked as they were seated in the hotel's restaurant, a simple room with a dark patterned carpet and beige walls.

It was the middle of the day and only one other table was occupied. Matt sat facing Blair, leaning back in his seat, appearing extremely relaxed. His answer was a question. "You okay?"

Blair stared at him. Although he seemed relaxed, his blue gaze was sharp and probing. "No." She stiffened. "I never intended to come home, I had no damn choice, and now look at what a mess this has become." She felt the roiling anger again. It was so intense, simmering inside of her, that she did not know what to do with it. But it was also mixed with despair.

Rick wasn't just dead, he was murdered, Jake seemed to know no bounds, Faith was an alcoholic, Dana had rudely reappeared in her life . . . Blair didn't know which issue to face first. And then there was Matt. With his steady, knowing eyes, his strong, solid body, always there, like an unwavering shadow in the Texas sun.

"Maybe this is good for you. Cathartic," Matt said, signaling the waitress. "Two coffees."

Blair slumped back against her chair. "That's easy for you to say."

"I agree. What did Dana want?"

Blair finally met his gaze. "I'm trying to figure that out. She says she's had a change of heart for years now, that she's been wanting to get in touch with me."

Matt fiddled with his spoon. He had large strong hands, Blair knew that firsthand, and long, lean fingers. Strong and capable, just like he was, solid, the salt of the earth.

She was startled by the sudden lurching, frightened feeling inside her chest. It was almost like being poised for the shock of an ice-water plunge. She glanced up and realized he was studying her. But she had no reason to be afraid of Matt. Or did she?

Maybe it was her own confused feelings that were frightening her. Or maybe it was the way he kept looking at her. "What is it? Why are you always looking at me that way— like you can see right through me, or right into me?"

He laid the spoon aside. And he said, "I hate seeing you this torn up. If I can help, I will."

Blair couldn't reply, but his simple words had the effect of knocking the wind right out of her.

He had big, strong shoulders. Blair told herself that she was very vulnerable right now. That otherwise she would never have thought of laying her head on one of them, or of being wrapped in his arms.

"Jake been terrorizing you again?" Matt asked.

Blair stared.

"I'm sorry, Blair," Matt said, grim. "I tried to warn you."

Blair didn't want Matt to have even an inkling of what had happened, but she heard herself defending Jake. "He hasn't terrorized me, as you put it. It was too uncomfortable being under the same roof with him. That's all."

"I see," Matt said. It was obvious from the look he gave her that he didn't believe a word she said.

Blair suddenly propped up her head with both hands. "You told me he hasn't changed," she whispered, wishing she could avoid the subject, but knowing she could not.

"No."

And Blair felt rotten to the core. "How long has he been with this Cindy Lee?"

It was a moment before Matt answered. "Does it matter?"

Blair had to meet his gaze. Something quickened inside her as she did, while something else kept right on dying. "What do you mean?"

Matt hesitated again. "I don't want to hurt you. But maybe a little hurting now is better than a whole lot more later. I don't know how long he's been carrying on with Cindy Lee. Because before Cindy Lee there was Theresa Vargas, and before Theresa there was Mrs. Pat Ryan, and the list just goes on."

Blair was not going to cry. She would not allow it. "Was he ever faithful to my sister?"

"You tell me."

Blair felt as if he'd punched her. She found herself staring into his eyes, but she wasn't seeing Matt, not really, she was remembering that night with Jake, just a few days before his wedding to Faith. "Oh, God," she said, wondering if she might throw up.

"It's not your fault," Matt said. "You were fodder, Blair, it's as simple as that."

Blair wiped a tear from her eyes and stared at the table. At that moment, the waitress set down their coffees and asked them if they wanted anything else. Matt ordered them two bran muffins. Blair said, "It takes two."

"Sometimes," Matt said.

Blair didn't look up as she fought for composure, aware of Matt sipping his coffee and giving her the time she needed to find it. A small voice inside of her head kept fighting the growing logic. Jake could change if he wanted to. It would only take the love of one good woman—it would only take true love—it would only take herself. She could change him, and they would have that future she'd dreamed of since she was a small child.

"Blair, does he know he's Lyndsay's father?"

Blair started, and she shivered. Matt's gaze was steady. "No. He doesn't." She knew Matt would never violate her confidence, her trust.

"That's probably a good thing," Matt said.

"He's not a bad person," Blair whispered.

"Blair. He's as selfish as they come."

Blair looked up, her eyes filling with tears. "Does Faith know? About the women?"

"Why do you think she drinks herself into a stupor every night?" Matt returned.

Again, the blow was unexpected; again, it hurt. Matt reached out and gripped her hand. "I'm sorry," he said.

Blair sniffed and shrugged it away. "I'm an idiot. I should have been prepared for this. You know, he never contacted me, not once in eleven years."

"I know," Matt said, not surprised.

Finally, Blair smiled slightly. "Are you always so astute?"

"Goes with the territory," he said, flashing a grin.

Blair tensed, leaning away from the table, staring at Matt

now. He had his own appeal, but why was she just noticing it for the very first time? She didn't want to notice how blue his eyes were, how engaging his smile. She didn't want to see that he was damned good-looking, too—just not flashy and out there, like Jake. But then, Matt had nothing to prove. And Jake had everything to prove, didn't he?

"It hurts," Blair heard herself say. "Thinking that Jake might have been involved in Rick's death." She was aware of avoiding the word "murder," and as aware that Matt knew it and wasn't correcting her.

"I hate to say this, but Jake wasn't with Cindy Lee when Rick was killed."

Blair gripped the cup of coffee. "She lied?"

"She did. Cindy Lee was at Sunset's that afternoon, watching her favorite soap operas, alone. Both the bartender and manager will swear to it."

"Oh, God," Blair said. "Matt, Jake is a lot of things, but he adored Rick—"

"Bull. You've been gone eleven years. Rick picked Jake up out of the dirt and grime, Blair, and got nothing in return."

"Is that fair?" Blair asked with real caution.

"He got a philandering son-in-law who made his daughter miserable. Who made both daughters miserable—and don't think Rick didn't know."

Blair was frozen. "He knew?" She was in disbelief. Rick had never once insinuated that he knew who Lyndsay's father was. Not once, in the many times he'd visited them.

"Honey, the whole town knows."

"I think I'm going to be sick."

Matt pushed her glass of water at her. "Jake never did an honest day's work in his life. But Rick hung in, finding him job after so-called job at the company offices. Blair, Jake's gone through a dozen titles in eleven years—if not more. Six months ago, Rick fired him. Told him not to set foot in Dallas again. I know. Rick cried on my shoulder, Blair. Literally. Because in spite of it all, he did love Jake, like a son."

Blair hugged herself. "But that doesn't mean he murdered Rick."

"No, it doesn't," Matt said. "Let's hope we find that rifle—and let's hope it doesn't belong to Jake."

Blair nodded. "But who else could it be? Who else would want to kill Rick?"

Matt smiled at her. "You do know I'm not allowed to discuss an official investigation with you."

"I thought that was only on TV." She found herself smiling back.

He laughed. Then he sobered. "What did Dana want?"

Blair stiffened. "Why did you run a make on her plates?"

He hesitated. "Because she reappeared in town last fall—and she and Rick took up where they left off eleven years ago."

Blair felt the room begin to spin. "I don't understand. Dana was still involved with Rick when she abandoned me?"

"Yeah. Drink some water," he said.

Blair obeyed. "Matt, you can't suspect my mother of being involved," she began. But she was trembling now, and she could not seem to stop.

"Rick didn't leave her a penny," he said flatly.

"She's wealthy."

"Is she? My understanding is she's heavily in debt, had a really bad prenup on the last one, and that she thought Rick would leave her the moon and the stars, not to mention a million or so and some shares in Hewitt Enterprises."

Blair was on her feet. Her mind was racing, spinning; she didn't know what to think. She didn't know if she could think. "This is a nightmare," she whispered. But suddenly she recalled a single moment from the very dark and bitter past.

Her mother with a rifle, her mother shooting the head off a snake at fifty feet. With Blair looking on, frightened and crying, not even five years old.

Her gaze wild and unfocused, Blair looked at Matt, wondering if he knew that once, a long time ago, Dana had been a crack shot. She knew she should tell him. She could not speak.

He was also on his feet, coming around the table, putting his hand on her to steady her. "I think you've had enough for one day," he said, as his walkie-talkie, hanging from one hip, began to cackle.

Blair didn't sit down. She was finding herself oddly breathless, but she kept telling herself that it was okay, everything would be all right, and Dana was not involved with Rick's death. Her mother was a horrible person. But she was not a murderer.

Matt was speaking into the radio. "Be right there." He looked at Blair as he laid some bills on the table. "Why don't you go upstairs and lie down?"

Blair wet her lips. "What is it? What's happened?"

He hesitated, grim. "Ben Ashkov was fishing out at White Rock Lake. He fished up a twenty-two-caliber rifle."

Blair didn't move.

"Go upstairs and get some rest," Matt said, his hand on her shoulder. And he was heading for the door with long, purposeful strides.

Blair ran after him. "Let me come with you."

He wheeled. "No."

She knew better than to argue. "Call me, Matt. Please. I have to know if the rifle belongs to Jake or not."

He nodded. And an instant later, he was gone.

Blair stepped out of the Honda, squinting against the sun at Rick's huge stone house. There were no cars parked in the drive in front of it. Blair could only assume that neither Jake nor Faith was at home.

She was about to get back in her car to wait, but then she thought about how the house was now hers. It was still unbelievable. Why had Rick done such a thing?

As Blair crossed the drive and stepped up onto the porch, she thought that Rick had loved her more than he had ever let on, and this was his way of showing it, even in death.

But he'd also hurt Faith. Blair couldn't understand that.

The front door wasn't locked and Blair stepped inside, where it was at least fifteen degrees cooler. She looked around, wandering first into the living room, and then back into the foyer and down the hall, into Rick's library.

Faith hadn't redecorated that room. It was still entirely masculine, with dark wood paneling and a stone fireplace and worn Navajo rugs. Blair sat down in one of the large chairs in front of the desk, tears filling her eyes.

If Rick hadn't died, she wouldn't be back in Harmony now, she wouldn't have seen Jake again, or Dana. It was hard to breathe. Jake wasn't a killer. That was impossible. But Dana?

That was impossible, too.

Blair tried to tell herself that she shouldn't care, but the lie was monstrous. Oddly, she did care, with every fiber of her being. Where had Dana been during the time of Rick's murder? Blair realized she hadn't asked Matt if her mother had an alibi.

"Hey. Saw the car. You okay?"

Blair leaped to her feet at the sound of Jake's drawl. For one instant, they stared at one another, Blair taking in the sight of him in his tight, faded Levi's, his worn cowboy boots, and a simple button-down shirt. He was still amazingly sexy. It wasn't just his whipcord-lean body or his face or his eyes; Blair thought it was some kind of sex appeal that could not be defined. She was aware of her heart racing faster than normal. "Can we talk?" she asked, folding her arms protectively across her body.

He smiled at her. "Why not?" He stepped over to the desk and leaned one slim hip against it. The huge silver belt buckle he wore drew her gaze. "Mind if I smoke?"

Blair did. But she shrugged and watched him light up with easy movements. She realized she was comparing his hands to Matt's. They weren't as large, but they were lean and dexterous.

An image flashed through her brain, of him behind her in the bathroom, his hands gripping her hips while he pushed his sex against her. Blair stiffened. "Matt went out to the lake," she whispered, her voice sounding raw to her own ears.

He dragged, but his gaze was sharp. "Yeah?"

"Some guy named Ashkov fished out a rifle, Jake. A twenty-two-caliber rifle."

He suddenly straightened, grinding out the cigarette in a Baccarat ashtray. "Shit."

Her pulse thundered now. "What does that mean?"

"It means shit, that's what it means." He rubbed his brow.

"Is it yours? Did you throw it in the lake?"

He flinched and faced her, eyes wider now—and hard. "So now you're accusing me of killing Rick, too?"

"I didn't say that," Blair said, feeling desperate.

"I think you did. Maybe you and Matt are getting a bit too cozy. He in your pants, Blair? Is that why you're taking his side in this?"

Blair inhaled, stepping back. "No. He is not in my pants, as you put it." She could not believe what he had just said. "I just need to know the truth."

"The truth is, I didn't kill him and damned if I know if that rifle is mine or not."

Blair managed to nod, lips pursed, arms crossed tightly over her chest again.

Suddenly Jake stepped forward, cupping her shoulders. "I don't want to fight with you, honey," he said. "I didn't do it, and you have to believe me."

Blair was still. His hands were uncompromising on her, and she found, to her surprise, that she did not like him holding her this way. Not now, not today. She tried to wriggle free, but he tightened his grasp. "I want to believe you," Blair said. "Please let me go."

"I don't think so," he said, and before she could react, he had pulled her close and was kissing her, hard and open-mouthed, one of his hands sliding down to grab her buttock, low and intimate.

Blair was so stunned that it took her an instant to react.

With surprising strength, she jerked free, ducking out of his reach and staring at him in shock.

"What the hell does that mean?" he demanded. "Why are you looking at me like I crawled out from under a rock?"

Blair fought to compose herself and to try to identify her emotions—which were a jumbled, rioting mess. But one feeling was standing out loud and clear. She did not want to be in his arms. Not in that moment, anyway. "This isn't the time or the place."

He stared. "So name a time. And a place."

Blair backed up another step. "Rick's dead. I haven't heard from you in eleven years. I don't think so." She realized she was trembling. She realized that she meant it.

"Then why are you here?" he leered.

She jerked. "Because I want you to be innocent." And then she heard herself say, "Because old dreams die hard."

He just stared at her with an expression that wasn't particularly pleasant. "Maybe you should go home, Blair. Back to New York City and your fancy job and fancy life."

Had he struck her, he couldn't have hurt her more. Blair was speechless.

"Sticking your nose in business that doesn't concern you isn't a good idea." Jake's gaze was ice.

"Rick was my father," Blair whispered.

"Yeah. So what? You were just the bastard, and now you're here, upsetting everything and everyone."

Blair bit her lip. She wasn't aware of upsetting anyone, other than Faith. Somehow she said, "I'll go when I'm ready to go."

His gaze hardened. And he said, "I don't think this is a good situation for Lyndsay, do you?"

Blair froze. His words rang in her ears. When she could speak, she said, "Lyndsay? Why are you bringing Lyndsay into this?"

"She's my daughter, too," he said calmly. Blair almost collapsed. He smiled at her, eyes narrowed. "I think you should take her home. A murder investigation like this is going to hurt a lot of people. Wouldn't want her in the way. Would you?''

Blair was reeling. ''Are you threatening my daughter?'' she cried.

''Our daughter,'' he corrected. ''I'm not threatening anyone, Blair. I'm advising.'' Giving her one last look, he spun on his heel and left the room.

Blair groped for the closest chair and sank down, dazed. And afraid.

Chapter Six

*B*lair was reeling. Jake knew the truth—what a fool she'd been not to realize it—and he had threatened Lyndsay. Hadn't he? Or had she misunderstood in the heat of the moment, distressed as she was? Blair prayed that was the case.

Her temples almost splitting, Blair stood and reached for her purse. When she looked up, it was to find Faith staring at her from the doorway, clad in a fitted pink sheath dress. "I didn't hear you," Blair began.

Faith's face was frozen, she did not move. But she said, "First you steal my home. Now you're trying to steal my husband?"

Blair cried out, "I didn't come here to steal anything, Faith, not this house and not Jake."

"Oh, please!" Faith stormed into the library. "The two of you were necking like teenagers on Cooper Street!" she accused, throwing her black alligator bag down on the sofa. "How dare you do this to me!"

Blair was stricken. "It was an accident. It will never happen again."

"Do you take me for a complete fool? I know Lyndsay is Jake's daughter. I know you slept with him before we married. Damn you, Blair, for doing this to me," she shouted. "But you've always wanted everything that I have, haven't you?"

For one moment, Blair could not respond. Faith's words cut; they hurt. And was she, maybe, right? "I was in love with him," Blair said unsteadily. "I'd loved him for years, ever since I was six or seven. I didn't mean to hurt you and

I didn't really know what I was doing that night. It just happened. I'm sorry I hurt you. And Faith, maybe you're right, maybe, once, I did want all of this.'' Blair glanced around. "But I have my own life now. Lyndsay and I, we have our own life."

"I want you to sell this house to me," Faith snapped. "If not, I'll see you in court."

Blair's pulse was banging, out of control. She wanted to say "Yes, I'll sell," but the words wouldn't come out. Even with the new décor, the house still felt like Rick's. His presence seemed to be everywhere, and it was more than comforting. And he had had a reason for bequeathing her the house. Blair still didn't understand—maybe she never would—and for now she said nothing.

"My father must have lost his mind when he wrote his last will," Faith said. "If your motives are so pure, you'd sell this house to me, at least. But your motives aren't pure, are they? You're just like your mother, Blair, a little fortune hunter who will stop at nothing to get what she wants. No matter who gets hurt in the process."

Blair inhaled, trembling. "I don't want to take this house from you," she finally whispered. "But I have rights, too." And she wanted to defend Dana. Dana who had reappeared in Harmony months ago, who was heavily in debt and driving a borrowed car, who had been Rick's lover yet again.

The look Faith sent her was scathing, disbelieving.

Blair turned away, feeling ill. But then, what did she expect? For Faith to love her as if they were real sisters, or old friends? She left the room, realizing nothing she might say would soothe Faith right now. As she did so, she thought she heard Faith beginning to cry. And Blair couldn't help it. She felt sorry for her.

And she wondered who had told Faith about that horrid kiss on Cooper Street. In a small town like Harmony, it could have been anyone.

Inside her Honda she locked the doors, turned the ignition, then gripped the steering wheel, unmoving except for the way her entire body trembled. She felt ill to her stomach and short of breath. Faith's words, her accusations, were haunting her, they would not go away.

She turned the air conditioner up full blast and let cooling air hit her face and chest. God. She regretted seeking Jake out in the first place—maybe she'd gotten what she deserved after all.

Blair closed her eyes tightly, against tears. She'd returned to Harmony and now she had to be honest with herself. She'd wanted to see Jake again because she'd never stopped loving him, and a part of her had hoped and yearned for his love in return, in spite of it all.

"I've been a fool," she thought grimly, blinking the tears from her eyes and finally driving away. But his words now kept echoing in her mind. What if he had killed Rick? Blair shuddered at the thought. He wouldn't hurt Lyndsay, he wasn't that kind of man. Would he? But maybe he'd try to take her away, just to get back at Blair. But for what? For spurning his advances? For coming to her senses after all these years? Or for appearing in Harmony again, and being an heiress who would deprive him and his wife of half their fortune?

Suddenly Blair wondered if Jake had even been honest with her about wanting a divorce from Faith. It was a horrible thought, both disturbing and unsettling, while reeking of the truth. The hairs stood up on her nape.

I need to get out of here, Blair thought. Automatically, her foot pressed down on the accelerator pedal. But she couldn't pack up and leave; Matt had ordered her to stay. It was hard to breathe. Blair realized she was going far too fast as a sharp curve appeared ahead of her and she took it recklessly, tires screeching, not in control. Instantly she hit the brakes and checked her speedometer as the car straightened out on the road, thanking God there hadn't been an oncoming motorist. If she wasn't careful, she was going to have an accident, and all because she was so incredibly upset and confused. Her life had been turned into a human drama that felt like an endless nightmare.

Matt's image flashed through her mind again and she

wondered if he'd seen the rifle yet and determined who it belonged to. Her heart sickened at the thought.

She had slowed the Honda to thirty-five miles an hour and suddenly she recognized the road ahead that bisected the highway she was driving on. If her memory served her correctly it was Figueroa Street. Eleven years ago Matt's parents had lived there.

The Honda slowed to a crawl.

Frank and Emma Ramsey, two of the kindest, most charitable people she knew . . . Blair wondered if they still lived at number 22.

Abruptly Blair took the turn, her pulse racing, compelled. If they were still living in the two-story country house, they would probably welcome her with open arms. She passed several whitewashed houses with large yards, an apple orchard, and a pasture with grazing Appaloosas. She stared, the Honda crawling. The house was ahead, on the left.

The large front yard boasted a green manicured lawn and was dotted with daisies, geraniums, and azalea bushes. Rosebushes climbed the white picket fence by the road. The house was whitewashed, two brick chimneys jutted up from the slate roof, and if Blair didn't miss her guess, someone had added an entire wing to the left side. An empty field was adjacent, filled with shady oak trees, a split-rail fence separating the properties. The old wood tool shed was still out back, and just visible. There was a garage attached to the house, and it was open. Blair saw the old Chevy station wagon inside it and almost fainted. They still had that car— Blair could hardly believe it. It was the first car Matt had driven when he'd gotten his license.

Blair turned into the short drive and parked beside a brand-new Seville.

She sat in the car and stared at the front door of the house, remembering being a child of eleven or twelve. Matt had brought her over a few times after school. They'd been doing some kind of inter-class project together, and Mrs. Ramsey had given them homemade cookies and then left them in Matt's room to study. She remembered sitting on the carpeted floor with him, their backs against the bed, their notebooks open by their legs. Posters had covered his walls, including one of Brooke Shields. His room had been a mess, filled with bats and balls, books and clothing, athletic trophies and scholastic awards. They'd both been so serious, Blair thought, suddenly wistful, and the project had garnered them an A.

But then she remembered writhing on the floor, Matt tickling her until she begged him to stop.

Blair forgot to breathe. A new memory surfaced. One she'd entirely forgotten about. Matt's body covering hers, their eyes meeting, Blair no longer laughing, and the sudden surge of adolescent hormones, the sudden desire and their mutual comprehension. And a brief, illicit kiss.

"Oh, my God," Blair said, getting out of the car shakily. She'd forgotten that incident; why had she recalled it now?

Knowing she had to say hello, Blair walked up to the front door and rang the bell. Matt's father, Frank, opened it almost immediately. "Yes?" he asked, not recognizing her.

He'd gained twenty-five pounds since she'd last seen him, and he was shorter than Matt by at least six inches, but he had Matt's eyes. Blair smiled. "Mr. Ramsey, hi. I hope I'm not intruding, but I had to stop by. I'm an old friend of Matt's. Blair Anderson."

His eyes widened and he beamed. "Blair? Little Blair Anderson in the dungarees and pigtails? That little Blair?"

Before she could nod, he'd pulled her into his embrace, hugging her so hard he lifted her right off her feet.

"Em!" he bellowed. "Come here. You won't believe your eyes!"

Blair was smiling as she stepped inside, immediately noticing that there was different wallpaper in the living room, new furniture, and a state-of-the-art entertainment center. Yet, in spite of the changes, everything felt exactly the same—which was warm, welcoming, familiar, and cozy.

Emma Ramsey stepped out of the kitchen, drying her hands on an apron, a plump woman with hair as gray as her husband's and spectacles perched on her small nose. She blinked at Blair.

"Em, it's little Blair Anderson," Frank said happily.

With a screech, Em Ramsey flew across the room and hugged Blair exactly as her husband had done.

To Blair's dismay, tears tried to fight their way to the surface again. She fought them. "I hope you don't mind my stopping by like this," Blair began.

Emma gripped her hand, but she was studying Blair far too closely. "We've been waiting for you to drop by. I told Matt just last night he should bring you over for dinner. He promised he'd do so, and soon."

"We're so proud of you, Blair," Frank said. "Matt's told us all about your career in New York. I hear you have a beautiful daughter, as well."

"Yes, I do," Blair said, wondering just how extensively Matt had talked about her to his parents.

"And when are we going to meet Lyndsay?" Emma asked. "When you come for dinner, dear, you must bring her, too."

Blair looked from Frank to Emma, and she nodded. Now she knew why she had come. The Ramseys hadn't changed. They were a real family, loving and warm, and Matt was so lucky to have grown up with parents like them. She couldn't imagine what it must feel like, to have a mother and father who would love you no matter what, through thick and thin.

Frank was studying Blair. He turned to his wife, exchanging a look with her that Blair caught but didn't fully comprehend. "Em, why don't you and Blair have coffee and some of those cookies you baked the other day? Go on, Blair." He smiled encouragingly. "Em's complaining I'm bad company these days. I'm in the midst of making some new shelves for the guest bedroom." He winked at her.

Blair found herself sitting in the kitchen with Em, fresh coffee brewing, a plate of cookies on the small table in front of her. She looked around at the white wooden cabinets, the white appliances, the blond wooden chairs. Then she looked out the kitchen window, past the tool shed, at the green field shaded by oaks. "You redid the kitchen, it's beautiful," she said.

"Frank retired two years ago," Emma said cheerfully, pouring two cups of fresh, fragrant coffee. "And he's been working on this house ever since."

Blair stared at her as she sat down, a smile on her plump face. "How many years has it been, Mrs. Ramsey?" she couldn't help asking.

"Oh! You mean me and the mister? Forty-three years," she said with a happy sigh. "I was fourteen when I met Frank and I've loved him ever since."

Blair nodded, close to tears again, and horrified over her lack of emotional control. "That's wonderful," she said, meaning it with all of her heart and wondering what it was like to be loved the way Em Ramsey was loved.

Immediately Emma clasped both of her hands from across the kitchen table. "Dear, you're so upset. I understand. We're both so grieved over Rick's death. He was such a fine man."

Blair felt herself begin to unravel. She nodded, looking down.

"It's not just Rick, is it?" Em asked compassionately. "I know your mother's in town."

Blair inhaled, and to her horror, tears slid out from beneath her closed lids.

"Oh, you poor dear," Emma said, standing and going around the table so she could cradle Blair against her bosom. She stroked her hair. "If crying helps, why, go right on and cry. It's good for the heart and the soul, dear."

Blair fought the tears and finally smiled up at her. "I'm sorry, Mrs. Ramsey. I don't know what's wrong with me these days."

"It's hard enough coming home after such a long time, but you've had to face a lot of memories—most of them painful, I'm sure."

Blair just regarded her. "You were always one of the kindest women I've ever known," she finally said.

"Seems to me there's never enough kindness to go

around." Emma smiled briefly. "Do you want to talk about it?"

Blair hesitated. "No. I don't think so. It's just that I'm so confused." She rubbed her temples, then glanced up. "I have these feelings for Matt," she blurted out.

Emma didn't seem very surprised and she smiled.

"Oh, God." Blair sat up like a rocket. She hadn't even realized the feelings growing in her own heart until she'd voiced the words aloud, and now she didn't know what to think or do. "I'm a wreck right now, that must be it," she finally said, but she didn't feel better, not at all.

Emma patted her hand. "There are worse things than falling in love with my son, dear," she said, her eyes bright and sparkling.

Blair stared. And she said, "Yeah, like thinking Jake Cutter's a lot better than he is, and making excuses for him at every turn."

Emma's smile vanished. "I won't talk bad about anyone, and God knows, poor Jake was dealt a bad hand once. But Rick loved him and did everything he could to give him a second chance in life." She nodded firmly.

Blair hugged herself. She could finish Emma's thoughts for her: But he blew it.

"This is interesting," Matt said from behind her.

Blair whirled, shocked, to find him standing in the doorway, tall and broad-shouldered and lean-hipped, an amused expression on his handsome face. His blue eyes were trained on her.

She prayed he hadn't been standing there for very long.

"Am I intruding?" he asked, entering the room. He went right to his mother, whom he kissed, while handing her a baker's carton. "Those bran and oat muffins you and Dad are so set on, the ones made with fruit juices instead of sugar."

"Thank you, son," Emma said, standing.

Blair realized she was staring at Matt, taking a close inventory of everything about him. The way he looked at his mother, his tone of voice when he spoke to her, the way he stood, at once casual but with a hint of easy athletic power, the way the pants of his uniform fit his buttocks, the way the gun in the arm holster seemed an extension of his body, the width of his back, his shoulders, the shortness of his haircut. Then she saw Em watching her. Blair flushed.

Em smiled. "I forgot a load of laundry in the wash," she said. "It's wet and needs to get into that dryer before I have to wash it all over again."

Matt grinned. "Yeah, Mom. Right."

Em hurried from the kitchen, humming a gospel tune.

Blair gripped her coffee cup, her heart racing with alarming speed. Why was she so nervous?

"I was surprised when I saw that rental in the driveway," Matt commented.

Blair had to look up—into his intent blue eyes. "It was impulse. Nothing more." Then, "I like your parents. I always have. They're wonderful, Matt."

"I know." He came around the table, toward her, slowly. "I like them, too." His gaze didn't waver from her face.

Blair felt her cheeks exploding with heat and she looked back down at her cup. Her knuckles were turning white, her pulse was deafening. She could hardly think.

"It's nice having you here," Matt said, stopping beside her chair.

Foolishly, Blair said, "It's nice being here." Then, glancing up, "It's safe."

He stared searchingly. "I'll always protect you, Blair. But there's more to a man and a woman than being safe."

Suddenly Blair leaped to her feet, almost knocking over her chair as she did so. "Man and woman?" she said, her voice comically high.

He studied her. "Why are you so nervous? I'm no hit-and-run artist like Jake Cutter."

Blair inhaled, managing a nod. "I know. The rifle?"

His expression changed. Became grim. "Running a trace. I'm sure it's Jake's."

Blair hugged herself.

His eyes darkened and his hands found her shoulders.

"You still want to defend him? After the way he's treated you—used you?"

She met his gaze. "No." She shook her head. "He knows about Lyndsay, Matt. I'm afraid. I'm afraid he'll take her away from me—just to spite me."

Matt's eyes widened. Then he brushed a knuckle over her cheek. And he brushed it over her mouth. "Don't worry. Jake's a loser. If he tried, there's no court that would give him custody of Lyndsay, Blair. Especially considering the way you've raised her, all by yourself. That you don't have to worry about. Trust me."

Blair couldn't reply. He'd brushed his knuckles over her mouth again, and the effect was shocking—searing right through her body, leaving a frightening urgency in its wake.

He knew, because he dropped his hands.

Blair took an awkward step back, away from him. "I do trust you, Matt. I think I always have." She glanced over her shoulder at the door. "I think I should go home."

She was about to dash for the exit when he said, "No."

Blair froze; Matt pulled her into his embrace. And the moment their bodies came into contact, his heat engulfed her, shocking her with its intensity. "No," he said again, but this time his tone was a soft, sexy murmur.

Blair tried to think of a protest as he kissed her. She tried to think if she even wanted to protest, really, and then, when the kiss became open-mouthed and wet, when they went tongue to tongue, when she could feel a hard, large erection pressing through the fabric of her jersey skirt, against her belly, between her legs, against her pubis, she just stopped thinking. Blair clung to his incredibly broad shoulders, her backside against the table. She began to spoon her softness against him, thighs spreading to accommodate every inch of him that she possibly could.

Even though she was dazed and stunned, the thought was there: why had this taken so long? Why?

He tore his mouth from hers, his breathing a raspy, uneven, loud sound. She met his gaze, mouthed a protest, which he cut off with another kiss, this one hard and sharp, followed by a fierce nipping. Matt abruptly framed her face with his hands and kissed her open-mouthed again and again, as if he wanted to suck something out of her and into him.

This time they both came up for air together, panting, shaking, almost laughing with the shock and disbelief. He threw his arms around her and pulled her more tightly against the rock-solid length of his entire body, his face against her ear. Their hearts seemed to be pounding in unison. "I have never in my life made love to any woman in my parents' house," he managed.

"That's good," Blair said, even though her knees were so weak she knew she would fall if he let her go, and that really wasn't good at all, because she felt on the verge of a huge climax and he hadn't even touched her, by God.

He drew away an inch or two to look at her with incredulity, his nostrils flared, his cheeks flushed, his entire face etched with the same urgency she was feeling. "Like hell," he said, taking her hand and pressing it to his distended penis.

The moment Blair felt him she started to see stars spangling in her mind as the first ripples of a climax began. She gripped the huge length he was showing her through the wool of his uniform trousers and her knees finally buckled. She sagged against the table, crying out. He caught her by the underside of both buttocks—beneath her skirt—and held her up, holding her wide open.

Blair cried out at the feel of his palms so low on her satin-clad bottom, exploding.

Matt cursed and fell to his knees, pressing his mouth to the vee made by the clinging fabric of her skirt, raining kisses there, tonguing her.

Her first climax, sudden and short, was barely over when the ripples began to unfold again. Blair cried out, unable to move, and she begged.

He shoved her skirt up, tore her bikini down, and slid his tongue between her lips, licking her, the tip of his tongue against her clitoris, and Blair came wildly this time, hugely, explosively, crying out and keening his name.

When she stopped coming, she was on the floor on her back, with Matt kneeling over her, his shirt hanging open, the gun holster still there, his hands frantically pushing off his pants and briefs. He finally threw pants and briefs on top of his boots and became motionless, one knee on each side of her hips.

Blair looked at every inch of him, then closed her eyes, wondering why she'd been so blind, so stupid, such a fool.

"Blair. I like it when you look."

She opened her eyes and looked some more.

He reached for her hand. She gave it to him, and let him mold it around his erection. Matt began to move then, in her hand, watching her intently.

He was slick and wet. The tip was a huge bulb, close to bursting. Blair let him thrust forward, until he was close enough to touch her lips. Then she sucked him down, all of him.

He withdrew and sliced into her and they rocked with abandon, their bodies growing wet with sweat, making slapping sounds, and then Blair knew she was coming and she told him, and he told her he was coming, too, and Blair held him, loving him, knowing now what was right and what was wrong, and she exploded, with her mouth on his, drinking him in, unable to get enough of him.

And when he had finished he rolled to his side, taking her with him, still inside her, holding her close.

Blair's breathing slowed. She kept her eyes closed, her cheek against his wet, hairy chest. Nothing had ever felt so right. She was stunned. Nothing had ever felt this way before. She'd never come so quickly, so easily. Inside her heart, there was a balloon, and it was filled with joy. Oh, God.

And with Jake, she'd never even come at all, virgin that she'd been at the time. She'd done everything she could to please him, so he would love her, never thinking of herself.

Recalling that, Blair felt sorry for the old Blair, the eighteen-year-old girl who had been so naïve and lost and desperate.

He was stroking her back, her buttocks. "What are you thinking?" he whispered.

Blair bit her lip and lifted her head so she could look up at him, into his eyes. "I'm thinking about you," she whispered, no lie. "That was so perfect. Words fail me, Matt."

He smiled, a beautiful, warm smile that creased his beautiful blue eyes. "Yeah. It was perfect. But then, you're perfect."

"Of course I'm not," Blair said, after their lips had briefly met.

"You're perfect for me," he said.

She just looked at him, trembling in the circle of his strong arms.

After a pause, during which she felt him growing in size and firmness, he said, "You do realize we're lying half-naked on my parents' kitchen floor?"

"Oh, God!" Blair shrieked, leaping out of his arms and to her feet, pulling down her very wet and ruined jersey skirt.

Matt sat up, clad only in his socks, his open shirt, and gun holster. He laughed softly at her.

She tried to ignore the lower part of his body, which kept growing. "Matt!"

"Honey, I know you didn't hear them, but my mom called out that she and Dad were going into town to do some shopping."

Blair knew she turned horrifically red.

Slowly, Matt stood up. He gave her a long look, then pulled off one sock, and another. Blair couldn't seem to move as she watched him. The muscles in every part of his body actually rippled beneath his tawny skin as he moved. She was mesmerized. And she wondered if this were a dream—because it suddenly seemed too good to be true—and she felt a moment of sheer panic.

Then he smiled at her, with promise, and as their eyes briefly held, Blair felt the panic receding, as something far more certain and immutable took its place. Her heart swelled with the joy and the love.

He had removed the gun and holster, laying it on the kitchen table. He was hugely erect now, the tip glistening with readiness.

Blair swallowed as he removed his shirt, carefully draping it over the chair, as if he were in no hurry at all. "What are you doing?" She meant to be teasing, but her voice came out strained and low.

"Making love to you another time—or two," he said calmly, reaching for her.

Blair let him pull her close, then she batted his penis away from her skirt. "You're ruining my outfit," she whispered.

"I'll buy you another one," he replied.

Chapter Seven

"Your mom should be along at any moment," Mary's mother said with a smile. She stepped out of her red four-wheel drive, a plump blonde in a yellow print dress, while both girls tumbled out from the curb side.

"Thanks, Mrs. Marley, I had a really great time," Lyndsay said, clutching a shopping bag that contained a new, cool pair of jeans with stars sewn on the front of each pants leg.

"We enjoyed your company, too, Lyndsay," Barbara Marley said, glancing at her watch.

Lyndsay looked at her own watch, a pink plastic Baby G, and saw that it was already five-fifteen. Her mom was fifteen minutes late. "She'll be here soon, she's never late," she announced.

Mary, also holding a shopping bag, poked her. "Maybe we can have a Coke at The Pegasus."

"I'm afraid not," Barbara Marley said quickly. "We have to go, Mary, I have to get dinner on before your father gets home from work."

Mary made a face that only Lyndsay could see.

Lyndsay felt a touch of anxiety then. "Mrs. Marley? You don't have to wait. Mom will be here any minute and I can wait in the lobby."

Barbara Marley hesitated, debating Lyndsay's offer. "I don't know," she finally said. "Even though Harmony's as safe as it gets."

Just then, Jake Cutter drove up in his black Chevy Blazer, rolling down the passenger-side window as he stopped adjacent to them. "Hello, girls, Barbara."

"Hello, Jake," Barbara said, smiling quickly and flushing.

"Hey, Lyndsay, need a ride?"

"I'm waiting for my mom," Lyndsay said, smiling at him. He was one of the handsomest men she had ever laid her eyes on, and she could understand why her mom always looked at him when they were in the same room. "She's late, I guess."

"Is she?" Jake smiled, studying them all. "Maybe I can help. Why don't I park up the block and I'll wait with Lyndsay until Blair returns?"

Barbara seemed surprised by the offer. Still, she hesitated.

"I am family, Barbara," Jake said with some exasperation.

She colored again. "I know that, and I appreciate your help." She was about to take Mary's hand and return to her car, when she faced Lyndsay. "Do you mind?"

"Not at all," Lyndsay said, excitement rising up in her. "Jake's my uncle and he's way cool." She blushed a little and gave him a sidelong glance.

Jake laughed. "I'm flattered," he said.

"Great," Barbara said with obvious relief while the girls quickly hugged, promising to call each other the next day. A moment later Mary and her mother had driven away and Jake had moved into their parking space. He stepped from the car.

Ruffling Lyndsay's hair, he said, "You know, I have an even better idea. Why don't we go get something to eat? I'm famished. I'll tell the desk clerk where we are."

"I don't know," Lyndsay said, wanting to agree because she was starved and she bet she could talk Jake into taking her to The Pegasus. If she went there with him, she'd be considered one of the coolest kids in town. On the other hand, she was supposed to meet her mother back at the hotel. Usually it was a bad idea to disobey Blair.

"Don't worry, kiddo, your mom will know where to find us. I'll be right back." He smiled at Lyndsay, who finally nodded, still a little scared and hoping her mom wouldn't get too mad, but deciding she shouldn't resist. Jake was also a lot of fun.

Jake strode into the hotel. Lyndsay waited outside, but the sun was hot, and Jake seemed to be taking forever. She hesitated, then after a minute or two, she followed him into the lobby.

It took her a moment to find him, because he wasn't at the front desk. She finally saw him chatting with an attractive woman off to the side by one of the room's seating areas, the woman laughing at his every word and making goo-goo eyes at him. Lyndsay couldn't imagine being so obvious. She assumed Jake had already spoken to the desk clerk.

Jake suddenly saw her, his eyes widening briefly. He left the red-haired woman and returned to her side. ''All set,'' he said cheerfully, patting her head again.

Lyndsay hoped he wouldn't keep doing that—it made her feel like a baby—but she smiled up at him and they left the hotel together.

Blair found herself humming along with Jewel as she parked her Honda in the hotel garage, forgoing valet parking. She couldn't stop thinking about Matt, and even though she was twenty minutes late, she'd somehow make it up to both Lyndsay and Barbara Marley. Oh, God. Blair burst into a smile as she walked up the ramp to the street, almost dancing a two-step as she did so. She felt wonderful. She'd never felt this way before, not even after that night with Jake.

Blair was in love.

And the best part was, Blair could count on Matt. He didn't have to say so, but she knew he loved her back. Loving someone and being loved in return was the most stunning feeling she'd ever experienced in her entire life.

Blair's smile faded when she didn't see Barbara and the girls on the street in front of the hotel. She glanced around, and saw no sign of Barbara's red Ford Explorer, either. A frisson of fear swept over her, but she shoved it away; there was no reason for her to worry. Blair looked up and down the street again, carefully. To her dismay, she saw Dana approaching.

Her exhilaration vanished. Tension overcame her. Blair did not want to speak with Dana. Not then, and maybe not ever.

"Hello, Blair. We have to talk." Dana seemed upset. "I'm so disturbed by our last conversation," she said, her eyes filled with anxiety.

Blair faced her mother warily. "How heavily in debt are you, Dana?"

"What?" Dana appeared taken aback.

"Does Matt know that you're a crack shot?" Blair asked bitterly, her heart careening with sickening force.

Dana gaped. "Are you accusing me of something?"

"I don't know. Matt tells me you're in debt. But you appear here, dressed for the society pages of *Vogue*. And you've been seeing Rick. Is it true?"

Dana wet her lips, her eyes beseeching. They clouded with tears. "Blair, I've always loved Rick. You know the kind of man he was. How could I not love him? Yes, we were lovers again—and friends. Best friends, I hope." She smiled while a tear slipped down her cheek. She opened her Chanel bag and extracted a tissue.

Blair wanted to believe her; at the same time, she didn't. Dana was very convincing, right down to the single tear. Blair decided she was a great actress. Hollywood had made a mistake in not accepting her into their ranks. "When was the last time you saw Rick?"

"The night before he was murdered," Dana replied, dotting her eyes carefully so as to avoid disturbing her makeup. "We spent that night together."

"Where?"

She seemed surprised. "At the house."

Blair's eyes widened. "Did Faith know?"

"Of course not. We were discreet. Jake knew, though," Dana said, her eyes darkening as she spoke his name.

"You think he did it?" Blair had to ask—dreading the answer.

"I think it's likely. He's very troubled, Blair. I know you're fond of him—"

"Not anymore." Blair couldn't believe how firm her tone was—and she'd spoken from the heart. Still, the last thing she wanted was for Jake to be so rotten that he was a murderer. She couldn't accept that, and she wouldn't, not until he'd been proven guilty beyond any doubt.

"I'm so glad you're over him," Dana cried, touching her.

Blair's heart raced even as she moved away from her mother's grasp. It was as if Dana cared. She seemed so genuine. And what if she did care? What if she had changed?

Life threw the oddest punches. Blair knew that firsthand.

Because never in a million years would she have imagined herself returning to Harmony and becoming involved with Matt Ramsey.

"Blair? I mean it. I've worried about you so."

Blair folded her arms across her chest, aware of being stubborn, but afraid to yield. She couldn't let Dana destroy her another time. The risk was too great. "It's too late."

"It's never too late," Dana whispered, her eyes heavy with sadness. "It's never too late to start over. Can't we try?"

Blair felt as if she were being pulled in two directions. "I have to find Lyndsay," she said, turning away.

"Oh, baby, please. I've changed, Blair." Dana followed her into the hotel.

Blair hurried into the lobby. "I don't know, Mother," she said. And then she was horrified. The word had slipped out of its own accord.

Dana stared, motionless. "Well," she finally said, unsmiling and wide-eyed, "this might be a start, after all."

Blair wanted to tell her not to count on it, but she couldn't speak.

Then she realized that Lyndsay was not in the lobby.

"Blair, what is it?"

Frightened now, she glanced at Dana, but didn't really see her. Her gaze was swinging wildly around the lobby as if she had somehow missed her daughter curled up in one of the armchairs or standing by the wall. "It's almost five-thirty. I was supposed to be here at five. Lyndsay was with Mary Marley and her mother at the mall," Blair cried. She strode to a hotel phone and dialed their room. There was no answer.

She then called the hotel operator for messages, her hands sweating now. There were none.

Blair faced her mother, a hand on top of her pounding heart.

"Darling." Dana touched her arm. "They're only late. Maybe they got delayed in one of the boutiques, or maybe in traffic. I'm sure they'll be here at any moment."

Blair heard her, but vaguely, because her mind was racing, and one thought kept looming large: something was wrong. Something had happened. Blair knew it.

Without answering Dana, she ran to the front desk and asked the clerk if he had seen Lyndsay, hoping her mother was right and knowing she was not.

And Blair got an answer she was not prepared for.

"She left the lobby with Jake Cutter," the young man said. "I'm certain of it."

"How's that burger?" Jake asked.

Lyndsay had eaten as much as she could. "I'm stuffed," she said. He was seated across from her at a small table in a restaurant and bar that was on some highway outside of town. Lyndsay didn't care for the place. She wished they'd stayed in town and gone to The Pegasus. This place was dark and smoky, crowded and noisy, and filled with cowboys and girls in tight jeans and short skirts. The table they sat at wasn't far from the bar, where most of the patrons were drinking beers and shooters and, in general, behaving in a manner Lyndsay had never seen before. There were also a few very frightening big, fat guys at the bar, in shirts that had the sleeves ripped off, ugly tattoos all over their arms, and Lyndsay knew they were the ones who had parked their huge motorcycles outside. There had been at least half a dozen in the dirt parking lot when they arrived. And the bathrooms were gross. Lyndsay had been careful not to touch anything when she'd gone to the toilet, the way her mother had told her to do. "Can we go?" Lyndsay asked.

"How about an ice cream?" Jake replied, his gaze steady upon her.

Lyndsay wet her lips. "But Blair's not here. It's almost seven. I think we should go." She meant every word. Not only did she hate this place, Jake hadn't been any fun. He hadn't said much, and the way he'd been watching her all evening had made her somewhat nervous. He hadn't smiled once, except at the *Baywatch*-type waitress.

"You always obey your mom?" Jake asked.

Lyndsay shifted uncomfortably on the straw seat of her chair. "Mostly. I think she didn't get your message, Jake. Can I call her?"

"We'll leave right now," he said, signaling the very blond waitress. "Your mom ever talk about me, Lynn?"

"No," Lyndsay said truthfully.

He stared. "You mean, she never told you that I'm your father?"

Lyndsay froze. Her heart went wild; she had to have misheard. "My father's dead. He died of cancer before I was born."

Jake finally smiled at her, but there was something cold about it, and Lyndsay gripped the table, unable to look away from him, mesmerized. "Your father isn't dead. I'm your father. Blair lied."

She couldn't seem to breathe. "My mom would never lie to me," Lyndsay said, fighting tears. But her mind was spinning. She'd always wanted a father. It was one of the things she'd yearned for desperately for most of her life. But knowing that her father had died before she was born, she'd wished and prayed for the next best thing, that her mom would one day marry, giving her the father she'd always dreamed of. But now Jake was telling her that he was her father, that Blair had lied to her. "I want to go home," Lyndsay said, hearing the tears thick in her own tone. Blair couldn't have lied. Not like this. Jake was wrong. But why would he say such a thing?

"I need my mom," Lyndsay whispered, trying hard not to cry. But tears burned their way out from beneath her eyelids, which she had squeezed shut.

"Don't be a baby," Jake said. "And don't you go crying now. I'm telling you the truth. I'm your father."

She started to cry, fat tears rolling down her cheeks. Her frightened, astonished mind suddenly thought of her aunt Faith. "But—what about Faith?"

"I made love to your momma before I married her," Jake said.

Lyndsay stared, panting. Jake was her uncle—but he was her father. Blair had lied. Sisters sharing one man. Her great-grandma had moved to New York to live with them, and before she died, Charlotte had made her go to Sunday school. Lyndsay didn't remember the details, but she knew that it was wrong, a sin, for this to have happened.

Blair had done something terrible, hadn't she?

And she had lied.

Lyndsay looked up at Jake through blurred eyes and saw that he was smiling at her, ever so slightly—strangely.

Chapter Eight

Dana's Jaguar screeched to a halt in front of Rick's house. Blair leaped out of the car before Dana had even turned off the ignition, and ran to the front door. Dana had offered her a ride after Blair had tried to telephone the house, only to find the line busy after several tries.

As Blair reached for the front door, she heard another car coming up the driveway. Hope overcame her and she turned, praying it was Jake with Lyndsay. It wasn't. Matt's cruiser halted beside her mother's Jaguar.

Blair didn't wait. She pushed open the front door. "Faith? Jake? Jake! Is Lyndsay here?"

There was no answer; the house seemed empty. But how could that be? Blair hadn't imagined the telephone being busy less than half an hour ago.

"Blair," Matt said from behind her. "What's happened? Dana said Jake's taken off with Lyndsay?" Unlike Dana, his expression was grave, as if he understood just how serious this development was.

Blair ran to him, gripping his shirt. "Lyndsay was supposed to be at the hotel with Mary's mother. Somehow, she took off with Jake. Matt! I told you he threatened her." She began to shake. Tears threatened. "If anything happens to her—"

"The Porsche is in the garage. I'll put out an APB on that Blazer of his." He touched her cheek briefly. "Calm down. Jake's a lot of things, but he won't hurt Lyndsay."

Blair didn't believe him. She couldn't afford to believe him. "Why would he threaten her and then sneak off with her behind my back? What does he hope to gain?" A thought struck her. "Oh, my God! The rifle?"

"It's Jake's," Matt said grimly. "And there's something else I haven't told you. I found a piece of fabric at the scene. The lab boys just got back to me with DNA results. It's Jake's."

Blair felt herself reeling. Matt reached out to steady her. "So he was there, with his rifle—when someone killed my father," she said unevenly.

Matt didn't reply. His gaze was searching.

"Is it proof?" she asked, overwhelmed now with the possibility that Jake was a murderer.

"It might be enough for a conviction. Only a jury can say for sure," Matt said.

"What conviction?" Faith slurred from the steps above them as Dana walked into the house.

They both turned. She was standing on the stairs in a pair of slacks and a beautiful white shirt, gripping the banister as if she might fall over otherwise. She was soused. And it wasn't even half past seven.

Blair stepped forward. "Where's your husband? He's taken my daughter, and I demand to know where he is!" she shouted.

Faith swayed where she stood. "How would I know where my husband is? If anyone does, it's you—the other woman." She was openly bitter, even in her drunken state.

Blair stiffened. She didn't look at Matt. "I'm not the other woman, Faith. I told you that before."

"Oh, please," Faith said with disgust. She came slowly, awkwardly, down the stairs. "Jake didn't kill my father. What do you mean, about a jury convicting him?"

"We found his rifle, Faith," Matt said gently, reaching out to help her down the last few steps. "He was at the scene."

Faith stared at Matt, tears filling her eyes.

Dana had left the front door open and Blair saw the black four-wheel drive at the same time that she heard it approaching. She stiffened, incredulous, as the Blazer stopped on the other side of Matt's cruiser. And then she ran.

To the door and outside and down the front steps. Lyndsay slipped from the passenger side, tears dried all over her face. Blair took one look at her and pulled her into her arms, holding her hard and tight, beginning to cry with relief and fear and anger, beginning to shake like a leaf. "Thank God," she whispered against her daughter's head. "Thank God! Lynn. Did he hurt you?"

Lyndsay looked up at her, crying now. "I hate him. He told me he's my father! But you said my father died before I was born," she cried accusingly.

Blair froze.

And when she could move, it was to place Lyndsay behind her and face the man she had once, foolishly, loved.

He was staring at her, his expression tight and hard and impossible to read.

"You bastard," she snarled. "If you ever come near my daughter again, I'll kill you."

He laughed. "You hear that, Sheriff?"

"Shut up, Cutter." Matt stepped forward. "You're coming with me."

Jake slowly turned to face Matt. "I need a lawyer?"

"You do. And I'm going to advise you of your rights," Matt said. "Anything you say can be held against you—"

"I didn't do it," Jake said, but his face was sullen and fixed.

Matt ignored him, reading him his Miranda rights from a small notebook he'd taken out of his pocket. Watching them, with Lyndsay now huddled behind her, no longer crying but riveted by the unfolding drama, Blair felt as if she were the observer of some surreal play. This couldn't be happening—but it was.

"Stop! Jake's not at fault!" Faith flew down the steps, stumbling in her inebriated state.

"Go back inside," Matt said.

But she ran to them, staggering. And when she halted, panting and out of breath, her gaze was on Jake—and he was staring back at her. Faith wet her lips. "It's all my fault," she said hoarsely.

Matt reached out. "Faith, you'd better stop right now until you talk to a lawyer."

"I don't need a lawyer," she cried, still looking at Jake, tears falling. And he never looked away from her, either. "It was my idea. I planned it. Jake did what I told him to do."

A shocked silence ensued.

Instinctively, holding Lyndsay tightly, Blair moved closer to Matt. How could this be happening? Faith and Jake, conspiring to murder Rick together?

And for one moment, something flickered in Jake's eyes. "Faith," he whispered, agonized.

Faith moved into his arms, weeping. And he held her, cheek to cheek, his eyes closed.

"Mom? Why did you lie? Did you lie?"

Blair sat on the bed in the guest bedroom where Lyndsay lay. She stroked her hair. "I did lie. I did what I thought was best, and maybe I made a terrible mistake. I did it for several reasons, one being that I never forgave Jake for marrying my sister. Stupidly, I loved him back then. But I was only eighteen. And maybe that reason was the wrong reason, but you're the best thing that's ever happened to me. I wanted to protect you, Lynn, because I didn't trust Jake and I was afraid one day he'd try to take you away from me." Blair felt her own eyes moistening.

Lyndsay was silent. She finally said, "He murdered my grandfather."

"Oh, honey," Blair whispered. "Can you ever forgive me?"

"It's okay, Mom. I think I understand. I don't like him anymore. He's mean and cruel. And he killed Rick." Tears filled her eyes.

"He'll never hurt us again, I promise you that," Blair said hoarsely, kissing her daughter's cheek. She meant it. She wondered what was happening down at the police station. Two deputies had taken Faith and Jake away, Jake in handcuffs, both of them in the locked back seats of police cars. Blair shivered.

Lyndsay smiled a little at her. "I love you, Mom. You're still the best."

"And you're the best daughter anyone could ever have," Blair whispered, meaning it. "I'm so proud of you. You're so brave."

Lyndsay smiled a little again. After a short silence, she said, "I always wanted a father. And now I've got one. This is really sad."

Blair bit her lip. It was hard to think of what to say, so she spoke from her heart. "Life isn't easy, Lynn. I've tried so hard to make it easy for you, but sometimes things happen that are unfair, things we don't deserve, and we just have to deal with them the best way that we can. I don't know why bad things happen to good people; I wish I had the answer to that. But at least we have each other. We'll always have each other."

Lyndsay yawned.

"Sleep tight," Blair whispered. After Lyndsay's traumatic experience, she had decided to stay the night at the house. It wasn't really an issue, because Jake and Faith were gone, and technically, the house was hers.

It was still unbelievable. The entire past few days remained incomprehensible to Blair. But one thing seemed certain. She didn't want the house. Not now. Not like this. There were other ways to hold on to Rick, to remember him and respect him. Like becoming an active part of Hewitt Enterprises.

Blair thought Lyndsay had fallen asleep when she said, softly, eyes closed, "And Matt."

Blair tensed. She knew he was still downstairs, waiting to talk to her, waiting to see if she and her daughter were all right. "What?"

But Lyndsay had fallen asleep.

Careful not to wake her, Blair eased off the bed. She turned off the lights, but left the door wide open. She would check on her every hour or so, to make sure she was sleeping soundly and not having nightmares after what she'd been through that day. And then she heard a loud thump from the master bedroom at the end of the hall.

Rick's room. She heard another thump—as loud if not louder than before.

Blair couldn't imagine who was upstairs in Rick's room. She was concerned. The help slept out. She walked quietly to his door, which was ajar, and slowly peered around it.

Dana, her face flushed with rage, threw a beautiful humidor at the wall. Several books were scattered around the floor; she'd obviously just thrown them.

Blair stepped into the room. "What are you doing in here?" she demanded—when she saw the safe on the wall. It was wide open.

Dana started, eyes wide, clearly surprised to see Blair. And she did not reply.

"I asked you a question," Blair said, walking over to the safe and checking inside. It was empty.

"That's right—it's empty. Empty!" Dana cried. She whirled, grabbed a vase and smashed it against the headboard of the bed. Colorful ceramic shards shattered across the heavy quilt covers. Dana was panting from her exertions.

"Stop it!" Blair cried. "How did you open the safe?"

"I figured out the combination ages ago," Dana said angrily. Suddenly she faced Blair, hands on her hips. "He let me wear this Bulgari necklace he'd bought for Elizabeth for an anniversary present some years ago. He said it was mine. He promised it to me. It's worth a quarter of a million dollars! But it's not in the safe! Do you know where it is?"

"I don't," Blair said, very still now, so still she could hear her heavy, drumming heartbeat. She stared with growing dread.

"You'll find it and give it to me, won't you, Blair?" Dana approached her, eyes eager. "Rick promised me millions of dollars. He said he'd take care of me, that I'd never have to worry about money again. He promised! And now he's dead, he left me out of the will—it had to have been a mistake—and the damn safe's empty, too! Blair?"

She was aware of the huge hurt inside her that had been born when she was only a small child and that had never really died. She recalled Jake's sullen face, and his even words: ''I didn't do it.'' Faith's image then flashed through her mind, so clearly, tears streaming down her face, having eyes only for Jake, telling them all that it was her idea, her plan. And she remembered the way Faith had moved into his embrace, and the way he'd held her afterward.

Jake could say whatever he chose, but Blair had seen the bond between them. They still loved each other.

And mostly, she recalled the flicker in his eyes when Faith had confessed—a flicker that she had not understood then. It had been a flicker of surprise.

Blair wet her lips, which were dry and felt cracked. ''Where were you when Rick was murdered?''

Dana had begun to pace, now she whirled. ''What? Faith confessed! Faith and Jake are the killers!''

Blair said, slowly, ''Faith loves Jake. I think Faith would say—and do—anything to protect him.''

''Then she lied—but it was Jake's gun, his shirt.''

Her heart beat harder, faster. ''How do you know about the shirt?''

Dana froze. Then, too quickly, ''Why, Matt told me, I guess.'' She smiled at Blair and moved to her. ''Baby, you're overwrought, and who can blame you? How is Lyndsay, is she okay? I can't believe Jake dropped that bombshell on her!''

''I didn't tell you anything, Dana,'' Matt said from the doorway, behind them.

Dana turned white. ''I thought you took Faith and Jake to town,'' she cried.

Matt stepped over to Blair. ''Maybe you knew about the shirt because you stole it, just like you stole Jake's gun. On one of those long, lazy afternoons you spent right here with Rick. Or maybe in the middle of the night—the day before he died.''

''That's absurd,'' she said through stiff lips.

Matt reached into his pocket and came up with a yellow

receipt. "Hertz car rental," he said. "I've impounded the vehicle, Dana."

Dana stared, eyes wide.

"She rented a four-wheel drive the morning Rick was killed," Matt said to Blair, never taking his eyes from Dana. "She returned it that evening. I didn't think much about it at first, until the lab boys came up with a tire imprint at the scene that matches the Hertz vehicle exactly. It's a safer assumption to say that Dana was at the scene than it is to say that Jake was there."

"Faith confessed," Dana said flatly, eyes glazed.

"Faith's in love with her husband and would take the rap for him if she could. Anyone could see that," Matt said quietly.

Blair hugged herself. This hurt worse than anything previously. Her mother . . . oh, God.

"You can't prove anything." Dana smiled, but it was cold and hard, and suddenly she looked older than her years.

"I beg to differ," Matt said. "Modern forensics are an amazing thing." He smiled. "There's a spot of blood on the front seat, passenger side. I never saw it. One of the lab boys got it right away. Now whose blood do you think that is?"

"Oh, my God," Blair whispered.

"It's Rick's, and it had to have come off the butt of Jake's gun," Matt said.

Dana was breathing harshly, her face white, nostrils pinched. "No jury will ever convict on such flimsy evidence."

Matt stared her down. "I've only just begun to build my case," he said.

Blair sat on her bed, her laptop powered on and open beside her. It was close to eleven. She couldn't sleep. She had no intention of even trying.

She'd cried for a while, for Lyndsay, for Jake and Faith, for herself, and maybe even for a small child who had been deprived of a mother, with only God knowing why. It would be a long time, she thought, before she could come to grips with her emotions. In the end, she felt sorry for Faith, and maybe for Jake, too, but she was relieved they weren't killers. As for Dana, she felt angry and hurt and betrayed all over again. But one thing was clear. Thank God she hadn't believed her offers of friendship, thank God she'd been wary and mistrusting, or the betrayal would be all that much greater now.

Blair looked at the laptop. She'd been composing a fax to her boss. She'd taken a week off, and now she wanted to extend that by another week. She wasn't ready to go home.

Blair looked around at the room. Rick's legacy was this house, Hewitt Enterprises, and all the good works he'd done for the town. Blair gripped the bedspread, close to tears again. The house belonged to Faith. There was no question about it.

Tomorrow Blair would sign the deed over to her for some nominal amount, just to make it legal.

She could pack up right now and go home. There was no reason to stay.

But whom was she fooling? There was Matt, and what they had just begun. Blair didn't have a crystal ball, so she couldn't predict the future, but how could she turn her back on him now? How could she simply walk away without even trying to make the relationship thrive? He was a very special man.

Blair hugged herself. She didn't even want to go back to New York. Not today, not tomorrow, not in another week. Harmony was a small town, where life was awfully simple, but God, it was home. For eleven years she hadn't had a home, Blair realized. But now she did. It had always been home and it would always be home and it felt good now, being able to think it and say it and feel it.

Blair cried some more.

When she had dried her eyes, she pulled over the laptop and quickly wrote a resignation letter. She plugged in the modem and faxed it off to New York, and when she was done, she felt as if a huge weight had been lifted from her shoulders, one she'd carried for far too many years.

She got up, stepping into her slides, and walked to Lyndsay's room. She was sound asleep.

Blair went quietly downstairs, not wanting to wake anyone, her car keys in hand. She was about to walk out the front door when she realized she was being watched. She turned. The living room was cast in absolute darkness and she strained to see.

Someone was there. A shadowy form on the sofa.

Blair walked to the threshold. A full moon was shining, and some of its light was streaming through one of the windows. Blair made out Faith sitting on the couch, as still as a statue.

She turned on one lamp, saw the drink in her hand and the tears on her face. "Are you okay?"

Wordlessly, Faith shook her head.

Blair hesitated. "Can I join you?"

Faith looked at her. "Why? To gloat?"

Blair came forward and sat down beside Faith, itching to take the drink out of her hand and throw it in the trash. Of course, she did no such thing. "Can we start over?" Blair asked impulsively.

Faith made a sound and drank.

Blair laid her hand on her half sister's knee. "The house is yours. I'll sign it over to you tomorrow, I don't want it."

Faith gaped at her.

"But I'm going to stay in town. He was my father, too, and it's clear he wants me to be a part of Hewitt Enterprises. I'm going to work with you, Faith. Not against you."

Abruptly, unsteadily, Faith stood. "This has been one of the worst nights of my life," she said, staring past Blair. Then she looked at Blair. "No. There have been worse nights. When Jake comes home at four in the morning, another woman's perfume all over his clothes."

Blair inhaled, hard.

"Have you slept with him?" she asked, mouth downturned, gripping the glass of scotch tightly. Her white knuckles stood out eerily in the dimly lit room.

"Only that one time eleven years ago. I'm sorry, Faith. So sorry that he treats you this way." Blair meant it.

She shrugged. "So am I." And she started to cry.

Not soundless tears, not small cries, but huge wrenching gasps of deeply rooted pain. Blair was on her feet. She didn't know what to do. She hardly knew this woman who was her sister. But she had never heard anyone cry this way—except maybe at a funeral. Finally, she reached out and laid her hand on Faith's small shoulder.

Faith finally stopped crying and moved away from Blair. "I'm sorry. Too much booze."

"You can always leave him."

Faith glanced at her. "I love him."

"He's not worthy of you," Blair cried, fists clenched.

Faith's face crumpled again.

Blair rubbed her back. It wasn't an easy gesture, it was like comforting a stranger. "Things will look differently tomorrow," she whispered, praying that would be so.

Faith nodded, but clearly she didn't believe it. "Is something going on between you and Matt?" she asked abruptly.

Blair knew she flushed. "Yes."

Faith studied her. "He's a wonderful man. You're lucky. I'm going to bed." She staggered to the door, clearly trying very hard to walk normally and failing. Blair hurt, watching her.

At the doorway, Faith paused. "If you and Lyndsay want to stay here instead of at the hotel, until you get settled somewhere, it's fine with me."

The two sisters looked at each other, their gazes meeting directly for one of the few times in their lives.

Blair wet her lips. "Thank you, Faith. I need to think about it. But maybe we will." She was overwhelmed by Faith's offer. It had to signify a new beginning for them.

Faith nodded. "Good night." She left.

Blair stared after her, her pulse elevated, hoping against hope, and then she left the house. Within moments she was driving down the road; fifteen minutes later she was parking in front of the sheriff's department, which was next to the courthouse. She didn't bother locking the car, and as she started up the sidewalk, she saw him, sitting in darkness on the limestone front steps of the courthouse, just outside of the circle of light thrown by the cast-iron street lamps.

Blair's strides slowed.

His head came up as he saw her.

Blair smiled.

A moment later she sat down beside him, shoulder to shoulder and thigh to thigh. It felt so right. "Are you okay, Matt?"

He studied her closely. "I was going to ask you that."

Blair smiled. "I'm good." Her smile widened; a song began in her heart. "Really good."

He wasn't startled, but his gaze roamed her features, one by one, slowly, in no rush.

Blair shivered, for the way he looked at her was so intense, and she reached for his hand.

He enfolded her smaller palm in his larger one. "If you've got good news, I'd like to hear it," he said softly.

Her heart beat. With life, with love, with certainty. This man meant everything to her—she had been waiting for him her entire life. "I just faxed my resignation."

Matt leaned toward her, sliding his arm around her. "I'm glad we got that one out of the way," he said with a smile.

"Me, too."

And they sat there together silently on the front steps of the courthouse, in the darkness cast by the vast and silent Texas night. It was a long time later before they got up, not to go inside his office, but to get into Blair's car and drive back to the house, and when they did so, a pink blush was staining the sky. It was a new day in Harmony, Texas.

Across a Crowded Room

❦ ❦

Judith O'Brien

Chapter One

*T*he main reason I, Nicole Lovett, decided not to attend the impromptu memorial service for my co-worker was simple. There was a very good possibility that I was the murderer. Or murderess, if one is a stickler about such things.

It would not have been a case of intentional homicide. It's just that, well, let's face it, I had plenty of motive. But let me back up first, so you can see how this whole mess got started.

The one thing you should know about me is I'm secretly ambitious. Not in an Eddie Haskell–obvious sort of way. No, I'm one of those people who graduated at the top of my class in both high school and college, and stood at the podium with the tassel flapping in my eye, enjoying the stunned expressions on everyone's faces.

My successes are usually unexpected by everyone but me. If I could be turned into a character in one of Aesop's Fables, it would be the slow-but-steady tortoise in ''The Tortoise and the Hare.'' Or if you blinked me into an old movie, I would be Eve Arden, the wisecracking friend of the heroine in the satin gown. In short, my style is to disarm with an absolute lack of a prethought style. And it usually works.

Not that I lack style, mind you. But when you're twenty-eight with strawberry-blond hair and blue eyes and freckles sprinkled on your nose, and more often than not you come into work on Monday morning with skinned knees from roller-blading or flying over the handlebars of your bicycle, femme fatale is usually not a viable option.

That's why everyone at the television station was so surprised when I applied for the weekend anchor position. Before you get all excited, let me explain a little about the station.

Years ago it was a UHF station, one of those channels on the second knob that went up to one hundred. The higher the number, the lower the ratings, budget, and frankly, the quality. It was known for poorly produced local ads and B movies from the 1950s. Then came cable, and even though it's still Channel Eighty-nine, it comes in clearly with basic service in Savannah. No need to pound the television set or to jiggle the rabbit ears anymore. The programming changed as well. The B movies have been traded in for long stretches of infomercials, religious chat, home shopping segments, and reruns of canceled network shows from the 1970s.

Now the big fear was that it would be bumped from basic cable for another station, most likely the All-Fishing Network from Tarpon Springs, Florida. As silly as it sounds, there are lots of people who are riveted by watching men in flack jackets and cheap aluminum rowboats, casting their lines into the water accompanied by background banjo riffs and dialogue such as "Whew, Bobby! You've got a real fighter there!"

That's where I come in. Channel Eighty-nine hired me from Channel Thirty-eight in Chattanooga ("Thirty-eight in the Great Tri-State!"), where I had been since getting my B.A. in communications. There I became known as a jack-of-all-trades, and when Channel Eighty-nine hired me at almost double my previous salary, it was with the understanding that I would help launch some original programming to keep the fish network at bay. They had been impressed with my sample reels from the Chattanooga station, and were delighted that someone with my experience would accept a job at such a low salary.

They had no idea, did they? The Chattanooga station was, in fact, a double-wide trailer on a rise behind the Piggly-Wiggly. We were close enough to a poultry processing plant to get feathers stuck to the satellite dishes and on the windshield of the "Great Thirty-eight" minivan, which doubled as a pizza delivery truck when the college intern used it on weekends. The upholstery always smelled of pepperoni the first half of the week. Nobody complained. The kid owned the van.

In spite of the makeshift atmosphere, I loved getting the chance to do just about everything there, from writing copy to designing sets and setting up the cameras. I sold advertising slots, produced the commercials, and made the clients' children look cute and talented as they lisped through the lines. I even appeared on camera a few times. Occasionally I was the weather girl in the studio, pointing to smiley-faced suns or cheerful umbrellas. Most of my airtime was outdoors, during storms or when the highways flooded. That was me in the yellow slicker, shouting over the rain and trying to remain upright during tornadoes and mudslides.

It was a handy first job. Chattanooga is my hometown and my parents still lived there. Everyone knew I lived at home, and my mom or dad drove me to work most mornings. They didn't want the car to get plastered with feathers by sitting in the lot all day. Fair enough. However, it did cut into my credibility as a serious journalist when I had to call my mom to pick me up at the end of the broadcast. Surely Edward R. Murrow never had to call *his* mom for a ride home.

The combination of a paltry non-union salary, college loans to repay, sending sample reels to other stations, and the costs of my fairy-tale wedding that never took place didn't offer much choice. No bachelorette pad for Nicole, even with roommates. Even on the outskirts of Chattanooga. Places with names like Soddy-Daisy were well beyond my means.

So by the time the Savannah offer arrived, I was absolutely thrilled at the prospect of a new job in a new city, a place with no memories. Even after all those years, it still hurt to drive by the hotel that would have hosted my wedding reception, or to attend church, knowing that aisle was the very same one I should have walked down in the beautiful, overpriced white dress. The time had come for a fresh start.

And Savannah had an extra added attraction: there was a place for me to live rent-free. In fact, it was one of those grand antebellum places on a square. Until a few months earlier it had been the home of my great-aunt, Adele Lovett. Before that it had been the home of generations of Lovetts, my father's family. Aunt Adele had been the last of her generation of Lovetts—her youngest brother had been my father's father. That's about all you really need to know about the Lovetts. They were an old Savannah family, and now there were none left to carry on, to live in the Lovett homestead.

Except, of course, for me.

Aunt Adele passed away without leaving a will, so the house automatically went to my father. He was thinking of selling the old place until my job offer came along. Not that my parents don't love me, but the truth is, they didn't enjoy driving me to work at six in the morning any more than I did. They were absolutely delighted with my new job. And it would eliminate, at least for the time being, the dilemma of what to do with Aunt Adele's rambling place. They would help me with the taxes, and in return I would play the on-site caretaker. With my new salary I could actually afford a car. All in all, it worked out pretty well.

Not surprisingly, the Savannah station was a lot like the Chattanooga station. It was a larger version of the double-wide trailer. They were just beginning to do local news reports and talk shows.

Still, the bread and butter of the station came in the form of infomercials and local commercials. They started to use me, first in the production, in writing the copy and organizing the shoots. And then, when Brynn Swann, the regular weather girl and occasional anchor, was unable to demonstrate products on camera, they turned to me, Nicole Lovett.

Brynn Swann was exactly what her name implied—tall, unnaturally blond, with a perfectly pitched voice and a burning desire to become the next Kathy Lee. I didn't blame her for the ambition. Hey, I was waiting to take over when Diane Sawyer called it quits. But I did blame her for backing out of the infomercials she felt were below her dignity.

Thus I was the one to demonstrate extra-wide peach-flavored dental floss. When it became stuck in my front teeth, I was forced to keep on praising the product, a full yard of string dangling down my chin like an otter at Sea World. The cameraman was doubled over in hysterics, but the advertisers loved it and asked to use that tape every time. For two years I sliced onions with miracle-choppers, mopped filthy floors with self-wringing sponges, pitched home courses for aspiring dental hygienists, made sock puppets from a kit, and stood in my yellow slicker during hurricanes.

And for two years I hoped that Brynn Swann would call in sick. Just once. So I could go on in her place, so I could dazzle the station manager and the news director and the viewers with my spectacular reading of the news.

Then it happened.

It was a Wednesday, and a local beautician had coated my legs with Hair-Go, her own formula spray-on leg wax. But she forgot the other step, Hair-Gone, the solution that removes the wax and, in theory, the unsightly hair. She had to go back to the shop to get the Hair-Gone. Meanwhile, my legs picked up every piece of paper in the studio—newspaper clippings, a candy-bar wrapper, wire-service copy, toilet paper. It was like being human flypaper—all very amusing.

Until the news director rushed in.

"You're on in five, Nicole," he shouted. "Brynn can't make it. She's had an allergic reaction to her eyelash glue."

"You're joking!"

"Do I look like I'm joking? Get over to makeup and cover those freckles!"

The freckles were to be hidden, but no mention of the Baby Ruth wrapper on my left knee.

Then it hit me—this was my big chance! My legs would be under the plywood newsdesk, out of camera sight. Suddenly I had visions of old show business legends, of going in a kid and coming out a star. Finally, it was my turn!

I was in and out of makeup in two minutes, settled behind the desk—legs slightly apart so the paper wouldn't rustle, and so they wouldn't get stuck together like a beached mermaid. I was all set, ready to go.

One minute until airtime. One more minute and . . .

"I'm here! I'm here!" Brynn's unmistakable voice wafted over the studio.

Someone yanked me from the chair, and next thing anyone knew, Brynn Swann, her eyes slightly puffy, did her trademark perky rendition of the day's major stories, remembering to frown if the report ended in death or dismemberment, smiling if the cat in the tree was rescued.

"Sorry, Nicole," mumbled a cameraman.

"Bummer. You almost had your chance," someone else said. My back was patted, heads shook at the opportunity lost.

"You'll get another chance soon," the news director smiled. "After all, hurricane season's coming up."

I shot him what I hoped was a murderous glance, but it was hard to look intimidating with refuse plastered to my legs.

That had been a low point. But a few weeks later, something miraculous occurred.

Brynn Swann announced she was leaving the station. Her contract was up, and she would be moving to Florida. Brynn Swann was going to be the new hostess for the All-Fishing Network.

Almost before the words were out of her lip-lined mouth, I was writing my application for her position. Even as I wrote, my own mouth was set into a grin. This was a mere formality, the application. Of course I would replace Brynn! I had been such a good sport, so patient. Not many women would put up with the indignities of demonstrating a cat toilet on television.

At last, it was my turn.

The guys at work took me out for drinks, all assuming

the job was mine. They were a bit surprised by how swiftly I had gotten my name in to the station manager. As I mentioned before, I'm quietly ambitious. So we drank fluorescent-colored concoctions with names such as Screaming Zombie and Samurai Revenge. I woke up the next morning with a hangover, a collection of oversized souvenir glasses from the drinks . . . and the news that the job wasn't mine after all.

They had hired a "name" to compete with the fish people. She was a former Miss Georgia. She had absolutely no experience beyond twirling a baton to John Philip Sousa music and waving from a float. Above all, she was someone I had known since ninth grade.

They hired Martha Cox. They hired my high school nemesis.

They hired the woman who stole my fiancé. And not incidentally, the woman whose death I would soon cause.

Now do you see why I couldn't speak at her memorial service?

Chapter Two

*E*very high school has a Martha Cox. Years later, the mere mention of that name still carries the power to evoke an uncontrollable shudder. It's the reason most people don't attend high school reunions, unless they are secure in the knowledge that their Martha Cox had gained a few hundred pounds or become a national spokesperson for alien abductions. A friend of mine had a Martha Cox who joined a motorcycle gang and had a devil tattooed below her left eye.

No such luck with my Martha Cox. She remained exactly the same as she was the first day I met her.

It was freshman year, and Martha Cox sat directly in front of me during the orientation assembly, flipping her perfectly trimmed hair in my face. The next four years were a continuous blur of hair flipping in my face. When I tried out for the lead role of Laurey in *Oklahoma!* it was, of course, Martha who got the part. Instead, I played Aunt Eller, a noble part to be sure, but one that consisted of churning butter on the porch, slapping my thigh, and commenting about the ''young'uns'' as I walked bow-legged off stage. She got to be Shirley Jones. I was Walter Brennan.

The next year I tried out for Sarah Brown in *Guys and Dolls*. People still rave about how Martha played the role. No one mentions me, the second streetwalker in the opening act and the angry hobo in ''Sit Down, You're Rockin' the Boat.''

She wasn't *that* good, not really. It's not as if she were an absolute beauty—she wasn't. Her nose was funny, as if someone smushed a ball of Silly Putty. Not flat, just a little odd for a nose. But men never seemed to notice her Silly

Putty nose or the way she flipped her hair. They just thought she was good-looking.

To her credit, she did have a certain charm, always laughing and blushing, batting her eyelashes and letting guys carry her books. Once I dropped my books, blushed, and told my boyfriend at the time they were too heavy for me to possibly carry. He suggested I get a backpack.

In hindsight, she must have hypnotized them.

Until junior year, Martha Cox was just annoying. Then she embarked on a new phase—boyfriend stealing. And I was her first victim.

That was the year of the big winter party, a turnaround dance where the girl asks the boy. I asked Mark . . . let me see. I can't remember his last name. Anyway, I asked him a little early just to make sure he could make it. It was a courtesy on my part, pure and simple. He seemed a bit surprised. Well, it was only September, and the dance was in mid-December. High school kids operate in their own time zone, much like dog years. So asking Mark to the dance a few months in the future was similar to asking a toddler where he would like to retire. But the point to remember was that he said yes. A clear, definite, stand-up-in-a-court-of-law yes.

After hours spent in the library during sixth period, we really got to know each other. A quirky guy, that Mark. He had a funny preoccupation with Jack the Ripper, and used to write me notes pretending to be Jack between jobs. Then he started hiding behind lockers and under stairwells, waiting for me to appear, whispering "It's me, Jack. I'm in Whitehall, the mist is swirling. And I perceive my next victim."

Come to think about it, he was a little weird, but hey, who isn't at sixteen?

The bottom line was the week before the dance, I knew something was up. He no longer wrote me notes signed in a slash, no longer crouched in the hallway. Then he told me. He was dating Martha. She had asked him to the dance. He, of course, had said yes.

"Hope you don't mind." He had kicked the toe of his tennis shoes against his locker as he mumbled.

Well, as a matter of fact I did mind. Ran all the way home from school in tears, in fact. This was the big dance, my dress was ready. My mother had even had her old pearls restrung, so when I walked into the living room, there was my midnight-blue dress spread out on the couch with the pearls. They looked perfect. But now I was officially dateless like those poor girls who write to the advice column in *Seventeen* magazine. Because of Martha Cox, I was one of those pitiful cases that made kind people wince and the less kind feel good about themselves.

In the end I went with another guy, and must confess we had a great time. The evening's big moment was when Martha and Mark broke up very publicly during the band's rendition of "Do You Really Want to Hurt Me." Still, this set a pattern.

The next year it was Olë, the exchange student from Norway. Then Ricky Dale Simpson. And at last I was finally free from the clutches of Martha Cox. We graduated from high school, and she went off to the University of Georgia and later became Miss Georgia.

Now this was where she got so sneaky. She was from Lookout Mountain, Tennessee, but she entered the contest for Miss Georgia. That never made any sense to me, although someone once told me it's much easier to win Miss Georgia than Miss Tennessee. Don't remember why, but that would be just like Martha Cox to go for the easy state.

I happened to see the Miss America contest on television that year, and she smiled and said although she was from Tennessee, she was so close to Georgia she could smell the peaches on a good day. The top ten finalists were named, but in the end she lost the big crown to a tap-dancing piano player from Texas. She remained Miss Georgia, cutting ribbons at shopping malls and giving inspirational, golly-you-can-do-it speeches at high schools.

Soon after that she stole my fiancé.

And now she was back in my life. Martha Cox. It just

didn't seem possible. It reminded me of a man I once interviewed who had been struck by lightning three times. The only permanent damage he suffered were singed eyebrows and the ability to pick up low-wattage radio stations with one of his back molars.

Martha Cox was my lightning. To her I lost roles in plays, my job, a handful of men, and as an aside, my self-esteem.

All in all, I'd rather have singed eyebrows.

The weeks leading up to Martha's appearance were like the moments before a bungee jump. I kept thinking there must be some way out of this situation. Other jobs crossed my mind; perhaps I should start sending my reels out. In truth, like all employees of small television stations, I never really stopped sending out my résumé and reels. Furthermore, getting a new job would make me a quitter.

Besides, I liked my job. This was my turf, my territory. And these people at the station, my friends for more than two years—they would support me. After all we'd meant to each other, the ups and downs and daily struggles, I knew I had nothing to worry about. These were my friends, companions through thick and thin.

"Hey, when does the babe get here?" Ben, the cameraman, asked.

I grinned. Ben was a great guy, in his mid-thirties, married with four kids. Flirting to him was as natural as chewing tobacco. Ben always brought me small game birds from his weekend hunting, and I always threw the burlap bags out unopened behind the station. It was the thought that counted. He even proposed to me at the last office Christmas party. Really a sweet guy.

"Hey, Ben. I'm here." I tapped the bill of his baseball cap.

"Nah. I don't mean *you*." He didn't even look up. "I mean our new Georgia peach."

Martha. She was already working her magic, hypnotizing the prey, and she hadn't even set foot on the linoleum.

Fortunately, a sense of perspective prevailed. My sanity was maintained by concentrating on all the good things in my life.

For one, whenever the time came and I met the right man, the wedding dress was all set. Yep. There it was, hanging in a zippered plastic bag in my closet, alterations completed and never worn. That was always such a comfort. And I had my health. Never underestimate the importance of health. My friends were all happy, my family content.

But no matter how determined I was to keep those positive thoughts in the front of my mind, right where they could do the most good, just behind those cheerful thoughts—just waiting to burst through at any moment— was the black-edged specter of Martha Cox.

The days passed almost as they do in old movies, the calendar peeled back by unseen hands, ominous music rising to a frenzy. Suddenly, somehow, against all of my fervent daydreams that she would decide to join the Peace Corps or marry one of the unclaimed Windsor princes, it was the eve of her arrival.

Similar to the Bigfoot phenomenon, there were increasing Martha Cox sightings reported in and around the Savannah area. My neighbor claimed to have seen her at brunch the previous Sunday. She was spotted withdrawing cash from an ATM, sniffing produce at a grocery store, dropping off dry cleaning and having her nails done.

There was no denying it. She was breathing down my neck; I could sense her presence everywhere.

I dressed carefully the Monday that was to be her first. Not that I don't usually dress nicely, but in all honesty, this time I really outdid myself. My hair was combed to perfection, the anchorperson suit had just the right confident yet jaunty air, and the makeup was so flawless, da Vinci would have been proud to claim it as his own handiwork.

As I walked into the studio, her presence was so powerful I almost turned back. But I would not. This was my time of reckoning.

"Hi ya, Nicole," said Stuart, the production assistant.

Then he stopped and did a double take. "You have a job interview or something?"

"No. Um, is she here yet?" I was so casual I almost fooled myself.

"Who? Mary Clare? Yeah. She's over by the—"

"No! Martha Cox."

There. I had said it, uttered her name out loud. And no lightning bolts had thundered from the ceiling.

"Martha Cox? Nah. Didn't you hear? She's been in Paris on a photo shoot or something. Been delayed for a few days. She's coming Wednesday."

"Wait a second. Hasn't she been in town for the past week or so?"

Stuart peered over his clipboard. "Nope. What makes you think that?"

"No reason."

Well, a two-day reprieve was better than nothing. I straightened my spine, and walked proudly to the studio, where I demonstrated wonton wraps and looked forward to the next forty-eight hours of freedom.

Chapter Three

*A*unt Adele was one of those relatives we only saw once a year, usually at Thanksgiving. Yet somehow her presence loomed over us the other eleven months and three and a half weeks of the year. A pink scarf at a department store would remind my mother of Aunt Adele, or some little souvenir spotted while we were on vacation would look just like something Adele would have in her house.

And it was impossible to think of Aunt Adele without her house, for it was quite literally an extension of herself.

She inhabited a world where she alone was comfortable—a place of perfume and chiffon and deep memories. Never did she concede the existence of other realms. Once you entered her house, you were enveloped in her universe. Time itself seemed to be different in Aunt Adele's home, with a large ticking clock and extravagantly framed photographs of men with starched collars and women with small waists. There were paisley shawls draped over bulky mahogany chests, floor lamps with fringed shades, and richly patterned carpets. Her home always seemed to be in soft focus, and indeed she kept the lights low and covered lightbulbs with floral scarves dabbed with her pungent-sweet fragrance.

Yet there was nothing dull about her. There was a vividness to her that you could almost touch. She resisted the years with stunning ferocity, and dressed the way she pleased, defying the current fashion or time of year or even the appropriateness of her dress to the occasion. No matter where she was going or whom she received at her home, she wore gauzy tea gowns of faint pastels. Her clothing seemed to flow and puff, trailing behind her as if she were continuously followed by a swirling mist.

Her skin was unnaturally pale, nearly translucent. That in no way inhibited a liberal use of rouge and fire-red lipstick. Adele Lovett was also an advocate of blue eyeshadow, which she would carefully apply to the arches of her penciled brows. Thus her face, painted and embellished, retained a peculiar Kabuki quality, ageless and surrealistic.

Then there was her hair. It never remained the same color for more than six months. Sometimes it was as red as her lipstick and nails. Other times she would favor an almost pinkish hue, or a blue-lavender. There was always a flurry of anticipation when we drove to Savannah, speculation as to what her hair color would be on this visit. Occasionally my parents even bet money, with my mother or father solemnly handing over a single dollar bill to the other within moments of Aunt Adele's answering the door. On some occasions nobody won, for who could have possibly anticipated the orangish-red shade, or the tricolor of purple, turquoise, and salmon?

So Aunt Adele remained a mystery to me, someone I saw but never knew. And as a kid, I seemed to have little reason to become better acquainted with her, this elderly aunt in strange clothes.

Sometimes she would stare at me and smile, her teeth discolored against the red lipstick and the whiteness of her skin. It was not an unkind smile. There was something almost conspiratorial about it, as if I should know a secret that we alone shared. A distant sadness would etch across her face, and I knew instinctively that whatever the cause of her sorrow, it had nothing to do with the present. Her pain was rooted in her past, and nothing now could touch it, alter whatever had happened.

Then her eyes, those large damp eyes with the robin's-egg-blue shadow, would hold mine, and after a while I would glance away in discomfort. When I dared to glimpse at her again, she would be watching the room with her usual set expression, the secret, sad smile gone.

There was something else about Aunt Adele that I sensed rather than knew. She made my mother uncomfortable. Whatever had happened to Aunt Adele, or whatever she herself had done, it made my mother hesitant to be around her. And then, in my early teens, I heard for the first time vague whisperings of her story. Little by little, as the years passed, I pieced it together, incomplete and sketchy.

It was rather a simple story, really. Back in the late 1920s, when she was a very young woman, she met a man. As if to make the story even more cautionary, he was a traveling salesman. He was not from Savannah. This was taken as a vital clue to his character, a pointer to his flaws. To compound the defect, he was from someplace up North. Some said a city, others said a farm. It didn't really matter. He was from up North, and that was about as bad as it could get.

Adele Lovett was lovely in her youth, from all accounts. It's difficult to tell, for without her trademark colors, she could be any one of a number of the small-waisted young women in the sepia-toned photographs.

The young salesman from the North swept her off her small feet (to her great pride, she always wore a size four shoe—whether or not they fit). Her parents were properly appalled. How could their only daughter marry a traveling salesman from up North?

But Adele demonstrated remarkable steel. She didn't care what her parents said. She was going to marry the salesman, and that was that.

It would be a small wedding. Adele was of age. Reluctantly, grudgingly, the Lovetts offered a tepid blessing. Not that the salesman had won them over. It's just that Adele had never been so determined.

They were to marry on a Saturday morning. Only a few close friends and family members were in the chapel—I never did find out in which chapel this event was to have taken place. And as the appointed time of the wedding came and went, and as the shadows grew long and one by one the guests shrugged and shuffled away, it became apparent that the traveling salesman was not going to show. Adele's brother—my grandfather—went to the boarding house where he had been staying, and was told the salesman had left early in the morning.

Adele said nothing then, nor did she ever say anything about the event. It was shortly after that she began to color her hair, and her first attempt was a brilliantly false henna that shocked all of Savannah. Even then, she was well on her way to becoming Aunt Adele.

Of course she never did marry, although some felt that she most certainly could have married had she wanted to. She just wasn't interested.

Then came the strangest part of Aunt Adele's whole saga. The fruitcake.

The first Christmas after Adele Lovett was jilted, she made a single fruitcake, packed it carefully in brown paper wrapping, and mailed it to someone up North. That became her yearly ritual, one fruitcake, packed up and shipped off. Then one year the fruitcake was returned, with a large "deceased" written in red ink across the name and address. That's why no one could read the name or address it had been shipped to. But that started her new ritual—baking the fruitcake, packing it up, sending it off—only to have it returned ten or twelve days later. No one asked why she kept sending the cake when the intended recipient was no longer alive.

As Aunt Adele got older, and as the people who had been at her thwarted wedding died one by one, no one could remember the salesman's name. Adele would not discuss it. And so, in the grand tradition of sequestered towns everywhere, rumors began to circulate.

At first the rumors were that Aunt Adele had, indeed, married the salesman. The jilting scenario had been invented by Adele Lovett herself to avoid unpleasantness within the family. So he lived in the basement, sneaking out only when the elder Lovetts were on one of their infrequent excursions. Someone claimed to have spotted him leaving the house past midnight, sample case in hand, no doubt on his way up

North to sell whatever it was he sold. The fruitcakes were said to be Christmas presents to the in-laws she would never meet, for they refused to budge from their city or farm, and Adele refused to ever leave Savannah.

Then a darker rumor began to circulate: that she had murdered the salesman and he was buried in the cellar, the sample case marking the spot, the only memorial the Yankee would ever have. But that story faded when the basement flooded one year, and no sample case or body bobbed out of the cellar, much to many people's disappointment.

Shortly thereafter the definitive version that remained until her death was passed around. Adele Lovett, the jilted bride, Savannah's own Miss Havisham, had murdered her wayward groom with poisoned fruitcakes. She continued to send the lethal fruitcakes up North even after his gruesome death in hopes of killing off the rest of his family. Since he was a salesman and a Northerner, no one in Savannah really minded. They just stepped aside when Adele Lovett walked down the street.

By the time I moved into the house, the persistent rumors had become reality in everyone's mind. Very few people attended her funeral, and I'm ashamed to say I was one of the absentees. I didn't even know where she was buried. She was so old by then, and it had been so many years since I had last seen her, that in my own mind she had passed away long ago.

It was with some guilt that I slipped into her house, into her world. How odd it seemed to be there alone, with all of the possessions that defined her life. My very first day there, the house still fragrant of must and the flowery pungent-sweet scent of her perfume, I opened a cupboard in the dining room. There were wrapped packages, dozens of them, it seemed. All had her return address, but the recipient's name and address had been carefully cut away.

Hesitantly, I opened one, almost afraid to look at what was in the box. It crossed my mind that it might be parts of the traveling salesman. Instead, it was an old fruitcake. Just an old fruitcake.

There was something so sad and forlorn about that solitary cake. It was as if by being unpacked after so many years, the poor cake was naked and vulnerable. Silly, I know. Still, I didn't want to just throw it away, poison or no poison. Instead I took out a crystal cake plate with a matching cover, and placed it in the center of the dining room table.

Almost right, but not quite. Something else was missing. So I rummaged through her carefully folded linens and found a lace runner, spread it out, and placed the fruitcake and its plate in the middle.

There. That felt better. And then I forgot all about the old fruitcake.

It had been one of the tougher days at work, that Monday that Martha Cox was a no-show. I came home from the studio exhausted, grateful to have the comfort of home. In the past two years I had gone from thinking of the house as Aunt Adele's to thinking of it as mine.

It's no longer one of the grander houses on the square, although that is my fault rather than Aunt Adele's. I just don't have the enormous funds it would take to restore it to its original splendor. And splendid it is, wrapped with ornamental iron banisters and fanciful brickwork, and surrounded by lush shrubbery with that rich earth scent peculiar to Savannah. The black wooden shutters still work, although a few slats are crooked or missing, and some shingles have long since vanished from the Gothic roof. The only changes I would make would be structural rather than cosmetic—although the house had stood for over a century and a half, there was always a nagging fear that one good slam of the front door would send the entire place crumbling to the ground.

There is nothing I would change about the interior, not the photographs—to which I had added some of my own—nor the paisley shawls and the funky Gloria Swanson lamps. I'd grown to love that place, and in a funny way I think it had grown to love me a little, too.

I'd even gotten to know Aunt Adele. Odd, how you can know someone after their death. Have you ever read an autobiography, or a really well-written biography, and put down the book feeling as if you had a new friend? You know details about their lives that even their closest friends didn't know. You feel as if you could be the best of friends, for you alone know the quirks and fancies. That's the way I felt about Aunt Adele.

Her personality was reflected in every corner of her home. Even the remaining family treasures were there simply because Adele had wanted them to stay. One by one other items of value had left the house, such as the silver biscuit box rumored to have been owned by King George III's physician, or the Turkish carpet with yellow tassels hanging on the staircase wall. They were gone because she hadn't particularly wanted them to stay. The things that remained, the Chinese vase covered with millions of cracks, and the strangely extensive tea caddie collection were still where she had placed them, ten years ago, maybe fifty.

Another odd thing about Aunt Adele was that she had left little notes to herself all over the house, tucked into drawers, folded into a cookbook or under a porcelain figure on a marble mantelpiece. Sometimes the slips of paper contained quotes, such as "a stitch in time saves nine" or "early to bed, early to rise" or "men seldom make passes at girls who wear glasses." Shakespeare, Ben Franklin, and Dorothy Parker were all equally represented in Aunt Adele's scribblings.

Other notes were more cryptic and, I suspected, her own creations. Some sounded familiar on a first reading, such as "never look a Trojan horse in the mouth." One stated "a friend in tweed is a friend indeed." Some were just plain odd, like "beware of strange men in lifts." I never could figure out whether she meant elevators or insoles on that one.

That afternoon I found a new slip of paper peeking out from beneath the bedroom carpet. I smiled. It was always fun to find one of her notes, like a never-ending Easter egg hunt.

This note was odd. "You will meet a stranger across a crowded room."

I read it twice before the doorbell rang. As far as I could recall, this was the first time she had quoted Rodgers and Hammerstein. She was branching out, our Aunt Adele.

The doorbell rang again, and I tucked the note into my pocket and went downstairs. A woman was there, her back to me. Before I could ask if I could help her, she turned to face me, a broad grin on her familiar face.

"Nicole Lovett!" Martha Cox squealed. "How wonderful it is to see you! How I've missed you!"

And then she hugged me.

Chapter Four

*I*t seemed a physical impossibility that such a slender woman could immobilize a full-grown adult in her death grip. But immobilize me she did, while simultaneously jumping up and down.

"This will be just like old times, won't it? Just like high school!"

And that, of course, was precisely my biggest fear. It was the nightmare of high school all over again, like a bad prom-night slasher movie. This was the sequel, every bit as unwelcome as most sequels. At that moment my only positive thought was at least I didn't have a boyfriend for her to steal. No boyfriend, only a job.

She pulled back to look at me, beaming.

Well, all right. So she was more beautiful than ever. Her complexion was positively luminous, her features more defined than before. The Silly Putty nose was actually rather, for want of a better word, charming. It worked on her. Each feature separately was a bit off, slightly gangly, but together they were absolutely stunning.

Her hair was lighter, expertly streaked yet still natural, and she wore it pulled back in a gentle knot, a few strands softening the look. Makeup had been applied with a conservative hand, highlighting rather than overwhelming her face.

And her linen suit was obviously expensive, cream colored with dull brass buttons, the sort of thing a bride would wear as a going-away outfit. Or, more to the point, the perfect apparel for a very successful network anchor to slip into before interviewing, oh, let's say, a head of state.

"Hi, Martha." I somehow managed to smile. "How the heck are you?"

Finally she stopped hugging me and stepped back. If I didn't know better, I'd almost think she was self-conscious. But then, I did know better and the mere thought of Martha Cox being uncomfortable was ludicrous. This was a woman who twirled a baton and kicked her knees over her ears on national television. Nothing could make her feel uncomfortable.

"I'm fine, Nicole," she said, glancing around. "Just fine. Wow. This is some place you've got here."

"Yeah. I'm pretty lucky. It was my aunt's."

"I know. She passed away a couple of years ago, right?"

That surprised me. I was curious to find out how she knew about my aunt, but not curious enough to ask.

"I love this porch. Is it wrought iron or cast iron?"

"Um, I think it's wrought, but I'm not sure."

"It's really fabulous." Martha seemed to be in no hurry to leave. In fact, she seemed quite prepared to set up housekeeping on my front porch, have her mail forwarded here.

There was no other option, really. "Would you like to come in for a few minutes?" I had to ask, hoping against hope she would say no. She must have someplace else to go, I prayed silently.

"I'd love to!"

I stepped aside so that she could pass, and couldn't help but notice she was wearing a gold ankle bracelet.

Now I don't know why, but ankle bracelets have always bothered me. There's something sinister about them. Think of Barbara Stanwyck in *Double Indemnity*. Fred MacMurray finds her wildly attractive, especially her ankle bracelet, and then she uses him to kill her husband, and ultimately kills him off as well. Only women who are up to no good wear ankle bracelets. They're a prelude to shackles.

Martha stood in the living room, her eyes taking in everything, it seemed. It was so odd to have her there, Martha Cox.

Obviously I had to offer her something, which seemed

ironic after all of the things she had simply taken from me over the years. But manners were manners, and there was no way out of it.

"Would you like some iced tea?" I felt like adding, "to go with my job?" or "Sorry, I'm fresh out of boyfriends. But can I interest you in a few of my more recent dates?"

"Iced tea would be a real treat."

Sure, iced tea would be a real treat. This coming from a woman in a Chanel suit and three-hundred-dollar hair. Yep, nothing beats a glass of iced tea.

We stood just looking at each other for a few moments. The ankle bracelet glinted. She brightened, as if she had come up with the right answer on *Jeopardy*.

"Is it always so hot and humid in Savannah?"

Part of me wanted to mention she shouldn't be so surprised. After all, she was a former Miss Georgia. One might be led to believe she grew up in, say, Tennessee rather than the state that entrusted her with their tiara and satin banner. Instead, I may have smiled politely.

"Oh, Martha. You'll get used to it." This was my chance. I went into the kitchen for the iced tea, and could hear her prowling into the dining room.

"This is darling, Nicole. Simply precious—with all the pictures!"

Standing on my tiptoes, I reached the iced-tea glasses and discreetly blew the dust out of the bottom of them before plunking in the ice.

"Yep. Pictures and everything." Heck, I even have running water.

"You're so lucky. They have me put up at a hotel. I don't even remember the name of it. It's all so impersonal."

I nearly dropped the pitcher of tea. The station put her up—in a real hotel? As far as I could remember, they had never done that. Never.

"Would you like anything in your tea?"

"Yes, please," she answered sweetly. "Do you have any of those little blue packets?"

"Nope. Sorry, only sugar and the little pink packets."

The only time I had the blue packets was when I took them from restaurants.

"No problem," she chirped. "I probably have a few from the hotel. I always steal them. Let's see. Here we go."

I entered the dining room and she was holding two blue sweetener packets with obvious triumph. "Want one?"

Actually, I did, sort of, but I smiled and shook my head. "No, thanks. Here." I handed her the glass, and she shook the packet back and forth for a few moments before tearing it open and adding it to her tea.

She looked at Aunt Adele's fruitcake for a moment and seemed poised to ask something, perhaps along the lines of why the hell do you have a fruitcake on your dining room table in the middle of September? But she said nothing.

We sipped the tea in silence, ice cubes clanking. The mantel clock ticked back and forth, click, click. I couldn't think of anything to say, at least not anything that wouldn't lead very quickly to an even more awkward silence. Every idea that popped into my head would take us directly back to high school. And that was certainly the last place I wanted to go at that moment, especially with Martha Cox.

Suddenly, she leaned forward and grinned. "Hey, do you remember that Mark guy we both used to date in high school?"

The iced tea went down wrong, and I began to choke. I couldn't believe she came right out and mentioned him! It would be like Elizabeth Taylor asking Debbie Reynolds what ever happened to that Eddie Fisher guy.

My choking didn't stop her from continuing. "Yeah, good old Mark. It was so embarrassing when he dumped me at the dance."

Although my eyes were still watering, I nodded. "I think they were playing 'Do You Really Want to Hurt Me,' weren't they?"

"I'd forgotten that! But I do remember that we argued about you."

"About me?"

"Yep." She sipped the iced tea before speaking. "He

said I was a bad sport because I wanted him to stop all this Jack the Ripper stuff. You know, notes and jumping out at me. He said you liked it, and he wished he had taken you to the dance instead.''

''Really?'' Now I smiled, remembering how the charm of his Ripper fascination had begun to wear thin on me as well. I looked at her, really looked at her. ''He was odd, wasn't he?''

''He sure was! And you got to go to the dance with that cute Randy Miller. You guys dated for a while after that, right?''

Funny, I'd forgotten all about Randy Miller. He had been pretty cute, in hindsight.

''You were so good in the school plays,'' she said. ''I always thought you would go on to be an actress.''

''Me? You've got to be kidding! I was always the odd character parts. You got to be the leads, sing all the great songs.''

''But I would have rather had a fun role, like Aunt Eller. I remember my mother made me go on a diet right before that show—I can't hear a single song from *Oklahoma!* without feeling my stomach rumble. The problem with those parts is that everyone was out to criticize you. It was no fun—I had to get the lead, because unless I got a scholarship, well, college would have been beyond my reach.''

At first I found it all hard to believe—like the pouty model who complains to an interviewer how very hard she has to work, but ultimately she really wants to direct, and that her unfortunate beauty has always held her back.

Then I listened to her. Really listened. And in truth, she really hadn't done all that much besides the Miss Georgia thing.

''But that's amazing,'' I said. ''You were great in the pageant.''

''You saw that?'' She actually blushed. ''God, it was awful. Twirling a baton—that's a valuable talent, isn't it?''

I couldn't help but laugh. ''You did make the finalist cut, right?''

'Rolling her eyes, she shook her head. "All I really needed was the scholarship money."

"I really don't understand," I confessed. Martha had been one of the wealthiest girls at the school.

"Yep. Dad left my mom for another woman—the old secretary cliché. It would have been funny, almost, but Mom really fell apart. The pageants were her idea, so I could go to college. It's not as if my grades were good enough to get an academic scholarship. It's not as if I was ever brilliant, like you."

"Like me?"

"God, how I envied you. All those friends. You were always so popular and smart. I remember that one chemistry final you aced and everyone else flunked. Remember that? Everyone else was ticked at you for throwing off the curve."

I vaguely remembered that final. Only faintly.

She was looking at the fruitcake again, and I was about to explain all about it when the phone rang.

"I'll be right back," I said, relieved.

It was not an important call, just a friend wanting to complain about her life. But I stayed on the phone much longer than necessary, simply to gather my thoughts. As Lucy rattled on about problems with her landlord, I thought about Martha.

Perhaps I'd misjudged her.

What an odd thought. After so many years of having Martha Cox to blame my every misfortune on, there was a chance—slight though it was—that Martha hadn't spent her life attempting to ruin mine. Maybe she just happened to be there in high school, our paths crossing by chance and mutual interests.

I heard the front door open and close, and checked my watch. Had I really been on the phone for twenty minutes?

"Lucy, listen. I've gotta run now," and I hung up.

Martha was gone.

And strangely, I felt terrible, a hollow feeling. I'd been rude to her, incredibly rude, leaving her alone. Actually, I was beginning to feel guilty for the previous fifteen years as well.

Maybe we wouldn't be best friends, but we could perhaps be friends.

I'd ask her to lunch the next day. That's what I'd do. She'd be new, and I could help show her around the station.

I felt better, as if a burden had been lifted from my shoulders. In fact, I felt better than I had for a long, long time. That is, until I walked through the dining room.

There, in the center of the table, was Aunt Adele's fruitcake, just where I had left it, just where it had always been.

Only now there was a single wedge missing. Crumbs were scattered at the place where she had been sitting.

Martha Cox had just eaten a good-sized slice of Aunt Adele's poison fruitcake.

Rampaging fear and blind panic can make a person do strange things.

Logically, what I should have done was call Martha at her hotel room and tell her, in the simplest, you'll-never-believe-this way, that she may want to trot on over to the nearest hospital and have her stomach pumped. And logically, I should have offered to drive.

But logic doesn't always rear its much-needed head at such times. To say I behaved badly is an understatement.

I didn't know what hotel she was staying in, since she herself couldn't remember the name. It's not as if I could just sit down and call every hotel in the area on the off-chance she was registered.

Of course I could call someone at the station and ask where she was staying, but wouldn't that seem peculiar? Everyone knew she got the job I assumed was mine, and they probably wouldn't give me information about where she was staying. They might assume I wanted to harass her with crank calls.

Then a strange thing happened. I convinced myself that nothing was wrong with the fruitcake, nothing at all. Poor Aunt Adele had been a victim of vicious rumors. That was it, plain and simple. Still telling myself there was nothing wrong with the cakes, I got a big black garbage bag and threw out the rest of the fruitcake, as well as the ones stacked in the cabinet, and put them outside. Tomorrow was garbage day, and by noon there would not be a single fruitcake in the house.

I would ask Martha out to lunch tomorrow, and we could have a big laugh over the whole thing.

There. I pushed the whole mess out of my mind and went up to bed, away from the dining room. All would be well tomorrow.

All was not well the next day.

By lunchtime, that magical hour that I had planned to make all right with the world, it became clear that Martha Cox was nowhere to be found. Mary Clare said there was no answer at Martha's hotel, and that her car was still parked in the hotel lot. Finally, Ben the cameraman announced the startling news: Martha Cox was missing. And the police had been called.

Somehow I managed to get through the day, shaking my head in perplexed worry with the rest of my colleagues, muttering about how sad it was.

And then something truly horrible happened. The station manager asked me to sit in as the afternoon anchor and announce that Martha Cox, a former Miss Georgia and a recent addition to our television family, was missing. Anyone with information, please contact the police or the station's main number.

My knees were trembling as I read. And I wondered if someone viewing would know that I had something to do with the missing Miss Cox.

Chapter Five

*B*y the time I'd pulled out of the station parking lot, I was shaking so violently the car was veering in all directions as if it were an accessory to my crime. The erratic driving was all but an invitation for some young police officer to pull me over, at which time I would surely crack and confess to all felonies in the history of mankind, including being present on the grassy knoll and handing Socrates his final mixed drink.

That's just what I needed, a drink.

Without further thought I steered the Toyota to the Bayou Cafe, a cozy place mercifully free of undue intimacy. There you could strike up a conversation or lower your head in feigned solitude with equal success. The solitude was sounding better by the moment, but not the relentless isolation of home.

People were just beginning to trickle in for the evening's live music, the lights of the bustling riverfront glowing in the old windowpanes, warming the rough stone-and-brick interior.

As I glanced around the room, faces were indistinct but I saw people laughing; everyone was there to relax and have a good time. They were in pairs or threes, and one large group had taken over a center table, pitchers of beer sloshing over heads as they were passed around.

It seemed I was the only person alone there, the only party of one.

And then I saw him.

I'm not sure why my gaze rested on him. It almost felt as if he had been watching me. You know that uncomfortable feeling at the nape of your neck when someone is staring at you, but you're not quite sure of the direction.

Perhaps he was so noticeable because he too was alone. He'd been behind another group, and when they went over to their table he remained just across the bar, on the opposite side of the room.

It was only with great effort that I looked away, then began to take in his appearance surreptitiously, pretending to read the chalkboard menu just over his left shoulder or out of the window just within peripheral view of him.

He wasn't drop-dead gorgeous, not in a traditional movie-star sort of way. Instead he was what you might call rugged without being bulky. He looked like the type of guy another guy would want to hang out with, or the sort of man a woman would make excuses to press her face against his broad shoulder, to sob her misfortunes.

It was tough to tell whether his hair was dark brown or black, but it was wavy and his coloring seemed to be . . . Well, it was hard to see in the muted light, but it seemed to be that wonderful outdoor-healthy complexion, as if he could hike ten miles and not break a sweat. His features were even, not maddeningly so, but nice and kind and handsome in a quiet, unobtrusive way.

In his dark green flannel shirt and jeans, he didn't look much different from the other men in the bar. Yet there was an intensity about him, a glint in his eyes as he too scanned the room.

Of course, it was possible the intense glint was simply because he was intoxicated.

Grinning to myself, I shook my head as if to clear my silly, fanciful thoughts, and pushed the stranger from my mind. I had more important things to think about tonight.

I ordered a white wine, a good choice whenever additional contemplation seems overwhelming. It was served in a plastic cup, a comforting notion, given the frayed state of my nerves.

Just as I was taking the first sip, a thought hit me.

I had probably killed someone, ended a life. Because of

my actions, a young woman was no longer alive, would not have a chance to experience the joys of the next decades, the normal ebbs and peaks that define a life. All of her hopes and dreams were erased, as were her fears and dreads and petty annoyances. In short, because I had been reluctant to utter a few words, such as "By the way, steer clear of the fruitcake—it may be poison," a beautiful young woman was dead.

But it was an accident, part of me interrupted. There was no plan to kill her, no premeditated blueprint. Her visit had been a complete surprise to me.

On the other hand, perhaps a small portion of my mind did indeed know exactly what it was doing. Although I can't recall a conscious thought of murder, maybe it was almost like when you're driving and a rabbit hops out in front of the car. You want desperately to avoid the bunny, but you don't have much time to methodically think through the options: are there any cars behind you, is there a brick wall you will hit if you swerve, is this a two-lane road, and are any other cars coming? You do the best you can, just react in a blink and hope no one gets hurt.

While I would do anything to avoid a rabbit, Martha was different. She was no fluffy bunny.

Maybe my crime was like that, a split-second decision that didn't have a chance to go through the usual moral steps. A corner of my mind took in the possibilities when I was on that long, unnecessary phone call with Lucy. Of course I had seen the expression on Martha's face as she saw the fruitcake. She was hungry. I had offered her nothing but iced tea and her own packet of sweetener.

In high school she used to take carrots and celery to school for lunch—rabbit food, how very ironic. Even then she had been conscious of her figure. And the pressure of competing in local beauty pageants, much less the Miss America Pageant, must have caused her to walk around in a state of perpetual hunger. She had even mentioned that when she was at my house.

And this I knew, at least subconsciously.

Plus I was angry at her, and had been for over ten years. Until that moment, sitting in the bar, the ferocity of my anger hadn't really been apparent. That's because, number one, I've never been in therapy, and number two, I've never admitted to myself how very much I blamed Martha Cox for every evil that had blighted my life since high school. Real or imagined, direct or indirect, it had all been pinned on Martha. From those roles in the school productions, to losing Jed my fiancé, to this job, it had all been her fault.

But in truth it hadn't, not really. It hadn't been that simple.

It didn't matter because now she would truly ruin my life. And this time, it *was* my fault.

And the very fact that I was now aware of what had happened, that part of me must have wanted to kill her, I could never pretend to be innocent. Not in a court of law, not even in my own heart.

I had killed someone. Now two lives were over, hers and mine.

The plastic cup slipped from my hand. Before I could make any attempt to recover it, I bumped heads with someone who had appeared, it seemed, from nowhere.

"Ouch!" My head felt as if it had been pummeled with a hammer.

"Whoa!" the hammer replied.

We both straightened. It was him, the guy from the other side of the bar.

Before having the chance to recover my limited supply of wits, he handed me the still-full plastic cup of wine. "Here." He winced, rubbing his forehead.

His eyes were green.

"Good reflexes." I touched my left temple to make sure it still existed.

"Sorry about that. I saw you from the other side of the room, and you seemed, well, a bit out of it." His voice had a lovely rich quality to it, as if anything he would say would be thoughtful and compassionate. "Are you drunk or something?"

Some compassion.

"No. I was just thinking about . . . things." I could only imagine what I must have looked like a few moments ago. And why had I worn such a stupid outfit this morning? It was my school-girl look, the pleated gray skirt and pressed white blouse topped with a blue blazer. Then I remembered selecting my clothes, standing at the wardrobe, wondering if by the end of the day, any outfit I chose would be replaced by an orange jumpsuit accessorized with handcuffs and ankle shackles.

"Oh. You must have been thinking about something important."

"Yeah, well. I suppose."

We stood in mutually awkward silence for a few moments, then he smiled, and I saw he had dimples. Oh, Lord, I thought, dimples? Why this guy with dimples, at this moment of my life? I'm only human. Dimples?

And he, this poor, unsuspecting man, had no clue he had just struck up a conversation with a soon-to-be convicted murderer. It was like Tyrone Power chatting up Ma Barker, Don Ameche sliding next to Bruno Hauptmann. He really had no clue. Had I been a more decent person, I would have left right then and there and not turned back.

But dimples, I must confess, are my downfall, murderer or not.

Next thing I knew he was extending his hand to me. "Forgive my manners. I'm Christopher Quinn."

Of course he was. What a great name! And his accent . . . well, it did seem to have a touch of a Northern twang, perhaps Midwestern. But let's face it, dimples and a great name go a long way toward mitigating any unfortunate geographical mistakes of birth.

His handshake was firm, with just the right amount of strength without leaving me yowling on the floor.

"Hello," I said, smiling, and he gave me a peculiar look, as if he almost recognized me, but then it passed. "I'm Nicole Lovett."

He looked down at our hands, clutching each other like

the end of an insurance commercial. Then he glanced again at me. "So, are you from around here?"

My hand went back to my hip, and then to circling the rim of the wine cup with my index finger. "My family is from here originally." Typical first-conversation bar chat, and I was somehow a bit disappointed. Thought he'd be more creative, which was ridiculous, but that's how I felt. "Where are you from?"

"Ohio," he said. "But now I live in Chicago."

"Interesting," even though it wasn't that interesting. "What's your line of work?"

"Well, at the moment I'm on sabbatical, trying to write a book."

"Based here in Savannah?"

"Yep."

"There's lots of that going around now, ever since that book about midnight in the garden and all that. Folks around here don't like people poking around much."

"I've noticed." He laughed, a deep, resonant sound to accompany the dimples.

Watch it, Lovett, I said to myself.

"Your family's from here, but you're not?"

Nodding, I explained. "I grew up in Chattanooga, but my father's family is from here. I actually live in the old home."

"Really? Interesting." He took a sip of his beer. "And what's your line of work, Miss Lovett?"

"Please, call me Nicole." I laughed. When was the last time a guy over the age of ten or under the age of eighty had called me Miss Lovett? "I work at a local television station, Channel Eighty-nine."

"Really? So do you know that woman who's missing?"

"No!" I hadn't meant to shout. The entire bar hushed, and my voice lowered, although the strange quivering remained. "Why would I know her? She never even came to work."

Slowly, almost languidly, he raised a finger to the bartender and mouthed "Another round." Then he turned back to me. "It's in all the papers. Her name is Martha Cox, and she's also from Chattanooga. About your age, I think. So you don't know her?"

Okay, there were a couple of options here. Once again, we were at the rabbit-hopping-in-the-car-path scenario—blink-of-an-eye moral decision time. And in that split second I decided I didn't want to lie to anyone, not to myself, especially not to this stranger I had just met. So instead of lying, I just came across as incredibly odd.

"Oh." I raised my eyebrows in an expression of surprise. "*That* missing woman. I was thinking of someone else."

"You mean there's more than one missing woman from Chattanooga who works at your station?"

My head started aching. "No, of course not. It's just that . . . well. Hum. This is hard to explain. Look—our drinks are ready!"

The bartender placed the drinks in front of us.

"But Nicole, you're not finished with your . . ."

At that I downed the entire plastic cup of house white, vintage last Thursday. My headache suddenly became the entire percussion section of the Philharmonic.

"Never mind," he murmured, handing me the new plastic cup. He stared at me for a moment, as if about to question something I had said or done, so I smiled idiotically and took a large swig of the new wine. That should keep him quiet, I thought as I fought back the urge to spit the wine back into the cup. Whatever he was thinking was bound to have been wiped from his mind by my majestic display of unladylike behavior.

"I was just thinking," he began, to my dismay.

"Were you?" I swallowed some more, but his expression remained the same. Mine, however, must have altered, for he narrowed his eyes.

"Are you feeling all right?"

"Fine. Great." I was content to have veered him off his path of questioning.

"I was just thinking," he continued, and I braced myself.

"Has anyone ever told you that you're a dead ringer for Ann Baxter?"

For a moment I just stared at him. "No, no one ever has." Had he suddenly morphed into an elephant, I couldn't have been more surprised. "But thank you. She's always been one of my favorites. No one remembers her now."

"It's a shame. Did you know her grandfather was . . ."

We said the name simultaneously. "Frank Lloyd Wright!"

Again, the bar hushed, but I only noticed it vaguely.

As you've probably guessed by now, I'm an old-movie nut. Much as I love new films, there is nothing in my mind that can touch the magic of old films, back in the days when there was something mystical about the art and the people of Hollywood. I adore everything about the dream factories, when the public only knew what the studios wanted them to know, and when movies were called "pictures" or, better yet, "talkies."

And never, in my entire life, have I ever met a man who loved them. But he did. We talked about obscure films, dead directors, favorite scenes, and all those character actors with names no one can remember. Still, I had an urge to test him, just to see if he really knew his stuff.

"So," I said coyly. "Who do you think murdered William Desmond Taylor?"

He gave me a blank look, and my heart sank a little. I knew it was too much to ask. In all honesty, that is why I was still single. I didn't lust after money, or power, or even good looks. All I really ever longed for is a man with dimples who knew Buster Keaton from Harold Lloyd.

"Well," he began, pulling out his wallet. "I know King Vidor thought it was Mary Miles Minter's mother dressed as a man. But personally, I've always thought Mable Normand may have known more than she ever let on."

My eyes must have glazed over a little as I slumped against the bar. This had never happened before. Then he grinned, dimples in full force.

My God, I thought. I think I'm falling in love.

"Would you like to have dinner with me tomorrow night? I just read an interesting account of the Fatty Arbuckle scandal . . ."

That's all I really heard. Of course I said yes, I would love to have dinner with him tomorrow night. Taking a deep breath as I listened to his voice but not the precise words, I idly watched him slip the bills from the wallet and carefully slide it back into his jeans pocket. He overtipped, as if he didn't want to open his wallet again for any change.

And later, when I came down from the clouds, I realized what I had seen in his wallet. For just a brief moment, I caught a glimpse of something shiny and metal.

It was a badge.

Christopher Quinn was a cop.

Chapter Six

Once home, in the embracing warmth of familiar surroundings—and the accusing empty cake plate—it became painfully clear that I had to get out of a dinner date with a policeman. The question was, how to get out of the date without arousing further suspicions.

The other question was more pressing. Did I really *want* to get out of a date with Christopher Quinn? Never had I met anyone like him. What if he's the one, the man who will . . .

Then I stopped this line of thought. How dare I even consider such indulgent, frivolous notions? I was a murderer. I had no right to think of human joy, of my own happiness. That simple right was forfeited the moment some element of my character decided to take a human life.

Still, well, it was indeed harder than I anticipated to stop dwelling on the image of Christopher Quinn. As I stood in the kitchen, conjuring the politically correct visions of one in my situation—eternal damnation, the flames of Hades licking my soul, interviews with tabloid news shows—aspects of the brief moments with presumed Police Officer Quinn kept intruding. There were his eyes, the sound of his voice, his interest in movies, and, of course, the dimples.

So there I stood, motionless, holding a damp dishtowel, trying to think of a punishment suitable to my heinous crime—with a large, sappy grin on my face. I know this for a fact, because I caught a glimpse of my ridiculous self in the window reflection.

That was a sobering sight. If the powers that be saw the

look of bliss on this criminal's face, there would be no punishment great enough.

It was then I made up mind. I would not run. I would not hide. I refused to play a coward any longer. It was time for me to own up to what I had done, to face the proverbial music.

Therefore, I would go on a date with Christopher Quinn. If it was destiny to be locked up by the authorities, well, I might as well let him do the locking.

As I drove to work the next morning, my mind had changed a bit.

In fact, my mind almost made my car drive past the station and head to Florida, where I could catch a plane or a boat to some remote Caribbean haven, or perhaps just keep going clear on to Argentina. They seem to welcome a certain criminal element, and I could rub elbows with minds as evil as my own.

Please don't misunderstand. I don't mean to sound glib. This was without a doubt the most awful thing I had ever done, and the magnitude was almost impossible to grasp. Whenever I'm cornered, I resort to a twisted sense of logic to get me through, and never had I felt so cornered. There was a terrible duality of the moral desire to suffer for my sins, and the innate human streak of self-preservation that makes the very same person long to flee, to escape retribution.

But instead of leaving the country, I went to work.

The buzz throughout the station was all on the Martha Cox case. Seems from the latest news reports, the only thing found in Martha Cox's deluxe hotel suite was a matchbook, and a single gold ankle bracelet.

"This is amazing. Imagine, a woman that young. So terrible. Where is the justice in this world? That's what I want to know," demanded Ben the cameraman, his red baseball cap clenched in his fist.

"I know, Ben. It's absolutely terrible," I agreed, shaking my head over his copy of the *Savannah Morning News*.

"Can you believe the station put her up at a hotel, and in a deluxe suite? And I'm still waiting to get my petty cash back for the six-foot hero I brought to last year's Christmas party. Terrible, that's just what it is."

Mary Clare, the receptionist who doubled as the office manager, shook her head. "We should do something."

"Like what?" came a voice from the control booth.

"I don't know. Maybe a memorial service or something."

"But there's no body," said Ben. "How can you have a memorial service without a body?"

"Well, that's just it, you see," explained Mary Clare, warming to her topic. "That's the difference between a funeral and a memorial service. At a funeral, you have a body. At a memorial service, you have memories."

We contemplated her words in silence for a few moments, and then another voice from the control booth—I think it was Ted the audio technician—said, "Nice logic. But we don't have any memories. She never worked here."

"Yeah," shouted Ben. "Her first day she was a no-show, and since then she's just plain gone. That just doesn't seem like the kind of employee loyalty that should be rewarded, does it?"

"Nicole knew her, didn't you, Nicole?" chirped Mary Clare. "They knew each other from Chattanooga."

"I thought she was a Miss Georgia?" a phantom voice from the booth asked.

"Chattanooga is almost in Georgia, and she went to the University of Georgia. Isn't that right, Nicole?" Mary Clare's voice was smooth as velvet over a knife blade.

All eyes, including unseen eyes from the control booth, were on me. "Yeah, well, I sort of knew her."

"How did you know her? Was it high school?"

"Yes. We went to the same high school. It was no big deal, really. Lots of people went to that high school."

"Was she gorgeous then?"

This was not the time to mention the Silly Putty nose. "Sure. She was captain of the cheerleading squad."

"Were you a cheerleader, Nicole?" Who was that? Ted again?

"Well, no. I was more interested in theatrical productions. Speaking of productions, aren't we supposed to be—"

"Was she in theatrical productions, too?" Mary Clare smiled brightly.

"Yes. As a matter of fact she was. Now, let's get going on the—"

"So you two were in plays together?" Mary Clare persisted. "What plays?"

"Oh, *Guys and Dolls* and *Oklahoma!*—the usual school stuff."

"I love those shows!" That was Steve, the station manager. "What parts did Martha Cox play?"

"Um, I think she was Sarah Brown and Laurey, but I don't exactly remember. Anyway, why don't we—"

"And who were you?" Mary Clare again.

There was an expectant silence. "I enjoyed the character parts. So I was a streetwalker and the second angry hobo and Aunt Eller. Okay? Are you satisfied?"

"There's a streetwalker in *Oklahoma!*?" mumbled Ben. "I don't remember that from my high school. We must have cut them out, being it was a religious school and all."

"No. There aren't streetwalkers in *Oklahoma!* I was Aunt Eller in that one."

Once more, the silence.

"It was a small but pivotal role. I was the one on the stage churning butter when the show begins. Remember? Crusty but lovable Aunt Eller?"

"Sure. The whole show revolves around her, right, Steve?"

"Oh, yeah. I hear Rodgers and Hammerstein almost called the show *Aunt Eller*—"

"But there was already a show on Broadway with the same name!" Ted was in fine form that morning.

Amid the general hilarity, the seriousness of the situation seemed to have been lost. "Excuse me," I interrupted.

"Please remember that we have a missing employee who may very well be dead."

"There's no body," Ben insisted. "And she was a no-show at work. Seems to me—"

"So will you, Nicole?" Mary Clare raised her voice.

"Will I what?"

"Will you say a few words at a memorial service? I'll get some candles at lunch. Does anyone have a Bible?"

"We're doing a commercial for a kiddy comic-book Bible. Will that do?" Steve offered.

They were still arguing when I left the studio. Although eight-thirty in the morning may have seemed a bit early for lunch, I needed to get away from them as soon as possible.

By the time I returned, Mary Clare had been forced to hold her own service, which was fine with me and consisted of a viewing of Martha Cox's baton-twirling at the Miss America Pageant seven years earlier and her sample reel that landed her the job. This was in place of a body.

Most thought it was peculiar that I refused to speak at Martha's makeshift service. I couldn't help but wonder what their reactions would be when they found out the whole truth.

Christopher Quinn phoned in the afternoon to confirm our date. While he was on the line, I knew there was a choice to be made, but I didn't want to back out on my decision. I would go with him, and whatever happened was my destiny.

"I hear there's a good place called Elizabeth, it's on Thirty-seventh. Hope you don't mind, but I made a reservation for two at . . ."

As I listened, I remembered one of Aunt Adele's strange little notes. I'd found it just the week before, and it said "Find Destiny on Thirty-seventh." Odd. At the time I thought she was referring to a birthday, and I had shrugged and wondered if I should plan a major party in a few years, book the ballroom now for my destiny.

"So does that sound good? I'll pick you up at your place,

or would you rather I pick you up at work?''

''How about if I meet you there? I have my car, and that will just make things easier.''

''You're not making me feel very chivalrous, first official date and all.''

And he didn't sound very much like a policeman, which was just fine with me. Not to mention the restaurant he suggested was way beyond Barney Fife's budget.

In all honesty, I don't recall the rest of our conversation, just that it was brief and I must have sounded like an utter space cadet.

Somehow I got through the rest of the day, freshened up, and drove out to the destiny. I mean, destination.

Christopher Quinn was already there, in a quiet corner table with candles glowing orange and a bottle of wine chilling. If this was what booking a suspect was like, law enforcement had certainly come a long way.

As I entered, he stood and smiled. He was wearing a sports jacket and a sweater, the collar of his shirt just slightly askew. It crossed my mind that he was on sabbatical, whatever that meant. The bottom line was that he hadn't come straight from an office. He dressed like this for me. As far as I could remember, no other man had ever put on a sports jacket for me. Ever.

Taking a deep breath, I extended my hand and his dimple deepened, his fingers closed over mine, and he pulled me toward him and kissed my cheek.

''Has anyone ever told you that you bear a striking resemblance to Irene Dunne?''

He held my chair, and for a moment I hesitated. Most of the guys I know only hold chairs if they intend to pull them back at the last instant. But he didn't. Instead, he placed a hand on my shoulder before returning to his own seat.

''Irene Dunne?'' I was suddenly in a terrific mood. ''No. But she's always been one of my favorites.''

''Mine, too. Especially in *The Awful Truth* . . .''

So that's how our dinner went. Talking movies, books, old television shows. He agreed that some *Twilight Zone*s are overrated, especially the ones with William Shatner, and that *Cheers* was never quite as good after Coach died. He also loved silent movies, collected antique books, and used to be an altar boy.

For over an hour, my real life ceased to exist and I was simply on a date with the most wonderful of men. The fascinating part was that being with Christopher seemed to make me a wonderful companion to him. He laughed at my comments, the type of comments people usually respond to with a blank stare and a quick change of subject. He understood what I was saying, even when I took a roundabout path. When I mentioned my career thus far, he said he was the same way, considered something of a plodder but always game to give it a shot.

See what I mean? He just knew what I was saying.

That's when I began to get suspicious again. So I turned the tables just slightly, and began to ask him about his job.

Oh, he was good. Very good. He discussed teaching in Chicago—night school at a small college. His students were all mature adults, some in their seventies but all with a desire to learn.

"What subjects do you teach?" A normal question, right? But he shifted a little in his chair, as if that made him uncomfortable.

"A little of this, a little of that," he hedged.

Now I've met a few college professors in my time, most notably when I was in college, and the one thing about them is they will go on ad nauseam, in minute detail, over every element of their courses. The course titles alone tell the whole story. They never teach just mathematics or history. It's "Dawson's Theory of Relative Statistic Manipulation as Applied to Modern Refrigeration" or "Middle Eastern Rites and Rituals Involving Women with Husbands but No Children Yet." You never get "a little of this, a little of that" anymore. Never.

"Interesting," I replied, and he glanced down.

"Well, yes, as a matter of fact it is." He looked back at

me and smiled. "Now tell me all about your family, especially the Savannah ones."

"Why on earth would you want to know any of that?"

"For my book. Any information will be greatly appreciated. And the names and identities of the characters will be changed to protect the innocent."

"Thank you, Jack Webb. But I really want to hear more about what you teach. Is it literature? Please. I'm really interested."

"Well, really—"

"And what about *your* family? Do you have any kids?"

I was grinning, and realized that he wasn't. "Well, yes. As a matter of fact I do."

It was as if someone had slugged me in the stomach. For a moment I thought I would be sick, literally.

"So you're divorced?" I ventured.

"No. No, I'm not divorced."

"So you're married?" My voice sounded like I had inhaled helium.

"No."

"But if you're not—"

His eyes met mine. "I'm a widower. My wife was killed three years ago in a car accident."

It takes an awful lot to render me speechless. All I could mutter was, "I'm so sorry."

A darkness came over his expression for just a second, then it was gone. "It's been rough, especially the first couple of years. The first Christmas, first birthdays without her. But we're coping. Oh, and I have a daughter—she's five."

"How wonderful." I knew my voice was hollow, but it was the best I could do. "What's her name?"

Finally he smiled again, a real smile, not a fleeting expression of less pain. "Her name is Adele."

The world seemed to lighten at the name. "Adele? Isn't that amazing! That's the name of the aunt who—"

"I know, I know. The one whose house you live in."

"That's right!"

The check came. He showed me a photo of Adele, pulling it out of his wallet. She was a beautiful child, dark curly hair and dark eyes.

"Her mother must have been lovely," I commented.

A wistful beam touched his lips, and I could almost feel my heart breaking. "She was," he said simply.

I was going to ask about the shiny metal badge, but couldn't, I just couldn't. We said nothing as he paid the bill. I did try to get a better look at the badge, but it was flashed so swiftly I didn't have much of a chance.

"Well," he said, holding my jacket as we left the restaurant.

"Would you like to come over to my place for coffee?" Was that me speaking, inviting a cop to get a firsthand look at the crime scene? Why didn't I just offer a DNA sample and a full confession instead?

Then he smiled again, and I realized that it had indeed been me offering the invitation. And I'd be delighted to make the offer again, anytime, just to see that expression.

"I would love to. Should I just follow your car?"

Nodding, I pointed in a vague direction and he seemed to understand. I was glad to have the relief of a few moments to myself in the car driving home, checking the rearview mirror every once in a while to make sure he was still there, following me.

He was a widower. It hardly seemed possible that a man so young could have lost his wife. But then, it happens all the time, newspaper reports of tragedy, of lives snuffed out through accidents and illness and . . . murder.

I almost missed my turn, and could see his confused expression as he made a sharp right to follow me. Then we were there, at home on the square. I got out first, he pulled into a spot a few cars behind me.

"Hey, Andretti. You might want to try turn signals," he called as he locked up. "A new invention. Very helpful when someone's trying to tail you."

Tail you? Wasn't that police lingo?

"Sorry. It's right over . . ."

But I didn't have to finish. He was already starting up

the right walk. He seemed to already know where I lived.

"I looked you up in the phone book," he answered my unspoken question. "Wanted to find a convenient place for us to meet—nothing too far away for you."

"Oh. Thank you." Pulling out my keys, I pondered his explanation as he touched the fence and inhaled the pungent scent of Savannah.

"I don't think any place on earth smells like this," he said quietly. "Why would anyone want to leave?"

"What do you mean?"

"You know, that girl. Martha Cox. That's why it must have been foul play."

I couldn't think of anything to say, so I flicked on the lights and let him in the hallway. "I'm going to make coffee. How do you like it?"

"Milk, no sugar. Mind if I look around?"

I shrugged. "Sure. Might as well."

He did a double take before walking into the room. I headed to the kitchen. Coffee. Coffee. Please tell me there is coffee around here.

"Great furniture!" he shouted. "What's the console? Eighteenth century?"

So he knew movies and antiques?

"Yeah," I answered eloquently. Coffee. Coffee. Sometimes I put it in the freezer, just to keep it fresh and . . .

"What happened to the fruitcake?"

For a moment I believe I died. Just for a moment—you know how your heart skips a beat and you feel the world tilting and you can't breathe?

"What fruitcake?" I attempted to say as casually as possible. Nothing came out. Of course it didn't. I had died.

Then I took a deep breath and cleared my throat, an emotional Heimlich maneuver. Adopting a false cheerful smile, I looked in the dining room.

"What fruitcake?" That time it came out.

Christopher held up something pinched between his thumb and index finger. "A green candied cherry. The only conceivable use for a green candied cherry is in a fruitcake.

And besides, there are crumbs all over the place, an empty cake plate. So again, where's the fruitcake?''

''Oh, well. I threw it out. It was bad.''

'' 'Bad' as in 'naughty,' or 'bad' as in 'not good'?''

''It was no good.'' There. End of discussion.

Then he grinned. ''How could you tell with a fruitcake?''

''What do you mean?''

''What I mean is that fruitcakes all taste alike, good and bad. How could you tell yours was a bad one?''

''Well. I mean, it was old. Really old.''

''All fruitcakes are old. How old is 'really' old?''

''Remember a few years back, when a slice of the wedding cake of Wallis Simpson and the Duke of Windsor was sold at auction?''

''Sure. Some fool paid a couple of hundred grand for a piece of sixty-year-old cake.''

''Well, this fruitcake was of the same vintage, without the historical value.''

He whistled through his teeth. ''That *is* old. Coffee ready?''

So that was it? End of the investigation? No fingerprint dusting or mug shots this time?

I eventually found the coffee, and we both had two cups and more extraordinary, marvelous conversation. Suddenly it was three in the morning.

He stood to leave, and I walked him to the door in silence. He reached for my hand. Very gently, he raised his other hand and pushed my hair from my face, and I closed my eyes, inhaling his scent, listening to him breathe.

I felt him coming closer, the warmth, and then his lips were on mine. Soft, clean, the warmth dissolved into heat. For the second time that evening, I believe I died a little.

His arms were around me, and I clutched at his back as if he were the only thing between me and drowning. And wonderfully, gloriously, he clutched me just as hard, held me just as closely.

Then, abruptly, he stopped and pulled back. There was

an expression of confusion on his face, and something else. Guilt, maybe? It was hard to tell.

Then he let out a deep sigh and looked at me, his lips pursed for just a moment.

"Anyone ever tell you you're a dead ringer for ZaSu Pitts?"

His voice was raspy, as was mine when I replied, "Oh, sure. I get that all the time."

Again, he reached out for me, and just when we almost touched, he dropped his hand.

"I'll call you," he said softly without much of an expression. Before I could thank him once more for dinner, he was gone, heels clicking on my sidewalk, bathed in the flickering street lamps.

"I'll call you" he had said.

And any woman worth her salt knows that meant one thing and one thing only: I would never see Christopher Quinn again.

Chapter Seven

*A*s restful, rejuvenating sleep goes, this night was right up there with the time my appendix burst, or when my roommate in college swallowed a dozen caffeine tablets and attempted to single-handedly revive the disco movement.

At one point I just wandered the house, opening cabinets, thumbing through linens. I found another of Aunt Adele's notes.

"He may not be the guy you think of as handsome."

I grinned. Almost Gershwin, Aunt Adele, almost. I folded it up and slipped it into my bathrobe pocket.

There was so much to think about, so much to ponder, both hideous and wonderful thoughts. For one, I was a murderer. But on the bright side, it was quite possible the man of my dreams had just entered my life. On the downside, I was still a murderer. And chances were the man of my dreams either had made an exit from my life forever or would book me for homicide during our next date.

Although I'm not generally a glass-half-empty type of gal, it was pretty hard to see anything beyond those basic facts. But then, around four in the morning, a revelation came to me. Why didn't I just call the police station and ask for Christopher Quinn? If he wasn't working for the Savannah department, I could call Chicago. It was so obvious, no wonder I hadn't thought of it before.

One particularly lovely aspect of this plan was that police stations are open twenty-four hours a day. I didn't have to wait until nine and call from work. So at a quarter to five in the morning, I called the Savannah Police Department.

"Hello," I said, disguising my voice. Don't ask me why,

but it seemed to be the thing to do at the time. "Is there an Officer Quinn with you?"

The woman on the other end seemed taken aback.

"What do you mean, 'with me'?"

"No, no. That's not what I meant." This wasn't going as planned. "I'm just wondering if there is an Officer Christopher Quinn working there." Whew. Got out of that one.

"Is there any particular reason you're asking, ma'am? Perhaps another officer could be of assistance."

"No, thank you." Now we were back on track. "I was just wondering."

"Do you mean that someone by the name of Christopher Quinn has been claiming to be a police officer?"

"No. Not really. But he seems to have a badge in his wallet."

There was a brief silence. "Does the badge state he's a member of the Savannah PD? And was he in any way impersonating an officer?"

"Well, not exactly."

"Did he claim to be a police officer?"

"No." I almost added that he claimed to be a college professor, but decided not to muddy the already murky water.

"In other words, Miss Lovett, you just saw something shiny in a man's wallet?"

"Well, in a way, but . . ." Wait a moment. She used my name. Was my phone tapped? Was there a surveillance van outside, with a fake exterminator logo on the side and a disk on the roof?

Carefully, I slipped over to the window and parted the curtains. The street was empty. No truck, no men with walkie-talkies. Only the lamps gleaming over the bushes and through the trees.

"Are you still there, Miss Lovett?"

"Yes." My voice was still disguised, now slightly hushed. "How do you know my name?"

"Caller ID, Miss Lovett. Everyone has it now. Cuts

down on prank calls. But getting back to the alleged officer—''

''Never mind. I've got to go now. Bye.''

''Good-bye then, Miss Lovett.''

I hung up, feeling like a total fool. Not only that, but the
call had been a mistake. At the very least, it was now on
record that I, Nicole Lovett, called the Savannah Police Department and asked if there was an Officer Quinn. So I was
either a stalker, or a calculating criminal, which would later
come out at my homicide trial.

Another fact was not lost on me. My question had not
been answered. I had no more information now than before
my vocally theatrical performance.

It seemed pointless to call Chicago. Just about everything
seemed pointless at that moment. Christopher Quinn might
not even be his real name. His entire personality might be
a fraud, from his love of old films to his daughter and his
deceased wife.

Getting ready for work, I finally admitted to myself that
the man of my dreams might very well have been nothing
but an empty fantasy.

The station was a frenzy of activity, but I didn't pay much
attention. Exhaustion had finally set in, despite four cups of
coffee and a bowl of sugar-laden Cheerios. Now I was wired
as well as debilitated by sleep deprivation.

''Nicole!'' Mary Clare grabbed my arm. ''There's a policeman inside to see you.''

Was it Christopher? I took a deep breath. ''Did he say
what he wanted?'' I brushed a hand through my hair, just
in case.

''He wants to talk to you about Martha Cox. He asked
me a few questions, too. I said you didn't seem to like her
much, and that you refused to have anything to do with our
memorial service.''

''Thanks,'' I mumbled, appalled. ''I sure appreciate it.''

Sarcasm was, in general, lost on Mary Clare. ''No problem! He's right over here.''

I straightened my back, steeling myself for coming face-to-face with Christopher Quinn. And then I saw him.

"Miss Lovett?" The officer was a very large man who looked startlingly like Mario from the video game. "I'm Officer Williams with the Savannah Police Department. I understand you're acquainted with Miss Martha Cox?"

Now there were two ways to go on this one. I could get it all over and confess, or I could hedge a bit and stall for time. The truth was, if I was going to be arrested, I'd much rather have Christopher Quinn do the job.

"Yes, I do know her," I said, trying to sound as nonchalant as possible. The problem was that between all the coffee and sugar, well, I was a bit nervous.

That's when my eye began to twitch. Not my eye exactly, but the lower left lid sort of leapt. Hopefully, Officer Williams wouldn't notice and would concentrate on taking notes on his little pad.

"So have you seen Miss Cox since she arrived in town?"

Now the funny thing about a twitching eye is that the more you try to stop the twitching, the more determined it is to twitch.

"Yes, as a matter of fact I did see her. She came to my house."

"Did she?" He looked up at me, and his expression altered from bland professionalism to mild surprise as he watched my eye.

As if jolted, he focused back to the pad. "And did she in any way indicate an intention to leave town?"

"No, not at all." The twitch was becoming a full-throttle spasm.

"What was the exact nature of your conversation?"

"Well, we discussed—"

He looked up at me. "Miss Lovett." His voice was stern. "I am a married man."

For a moment I was perplexed, then it hit me. He thought I was winking at him.

"No, no!" I tried to figure out a way that would contradict his thoughts without insulting him. "As attractive as I find you, I just have this thing—"

"For married men?"

"No! A twitch. When I get nervous, my eye twitches."

"Are you nervous, Miss Lovett?"

"Of course not," I replied indignantly, traitorous eye notwithstanding.

"If you can remember anything that could be of help in locating Miss Cox, please contact us."

"You bet." I winked.

Officer Williams paused for a moment, as if wondering if there was such a thing as felonious facial movement, then snapped his pad shut.

As he turned to leave, a thought crossed my mind. "Excuse me, Officer?"

"Yes?"

"Do you know a Christopher Quinn?"

"Christopher Quinn? You mean that guy in *Zorba the Greek*?"

"No, that's Anthony Quinn. I mean a real person, a policeman named Christopher Quinn."

"You mean here in Savannah?"

I nodded encouragingly, as if giving clues in a game of charades.

"What does he look like?"

"Sort of dark hair, tall, nicely built, intense green eyes. He's not really the sort of guy you'd think of as handsome."

He thought for a moment. "But to your heart, he carries the key?"

It was a strange instant as he looked at me, completing my own thought before I could finish.

"Ira Gershwin," he said. "Great lyricist overshadowed by his younger brother George. Just the way Johnny Mercer is so overlooked. A shame, really."

"Yes it is." This conversation had taken a definite turn for the bizarre. "But anyway, do you know of anyone like him?" I tried to keep it light.

"Nope. I'm afraid I can't help you."

"Well, if you remember anything that could be of assistance, could you give me a call?"

"You bet." He smiled and held two fingers to where a hat brim would be, had he been wearing a hat. Then he left.

I'd also wanted to ask him more about Martha, about any ideas they had as to where she might be, but I was afraid of arousing suspicions. One fact was clear—when Mary Clare had mentioned the memorial service, the police officer was not quick to dismiss the notion of Martha Cox being dead. Perhaps they even had the body, they were just trying to flush out the murderer by pretending she was missing.

The truth was, I'd been thinking a lot about Martha. Not in the way I had before, viewing her as my enemy. No, when I thought about Martha now, it was entirely different, as if watching an old film and discovering a new scene.

Looking back, I recalled there were times when she had tried to be my friend. But I was the one who rebuffed her. There was one cast party, I can't remember for which play, when Martha had come up to me, smiling, saying something about what a wonderful job I had done with my character. Instead of being gracious, I turned to my friends and made fun of her. While I don't remember exactly what I said, I do remember the expression on her face, especially in her eyes.

There were other occasions, too, but somehow I had managed to block them out for all those years. It was much easier to think of Martha Cox as the undiluted enemy. That made me the victim, and eliminated my need for accountability.

With Martha Cox as a scapegoat, I didn't have to look too closely at my own behavior in the past. I could just point a finger at Martha, and shower myself with sympathy. It had all been so convenient, all so very easy.

Even with Jed, my fiancé. Jed. Our relationship never should have gotten as far as it did. It was more a matter of inertia than anything else. We never bothered to break up after college. And when it seemed time to get married, well, we got engaged. And then I threw myself into the externals, of planning a grand wedding as would befit a future anchorwoman. I became so focused on the wedding that I ignored the entire issue of the marriage.

No wonder Jed had left. No wonder he had to leave. No wonder he had been unable to explain why, because I would not have listened, and he knew that.

And no wonder he had dated Martha. But he had also dated others. And Martha, who had been out of town when Jed had stood me up, stopped dating him when she learned we had been engaged. She may have really liked Jed, perhaps she was even beginning to love him, but she broke off their relationship.

I had forgotten about that. Instead I had blamed his no-show at the church on Martha, and in reality she hadn't even been within a hundred miles.

Even the other day, when she stopped by, I hadn't given her a chance. If I had, she would still be alive. If I had, how different things might have been.

It was then I made up my mind. If Christopher Quinn ever called, I would turn myself in. And if he didn't call within the next two days, I would simply go to the police station and turn myself in.

Maybe it was a bit late in the game, but finally, I was going to take responsibility for my own deeds. Finally.

Chapter Eight

*O*bviously Christopher Quinn, whoever he was, was ignorant of the rules. His parting words to me had been "I'll call you." Therefore, when he actually called toward the end of the day, I was completely befuddled.

"Hello," he said. There was something strained about his voice, something not quite right. "I know this is last-minute, but are you free for dinner tonight?"

Ah-ha, I thought. This is it. Enough of this playing around—he was planning on booking his suspect, and hopefully having a decent meal before leading me away in handcuffs.

But I was ready. "Of course I'm free," I answered. Not for long, but for the moment I was indeed free.

"Great." Again, he sounded tired, not quite himself. He suggested a cute French bistro on Congress Street, and as we did before, we agreed to meet there.

There were still a couple of hours before our date, so after work I went home and had a large cup of tea. There was so much to think about, but really no point in dwelling over every issue. My life was about to change forever, and there was a feeling that I should be doing something monumental in acknowledgment of the upcoming transformation. But nothing seemed right, from jotting down notes to paying off my latest bills.

What did other people do when confronted with the same situation? Instead of performing an important, meaningful deed, I had a second cup of tea and stared down at the design on the kitchen tablecloth.

Then my parents called. I almost told them everything,

but realized that would be a relief only to me, not to them. Let them linger just a bit longer in their happy world. Soon enough it would be shattered.

It was time. I took one last look at the house, wondering when I would see it again, if I would see it again.

The drive to the restaurant was strangely calming. This was my choice, to come here and meet Officer Quinn. No matter what, I managed to overcome the desire to flee. There was something of a small triumph in that, in steering my own fate, at least to a certain extent.

As with dinner before, he was waiting for me in the bistro, again looking impossibly wonderful. There was an early chill in the air, and again he was wearing a jacket, his hair slightly tousled. Suddenly I had an image of him as a father, as a loving husband, having his entire life shattered.

How awful this case must have been for him. There must have been moments when dealing with senseless deaths—from his wife's to Martha's—had become too much, yet there was probably no one for him to speak to, no one with whom to share his troubles.

He stood as I approached the table, then smiled and we sat down.

"It's good to see you, Nicole." He placed his hand over mine.

"And it's good to see you, too." In spite of the circumstance, I meant it. "I hope your day went well."

The waiter handed us the menus. "In all honesty, I've had better days." Christopher glanced at me, then looked away.

So he knew what he had to do. "I understand," I said quietly.

"Do you?"

I nodded. "It's not exactly what you were expecting, is it?"

He looked directly at me, those intense eyes of his so close. "No, it isn't. I just thought it would be easier."

"How long have you known?"

He shrugged. "All along, I suppose."

"I never guessed. I mean, that you knew."

"Well . . ."

"And the fruitcake must have cinched it."

"The fruitcake?" He put the menu down and stared. "What the hell does a fruitcake have to do with it?"

The waiter had returned, his face expectant. After one look at us he held up his hand, indicating he would return later.

"A fruitcake?" Christopher repeated.

"Well, that is the murder weapon, of course."

"The murder weapon?" The beginnings of a grin were tugging at the corners of his mouth. "My dear Nicole, what are you talking about?"

"The Martha Cox case. I killed her by allowing her to eat a piece of Aunt Adele's fruitcake."

Confession complete. A strange lightness overtook me, a sense of freedom. The worst was over. I had confessed all.

Christopher Quinn gaped for a few moments, then he began to laugh, a quiet chuckle at first, then a full-throated roar.

All I could do was stare. This had to be a first, the arresting officer cracking under the pressure as the suspect remained eerily calm. Other diners turned to look, uncertain smiles on their faces as they saw a man in gleeful hysterics and a woman with her hands solemnly folded over an unopened menu.

Finally his laughter died down to a grin and only an occasional chuckle.

"Thank you, Nicole," he said. "I can't tell you how much I needed that."

"Well, good." Then I ventured one step further. "So when will I be arrested, Officer Quinn?"

The smile began to fade. "Who is Officer Quinn?"

"You."

"Where on earth did you get that idea?"

"You're a policeman, aren't you?"

"I repeat, where on earth did you get that idea?"

"Well, from everything. Do you want me to explain it all?"

He nodded just once, and I began. "For one, you came out of nowhere the first night Martha Cox was missing. I saw something shiny in your wallet, clearly a badge. Your interest in me is professional—you've managed to keep me off balance enough that I've probably all but confessed several times. You even found evidence of the missing fruitcake. You know, the green candied cherry and the telltale crumbs. You have a terrible cover story about being some bogus teacher. Really, Officer Quinn, you should find a better description of your courses than 'a little bit of this and that.' Do you want me to go on?"

His expression was unreadable. All I knew was that his dimples were gone.

The waiter came back, took another look at us, and crept away.

For a few moments Christopher simply looked at me, and then, very slowly, he reached into his jacket pocket.

I held my breath. Would he pull out his weapon here, unprovoked, at the table? Or was everything I had just said considered some sort of offense, such as taunting an officer? Maybe he had handcuffs. Maybe . . .

His wallet flipped on the table. "Would you like to open it?"

"There's really no need," I answered stiffly. In truth, I was dying to see what was in there. The official police identification and the badge and all sorts of fascinating information were just waiting for me to discover.

But no. I looked away, almost afraid of the temptation.

"Please. I insist." With a finger he pushed it closer to me.

"Really. This is just silly."

"I agree. So will you please have a look?"

Clearly this man would not let me avoid the wallet hazard. Again, I glanced around the restaurant. No one seemed to be watching us anymore. And then I touched the wallet, gingerly at first. It was still warm from being close to his body.

"Okay," I whispered. "Here goes."

Like a well-thumbed book, it flopped open with only a touch. And there it was, the badge. I looked up at Christopher, but his eyes remained fixed on me, not on his wallet.

"Read it out loud," he said softly.

I was reluctant to look away from his face. Because after I had seen his wallet, once the information was mine, there was no more pretending. This would be the end of my secret fantasy of a normal life with him, a dream of such importance I had only just then realized how badly I wanted it to come true.

Then I looked down. It took a moment to focus, but there it was, a star, gleaming in the romantic light of this little bistro. But something was wrong. I held the wallet so I could read the words embossed on the badge.

" 'World's Number One Daddy.' "

"Huh?"

"I thought you might say something like that. My daughter gave that to me last Father's Day. It entitles me to take her to the park on Saturday mornings and make pancakes, not to solve crimes."

"I don't understand," I mumbled, in what had to have been the biggest understatement of my life.

"Look at the photo ID behind the badge," he instructed. It was a laminated card with his picture—not a bad one, actually—and some sort of official-looking seal. "LaSalle College," it said. In smaller letters, "Christopher P. Quinn, PhD."

"What does the *P* stand for?" I asked idiotically.

"I'm not telling," he replied. "Suffice it to say I logged a lot of time in school yards defending my masculinity because of my middle name."

A strange giddiness settled over me. He was not going to arrest me! Everything I had assumed over the past few days had been wrong. But then, what *was* he doing there?

And again, the truth of his identity in no way detracted from the same basic fact that I was a murderer.

He ordered a nice bottle of wine, not that I would have noticed if it hadn't been nice at that point, and asked me to explain everything about Martha Cox. Unfortunately for him, I did—from that first day at the orientation assembly to the moment I realized she was gone and had eaten Aunt Adele's fruitcake. He listened carefully, asking for clarification on some points, questioning others.

Finally I had finished, my first course of some sort of soup untouched. He had gone through a full basket of bread and was awaiting a refill.

"So now you know," I said at last. "You know what a cowardly murderer I am." It felt good to have it out in the open, to share it with him.

He remained silent. "Well?" I prodded. "Please, what do you have to say?"

He had made a small pile of breadcrumbs and pushed them from side to side. Then he spoke. "Mike Gigante."

It took a moment for me to respond. Had I missed something? Was Mike Gigante a name I should somehow know?

Without waiting for my questions, he continued. "I think the first time I met Mike Gigante was in sixth grade. He tied my shoelaces together—this was in the days before Velcro. I stood up, fell down, and vowed to hate him for the rest of my life."

"Really? Then what happened?"

"I kept the vow for about four years. We played on the same football team, had some of the same friends, and managed to get into at least one a fight a year. No major battles, just the obligatory bloody nose and one chipped tooth. Then my second year of high school I left something in the locker room. The place was empty, but I heard someone in the showers. Someone was crying. I went in there, and Mike Gigante was sitting, fully clothed, against the tile wall, his head in his hands. Seems his grandmother had just died. He wanted me to go, but I stayed, sat next to him. We didn't say much. Finally I had to get home, and he didn't even look up when I left. Then the next day after practice he was waiting for me. I assumed he was going to jump me, so I put down my backpack and got ready for the first punch.''

''What happened?''

''Nothing. He just said thanks, and went home. But eventually, little by little, we became friends. Actually, it started out that we simply stopped being enemies. We no longer pounded each other or spit in each other's path. Friendship took a while longer.''

''You made the first step, though.''

''Well, I guess you could say that. But so did he, in a way, that afternoon in the shower. He could have pushed me away, but he didn't.''

I finally began to spoon some of my now-cold soup, thinking about how things would have been different had I been a better person, or at least less self-defensive. Maybe I had waited too long. High school was a long time ago.

''Are you and Mike still friends?''

Christopher smiled. ''We are. In fact, his younger sister was my wife.''

''Wow.'' I couldn't think of anything else to say. His wife again. His ability to forgive had led him directly to happiness. My inability to forgive had led me, well . . .

''Nicole.'' He leaned close, so close his breath ruffled my hair. ''I'd be willing to bet anything that Martha Cox is alive and well.''

''Then where is she?''

''Who knows? Lives are complicated. She probably had her own reasons for skipping town. But I'll tell you one thing—whatever her reason for leaving, I doubt very much it had anything to do with a fruitcake.''

''Do you really think so?''

He nodded. ''Absolutely. In fact, if you want me to, I can help you find her. I've always wanted to be an amateur sleuth. I've probably seen too many Dick Powell movies, but I'll be glad to help.''

''Really? Where do we begin?''

''Well, first off we finish dinner. Then we have coffee,

and figure out why a newly employed former Miss Georgia would want to leave, and where the destination would be. Does that sound good?''

''Sure. But how can we discover what the police—the real police—can't? They've been working on this for a few days, and still no Martha Cox.''

''True. I wonder, though, how hard they are looking. This has been a slow news week—not much else in the papers. So for the moment they seem to be conducting an investigation, right? On the other hand, there doesn't seem to be any evidence of foul play. She's gone; that's hardly a crime when the missing person is an able adult.''

''Maybe.'' Actually, what he was saying made a lot of sense.

''But let's put it this way,'' he continued. ''The whole situation makes it extremely unlikely that she's been poisoned. Had that been the case, she would have been found in her hotel, right? Or by the side of the road in her car, fruitcake on her breath. That wasn't the case. And remember, deathly ill people usually don't pack up their bags and leave quietly.''

For the first time in days, a ray of hope seemed to exist. Maybe he was right. He had been right about other things. And there was something about him that I trusted instinctively. He just seemed to be, for want of a better word, good. Not in the dull, holier-than-thou sense of the word, but good as in a decent, honest human being.

And here we had been for the better part of an hour discussing my problems. I put down the spoon.

''So tell me, why was your day so rough?''

He raised his eyebrows. ''We're back to me now, eh? It wasn't a horrible day in terms of what you've been going through. I haven't been walking around, willing to confess to a murder. It's just that . . .''

''Just that what?''

''I've finally come to the realization that I don't have the makings of a novelist. I had come here hoping to find some sort of inspiration. But I haven't. And it's not Savannah, it's me.''

''But what were you looking for? What sort of inspiration?''

''I wasn't sure. Just thought I'd give it a chance, one last shot. These past few years have been such a strange time. I've done a lot of thinking, a lot of praying for answers. For some reason I had an urge to come down here. No logical reason, really. It's just that I've learned to be more open to my more illogical whims, to give them a chance and see if anything pans out. Doesn't matter, really. I'm teaching again next semester, back to routine.''

''Maybe you'll find something.'' I reached out and touched his hand. Slowly, gently, he took mine, rubbing his thumb against the top of my hand.

''I think I already have,'' he said softly.

Before he could say anything else, the main course—which we had been putting off—finally arrived. For the first time in days, I was absolutely ravenous.

We never did get around to working on the case of the missing baton twirler. Not that night anyway.

It was all sort of a haze. All I know is that he came back home with me, and we sat for hours, his arm around my shoulders. It felt so right, so perfect and natural.

There was no real shift from just sitting on the couch to everything else. It was a seamless transition, from a gentle feathery kiss to something much deeper. Yet still there was an ease, a comfort. He didn't frighten me, this man whom I had known for such a short time.

It was just so right.

When morning came he finally left, reluctantly, I think. At the front door he gave me a last kiss. His eyes were still foggy when I asked him the question.

''So, what does the *P* in your middle name stand for?''

He answered without hesitation. ''Phinneous.'' And then he was gone.

I watched him walk away, a smile on my face. This time there was no doubt. I would see him again. Then another thought crossed my mind.

Phinneous?

Chapter Nine

*T*here was nothing more appealing than the thought of playing hooky. All I longed to do was sit around in my old bathrobe and replay the previous night in my mind, an expression here, a touch there, some of his words and thoughts.

In the daylight it was clear how very little I knew him in some ways. There were massive chunks of basic information that were blank, important things such as what his marriage had been like, how he coped after the accident, whether his daughter liked dolls or video games or movies like her father.

I didn't know if his parents were still alive, if he had siblings, and if he liked pasta or long walks on a misty beach. But in spite of the factual gaps, I felt as if I did know him—better than most people who had been my friends for years. Strange as it sounds, there was a sense of spiritual knowledge that had nothing to do with chronological timelines or fundamental events. Those bits would be filled in eventually, with some luck. Everything else was already in place.

Although I was still exhausted, panic was no longer my primary motivator. And in the calm sanity of the morning, everything Christopher had said the night before made sense. If she had been poisoned by a deadly wedge of fruitcake, naturally she would have been found in her hotel room. So she must have gone someplace, but where?

Getting ready for work, I tried to recall that last conversation. I'd been so stunned by her mere presence, the only clear recollection was that she had talked about high school as if it had been the last important phase of her life. For Martha Cox, the years since high school had been a slow come-down.

Maybe there was something to that aspect. The phone rang as I was slipping on the second leg of my stockings.

"Can you think of anyone from high school she might want to visit?"

I smiled. Of course it was Christopher, not even bothering to identify himself and launching into the conversation as if we had been sitting together for hours. It wasn't annoying—it was intimate and wonderful.

"Good morning to you, too." I pulled on the left leg. "But I was just thinking along those same lines."

"Did she have a lot of friends?" It sounded as if he were sipping coffee on the other end.

"Funny, now that I think about it, not really. She was always popular, but with groups that were always changing. One moment she would be the queen of the football team. The next, she'd be hanging out with the guys from the theater club. I can't remember any constant friends."

"That's sort of sad."

"Yeah, it is."

"I've been thinking over a few options. Her car was still in the hotel parking lot. So that means wherever she went, it's either very nearby or far enough away to require an airplane."

"Could she be in another country?"

"Don't think so. The police would have found that out already. And with the security checks required on domestic flights these days, my guess would be that she's within a few miles of here, or she went someplace on a private plane."

"What about the bus or train?"

"Maybe. But from what you've said, Miss Cox doesn't seem like a Greyhound sort of gal. Now getting back to high school, was there anyone there who has made it financially?"

"A few people. Why?"

"I think she was looking for security, and financial security is usually very appealing to people who don't realize they want emotional security."

"Can you run that by me again?"

He laughed. "Never mind. But is there anyone you can think of who has money to burn?"

"Other than me, of course."

"Naturally."

"Let's see, does it have to be male or female?"

"Either, but I'd take more of a bet on a male. And if you happen to know any filthy rich and eligible females, just pass me their names and phone numbers."

"Very funny." I smiled. "But wait—there was a guy. Nah. It couldn't be him—he's married."

"All the more reason to check up on him. Who is it?"

It was almost impossible to imagine Martha Cox with Boo Boo Myers. He was one of those guys who wore Buddy Holly glasses before they were fashionably retro, always held together with a bent safety pin or a roll of white tape. He was president of the computer club in school, went to a couple of years of college at MIT before dropping out and designing software. His most successful design, BlickFlick, is that program used by everyone on Wall Street, and thus the world. If you look carefully at the box, there's a little hologram of Boo Boo, crooked glasses and all.

He married a girl he met at MIT—she was something like sixteen and doing postgraduate work. Rumor had it she designed most of the software, but they relied on Boo Boo's personality to market the goods. It was always something of a shock to pick up a copy of *Business Week* and see Boo Boo Myers on the cover, and always more of a shock to think of Boo Boo with a winning personality.

I gave the information to Christopher, who seemed intrigued by this angle. He asked me to keep on thinking of others, and I said I would, although it seemed far-fetched at best. Maybe he was right—he'd seen way too many detective movies for his own good.

There was no more information at work about the missing Martha Cox. After just a few days, the excitement was fading, and we were all back to the same routine. Even Ben the cameraman was no longer interested. This was the first morning that the newspaper didn't feature her on the front page. Instead she was on page nine, below a piece about planting winter bulbs.

All in all, there was something rather depressing about the general lack of interest. Here she had made a spectacular, if mysterious, exit, and no one seemed to care anymore.

Now that I was quite certain of my own innocence, I couldn't help but feel indignant about Martha Cox's obscurity.

"It just seems all wrong," I complained to the station manager. "Don't the police have a better chance of locating her if we keep her story alive?"

"Sure they do," he answered. "But we only have that baton-twirling tape and that sample reel. There are only so many times we can force our viewers to watch that stuff." Then he gave me a second look. "Now if *you* should ever end up missing, well, we'd be in real luck. Can you imagine all the clips we could show? Why, we could have a Nicole Lovett marathon—from storm reports to ant-farm hygiene."

"Thanks, Steve. I appreciate the thought."

"You know, that would be great, wouldn't it? We have you in a swimming suit, in a bath towel, in that Carmen Miranda hat. Remember when you fell off the pony? Or when the raccoon clawed that silk jacket of yours? Now that was entertainment. Yep. You can betcha if anything happened to you, God forbid, it would be a real ratings bonanza. Maybe we should prepare a little something, just in case." He smiled hopefully.

I just smiled back and pretended to ignore the look of raw ratings hunger on his otherwise bland features.

Still, it seemed as if we had to do something to help Martha. What if she had lost her memory? Or what if she had been kidnapped?

When I ran those possibilities by my co-workers, they all rolled their eyes.

"Drop it, Lovett," said Ted in audio. "And aren't you glad you finally have the job?"

"What job?"

"He didn't tell you? They've decided to go with you as the anchor. That is, for as long as we do news. Seems we may be taken over by that shopping network."

Ted had delivered both bits of news casually. I got the job I had wanted, but we may all be out of a job soon.

"No. I don't know that," I said quietly. This felt all wrong. Not just the shopping network, but the way the anchor job finally came to me. It wasn't the way I had wanted it, but if you'd asked me a few days ago, I wouldn't have blinked.

What had happened to me? But of course even as I thought the question, I knew the answer. Christopher Phinneous Quinn, that's what had happened to me.

"Okay, Nicole. You're on in ten."

I applied my makeup, the lipliner and dark eye shadow and the contour blush. My hair was sprayed to the point of being bulletproof, and then I was ready.

It was the usual news report. There was a school closing because of a flooded basement. An art gallery was featuring a hands-on exhibit for the blind. It was the one hundred and second birthday of a nursing home resident. I read professionally if a bit fast, and Steve made the "extend" sign, meaning I would be finished with copy before we had used all the airtime.

That had been my intention.

"Finally, on a personal note," I said, looking directly into the camera. Someone had once said that the most successful news reporters were the ones who made the camera their best and most trusted friend. I had never seen it that way before, until now.

The camera was my best friend in the world. I implored with my eyes, didn't flinch the way I usually did under the lights and the stress.

I pretended the camera was Christopher.

"A member of our Channel Eighty-nine family is still

missing. It's no longer a front-page story, but Martha Cox has not been located yet. Martha, if you're listening to me, please let us know how you're doing.''

Steve was making frantic gestures that I studiously ignored, slashing his finger across his throat to ''cut,'' jumping in his crepe-soled shoes. I continued.

''There's a chair waiting for you at the news desk—I'm keeping it warm for your return. I beg you, please contact us at once, or at least contact me.'' Finally I smiled. ''That fruitcake you swiped was not good, although as someone pointed out, with a fruitcake it is hard to tell.''

The red eye blinked off, and Steve's face was red. ''What was that? This isn't the personal-message network, for Christ's sake! What kind of a stunt was that? Man, if you had any chance of selling discount cultured pearls when the new guys take over, you just blew it big time.''

I said nothing as I gathered the copy and left the desk. Everyone was staring at me, not saying a word just in case my unpopularity with the boss happened to be contagious.

Wish I could say my little on-air appeal worked, but it didn't. The switchboard did not suddenly light up. No one called to report seeing Martha wandering lost and confused on the highway. The only thing accomplished was that I was now in more trouble than I'd been in since accidentally driving the family car into the side of the garage.

But then Christopher came by to pick me up for lunch.

''That was nice,'' he said softly.

''You were watching?''

''Of course I was. I've been watching you for a long time, but I wasn't going to admit it. Can you get away for lunch?''

''Sure. I think I can get away for a lot longer than lunch. I may be out of a job by the end of the day.''

We picked up sandwiches and sat on a bench in Oglethorpe Square.

''It's beautiful here,'' he said sipping his coffee.

I nodded. ''What did you mean that you had been watching me? Do you mean even before we met?''

"Yes."

"How? I mean, why on earth didn't you mention this before?"

"I didn't want to come off as a stalker. But I'd been watching your show. That was really great the way you used that plastic food sealer. I came this close to ordering one for myself."

"Thank you. That's quite a compliment." Although it really didn't seem like one. "So you were interested in me for some other reason after all, right? Very few people are that fascinated with plastic food sealers. Maybe you weren't going to book me for murder, but there was some other reason."

"Yes, as a matter of fact there was." He started to reach for his backpack, then paused. "You see, my grandfather always talked about Savannah with a great deal of affection."

"Did he?" Now where on earth was he going with this tale?

"Indeed he did. He was only here briefly, but it made quite an impression on him. He was especially fond of a young woman by the name of Adele Lovett."

"Aunt Adele?" Was it possible? "Was your grandfather a traveling salesman from up North?"

"Yep. From Dayton, Ohio, as a matter of fact."

"Why did he stand her up at the altar?" Suddenly I felt angry on behalf of poor Aunt Adele. "Didn't he realize he ruined her life?"

"The whole thing ruined his life, too, if that's any consolation. He had to leave the woman of his dreams to go home to his wife and small son, my father."

"He was married?"

"Bad timing, wasn't it? He had no idea how hard he would fall for Adele. So hard, in fact, that he almost committed bigamy. He went home to Dayton, had a few more kids, and spun Walter Mitty–like tales. He's the one who took me to my first movies when I was little. I think that's where I get my less practical side, from Grandfather Ralph."

"How did you hear about all this?"

"The fruitcakes. Your aunt sent them every year, and Grandfather Ralph loved them—that is, until his wife found out. She caught him eating one in the barn just before Christmas one year, and that was the end of his yearly fruitcake indulgence. Then she had her friend at the post office stamp 'deceased' all over the packages, and return them unopened. I think that was illegal, but Grandma was a very determined woman. Granddaddy assumed your Aunt Adele had passed away once he stopped getting the cakes, and he mourned for her. Quietly, of course—Grandma had a mean left hook. But once, just before he really died, he told me all about her, Adele Lovett. He said she used to dance the Charleston and roll her stockings. They would sneak out and smoke cigarettes, two grown adults behaving like wayward kids. That must have been part of the appeal—Grandfather never had much of a childhood. And being married to Grandma, well, he didn't have much of an adulthood, either. But just before he passed away, he made me promise that if ever I had a daughter, I'd name her Adele. Actually, he requested the name for a child of either sex, but luckily Adele was born female."

"That still doesn't explain why you're here."

"Well, that's a little more difficult. You see, through my grandfather, I had always seen Savannah as a magical place, a place of romance and wonder. I'd wanted to come here to see it for myself, but one thing led to another and I never had the chance until now."

"What about your book?"

"I was thinking of writing a novel based on their story. It just seemed so touching, so sad. Grandfather Ralph was an amazing character, and it seems your aunt was, too."

"She was, I think."

"I'd been thinking of this book for a long time. And then, after the accident, it was all I could do to keep myself sane. I didn't have the energy to attempt a project, even one that might prove healing. It was too overwhelming until recently. I have to make some decisions very soon about teaching, where we'll live. It was either now or never."

Birds were chirping in the trees, people were strolling through the square.

"I don't know what to say, where to even begin," I said at last.

"You don't have to. I'll be going back to Chicago tomorrow."

"Tomorrow?"

"Yep. I have to get back to Adele—she's been staying with her Uncle Mike. I have to get my classes in order."

"What do you teach?"

"Believe it or not, I wasn't kidding. A little of this, a little of that. LaSalle isn't exactly Harvard, but they have been there for me. I teach American film mostly, and a few years ago I added a course on coping with grief."

"Those are the adults you teach," I stated.

"Yep. Most of them are widowed, like me. Some have lost children, something I can't even imagine. It's rewarding. But I was ready for a change."

"Savannah?"

He nodded, then added, "And I might go back to my old job, the one I had before LaSalle."

"Really? What was that?"

For the first time since we reached the park, he grinned, the dimples forming gloriously at either side of his mouth. The wind blew his hair, and I wanted to kiss him more than I'd ever wanted to kiss anyone in my life. But I didn't. I just waited for him to speak.

"My dear Nicole," he said and laughed. "I was with the Chicago Police Department. Would you like to take it from there?"

"Homicide," I said, still stunned by the whole afternoon. "You were a homicide detective."

Then, right in the middle of Oglethorpe Square, he kissed me.

Chapter Ten

*H*e was leaving the next day.

No matter how hard I tried to concentrate on work, how determined I was to get back on my bosses' good side, the plain and brittle truth was that he was leaving. I'd been a fling, maybe a strange last gesture for his grandfather Ralph.

There hadn't been anything deliberately cruel in his hit-and-run wooing of me, complete though it was. Maybe it was a family trait, like night blindness or big ears. The Lovetts were pushovers for the Quinns, and that was that.

He was leaving, and I would remain in Savannah, alone, perhaps selling cultured pearls and silk pants suits on television. If I was lucky.

To give myself a dash of credit, I had stumbled on the truth earlier when wondering if Christopher Quinn had been the product of my imagination. Oh, he was a real person. It wasn't quite as bad as inventing a whole person, an imaginary friend. But I did something nearly as destructive and hopeless by inventing a romantic chemistry. If it was real, I seemed to be the only person aware of it. Had there really been anything between us, he would have noticed.

So he had been a homicide detective. In spite of my pain, I smiled at the thought. At least I had been right about something. No wonder he had taken a leave after his wife died. But now he seemed ready to go back to it, ready to move on.

When he had left this afternoon, he didn't even bother to say he'd call me. Funny, I didn't even know where he was staying. Never had the chance to ask.

Mary Clare handed me a cordless phone. "There's a call for you on line six."

"Nicole Lovett," I answered.

"Boo Boo Myers has an airplane."

It took me an instant to reply. "And Bill Gates owns an island."

"Furthermore, Mr. Boo Boo has been in town, did you know that?"

He was acting as if he weren't leaving in a few hours, as if things down here mattered. "No, I didn't know he was in town. I wonder why he didn't call me to say 'hey'."

"Maybe he was involved with another illustrious member of your graduating class," Christopher proclaimed.

"Nah. I just can't see it. Not Boo Boo. You know what would make sense?"

"I'm listening."

"A politician." I was warming to the topic. "Are there any senators hanging around? A congressman or two?"

"But they don't always have money, my dear."

"Doesn't matter. I've been thinking about what you said, about security. She doesn't want financial security, she wants a daddy, a father figure, someone to give her unconditional approval."

"And you don't think Boo Boo is our man?"

"Absolutely not. He may be wealthy and powerful, but to everyone back home he's still just good old Boo Boo."

"Politicians, you think?"

"Yeah. But that's just a guess."

"Okay. I'll see you later."

Then he hung up. So maybe he was, indeed, leaving the next day, but somehow I'd see him one last time.

That simple thought put me in a terrific mood for the rest of the afternoon.

He was on my front porch when I got home.

"You know, you're looking just like Blanche Sweet this evening."

"Thank you. And you're looking very Buddy Rogers."

"Must admit, I've never been called Buddy Rogers." He had the black backpack over his shoulder, every inch a man on his way out of town. And of course, that's exactly what he was.

But I refused to think about it any further. There would be plenty of time for that once he was gone, plenty of time to adjust. Plenty of time to throw my hairbrush at the wall and shoot hostile looks to people on the street.

"I brought you something." He reached into the bag and pulled out a familiar brown paper package.

"My God, a last fruitcake! How did you get this?"

"As I mentioned, Grandma intercepted them and sent them back. But one year she visited her sister in Milwaukee. Hence, the last fruitcake."

"Oh, Christopher, thank you!"

"You're welcome."

This cake had the address, to Mr. Ralph Quinn. I was torn between wanting to unwrap it and place it on the cake plate, or leaving it wrapped with the address.

"You can always keep it wrapped on the plate."

The perfect solution. We went inside, and as I placed the cake on the plate he walked over to the photographs. "That's my grandfather." He pointed to one of the stiff-collared young men. And I could have guessed that, had the thought of Granddaddy Ralph being one of her prized pictures ever crossed my mind. That particular picture happened to be my favorite, a handsome, dapper young man holding a croquet mallet as if it had been a baseball bat. His smile is slightly crooked, but unlike the other photos it's unposed and natural.

Aunt Adele had slipped it into the nicest frame, a silver Art Deco number, and as long as I could remember it had always been right up front, crowding out the more formal studio portraits.

"This one of your Aunt Adele is nice," he commented.

"Which one is that?"

"Here." He placed a smaller picture of a sedate young woman next to his grandfather. No wonder I had never recognized her, Aunt Adele. No color, no wild hair or chiffon. But on closer examination, there was a distinct spark in her eyes that even the starched shirtwaist and prim brooch couldn't belie.

"Are you sure that's Aunt Adele?"

The slight smile faded from his face. He needed a shave. His hair was uncombed. His shirt collar was pointing out.

In short, he was perfect.

"I'm pretty sure that's Adele. I found the same picture in my grandfather's things when he died."

"You don't suppose he courted another woman in town, do you? Since he was already married, maybe he just used Savannah as his one-stop fantasyland." My voice became unintentionally harsh. "It was a perfect setup, really, a place where he could be whoever he wanted to be for whichever young woman struck his fancy. Then he could just bolt. It's possible."

Christopher looked back at the photograph of his grandfather and tilted it toward the light. "Nah. He wasn't like that."

"But he was, don't you see? You knew him as a nice guy, a sweet man who took you to the movies and plied you with Milk Duds. I know him as a man who destroyed my aunt's happiness, who left her a laughingstock. Worse— an object of pity. She had no choice but to go from that pretty young woman in the photograph to an eccentric creature with purple hair."

"Purple hair? Don't think old Ralph would have liked that much."

"Old Ralph had no say in the matter, don't you see?" When had I started to shout? There was an unfamiliar edge to my tone, a ferocity. "He had no right!" I pulled the photo of Aunt Adele off the chest with the others and marched to the other side of the room, clutching her to me.

At that point I realized how ridiculous it was. My lower lip was trembling, and I could tell by the awful, familiar sting in my eyes that hot tears would appear in a matter of seconds.

Of course Christopher should have laughed at that point. He should have, really. Instead he picked up the picture of his grandfather and held it up.

"Now see what you've done?" he admonished. "You've really messed up this time, Ralph. Just because you fell deeply in love with Miss Lovett, that did not give you the right to act on your emotions. You never did learn, did you?"

Lowering the photograph, he looked straight at me, green eyes reflecting the warmth of a floor lamp. "You had so many problems, so many issues. You thought it would be better for you to leave rather than give her the chance to help you. Sure, it would have been hard. Maybe even impossible. But now you'll never know what could have been, will you?"

"Maybe it wasn't all his fault," I said softly, looking down at Aunt Adele. "Maybe she didn't know how to reach out to him, to let him know she could have helped. She might have been one of those brittle people who spend their lives blaming others for their misfortune. It would have been ghastly and strange at first. She would have learned about intimacy and sharing and love. It would have scared the hell out of her, but maybe they could have been happy."

"Ralph had been married," he stated flatly. "Nothing can ever change that. In some ways he doesn't know how to go forward. He's been defined by circumstance, and in some ways that's been a comfort. It eliminates a need to try."

"It's time to move on. For everyone's sake. For yours, for Adele."

"Don't you see? I'm afraid, Nicole." His voice was a rasp. "I've loved before and trusted before and thought I knew what life held. Then everything changed in a split second, and that nearly destroyed me."

"You have to try. You have to take a chance."

"So do you."

In a few steps he was at my side. Gently, very gently, he pried the photograph from my hand, and after looking at her for a moment, placed it on a shelf. Then he put his grandfather's picture beside it, and smiled.

"There. Now don't they make a nice couple?"

"They have a lot to work out." Although I had to admit, they did look right together. "He's married. Her parents don't approve. They're both dead. All those little kinks that make relationships so tricky these days."

With no warning, he leaned down and kissed me, a soft, tender touch. All of my anger and hurt and fear evaporated, and all I could do was revel in the moment. This was real, now was a time to savor and not squander. And somehow, that kiss made everything else seem utterly possible.

We spent the evening studiously avoiding the topic of his leaving. It wasn't particularly hard, especially for me. That was the last thing I wanted to discuss.

So instead we talked about everything else as I made dinner out of linguini and a jar of tomato sauce that wore an expiration date of last spring. We debated the use of black-and-white film for a modern feature, the evils of colorization (it annoyed him too when a character in a colorized film opened his mouth to reveal a still–black-and-white tongue), and whether James Dean could have had a successful career as an older actor. Just as the linguini was done, the doorbell rang, followed by a series of staccato knocks.

"Dang," I mumbled, dumping the cooked pasta into the colander.

Christopher followed me as I answered the door.

And there she was.

"Martha Cox!" I shouted. "Where have you been? Everyone's been looking for you, the police, everyone. You were on the front page of the *Savannah Morning News*, did you know that?"

She was not smiling. "I *was* having a wonderful time. Almost." Without saying hello, she stepped into the house and closed the door. Then she noticed Christopher. "Who is he?"

"Oh, um. He's a friend. Don't worry. Christopher, this is Martha Cox. Martha, Christopher Quinn."

He didn't bother with niceties. "So where were you?" There was excitement in his voice, an expectant tension like a taut rubber band. "Were you with Boo Boo Myers?"

For the first time, she grinned her full megawatt smile. "Boo Boo Myers? You've got to be kidding! Is he kidding, Nicole?"

"No, I'm afraid he's not."

"Boo Boo Myers! As if!"

Christopher seemed slightly crestfallen. "I really thought . . . well, never mind."

"May I sit down?" she asked. "I've been under the weather lately."

She sat down in the closest chair. "I wanted to come to you first, Nicole. I heard you were worried, and, well, thank you. I didn't know anyone would notice if I left for a few days."

"Well, they did." Christopher and I both sat on the couch. "Where have you been?"

"Okay, this is not for anyone else. I'm going to tell the station and the papers another story. But what really happened was—God, I feel stupid."

"Go on," I urged.

"There's this man. A senator from . . . let's just say a New England state. We've been seeing each other for about six months and he told me he was going to ask his wife for a divorce, but that he wanted to wait until after the elections. You can guess the rest. I don't think he ever intended to divorce his wife. She's wealthy and politically connected."

"So what happened?" Christopher asked.

"I was going to fly up to Washington to talk to him. We'd just been to Paris and everything, and I couldn't believe he was calling our whole relationship off. If only I could see him, I thought, I could change his mind. Pretty pathetic, eh? It wasn't very professional, the day before a new job and everything. But I planned to be back here by the next afternoon. That wouldn't have been so bad, would it? I came here to tell you, Nicole. I was hoping you could give them some excuse at the station—anything. But then I lost my nerve when you were on the phone. I mean, you have so many friends and all. How could I expect you to cover for me? I realized it was unfair. So I left."

"Did you go to Washington?" I asked.

"Nope. Never made it. I called this guy I met—he's a doctor, a bit older but really nice. I asked him to give me a ride to the airport, but by the time I was packed and got my luggage into his car, I was feeling pretty terrible. The doctor says it was poisoning."

"Poison!" I shouted. Christopher shot an accusatory glare at Aunt Adele's photograph.

"Yeah. I'd had some of those raw oysters at lunch and . . ." Her complexion paled. "Sorry. I can't even talk about it. The doctor thinks I probably got a bad one. I hardly remember the last couple of days. It was awful. But the doctor, he's wonderful. He took care of me, and he's going to write a note to the station to explain how sick I've been. I was hoping to spend a few more days with him, but then I heard you were going all over the place asking for me. You flushed me out, Nicole."

"So it wasn't the fruitcake you ate here?"

"Heavens, no! Is that what you thought, Nicole? Not at all. Actually, it looked so good just sitting there. I just took a little slice. Hope you don't mind."

"No, not at all. Didn't even notice." Aunt Adele, vindicated at last!

She stood. "Well, I have to be going. The doctor's waiting in the car outside." Again, she smiled. "Think they'll fire me?"

"I don't know," I said honestly. "We might both be out of a job. We'll figure it out tomorrow, okay?"

"Okay." Turning to leave, she looked over her shoulder at Christopher. "Boo Boo Myers? As if!" And then she was gone.

Christopher shoved his hands into his pockets. "Guess I'm a little rusty."

"You'll be fine." I began to walk back into the kitchen.

"Wait a moment." He pulled my arm. "I found out something else."

"Yes?"

"I found out where Aunt Adele is buried. I wrote the cemetery down—she has this little headstone. Thought maybe we could go out and see her tomorrow morning."

"Before you leave?"

He nodded.

"Sure. That would be great."

"I have someone I'd like her to meet."

With that he got his black backpack and pulled out a sealed jar.

"That's not . . ."

"Yep! Grandpa Ralph, meet Nicole Lovett."

"That's him? You've been walking around with his ashes?"

"Well, almost." Tilting the jar, he held it up to the light. "The dog knocked him over a few years back. But this is most of him, with a little dust from under the couch."

"And just what do you plan to do with Gramps?"

"I thought we could leave him with your Aunt Adele."

"Absolutely not! He's a married man! Adele would never, ever approve. It's just not decent."

Christopher put the jar down. "I guess you have a point." He tapped the lid. "But can he visit? Not overnight. Just for an afternoon."

I crossed my arms. "Maybe. I have to think about it."

"Thanks."

We were both silent, and the mantel clock in the living room ticked and tocked, as if measuring the length of time that we stood there. So many thoughts crossed my mind, there was so much I wanted to say before he left. I wasn't sure how to begin, and once I started, how it could ever end.

"You know I have to go back," he said at last.

"I know." Not really, but it seemed to be the right thing for me to say.

"There are things to settle. I owe that to LaSalle, and to the force in Chicago."

What was he saying?

"It's not going to be easy, you know. There will be times you will wish I'd never come. But then when you meet my Adele, you'll think it's all worth it."

Again I said nothing, afraid I had heard him wrong.

"I can teach here. Oh, and I have a job offer from the Savannah department. An Officer Williams is a great fan of yours—says you tried to pick him up, and that I should come down and keep an eye on you."

This was crazy, insane.

"We'll move into an apartment at first, me and Adele. She'll need to settle into school, and we need to give her a chance to adjust. To give us a chance to adjust. But then, maybe. Well, I've been thinking."

Finally, I dared to speak. "Yes?"

He grinned, those dimples, and I believe I would have fallen had he not caught me in his arms. "Has anyone ever told you that you're a dead ringer for Nicole Quinn?"

When the sun filters through the rustling leaves at Bonaventure Cemetery, you can almost imagine statues moving, as if they could leave with the other visitors, but prefer to stay.

It was Christopher's idea to use his book advance on commissioning a grand memorial to Aunt Adele. Of course it won't be ready for a year and a half, which is about the time the book will be published. And the shopping network has already promised to feature it, so Martha Cox can hawk it while I read the serious news on a local network affiliate.

Meantime we visit my aunt often, sweep the dirt and leaves off her name and rest fresh flowers across her grave. We poured her a bit of champagne when we married, and sometimes we bring Ralph with us. Not always, just sometimes.

And when I'm alone in the house, before Adele comes home from first grade and when Christopher is still at work,

I can almost see my aunt in her chair, watching over everything in her own little world. This is the universe she created, the only place that could have brought us together.

I remember her smile, the secret look she would sometimes give to me when I was a little girl. And please forgive me, Aunt Adele, for being so late. I didn't understand. You deserved so much, and as with everything in your life, this is well overdue.

But finally, at long last, I'm smiling back.

The Return of
Travis Dean

KATHLEEN KANE

Chapter One

THOUGH TRAVIS DEAN DOESN'T REST HERE,
THOUGHTS OF HIM ARE ALWAYS NEAR.
NOW HE'S GONE, BUT NOT FORGOTTEN,
WE THINK HE'D LIKE THIS STONE WE BOUGHT HIM

*T*ravis Dean's eyebrows lifted high on his forehead as he silently read the epitaph on his tombstone one more time.

A soft breeze rippled through the graveyard at the edge of town, quivering the leaves of the old maple—the Spirit Tree they'd always called it—that stood sentry over the graves.

His grave, for God's sake.

He shivered a bit in response to the eerie sensation of staring at his own name carved into a headstone. Jesus, they'd *buried* him?

"And who the hell wrote that epitaph?" he asked himself. " 'Forgotten' and 'bought him' don't even rhyme."

Four years he'd been gone from Tempest, California. And in those four years, he'd dreamed of his return countless times. He'd wildly imagined brass bands, the mayor turning out to shake his hand, old ladies weeping, young girls swooning, and Katie . . . his Katie . . . jumping into his arms to kiss him senseless.

He frowned and glanced at the tombstone again. Not once in any of those dreams had he imagined himself a buried memory in a well-tended graveyard.

Yet, here he was, smack in the middle of the town cemetery with only the dead for company. And speaking of company . . .

Travis's gaze slid to the grave beside his and his eyes widened. A spurt of indignation shot through him. "Whose idea was it to lay me down alongside Hester Morgan for all eternity?" Hell, he still had nightmares about her classroom. The meanest damned schoolteacher in all of California, "Monster" Morgan had made his life a misery when he was a boy. And as he recalled, there hadn't been a single mourner when she was laid to rest here.

He scratched the back of his neck and took a step away from the woman's grave, half expecting her to reach out of the grassy mound and give him a good shake for old time's sake.

Apparently it wasn't enough just to tuck him away into the graveyard. Whoever had planted his memory in the thick, dark earth had chosen to settle his name beside the one person who could make him miserable for centuries to come.

Now who hated him *that* much?

"What in hell is going on around here?" he wondered aloud. Giving his empty grave a wide berth, he walked to the nearby whitewashed fence surrounding the cemetery. It had only been by pure chance that he'd noticed his own name on that stone. Minding his own business, intent on reaching home, he'd given the familiar graveyard a casual glance only to see his own name staring back at him.

An odd feeling to see yourself buried good and proper.

The hairs at the back of his neck bristled and he clapped one hand to them. After all the times he'd managed to avoid death over the last four years, to find himself buried here at home was just too damn much. He clambered over the short fence, eager to put some distance between himself and that tombstone, and looked toward Tempest, not half a mile away.

It was Sunday morning, so most folks would be in the small church at the end of Main Street. Most, he thought with a brief smile, but not all. No doubt a few of the "heathens" would be sprawled in chairs on the boardwalk outside the saloon. Idly, he wondered if they'd kept his chair empty, waiting for his return. Or had his friends too neatly tucked him away in the cemetery?

It didn't matter, he reminded himself. His wayward days were over. He was a changed man. Lifting his chin and squaring his shoulders, he renewed the pledge he'd made four years ago. "No more wastin' time, I swear it. I'm gonna marry my sweet Katie, make some babies, and turn that ranch into a prizewinner."

Just saying it out loud made him feel better.

He gave his tombstone one last look. Damn. Made a man think. Here he'd been working like a madman trying to get home, and all the while, his friends and loved ones had consigned him to memory.

Well, he thought, they'd just have to get used to having him back in their midst. Because now that he'd finally come home, he'd be damned if he'd leave again. That thought firmly in mind, he set off at a brisk walk. His boots against the dirt seemed to pound out a rhythm. *Almost home, almost home, almost home . . .*

Four years.

Frowning to himself, he wondered what else had changed . . . besides him being a dead man and all.

Behind him, the wind whispered across the leaves of the Spirit Tree, sounding like the echo of voices long silent.

"He's back," Eli said.

"About damned time," Addie answered.

Thankfully, the preacher didn't seem to be headed into one of his more long-winded sermons. Already he was tugging at his white collar, a sure sign that services were nearing the end.

Katie sighed, reached out one hand, hooked a finger under her son's suspenders, and dragged him back into the pew. He threw her a grin and tried to escape again. She tightened her hold determinedly and swallowed a smile. It wouldn't do to let the little rascal know just how much she enjoyed his sense of independence . . . his spunk. The soles of his feet scraped and clattered against the wood floor, making enough noise for an army of mischievous little boys.

From the next pew up, Maude Simpson turned her iron-gray head and scowled at the boy. Katie winced. Little Jake stuck his tongue out. Maude sniffed, narrowed a furious gaze at Katie, and whipped back around to give Preacher Davis her attention.

Katie rolled her eyes, grabbed hold of her son, and plopped him onto her lap. Grinning at the back of Maude's head, she wished she had the nerve to stick her own tongue out.

"Suffer the little children to come unto me," the reverend was saying.

Jake's feet kicked at Maude's pew in accompaniment.

"Suffer is right," the old woman muttered.

Katie stifled another smile and reached to lay her hand on Jake's legs to quiet him. Was it her fault if Sunday services, even the shorter ones, were too long and too boring to keep the attention of an active three-year-old?

"Give him to me," Arthur said quietly.

She looked at the thin, bespectacled man beside her and tried not to sigh inwardly. Arthur meant well, she knew. But Jake was all boy, full of beans, and would make short work of the gentle schoolteacher. Besides, she knew darn well her sweet little boy absolutely terrified the man. Smiling her thanks, she shook her head and tightened her hold on the boy.

Bending close to his ear, she whispered, "Be still, Jake. It's almost over now."

"I wanna drink," he said in a voice that carried throughout the small church.

From somewhere up front, a man whispered theatrically, "Amen, kid."

A sprinkling of chuckles rose up and Preacher Davis, sensing he was fast losing his audience, quickly wound up his sermon. "That's all for this week, friends. Until next Sunday . . ." Picking up his Bible, he turned and left through the side door.

Instantly, the congregation stood up and hurriedly headed

for the wide front doors, as if afraid the preacher would change his mind and rush back in with a fresh sermon. Babbling voices rose up as neighbors chatted in the blocked aisle, catching up on the latest news and gossip.

Standing up, Katie perched Jake on her hip and only half watched Arthur try to hurry outside to hitch up the carriage. A nice man, she told herself firmly. A good, kind, steady man.

Then she shook her head as Arthur tried and failed to join the throng of people filling the center aisle. No one seemed to notice him. People jostled and pushed, intent on leaving, paying no attention to Arthur's pitiful attempts to join them. His tall, too thin body ricocheted off the crowd like a small pebble off a still pond. And, like every Sunday, Arthur ended up standing perfectly still at the end of the pew, waiting for the church to empty itself.

As usual, they would be the last to leave.

Sighing, Katie thought tiredly of all the things she had to do when she got home and tried not to resent Arthur's patient plodding.

"Katie," Maude said as she stood up and whirled around to face her.

Almost grateful to have her thoughts disrupted, Katie glanced sideways at the woman and waited for what she knew was coming.

"You ought to be ashamed of yourself, lettin' that child disrupt services every blasted week."

"He's only a boy, Maude," Katie reminded.

"Boys have to learn when to hush up."

"Hush!" Jake echoed.

Maude shot him a look.

Katie grinned. "I'm sorry, I'm sure he didn't mean you in particular, Maudie."

"I'm not so sure," the older woman said, considering the child. "The boy needs a father, Katie. A strong hand and a deep voice go a long way, you know."

A father.

Katie stiffened slightly. "I've been seeing Arthur and—"

"Piddle!" Maude sniffed and ran both hands down the front of her flower-sprigged gown. "Arthur Featherstone's no match for that boy. He's afraid of the child. A blind man could see that!"

True, Katie thought with yet another inward sigh. In the two months Arthur had been courting her, she could count on the fingers of one hand the times he and Jake had spent any amount of time alone together.

"And a more unlikely schoolteacher I never saw," Maude went on, warming to her subject. "Why, his students have tied him into the school outhouse so many times, folks in town are calling it 'Featherstone's Folly.' "

"He's a gentle man." Katie felt duty bound to defend him.

"Gentle's one thing," Maude argued. "Scared spitless is quite another."

Katie glanced toward the crowd. Arthur trailed along at the end, like a puppy on a short leash.

"Marryin' him after what you already had," Maude went on more quietly, "is like bein' offered a steak and settling for a fried-egg sandwich."

"Maybe," Katie admitted, "but at least the egg sandwich is here. Now."

"If you ain't the stubbornest woman I ever met . . ."

"Kiss!" Jake demanded and leaned toward Maude, arms outstretched.

"You little hooligan," the woman muttered.

"Kiss!" he said again, waving his arms impatiently.

"Think you can sweet-talk your way out of anything, don't you?" Maude asked, reaching for the boy. As Jake gave her a big, wet kiss on her powdered cheek, the woman laughed and shook her head. "Just like your pa, aren't you? A good, thick steak, clean to the bone."

Katie inhaled sharply.

Jake tipped his head to one side, looked up at Maude through lowered lashes, and gave her a lopsided grin that was so much like his father's Katie's heart twisted.

He was his father's son, all right, she thought. From that wild streak of his to the grin that had saved his hide from a tanning more than once.

But unlike his father, Jake was going to grow up with a sense of responsibility. She would see to it that her son kept both feet on the ground. He wouldn't become the kind of man who would simply walk away from everyone who loved him.

Like his father had.

While her thoughts churned, a part of her mind noted a building babble of voices from outside. It was not the usual small talk, however. These voices were shouting, yelling, as if everyone in town were trying to outshout everybody else.

"What in heaven?" Maude asked as she started for the front door, Jake still perched on her hip.

"Heaven!" the boy shouted.

Katie fell in behind them, hurrying as the crowd moved quickly out of the church. Apparently, everyone was eager to find out what all the excitement was about.

She lost track of Arthur in the press of people and bumped into Maude's back when the woman came to an abrupt stop on the wide front step.

"Katie . . ." She sounded odd, her voice strangled.

"Maudie?" Katie asked, looking into her friend's eyes. "Are you all right?"

"I'm doin' fine, honey," the woman said softly, "but you might want to sit down."

"What?" She frowned and shook her head. "Why?"

"Because," Maude said, her gaze fixed on one particular face in the crowd. "It looks like you've got steak for supper tonight after all."

"What are you talking about?" Katie turned her head, followed Maudie's gaze, and felt her hard, solid world crashing down around her.

"He's back," Maude said unnecessarily. "Travis Dean is back from the dead. We should have known nothing could kill him."

Chapter Two

*H*e can't be back, damn it.

He'd ruin everything.

Yet, there he stood, big as life and twice as tempting.

Oh, good God.

Katie's gaze locked with his and for one heart-stopping instant, she felt a rush of joy she hadn't known in four long years. Her blood pumped fast and hot in her veins and even her knees trembled slightly. Lord, how could he still have such an effect on her?

Taller than she remembered and leaner, too. Travis's night-black hair was a bit too long and his unshaven cheeks and dusty clothes spoke of some hard traveling. But he was as handsome as the devil and as inviting as the road to hell itself.

Then he gave her that wicked grin of his and had the nerve to actually wink. That brought her back to her senses.

She'd been swayed too often in the past by that rascally look of his. And she wasn't about to swoon over it again.

Katie's teeth ground together and she felt a slow burn start at the tips of her toes and slowly spread to the roots of her hair.

Joy settled into the pit at the bottom of her stomach and was quickly covered by a fresh layer of temper. How dare he wink at her as if the two of them had been playing a game and now it was over? Gone four years without so much as a single letter letting her know he was alive, damn him. Was he now going to try to stroll back into her life? How dare he assume that everything between them was the same as it had been the night he'd left?

How dare he come back at all?

Damn it, didn't he realize that along with his name, she'd buried his memory in that graveyard?

"Mama?" Her son's voice cut through the commotion in her brain, reminding Katie of what was important. Jake. He was all that mattered. And she had to make sure she got to Travis before he could say something that would ruin her reputation and her son's future.

Travis didn't even feel the slaps on his back. He could hardly hear the laughter or the excited shouts he'd dreamed of hearing. The town, the crowd, everything around him went unnoticed. All he could see—all he *wanted* to see—was a pair of emerald-green eyes, now wide with shock.

Should've written to her, he told himself, not for the first time. Hell, he should have warned her that he was returning. That he'd soon be home again to pick up his life, and her, where he'd left them.

But he hadn't wanted to take the chance of giving her hope and then letting her down. His life hadn't exactly been safe and secure these last few years. His chances of making it home had been so slim, even he had lost hope a couple of times. And then, when he was only a week or two away from her, he'd decided that he'd rather surprise her.

And by the looks of things, he had.

Damn, she looked even better than he'd remembered.

Long red hair shining like a fire in the sunlight, the ends lifting and dancing around her head in the soft breeze. Her creamy white skin sported a dusting of freckles across her nose—and he recalled with an inward smile that there were a few more freckles hidden where no one but he had looked. Golden-red eyebrows arched high over the green eyes that had haunted him waking and sleeping. Tall and slender, she stood proud and wore that ugly brown dress like a queen's robes.

As he watched, she lifted her chin defiantly, squared her shoulders as if preparing for battle, and narrowed those eyes of hers to slits. A thread of foreboding snaked through him.

He knew the signs, better than anyone. Katie's legendary temper was rising. Well, hell. He'd known he'd have to do some fancy fast talking to smooth her ruffled feathers.

But nobody could get around his Katie like he could.

"Travis, boy!" a voice from close by shouted, "Where you been? Hell, we heard you was dead!"

"Not yet," Travis said with a grin and took a step or two closer to Katie. To home.

Hell, he didn't care if she was mad. They'd get past it. They always had before. Foreboding forgotten, he told himself it'd be a real pleasure to watch her temper boil. Lord, how he'd missed arguing with her.

Stubbornest woman he'd ever known, seemed like he'd loved her forever. They'd been engaged to be married when he left town for that fateful trip to San Francisco four years ago. And damned if he wasn't going to drag her to a preacher just as soon as he could.

There was too much lost time to make up for.

Everyone around him was happy, except her. Why wasn't she smiling? Why wasn't she acting like his dream Katie and racing to meet him, arms thrown wide in welcome? Sure, he'd expected her to be mad . . . but he'd also expected her to be a *little* glad to see him.

"Did ya see your tombstone?" someone else called out.

"Yeah," Travis said, loud enough for everyone to hear. A shiver coursed up his spine at the memory. Too many times over the years he'd come real close to actually needing a headstone.

"Soaker Thomas come up with the sayin'," a man beside him offered.

Well, that explained it, Travis thought. Soaker hadn't been sober more than two days straight in ten years. No wonder his epitaph didn't rhyme. He frowned to himself. Who the hell had let the town drunk come up with the words?

"It was a right nice funeral," a woman from the crowd said. "You should have seen it."

"Sorry I missed it," Travis said, nodding at her.

Hell, he was sorry for a lot of things. For ever leaving Katie. For being gone so damn long. For not having her in his arms right this minute.

Well-wishers kept stopping him. Familiar faces in the crowd, all of them smiling. All of them surprised, shocked, pleased. All but Katie.

He kept his gaze on her as he walked, pushing through the people, eager to reach her. To finally touch her and put the last four years to rest. His whole body ached for the feel of her in his arms. All he wanted now was to marry her and settle down on the ranch like they'd always planned.

Make a home.

Make some babies.

As if they'd finally realized his intentions, the crowd parted before him, leaving a wide path leading straight to Katie.

His gaze locked with hers, searching for the welcome he'd yet to see on her face.

Every step took him closer.

He noticed Maudie, a small boy on her hip, give Katie a little shove.

She hesitated for a long minute, thinking, and Travis aged another year while he tried to read the expressions darting across her features. Then, just when he'd convinced himself she was going to have nothing to do with him, she hurried down the porch steps and ran straight at him.

Relief swept through him. Relief and a high tide of pleasure so wide and deep, he thought he might drown in it.

He opened his arms and brought her close, inhaling the soft, sweet scent of the rose-scented soap she always used. The feel of her pressed against him was familiar and strange all at once. So many nights, he'd imagined this moment and none of his imaginings had even come close to the reality.

For the first time in too long, Travis breathed easy. He was home. Where he belonged. With Katie.

But over the roar of applause from the crowd, he tensed as she whispered in his ear. "Don't you dare say one word about anything, Travis Dean. Not until we've talked."

"Who the hell feels like talkin'?" All he wanted was a quiet corner somewhere so he and his Katie could find each other again.

She tensed in his arms, pulled her head back, and glared up at him. "We *have* to talk, Travis. So don't you say a word to anybody until then."

Don't say a word about what? he wondered, even as he warily noted the glint in her eyes.

"Travis Dean," Maude called out, dragging his attention from the woman in his arms.

The crowd went suddenly quiet. Like everyone had taken a breath and held it at the same time.

All right, now he was beginning to feel a little edgy. Dozens of pairs of eyes locked onto him. He felt each one of them and noticed a few expectant smiles on the faces of his friends. What was going on around here? Why was everybody acting so strange?

Maudie pushed through the crowd, still holding that boy to her hip. She stopped alongside Travis and handed him the child. He looked from Katie, to Maudie, to the boy. Then he understood.

Eyes as blue as his own stared back at him. The kid's short, wavy black hair was the same shade as his. A curl of alarm unwound inside him. When the boy suddenly grinned at him, Travis felt his knees go watery. It was like looking into a mirror.

A son?

He had a son?

Holding the boy as he would a hot rock, arms stiff and straight out in front of him, he shifted his stunned gaze to Katie.

She nodded at him as if to silently say. "See? I told you we had to talk."

Over the roaring in his ears, Travis heard Maude say proudly, "Travis, meet your boy. Jake, this here's your pa."

Pa?

"Look at him," Adelaide snorted to the ghost who'd accompanied her on the trip from the cemetery. *"Gone four*

years and he stands there dumb as a stump.''

"It's a big day for a man when he finds out he's a father,'' Elijah said in his nephew's defense.

"How would you know, you old coot?'' Adelaide turned
on him. "You didn't even show up for our wedding.''

"I explained all that as soon as you died, didn't I?''

"Yes,'' she allowed, softening some toward the old goat
she should have been married to for forty years. If, of
course, he hadn't broken his neck in a spill from his horse
on his way to the ceremony.

Until the day she died, Adelaide had cursed him for jilting her. It was only after she was dead she'd discovered the
truth. That her Elijah had died in an accident before he
could marry her.

"The point is,'' Adelaide said, willing to let bygones be
bygones for the moment, "if we don't get the two of them
together, we'll never be able to leave town and that durn
graveyard.''

Elijah was silent, thinking it better not to remind her that
it was her own fault their spirits were still tied to earth. If
she'd just had a little more faith in him. If she hadn't had
such a temper. If she hadn't heaped so many blasted curses
on him, neither one of them would be here now. They'd be
in heaven, hip deep in gold harps and angel's wings.

But, no sense in whining. Best to just get busy earning
their way upstairs.

"At least he's come home,'' Elijah said. "Now we've got
a chance to fix things.''

"As mad as Katie is, it won't be easy,'' Adelaide mused
thoughtfully, leaning in close to study the furious expression
on her niece's features.

Elijah shook his head, leaned in close, then shifted his
gaze to the woman he'd loved for what seemed forever.
"She's just like you, Addie. Temper hot enough to fry an
egg on ice.''

One of Adelaide's eyebrows lifted as she glanced at
Travis, still looking at his son as if he expected the child to
grow another head and start howling like a wolf.

"And he's the spittin' image of you," she said, with a slow shake of her head. She remembered all too well the temptation of Elijah Dean coming to call on a soft spring night. "Lord help Katie."

"He loves her as much as I do you," Elijah said with a wink, then took Adelaide's hand and gave it a kiss.

She frowned at him, despite the tingle of pleasure that rippled along her soul. "You Dean men always were too smooth-talking for your own good."

"Yep," Elijah countered, "and you Hunter women love it."

Adelaide glanced at Katie again and noted the high color in her cheeks and the sparks shooting from the depths of her green eyes. "I reckon we do at that," she said.

And that fact was the one thing that would help them get this job done.

Chapter Three

Katie didn't know how she'd managed to get Travis out of town so quickly. Panic must have given her magical powers of persuasion. Why had he come back? After four years, what had made him decide to stroll back into her life?

And for pity's sake, why had he insisted on announcing his presence to the whole blasted town?

Now, in a too small carriage, sandwiched between the man courting her and her supposed-to-be-dead . . . *husband,* Katie silently made and discarded hundreds of plans. Arthur, naturally, had insisted on driving her home. And being Arthur, he'd also graciously included Travis in the invitation. Although, to be fair, what else could he have done?

She felt Travis's gaze as surely as she did the press of his hard thigh against hers. Those sharp blue eyes of his shifted from Jake to Arthur and then to her with an eerie regularity. Oh, being this close to him again wasn't helping her think more clearly. And if she'd ever needed to think, now was the time.

"So what'd you say your name was again?" Travis asked suddenly and Arthur jumped in his seat as if he'd been shot.

Katie nearly groaned at the man's skittishness. For heaven's sake. He'd done nothing wrong. He had no reason to be as nervous as a long-tailed cat in a room full of rocking chairs. If anyone should be jumpy and apologetic, it was Travis!

"This is Arthur Featherstone," she said, when it became clear the man was incapable of speech. "He's our school-teacher."

"Ahh . . ." Travis said and nodded slowly before narrowing his gaze on the man. "Good of you to take Katie into church. Do it often, do you?"

Arthur squirmed on the seat and spared one hand from the reins long enough to run one finger around the inside of his collar. Katie could practically feel him tremble. A flash of temper directed at both men scuttled through her. Arthur could be irritating, but at the moment, it was Travis Dean she wanted to smack in the nose. But since a woman hitting a man would no doubt send poor Arthur into fits, she settled for saying sharply, "Yes, he does."

One of Travis's eyebrows lifted as he watched her.

"As a matter of fact," she went on, giving in to the urge to wipe that half-smile off his face, "Arthur is—has been— *is* courting me."

"Is that so?" Blue eyes stared hard into Katie's and she glared right back. Four years gone, he was. Had he expected her to sit idly by the fireside, mooning over his daguerreotype, quietly pining away?

Of course the fact that she had spent the first two years of his absence doing just that was beside the point.

The schoolteacher cleared his throat loudly, and both of them turned to look at him.

"As to the courting, sir," Arthur said with formality, "we were of course under the impression that you were dead, Mr. Dean."

That black eyebrow arched again. "As you can see," Travis pointed out tightly, "I'm not."

No, he certainly wasn't. In fact, he seemed more alive than ever. His skin darkly tanned, muscled shoulders straining in the confines of his shirt, Travis appeared the picture of health, damn him anyway.

Not even a limp or an old bullet wound to explain away a four-year disappearance.

Arthur deliberately kept his gaze on the road ahead. "Naturally, now that you've returned to your family, I will step aside."

Katie stared at the schoolteacher for a long minute, then

shifted to look at Travis. Blast if he didn't have a self-satisfied smile on his face.

"Well, good," Elijah said from his seat on the rump of one of the horses. "At least we're rid of this 'Nancy' fella. Now we can get down to business."

Adelaide looked at the people seated opposite her and shook her head. "You old fool. Can't you see Kate's face? If she don't have murder in her eye, I'm not a ghost."

"Hell, she always did have a temper, your niece." He paused. "Or is it great-niece?"

"What difference does that make?"

"None," Eli agreed. "The point is, Travis is used to dealing with Kate."

"He ain't done too fine a job so far, I'm thinkin'."

"That wasn't rightly his fault, Addie."

"His fault he left, isn't it?"

"He come back, didn't he?"

"Finally."

"Give the boy a chance," Eli said, leaning across the harness chains to take his sweetheart's hand in his. "You'll see, he'll do us proud, and pretty soon we'll be standin' at the Pearly Gates."

"So you say," Addie muttered. She'd been dead nearly ten years and she still wasn't used to this ghost business. Of course, having Elijah with her was a great comfort, but still, she'd always planned on going straight to heaven. This waiting around to earn your way in could get right wearying.

Especially when the people you need to bring together aren't helping you a damn—durn—sight.

"Anyways, least we're outa town. Nice to get out once in a while, don't you think?"

"It surely is, Eli, honey . . ."

The now silent schoolteacher steered the carriage into the rutted drive leading to the ranch and Katie held her breath, waiting for Travis's reaction. After all, he hadn't seen his family's home in four years.

After he'd disappeared, Katie had moved into the empty

house and then worked herself nearly to the bone to keep the ranch up and running. It would be Jake's someday and she was determined to see that her son inherited *something* from his ne'er-do-well father besides his blue eyes and dimples.

And why it worried her what Travis would think about her efforts now she couldn't say. But she found herself holding her breath, waiting.

"What's happened to the place?" Travis finally whispered, letting his gaze drift across the ranch yard.

She should have known. Katie stiffened slightly, and as Jake squirmed on her lap, she tightened her hold on him. Fine. So her home wasn't a showplace. The roof on the house sagged in the middle and the barn doors hung drunkenly on broken hinges. But the horses were healthy, the fences were strong, and he had no right at all to sit there looking disappointed.

Where had he been during the rainiest summer they'd ever known? When she'd had to stay up nights just to empty the buckets set out to catch the drips? Where had he been when the south fence blew down and her best mare had broken a leg trying to jump it? Where had he been when she'd strapped Jake to her back like an Indian papoose and strung barbed wire?

Hell. Where had he been?

"Four years happened," she snapped.

"Looks more like forty," he murmured, shaking his head.

Any softening she might have felt toward him disappeared.

"Y'know, Travis," Katie started, feeling her temper build. As always, no one could make her mad quicker than the man who just as easily turned her bones to water and set her blood to boiling.

"Although," he interrupted smoothly before she could get up a head of steam, "after the last few years, it's a sight for sore eyes."

She really looked at him then and saw the pleasure shining in his eyes and the soft smile curving the lips she used to dream of kissing again. Like a blind man suddenly given his sight, Travis looked at everything as though he were seeing it for the first time.

Wherever he'd been, she decided silently, if he hadn't missed her, he sure had missed this ranch.

"Well. I'm sure you have many things to discuss," Arthur put in just then and Katie and Travis turned to look at him in surprise, having almost forgotten he was there. But then, the man was always so quiet, it was easy to overlook poor Arthur.

"That we do," Travis said and leaned across Katie to stretch out one hand toward the man. "Thanks again, Mr. . . . um . . ."

"Featherstone," Katie told him. "Arthur Featherstone."

The schoolteacher's narrow hand was swallowed in Travis's hard grip, but to give him his due, he only winced slightly.

"Well, we sure appreciate the ride," Travis said a moment later as he jumped from the carriage with obvious haste. He turned to help her down, and as his fingers closed over hers, Katie's heart skipped a beat, as it always did around him. Her breath trapped in her chest, she lifted her gaze to his and saw that he'd noticed—and enjoyed—her reaction to him.

Blast it! She snatched her hand back and whirled around to scoop Jake off the bench seat. Only then did she look at poor Arthur. And why, she wondered, did she always think of him as *poor* Arthur?

With Jake propped on one hip, she shot the man a smile just as he wheeled his horses around and nearly galloped them out of the yard, leaving only a cloud of dust rising up in his wake.

And just like that, she was alone with the man who'd deserted her four long years ago. Well, almost alone.

"Down!" Jake pushed against his mother's grasp and wasn't satisfied until she set him on his feet. Tipping his little head back, he gave his father a long, thoughtful look, then turned and scampered off toward the barn where a new litter of puppies awaited him.

Katie watched the man beside her. A bemused smile on his face, Travis stood looking after the boy long after he'd disappeared into the barn. Her heart twisted unexpectedly as she noted the regret carved into his features.

"He's a good-looking boy," he finally said as he slowly turned his gaze on her.

"I think so," Katie said, swallowing hard.

"How old is he?"

She bristled slightly. "Three and a bit."

Nodding, Travis said, "So he's mine."

What kind of thing was that to say? He knew damn well and good that he'd been the first—the *only*—man Katie'd known that way.

She squared her shoulders, folded her arms across her chest, and looked him dead in the eye. Before they talked about anything else, there was one thing he had to understand right off. "No, Travis," she said flatly. "He's *mine*."

"He's the spittin' image of me," he pointed out, waving one hand at the barn.

The tip of one of her worn black shoes tapped against the dirt. "Giving a boy your dimples doesn't make you his father."

He snorted. "I'd like to know what does, then."

Would he really? she wondered.

"I'll tell you what does, Travis," she said and charged him, stabbing his chest with her forefinger. "*Being* here, day in and day out. Walking the floor with him when he has croup so bad he can hardly breathe . . . applauding when he takes his first steps . . . telling him bedtime stories and chasing monsters out from under his bed . . ." She took a deep breath and would have continued if Travis hadn't reached out, grabbed hold of her shoulders, and given her a good, quick shake.

"Do you think I *wanted* to be gone, Katie?"

"What else was I supposed to think, Travis?" she snapped, tilting her head back to glare at him. "You went

to San Francisco for a four-day business trip and instead
you were gone four *years*!''

"That wasn't my fault, damn it," he said, his fingers
gripping her tighter. "I can explain."

"It's too late." She cut him off and jerked herself free
of his grasp before the warmth of his touch could undermine
her hard-won defenses.

He shoved both hands through his hair and Katie steeled
herself against noticing the play of his muscles as he moved.
Wherever he'd spent the last four years, he'd been working
hard. But she didn't care, she reminded herself. Didn't care
where he'd been and didn't care that he was back.

"Katie," he said and let his arms fall to his sides. Shaking his head, he went on, "This isn't how I imagined my
homecoming."

"*I* didn't imagine it would ever happen."

"I should have written."

" 'Should have' doesn't mean a damn thing, Travis."

"I never meant to hurt you," he said softly.

But he had. More than anyone else had ever done, Travis
Dean had hurt her desperately. She'd trusted him. Loved
him. Waited for him like a damn fool.

Yet dear God, his voice still had the ability to rumble
along her spine like a feathery caress. She remembered
warm summer nights, wrapped in his arms, as they lay in a
meadow watching the stars. She remembered the touch of
his hand, the brush of his lips, and the hard, solid feel of
his body claiming hers.

Just as she remembered being pregnant, alone, and waiting futilely for his return.

She stiffened.

"It's been a long time, Katie."

"Too long, Travis."

He shook his head, reached out for her, and drew her
close again before she could pull back. Pressed to his chest,
she felt the thundering of his heart pounding in rhythm with
her own.

"Four years or four hundred, Katie," he whispered,

bending his head down to hers, "it's still magic between us."

God help her, she thought as his lips met hers in a soul-melting kiss that weakened her knees and curled her hair. Four long years dissolved in a hot, liquid pool of desire that crashed against her insides like high waves breaking on the shore.

Then, before she could end it—which she would have, in the next minute or two—Travis pulled his head back, looked down into her eyes, and said, "Now, Katie darlin'. Why don't you tell me about my funeral, our wedding, and our son? Not necessarily in that order."

Chapter Four

*H*is son.

Just saying the words aloud made Travis's head swim.

He'd had a son and he'd missed it all. Watching Kate's body round with their child. Pacing nervously as he awaited the birth. Holding a tiny, red-faced infant as he took his first squalling breaths.

Tears stung the backs of his eyes and Travis sucked in a gulp of air, hoping to keep them at bay. Damn it. He'd missed so much.

"Jake was born eight months after you left."

That piece of news staggered him. She'd known about the baby before he'd left and hadn't said a word. If she had . . . what? Would he have canceled that trip? Stayed home? No, he thought honestly. Probably not. But at the very least he might have hurried home rather than staying an extra day. And if he had, he wouldn't have been in town to visit the saloon where his whole world had changed.

"Why didn't you tell me you were pregnant?"

She snorted and took a step back from him, raking him up and down with a look that should have scalded him. "You're trying to say this is *my* fault?"

Travis raked one hand through his hair then shook his head. "Of course not," he snapped. He knew damn well whose fault this whole mess was. "But you could have told me."

"I didn't know myself," she said and turned away, facing the house. Her spine was so stiff, it was as though a pole had been shoved down the back of her dress.

A slight wind kicked up, tossing the hem of her skirt

around her legs and lifting the ends of her bright red hair into a tangle of curls. He wanted to reach for her, just as he had dreamed of doing so many empty nights. He wanted to hold her, bury his face in the crook of her neck, and lose the next four years simply being with her.

"Where the hell were you?" she muttered, her words drifting to him on the same breeze that carried her scent.

"Where haven't I been?" he whispered, thinking of the dank, black holds of countless ships. The tropical islands and cold cities he'd seen, the strange yet somehow appealing world of the Orient. He'd been so far away for so long, he hardly knew where to begin to explain it all to her.

Before he could even try, she shook her head. "Never mind. It doesn't matter anymore, Travis."

"You're right," he said, moving to stand directly behind her. His palms itched to touch her. "All that matters is I'm back. To stay."

"No." Katie turned around then to face him and he saw the determined glint in her green eyes flash out a warning. "What matters is that I've buried you and moved on."

"But I'm not dead," he reminded her, thinking again of his tombstone.

"You are to me."

"Oh, ain't this dandy?" Eli said as he leaned in close to Katie.

"Can't hardly blame her," Addie told him, watching her niece with more than a little sympathy. She knew only too well what it was like to wait in vain for the man you loved. Still, if Kate didn't forgive him and take a chance on him again, she'd be destined to lead the same lonely kind of life Addie had. And that wouldn't do at all.

"This isn't goin' to be as easy as I'd thought," Eli said thoughtfully as he walked slowly around the couple.

"Nothin' about love is easy," Addie reminded him.

"Oh, the lovin's easy enough, it's the livin' that's hard." He wiggled ghostly pale eyebrows and Addie had to smile.

"Just out of curiosity," Travis said tightly, "what did I die of?"

"It was an accident," she told him in a sweet voice that didn't match the nasty gleam in her eye. "A terrible mishap at a sawmill outside San Francisco. You suffered horribly, by the way."

A *sawmill*? Travis winced as his imagination created dozens of unpleasant images. He'd guess he *had* suffered horribly. Narrowing his gaze on her, he asked, "How long exactly did you wait before deciding to kill me off?"

The smile slipped from her face like rainwater off a duck's back. "Three months," she said shortly. "At first, I kept telling folks you'd been delayed. That you were doing everything in your power to get home . . ."

Her voice broke slightly and Travis's heart ached.

"But after three months without a word, I had no choice."

"I would have written if I could have," he started.

"I told you, I'm not interested." With that, she took off for the house, her quick strides kicking the hem of her dress out into a bell shape around her.

Travis was only a step or two behind. "Hey!" he called. "Are you just going to leave the boy alone in the barn?"

She stopped suddenly and looked over her shoulder at him. That look clearly said it was none of his business what she or his son did. But she answered him anyway. "The boy's name is Jake. And he's not alone. Henry Winters is in there, too."

"Henry?" Travis's gaze shot to the barn as if he could see beyond the walls to his old friend inside.

"That's right. He works for me now."

"That's good, Katie," Travis said.

Both of her red-gold eyebrows lifted high on her forehead. "I'm so relieved that you approve."

Oh, for . . .

She started walking again and Travis hurried after. Damn woman was going to listen to him whether she wanted to or not.

"When you didn't come home," she said, her voice

carrying back to him easily, "and I realized I was carrying Jake, I had to do *something*."

Just thinking about what she'd gone through alone, what she'd worried over . . . what she must have thought of him, sent a wash of shame over him.

"Jesus, Katie, I'm sorry." Sorrier than she would ever know. But damn it, he'd paid his penance, hadn't he?

At the front porch, she wiped her feet on a threadbare rug, then opened the door and stepped inside. "I told people that we'd been secretly married before you left."

"And they believed you?"

She shot him a glare before heading straight across the main room to the door leading to the kitchen. "There was no reason not to. Everyone knew we were engaged."

He kept up with her, hardly noticing the small house he'd called home most of his life. But from the brief glance he did give the place, he noted that the inside, much like the outside of the ranch, had seen better days.

Snatching her apron off a wooden peg pounded into the kitchen's plank wall, she settled it in front of her and tied the strings around her narrow waist into a bow at the small of her back.

God, she looked good enough to eat.

Sparing him another brief look, she marched to the stove, picked up the coffeepot, and carried it to the sink. Sunshine spilled through the nearby window, gilding her red hair into a color that reminded him of a hot fire on a cold night. As she dumped the cold coffee and pumped fresh well water into the pot, she went on, speaking loud enough to be heard over the sound of rushing water pouring from the spout.

"Before you *died*," she was saying, "the whole town was excited about the baby." She laughed shortly, humorlessly. "They all knew how pleased you'd be to be a father."

Regret stabbed at his insides again and Travis had to swallow it back like a dose of castor oil.

"I moved out here," she said as she released the pump handle and it settled back into silence. Her voice quieted, too. "Thought you'd come here first, when you did come home."

She was wrong, he thought, fisting his hands helplessly at his sides. He would have made straight for her. As he had today.

"But like I said, when there was no word after three months, I figured you weren't coming back."

"Katie . . ."

She shook her head, walked to the stove, and finished getting the coffee ready. Then, with slightly trembling hands, she set the pot on the back of the stove to boil and looked at him.

"I pretended to get a telegram." She shrugged. "Tempest still doesn't have a telegrapher, so it was easy to get away with saying the wire had been delivered from Sacramento." Her hands were still trembling, he noticed, as she folded her hands together at her waist.

He braced his feet wide apart on the freshly swept floor and jammed his own hands in his pockets. "And this 'wire' told you I was dead."

She met his gaze squarely. "Yes."

Travis supposed he couldn't really blame her.

Jaw tight, she added, "I preferred being a respectable widow to being an abandoned, pregnant fiancée."

Damn, he'd put her—them—through a lot.

He watched her as she turned away to feed kindling into the stove's firebox. The hungry snap and crackle of flames licking at fresh fuel filled the kitchen.

After a long moment, Travis heard himself ask, "How'd you bury me without a body or a coffin?"

Katie straightened up and gave him another small smile. "Oh, your tombstone is just a memorial. We didn't actually bury you."

Some comfort, he thought grimly.

"After that sawmill accident," she went on, "there wasn't enough left of you to bury proper."

"Jesus!" He looked at her, horrified. When Katie Hunter held a grudge, nobody could say she wasn't thorough.

Katie hid a smile and turned to the table. His reaction was well worth all the time and trouble she'd gone to to come up with a particularly grisly imaginary death for him. At the time, as angry and hurt as she'd been, it had given her some comfort to know that at least in her mind, she'd hurt him just as severely as he had her.

Now, though, he was back and no amount of pretending would change that. But she wouldn't let him hurt her—or Jake. Not again. So somehow, she had to keep Travis Dean from stealing back into her heart. The secret, she told herself, was to keep busy. Then she wouldn't have time to remember how much she'd loved this man. How long she'd hoped he'd come home to her.

"Katie," he said and she closed her eyes against the warmth in his voice. How was it possible, she wondered, that four long, lonely years hadn't been able to destroy her reaction to him? "We have to talk about what we're going to do."

She stared down at the kitchen table, focusing on the fresh bread, the basket of eggs, and the slab of bacon waiting to be sliced. Everyday things. Ordinary things. Dinner to be cooked, horses to be fed, Jake to be tended . . . *anything* other than the fact that Travis was standing right behind her. Deliberately, she picked up the knife, set the bacon on a carving board, and cut several thick slices.

"We have to think of Jake," he said. "What's best for him."

Didn't he think she knew that?

"There's only one thing we can do, Travis," she said softly and set down the knife again before turning around to face him.

"I think so, too," he said.

"Good," Katie said. "Then we're agreed."

Travis reached out and laid both hands on her shoulders. Heat sizzled through her, but she valiantly fought against the sensation. If she surrendered in the slightest, she'd lose her heart to him all over again. She'd made that mistake before. Making the same mistake all over again would just be stupid.

They stared at each other for a long minute, then spoke at the same time.

"We'll get married for real," Travis said.

"We'll get a pretend divorce," Katie said.

"Oh, for pity's sake," Addie moaned.

Chapter Five

*F*our days later, the words "pretend divorce" still echoed in Travis's mind.

Grimacing tightly, he picked up his glass, swallowed down the last of his lukewarm beer, and set the empty down onto the scarred bar top again. The noise and confusion of the Last Dog saloon swirled around him, but he paid no attention. Instead, he stared at his distorted reflection in the bar mirror and wondered idly if his head was really as misshapen as all that or if perhaps he'd had one too many beers.

Sam Fuller, the bartender, stepped up to him, grabbed his glass, and refilled it. Setting it down in front of Travis, the big man leaned his forearms on the bar and asked with a grin, "So how come you're here instead of at home with that pretty wife of yours?"

Visions of Katie swam to the surface of his beer-soaked mind. Well, now, he couldn't hardly tell Sam the truth, now could he? Everyone in town was so damned pleased that he and Katie had had a happy ending, no one would believe that Travis had spent the last three nights sleeping in the barn with nothing but the sound of Henry Winters's snoring to keep him company.

Hell. He hardly believed it himself. Four years of being without her and as soon as he got home he was further away from her than ever before. Where the hell was the justice in that? he wanted to know. He missed her more now than he had all the time he was gone. Because now he got to see her every day. Hear her voice. Watch her walk across the yard with her long, determined stride. See her touch their child with all the tenderness he longed for.

And every night, he took those images of her with him to his empty bed. Damn her for being so blasted stubborn. She wouldn't even listen to his explanation! Kept saying it didn't matter. Well, of course it mattered! *They* mattered. If there was one thing he'd learned in the last four years, it was that what they'd had together was the only thing in the world that counted for a damn.

"Travis?" Sam asked, bending his head a bit to look into the other man's eyes. "You all right?"

No, he wasn't. And doubted he would be anytime soon. But he wasn't about to say so. Travis wiped one hand across his eyes, hoping to clear up the impression of *two* smiling Sams, before saying, "You know how it is. A man needs to get out and see his friends sometimes . . ."

Sam shrugged and wiped the bar top with a clean white towel. "Up to you, I suppose," he said. "But if it was me, I'd purely rather be at home with Katie than here with this bunch." Then he moved off down the bar to satisfy the thirsts of other men looking to lose themselves in liquor for a while.

The bartender's words still ringing in his ears, Travis let his gaze slide to the left of the mirror. The reflection of the room behind him wavered and danced unsteadily, but he saw it clearly enough to realize it was no different from any other saloon in any other town. Tables with men hunched over games of poker, women dressed in feathers and bangles, smiling over the winners and consoling the losers. A piano player in the corner paused long enough to take a sip of the whiskey he kept nearby. And over the milling crowd hung a thick cloud of cigar smoke and cheap perfume.

He scowled to himself and tightened his grasp on his beer. He hadn't been inside a saloon since that last night in Frisco when a friendly stranger had bought him a drink that had tasted a bit off. The rest of that night was still a blur. But he sure as hell remembered waking up the next morning . . . in the hold of a ship bound for China.

Shanghaied. Just like some green-as-grass kid let loose in the big city for the first time.

"And ya didn't learn a damn thing from that, did ya?" *someone asked.*

Travis straightened up and glanced uneasily around him. But no one was there. He snorted and shook his head. All right. Now he was hearing things. Had had enough beer, apparently.

"What're you doin', boy? Why aren't you home straightening things out with your missus?"

He set his beer aside with a jerk that spilled the liquid all over his hand. He wasn't imagining things. He'd heard that voice coming from nowhere and everywhere all at once.

Taking a half-step back from the bar, Travis shot a look at the man closest to him. A tall man with a hard look to his face and a belly that overlapped his belt buckle by a couple of inches glared at him.

"What?" he demanded.

"What do you mean, what?" Travis asked. "You were talkin' to me."

"Mister," the big man said flatly, "you're drunk."

"Maybe, but I ain't deaf."

"Just stupid."

The man's lips hadn't moved when he spoke. How the hell had he done that? "Who are you callin' stupid?"

"Travis," Sam called as he scurried from the other end of the bar, eager to prevent a fight that would only serve to destroy his place. "Calm down. Nobody said you was stupid."

"Somebody did," Travis told him, shooting him a look that took in the bar mirror and the reflections of the faces in the crowd that had turned to stare at him.

"I did," one of those faces said.

Travis's gaze narrowed on that face just before he turned to confront the tall, thin man standing behind him. But there was no one there. He swallowed heavily, turned again to look into the mirror, and saw him, plain as day. Clearly disgusted, the man looked back at him and shook his head.

But when Travis shifted his gaze to the spot behind him, the man had disappeared. He squinted desperately, but all he could make out was the vaguest impression of a shadowy figure.

Damn. He rubbed both hands across his eyes. Not only drunk. Crazy.

"Maybe you best go home, Travis," Sam suggested.

"Yeah," he agreed, suddenly anxious to get out of the saloon and start sobering up. "Good idea."

"About time," that voice said again and spurred Travis into action.

Pushing his way past the crowd, he slammed through the double doors, stepped onto the boardwalk, and took a long, slow, deep breath of the cool night air. This was all he needed, he thought. Fresh air. Too damn stuffy in the saloon. Make a man think all manner of things. Tipping his head back, he stared up at the sky, watched the stars turn and whirl past his vision and told himself that that was the last time he'd look for solace in the bottom of a glass.

"That's what you said when you woke up on that ship."

"Christ." Travis straightened up and stared all around him at the night. Storefronts faced him with blank, darkened windows looking like blinded eyes. A stray wind whistled along the street, kicking up dust and plucking at the edges of his coat. A horse stamped its feet impatiently and huffed out a breath.

Everything was just as it should be, he thought. Except for the fact that he was hearing voices from someone who wasn't there.

"Oh, I'm here all right, and gettin' plenty tired of bein' here, too."

Travis closed his eyes tightly and, even knowing he wouldn't see a thing, slowly turned around toward the sound of that voice.

But the tall, thin man stood not an arm's reach away. And before Travis could say a word, that suddenly very substantial man slammed a fist into his jaw that sent him sprawling into the dirt.

* * *

"Mama!"

That young voice splintered her delicious dreams of Travis and jerked Katie into reality. She sat up straight in bed, staring blankly at the shadow-filled bedroom she'd known for four years. Head still foggy, her insides warm and silky from the dream-Travis's attentions, she fought for breath and attempted to still her pounding heart.

"Mama!"

Jake. Instantly, she threw the blanket back and leaped out of bed. She barely felt the sting of the cold floor against her bare feet as she ran to Jake's room just down the short hall.

She threw the door open and paused to savor the relief of finding him safe. Sitting up in bed, Jake rubbed both hands over his eyes fitfully, and even from a distance, she saw his small shoulders trembling. A nightmare, then. Moonlight poured through the window alongside her son's bed, bathing him in a pale, silvery light that seemed to shift and play across the boy like a ghostly hand trying to offer comfort.

Shaking her head at the notion, she hurried across the room.

Sitting on the edge of the mattress, Katie pulled him onto her lap and sighed gently when his short arms came around her in a fierce hug.

"You went away," Jake accused and snuggled his head against her chest.

"Ah, sweetie, it was just a dream," she cooed, smoothing his hair back from his tear-streaked face.

He shook his head and she looked down at him. "Uh-uh. You left."

In the quiet of the night, Katie's heart twisted as it always did when she looked into those blue eyes. She couldn't imagine her life without him and loved him with a depth she'd never thought possible.

"I'd never leave you, Jake," she told him and meant every word.

"You did too," he said, obviously recovered enough to indulge in his favorite pastime . . . arguing.

"Dreams can feel real, Jake," she said and briefly thought about the dream *she'd* been having. A quick, lightning-like flash of desire raced through her, leaving her as breathless as she'd been on awaking.

"I felt you," he insisted. "You kissed me and you went away."

Katie smiled. As hardheaded as both his parents, Jake would never surrender an argument. She wiped his tears away with a gentle swipe of her thumbs. "Well, I'm back now, so you can sleep again, all right?"

He nodded jerkily against her, but didn't fight when she laid him down and tucked him in, setting the edge of his blanket just beneath his chin. He opened his eyes and looked at her warily. "You stay?"

"I'll stay," she promised and settled back against the wall. It wouldn't be the first night since was born that she'd slept sitting up.

Jake sighed, nestled deeper into his bed and, eyes closed, asked, "Papa, too?"

Katie stiffened and gritted her teeth before saying tightly, "Papa, too."

Obviously satisfied, Jake drifted into silence, and in just a few minutes, his deep, even breathing told her he was again asleep. Katie shook her head and watched him, wishing she could be as accepting as Jake. As forgiving.

However she might feel toward Travis, their son had readily forgiven four years' absence. Delighted to have a father, the little boy followed Travis around all day, like a tiny shadow. He aped his father's walk and had even asked for "a big boy's hat," so he could look more like the man he so clearly adored.

She tucked her bare feet up under the hem of her nightgown and stared hard at the moon-cast shadows on the wall opposite.

For Travis's part, Katie had to give the man credit. Not only did his patience with the child never waver, he actually seemed to enjoy spending hours with his son. Seeing the two of them together made her heart ache for what might have been, and awakened, though she was ashamed to admit it, tiny seeds of jealousy. Their relationship seemed so easy. So effortless. Yet she and Travis were further apart than they'd been when he was who knew where. It wasn't fair, but *she* was the one who felt like an outsider.

Now that Travis was back, even Henry went to him with questions or problems. The years when she and the older man had worked as a team to keep the ranch going had apparently meant nothing to the old cowhand. Oh, he was as friendly and polite as ever, but he treated her like . . . like . . . Travis's *wife*.

"Isn't that what you are?" a woman asked.

Katie sat straight up in bed, cast a quick look at her sleeping son, then shifted her gaze to sweep the room. She hadn't imagined that voice. She wasn't crazy. Or drunk. Or dreaming.

So, what did that leave?

"Me." The voice came again.

Katie's gaze settled on the wall opposite, where, as she watched, shadow and light twisted together in a weird sort of dance. She held her breath and counted each beat of her heart. Her eyes burned from staring, but she didn't dare blink. Stretching out one hand to lay protectively on Jake's back, she stared at the thickening slice of moonlight as it slowly shaped itself into something—some*one*—very familiar.

Katie swallowed heavily, looked the figure up and down, and then again, just for good measure. Somehow, she managed to squeeze two words past her tight throat. "Aunt Addie?"

"In the flesh," the woman said, then caught herself and laughed shortly. "Well . . . so to speak."

Chapter Six

*T*ravis shook his head and clapped one hand to his throbbing jaw. Staring up at the man standing over him, he asked, "Who the hell are you?"

"I'm your uncle Eli, boy, and I am plumb fed up."

Working his jaw carefully, Travis pushed himself to his feet, staggered a bit, then balanced himself carefully on ground that seemed to be tilting precariously. "Elijah Hunter died long before I was born."

"True," the man said and took a step closer.

Ridiculous. If his face wasn't still aching, Travis would be convinced that this whole conversation was some kind of drunken, waking nightmare. As it was, he owed this stranger a good sock in the nose.

"Well, you pack a helluva punch for a ghost, mister," he said and brought his right fist up to connect with the other man's chin. But as his hand sailed right through the other man as if he were nothing more than a shadow, Travis staggered, eyes wide. "Sweet mother," he whispered, and stared from his fist, to the man, and back again.

"I told ya I'm a ghost, boy. You can't hit me."

"Too much beer, not enough food . . ." Travis headed for his horse again, determined now to ignore the figure walking along beside him.

"I'm here to see to it you and Katie work things out."

Travis snorted a choked laugh. "You're doin' a helluva job so far . . . *Uncle.*"

"You ain't helpin' me any," Eli countered. *"Hell, I've been waitin' for you to get back to town for four years. And now that you are, you ain't doin' a thing about it."*

He stopped beside his horse and bent down, resting his aching head against the cool leather of the saddle. Sliding a sideways glance at the "ghost," Travis said, "Maybe you don't know this, but Katie wants to divorce me."

"Yeah, I know."

Travis took some comfort in the fact that dear old ghostly Uncle Eli looked as disgusted as he felt. "Divorced before I'm married," he said thickly. "That's different."

"She wants to marry that teacher, Featherfield."

"Feather*stone*," Travis corrected, though it cost him. Just the thought of that nervous, skinny little dude and his Katie together was enough to make him want to turn around and head back into the saloon. But if he kept drinking, who knew how many ghosts would show up?

"You got to woo her back, boy," Eli said and slapped Travis hard on the back.

He glared at the wispy figure beside him. How the hell could he hit that hard if he was dead? Shaking his head, he said, "She won't hardly talk to me." A bitter pill to swallow, but there it was. Since he'd been home, she'd done everything possible to avoid him. Even at meals, when she was forced to see him, she spoke only to Henry or Jake.

Jake. His son.

Travis's heart swelled at the thought of the boy. In the last four days, he'd discovered a whole new world just by looking at it through Jake's eyes. Katie had done a fine job with him. He was full of beans, but he had a kind spirit and an easy laugh. It tore him up to know how much he'd missed. How much he would go on missing if Katie had her way.

She'd asked him to go on pretending to be married and he'd agreed. Mostly because he wouldn't harm her or the boy for anything. But also because a part of him hoped that she'd become accustomed to having him as her husband and come to want to continue that way.

But his Katie was nothing if not stubborn. She was bound and determined to go on pretending to be married only long enough to get a pretend divorce. Why he hadn't fallen in love with some weak-kneed, quiet, mousy little thing, he didn't know.

"You know damn well why," Eli said. *"Because that kind of woman ain't worth the wind to blow her away. Any real man wants a strong woman by his side. One with a mind of her own and the gumption to stand toe to toe with him from time to time."*

He hadn't realized ghosts could read minds.

"Now you do."

"Well, cut it out." Travis lifted his left foot and tried unsuccessfully to stab the toe of his boot into the stirrup. Once, twice. He wobbled, staggered, then curled his fingers around the saddle for support. Grabbing hold of the horn with his right hand, he held his foot with his left and guided his boot into the stirrup. Then he dragged himself up into the saddle and swayed unsteadily for what felt like forever.

From somewhere nearby, he heard a window being thrown open. Not trusting his balance, he didn't look up when a familiar female voice shouted down to him.

"Travis Dean, who in tarnation are you talking to?"

Maudie. He inhaled deeply, pulling the clean, cold air into his lungs and hoping it would clear his head. It didn't. "Say hello to Uncle Eli, Maudie," he said, still not looking up to where the older woman no doubt had the upper half of her body leaning out her window.

"Shoot, boy, Eli's been dead longer than you've been alive."

He glanced at the ghost and nodded. "See?" he said. "I told you you were dead."

"Think I don't know that?" Eli's gaze lifted to the woman. *"Old busybody hasn't changed in forty years."*

Travis snorted and called out, "Eli says you're a busybody, Maudie."

"And you're a drunk, Travis," she retorted. "Go home so we can all get some sleep!" She slammed her window shut again.

In the sudden silence, he looked down at his late Uncle Eli. "Since you'll be gone when I sober up, I'll say this now. Good to meet you, Uncle Eli. Don't ever hit me again.''

Elijah shook his head and slowly lifted off the ground until he was eyeball to eyeball with his nephew. He ignored the stunned surprise in Travis's eyes and said, "Understand me, boy. I can't go anywhere until you make Katie see some sense.''

Travis reached up, pulled the brim of his hat down firmly on his forehead, and gathered up the reins. Giving his horse a nudge in the ribs, he said, "Then I guess you and me are gonna be friends for a *long* time.''

"Heavens, girl, haven't you ever seen a ghost before?''

"No,'' Katie whispered and eased carefully off the bed. Aunt Addie, she told herself, was no one to be feared. But her spine tingled anyway. Quickly, she left Jake's room, hoping to draw her strange visitor away from the sleeping boy.

Moonlight flooded through the three windows facing the ranch yard, making the main room almost as bright as day, but with an eerie, magical quality that somehow made the idea of a ghost more believable.

"Why are you here?'' she asked as she turned to face the woman she'd loved and lost ten years ago.

Addie smiled and shook her head. "Always could count on you to get right down to brass tacks. I'm here to see to it you and Travis get back together. Like you're supposed to be.''

Katie plopped down onto one of the chairs. "Then let me save you some time. We're not going to be together.''

The light surrounding the older woman shifted, pulsed, and wavered weirdly.

In spite of herself, Katie shivered. She really needed to get more sleep. This was all Travis's fault. If he'd never come back, she'd be able to rest. She wouldn't be lying awake all night, every night, remembering his every touch, his every kiss. Her body wouldn't burn. Her soul wouldn't weep for chances lost. For love missed.

"And you don't have to," Addie said.

Of course ghosts could read minds, she thought. Why not? "Go haunt someone else."

"Honey, I ain't even started haunting, yet."

Katie looked toward her aunt, but the wispy blend of light and shadow was already gone. All that was left was the moonlight dancing on the walls. She sighed, swallowed heavily, and put the whole episode out of her mind. Obviously, she was even more tired than she'd thought. Imagining that Addie of all people would want Katie to forgive Travis was ridiculous. Hadn't her aunt spent the last forty years of her life cursing the man who'd left her standing at the altar?

If anything, if Addie were really a ghost, she'd be more likely to cheer Katie on and tell her to stand firm. No backing down. No forgiveness for a hurt that could still draw blood so many years later.

Curling up in the chair, Katie dragged a knitted throw over her, pulled it up to her chin and eased her aching head down against the chair back.

No point in going to bed if she wasn't going to sleep anyway.

"Papa's here," Jake crowed in a voice loud enough to shatter glass.

Katie opened gritty eyes warily, half expecting to see that dream image of Addie again. But in the soft morning light, all was as it should be and her son's face was just inches from hers.

"Why you sleepin' inna chair?" he asked, cocking his head to one side in an unconscious replica of his father.

"I was just resting," she said and groaned as she uncurled her legs and stretched. Resting. If you could call running from one dream of Travis to the next resting.

Jake jumped off the chair, grabbed one of her hands, and tugged for all he was worth. "Papa's cookin'. Come eat."

"I'm not hungry," she said, with a quick glance at the open doorway to the kitchen. She couldn't see Travis, but she could hear him, talking to Henry, rattling pans. The scent of fresh coffee drifted to her and she savored it.

But as much as she wanted some, she wasn't prepared just yet to face the man her dreams were filled with.

Her son frowned at her and tugged again. "Breakfas'," he insisted.

Looking into those determined eyes, she conceded. After all, it was easier than trying to explain to a three-year-old why you suddenly didn't consider breakfast an important part of the morning. "Fine," she said. "Just let me get dressed."

Jake shook his head. "Papa says now."

Papa says this. Papa says that. Katie gritted her teeth and tried to ignore the stab of resentment that shook her to her toes. Hadn't even been here a week and Travis had already wormed his way into Jake's affections.

But then, she reminded herself, he was good at that. It was the sticking around that came hard to the man.

"Jake," Travis called and stepped into the doorway. He looked directly into Katie's eyes. "Hungry?" he asked and she knew it was a challenge. She also knew that he'd been into town the night before and had probably spent hours in the saloon. Naturally, he didn't look any the worse for it. Travis always had had the devil's own luck that way.

Standing up, she draped the throw around her shoulders and knotted it between her breasts. She might have to sit across the table from him in order to save face, but she wasn't going to give him a chance to stare at her breasts. At that thought, her nipples tightened and tingled in anticipation. Damn. If her own body betrayed her in an instant, what chance did she have to stand firm against the temptation that was Travis Dean?

As if he could read her mind, he smiled, slowly, savoringly, letting his gaze roam over her from head to toe until finally meeting her gaze again. "I forgot how good you look in the morning," he said.

His voice rumbled along her spine and she stiffened instinctively. "You forgot a lot of things," she said as she followed her son into the kitchen, brushing past Travis. "Like coming home when you said you would, for instance."

She heard him sigh and smiled inwardly. It wasn't much, but at this point, she'd take her satisfaction where she could find it.

Henry stood up from his seat at the table. Gray hair in a wild halo around his head, he gave each of them a cautious look. He hadn't said anything yet to anyone about the strangeness of a newly returned husband sleeping in the barn, but Katie knew he was thinking about it. And once Henry started talking, there'd be no stopping the gossip.

She quailed a bit at the thought, but not enough to have Travis sleeping in the house. Besides, once the gossips got busy, she'd just tell everyone in town about the divorce she was planning to get. Sure, a divorced woman was a bit scandalous. But that was nothing compared to being the fallen woman who'd delivered an illegitimate child.

Henry's gaze sharpened as if he were looking at the two of them, trying to figure out what exactly was going on. Then he seemed to reconsider and reached out to snatch up a couple of pieces of toast. "I'll just go on out and get started, boss," he said.

"Fine," Katie answered.

"Good," Travis told him at the same time.

They stared hard at each other for a long minute. Katie glared, but Travis didn't back down. He seemed to think that just by showing up again, he had the right to reclaim everything he'd given up. Well, she told herself, silently fuming, he had another think or two coming.

Henry cleared his throat, grabbed hold of Jake's hand, and muttered, "Come on, boy, let's you and me go out to the barn."

"See the puppies?" Jake asked, clearly delighted at the prospect.

"Sure, sure," Henry promised, scuttling for the door.

In seconds they were gone, leaving Katie and Travis alone in the suddenly silent kitchen.

After a moment's hesitation, Travis poured two cups of coffee, set them down, and took a seat. Nodding at her, he said, "We have to talk sometime, Katie. Might as well be now."

Since she needed the coffee desperately and refused to give him the pleasure of seeing her cut and run, she sat down. Picking up her cup, she took a long, satisfying swallow and felt life rush back into her veins. Another sip or two and the fog clouding her still-tired brain might lift, too.

"We don't have anything left to say to each other, Travis."

"That's where you're wrong, Katie," he said, leaning his forearms on the table and meeting her gaze steadily. "I have lots to say and you're going to listen."

She curled her bare toes on the cold wooden floor and held on to her coffee cup with both hands, more for something to do than for the warmth it offered. Looking at him now, she felt the old, familiar swell of heat rising inside her. But she fought against it. Once, she'd paid a price for loving him. Now, there was more than just herself to consider. There was Jake. And she wouldn't let this man who had hurt her so badly do the same to her son.

"Anything you have to say to me, I don't want to hear."

"Too bad," he said, reaching across the table and covering one of her hands with his. "I should have said all this four days ago. But I wanted to give you time. Give us time. I've waited four long years to say this and—"

She snatched her hand back and glared at him. Any lingering traces of warm, cuddly feelings withered and died. "*You've* waited?" A wild, crashing wave of pure fury rocked her to her toes. "Excuse me, but I think you're forgetting something else here, Travis. You were the one who left. *I* was the one waiting." He flinched, but she didn't care. "I waited for the man who'd said he loved me to come home. When I needed you more than I'd ever needed anybody, Travis, you were gone."

He pushed back from the table, his chair legs scraping harshly against the floor. In an instant, he was at her side, pulling her to her feet. His hands on her upper arms, she felt the impression of each of his fingers, digging into her flesh. Felt it and, damn him anyway, loved having his hands on her again.

"I didn't know," he ground out. "How could I have known?"

She heard the pain in his voice, but it was nothing compared to what she'd gone through. What her son had gone through, not having a father. He'd left them without a thought. And if she hadn't come up with the lie about them having married, Jake would now be known as "Travis Dean's bastard."

His eyes mirrored the pain she'd heard in his tone, but she steeled herself against reacting to him as she always had and pointed out, "You couldn't have known about Jake, you're right. But that doesn't come into this. You should have come home anyway, Travis. To *me*." That was what hurt. He'd held her and loved her and made promises and plans—and then disappeared from her life.

"I wanted to," he said. "You'll never know how much." His gaze moved over her features with an intensity she felt as well as saw.

Her heart turned over in her chest. "But you didn't," she reminded him.

"I couldn't."

"So you say."

"Damn it, Katie," he whispered hoarsely, giving her a shake. "Listen to me. Let me tell you why I stayed away."

Maybe if she heard him out, he'd leave. Maybe he'd go along with her plan for a pretend divorce and go away before he made more promises he had no intention of keeping. Leave her and Jake to go back to the nice, quiet life they'd built for themselves.

It was a chance she had to take.

"All right," she said tightly, "I'll listen. But I won't promise to care."

Chapter Seven

*N*ow that he had her attention, he wasn't sure where to start. How to tell the story without admitting what a damned jackass he'd been. His mind raced for a minute or two before he finally conceded there was no way to both tell the truth and avoid humiliation, so he dived right in.

"I was shanghaied."

Obviously, she hadn't been expecting that. Her eyes widened and her jaw dropped. "What?"

"Shanghaied." He released her, shoved both hands through his hair, and started pacing. Amazing how really small the kitchen was. He'd never actually noticed before.

"I'd decided to stay in the city an extra day," he said aloud, memory taking him back four long years to the cold, windy night in San Francisco. "Made a good deal on the horses." He paused thoughtfully. "Don't know what happened to them or the money . . ."

"What happened to you?" she demanded and he almost smiled. She hadn't promised to care, he thought. But she did.

He looked at her, filling his soul with the sight of her. So many times over the years, he'd brought her image to mind in the hopes of dimming the reality he was living through. And now he was here, within arm's reach of her, and she was farther away from him than ever.

"Jesus, Katie," he whispered, "I missed you so bad, it hurt."

She flinched and turned those incredibly green eyes away. "Just . . . tell me, Travis."

He pulled in a shuddering breath and said, "Some fella in the saloon bought me a drink."

"Who?"

"I don't know who he was. I'd already had a few," he remembered, "celebrating the horse deal and"—he shot her a look—"you. With that deal, I knew we'd have a good start on our life together."

She folded her arms over her chest, drawing that knitted shawl tight across her breasts. "I didn't care about that deal, Travis. I only wanted to marry you."

"I know." He groaned tightly, letting his head fall back on his neck. "And don't think I haven't thought about that for four years. If I hadn't gone . . ." He shook his head and looked at her again. "But it's pointless to think about that now."

She nodded.

"Anyway," he said quickly, "after I sucked down the stranger's drink, I felt odd. Sort of tired."

"What happened?"

"I woke up in the hold of ship bound for China." He scowled to himself as the memory of that stinking blackness rose up in his mind again. The stench of rotting wood and the unwashed bodies of the others who'd been shang-haied along with him came flooding back. Instinctively, he walked to the nearest window and stared out at the sunlit yard and the open spaces behind the barn. Several deep breaths eased the racing of his heart and he started talking again. Telling her everything. From that first morning when he'd faced the captain angrily and had experienced the bite of a whip on his back. He told her about the two years he'd spent slaving for the man who'd destroyed his life and about the night he'd jumped ship in Canton. As he told the story, he relived it all, remembering the fear that had clawed at him as he struggled to survive in a country where he couldn't speak the language.

"How'd you get home, then?"

He glanced at her before turning his gaze back on the windswept land stretching out for miles in every direction.

"I found another ship. Volunteered to work my passage home. Took another two years. It was a merchant vessel. Stopped at every port all over the world." And at every stop, the delays had chafed at him. Though he hadn't had to worry about being whipped and the captain had been a fair man, the voyage had lasted an eternity. "When we finally put in in San Francisco, I came right here."

"Why didn't you write to me?" she asked quietly. "Let me know you were alive."

He turned toward her and saw the hurt, the confusion on her face. But at least most of her fury had gone. That was something, he supposed. "The first two years, I couldn't," he said. "Hell, I was lucky to get abovedecks. The captain didn't let us wander off. When we were in port, we were locked in the hold to keep us from escaping."

"How did you get away?"

He snorted a choked laugh. "Talked my way into his confidence finally. Convinced him I was a better deal maker than the first mate. He let me try and I proved myself a time or two. Then the first time he let me go ashore alone, I disappeared."   .

"Fine," Katie said, walking quietly across the room to stand beside him. In the sunlight shimmering through the open window, her hair blazed in a wonder of color. Travis had to fist his hands in his pockets to keep from reaching for her. She wasn't angry anymore, but there was no welcome in her eyes.

"Once you'd escaped that ship, you could have written to me."

"Maybe I should have," he said tightly. "But damn it, there was a better than even chance that I'd never get back. I figured there was no point in telling you I was alive if I wouldn't be for long."

She shook her head. "You owed it to me, Travis. You owed it to Jake."

"I didn't know about Jake, damn it." His own frustration mounting, he took a long, deep breath, hoping for calm.

"Look," she said, her hands gripping the threads of the

knitted throw, "I understand what you went through. And I'm sorry. But it doesn't change anything."

He felt as though someone had slugged him in the stomach. Briefly, he wondered if the ghost he'd imagined the night before had slipped into the room. But no. It was Katie's quiet dismissal that had robbed him of breath.

"Maybe it wasn't your fault that you were gone so damned long," she went on. "But it was your fault that you left in the first place. I asked you not to go." Her words came faster, and as she talked, he could see her temper building again. "I told you we didn't need that stupid horse deal you were so set on."

"It wasn't stupid," he countered quickly. "We needed that money to get married."

"*We* didn't need it, Travis," she snapped. "You did."

"A man's got a right to provide for the woman he loves."

"I trusted you to come back."

"I was going to."

"But you didn't."

"I was shanghaied!"

"Because you were so set on that damn deal, you put it ahead of me and Jake," she shouted, leaning in and glaring at him.

"How many times do I have to say I didn't know about Jake?"

"You knew what we'd done, though, didn't you?" she asked, furious. "You knew we'd been together and that we might have made a baby."

"I wasn't thinking about babies that night, Katie," he said as the memories crowded in on him. Hushed whispers, fevered kisses, hands exploring, bodies melding . . . He took a breath. "And neither were you."

She flushed and he wanted her so desperately he thought he might die if he couldn't hold her. Taste her.

"It doesn't matter," she said at last and shook her head. "None of this matters anymore. What we had is over, Travis."

Over? How could it be over when every time they were in the same room together, he felt the sparks fly?

"All that counts with me now is Jake."

"And that schoolteacher," he ground out.

"Leave Arthur out of this." She turned away from him and Travis reached out, grabbing her arm to spin her back to face him. Her red hair swung free around her shoulders and framed her face in a riot of untamed curls.

"You can't be serious about that man," he said, and his gaze locked on the throbbing pulse point at the base of her throat. She felt it. Whether she wanted to admit it or not, she felt the magic that lay between them. She could tell herself it was over until the end of time, but what they had would never be finished.

She flipped her hair back over her shoulder and stared up at him, lifting her chin defiantly. "Arthur is a perfectly nice man."

Travis snorted. "Christ, Katie, you're too much for him and you know it."

"He has a good job."

"As a schoolmarm?"

She scowled at him. "He'll be home every night."

"Who else would have him?"

"He'll be a good father to Jake."

Fury burned inside him. "*I'm* his father!"

She pulled free of his grasp. "Arthur loves me."

With those words hanging in the air, she whirled around and flounced toward the doorway. It only took Travis three quick, long strides to catch her. He grabbed her, turned her to face him, and pulled her close. As their bodies pressed together, he felt the hard, rigid tips of her nipples jutting into his chest and just managed to swallow the groan rippling up his throat.

"He may say he loves you, Katie," he said, his gaze moving over her features with a frantic intensity, "but what he feels for you isn't a pimple on what we have together."

She shivered. "*Had.*"

"Have," he insisted. Then whispering, he went on.

"You don't want Arthur, Katie," He lowered his head to within an inch of hers. "You want me. Almost as bad as I do you."

She licked her lips and shook her head. "You're wrong."

"Am I?" Hell, he could feel her trembling in his hands. He knew damn well he was right about them. And if there was just a tiny thread of worry worming its way through him, Travis ignored it. "Let's find out."

He took her mouth in the kiss he'd been dreaming about for four long years. Her hands flat against his chest, she made a token effort to push him away, but in less than a second, she'd run her hands up over his shoulders to his back and was holding him.

Travis shifted one hand to the back of her head, his fingers tangling in the mass of curls. He held her still while he used his mouth to stake a renewed claim on her heart and soul.

On a sigh, she parted her lips and his tongue swept inside her warmth and he knew he'd finally come home. She was everything he'd ever wanted and all he would ever need. He couldn't taste her enough. He explored her mouth, her lips, her teeth. He sighed as she moaned gently and moved into him.

His body leaped into life and he lowered one hand to the small of her back. Then, holding her tightly to him, he let her feel the strength of his response. The need catapulting through him. The desire that was always hers.

He wanted more. He wanted all of her. Here. Now. On the kitchen floor, he wanted to bury himself inside her again and feel once more the completion that only she could provide.

Tearing his mouth from hers, he slid his lips down the length of her throat, tasting, kissing. She groaned tightly and tipped her head back, granting him access.

"I love you, Katie," he whispered against her skin and watched as goose pimples dusted her flesh. "I've always loved you."

"Travis . . ."

He ached for her.

"Love me, Katie . . ."

"Oh, God help me," she murmured, "I—"

"Papa!"

The back door swung open, slamming into the wall with a crash. Katie jerked herself free and took a step or two backward, just for good measure. Blood rushing, heart pounding, she stared at Travis and knew that if it hadn't been for Jake's interruption, she would have taken Travis back into her bed.

Good God. Hadn't she learned anything?

Jake hopped from foot to foot, excitement pulsing through him. "Henry says to come. He says the baby horse is coming."

Travis's gaze remained fixed on her and Katie shifted uncomfortably beneath his hooded, desire-filled stare. Not even glancing at his son, he said, "Tell Henry I'll be right there."

"Awright," the boy said, then spun around and raced for the barn, leaving the door wide open.

A slash of sunlight spilled through and lay across the kitchen. From outside came the familiar sounds of the ranch waking up. But Katie hardly heard it. Pulling in a deep breath, she said, "That kiss didn't mean anything, Travis. I still want a divorce."

"You can't divorce me," he countered. "We're not married."

"I made everyone believe we were married. I can do the same with a divorce."

"Not if I tell everyone the truth," he said, and Katie's knees turned to water.

Chapter Eight

*H*e was already out the door before Katie shook off the shock holding her rooted to the floor and raced after him. Clutching at his arm, she dragged him to a stop at the foot of the back-porch steps.

The rocky dirt was cold against her bare feet and sharp-edged pebbles dug into her flesh, but she hardly felt them. Cold morning air, still heavy with damp, clung to her night-gown and had her chilled clean to the bone in a matter of seconds. And none of that mattered, she told herself as she looked up into his eyes.

"You wouldn't," she said flatly.

"Why wouldn't I?"

Why? Because the truth would ruin everything, that's why. Everyone in town would know that she'd never been married. That Jake was illegitimate. Her reputation would be in tatters and her son's future clouded.

"You know the answer to that question as well as I do."

His jaw tightened and she saw a muscle in his cheek twitch.

"How could you even think about doing it?" she demanded. "You say you love me. That you want to be a father to Jake. And then you threaten to do this?"

"You think I want to?" he asked. "You're not leaving me much choice, Katie."

She looked up into hard blue eyes and tried to determine if he was bluffing. But Travis had always been a fine poker player. If this was a bluff, it was a damned good one.

Taking a step back from him, she eyed him warily for a minute and tried a bluff of her own. She'd pretend she didn't care. "You won't do it, Travis," she said, pleased at how calm and reasonable her voice sounded. "I know you well enough to know you won't hurt a child just to get even with me."

He snorted a laugh and shook his head. "You think that's what this is about?" he asked. "Getting even?"

"What else?" She shrugged and ignored the temptation to shiver as her now thoroughly damp nightgown settled onto her skin and clung there like seaweed to a piece of driftwood. "I didn't welcome you home with open arms, so now you want to get back at me."

"You're really something, you know that, Kate?"

He laughed, but didn't sound amused. She kept her gaze fixed on him as he took one step, then another, closer. He didn't stop until there was less than a breath separating them. So much heat leaped into life between them, Kate wouldn't have been surprised to see steam rising up from her sodden nightgown.

"I'm not here to get back at you," he said, dipping his head until they were eyeball to eyeball. "I'm here to get my life back. And that means you. And Jake."

She shook her head, despite the sizzle of want and need rocketing around inside her. "And you're planning on winning my affections by shooting your mouth off and making me look like the town tramp?"

"Only as a last resort," he assured her, but she didn't take much comfort in that. "There's another way to handle this," he added quietly, and his whisper rippled along her spine, giving her a whole new set of chills that had nothing to do with being cold and damp.

"What way is that?" she forced herself to ask.

"You can marry me for real," he told her.

She sucked in a breath. She should have been expecting that, she told herself. She used to dream about marrying him. About living with him, waking up beside him every morning, falling asleep cuddled into his warmth, feeling his hands and mouth claim her body in the darkness. But that was before, she reminded herself. Before he'd left her to carry on as best she could with a son he hadn't even known existed.

Now it was too late. She wouldn't be tricked into marriage or forced into it or any other damn thing. She'd learned how to survive on her own and she'd done a damn fine job of it, too. He'd just have to get used to life as it was. She'd had to. "Marry you or . . . ?"

A slow, wicked smile curved one corner of his mouth. "Marry me, or I tell everybody in town the truth."

Kate gritted her teeth and shot him a look that should have singed his boots. "You son of a bitch."

"Why, Katie, my love," he said, feigning shock, "such language."

"That's blackmail."

"That's right."

"Well," Addie said, *sarcasm icing her voice, "isn't that the most romantic thing you ever heard?"*

"The boy's desperate," Eli said in his nephew's defense, though in truth he thought it had been a pretty foolish maneuver. You'd never win over a Hunter woman by ordering her around.

"Desperate and crazy. Katie'll never go along with this. She'll just get madder and none of us'll get anywhere."

"Then we'll just have to figure something else out, won't we?" Eli said, and judging by the twinkle in his eyes, Addie figured the old coot already had something in mind.

Travis started for the barn again, this time with a spring in his step. He had her now and he knew it. Hell, he should have done this days ago. Katie would never take the risk of being at the business end of a town full of wagging tongues. She'd surrender, they'd get married, and they'd damn well live happily ever after.

He heard her bare feet on the ground as she chased him. Darting around in front of him, she stopped dead, put both hands on his chest to keep him still, and glared up at him.

"I'm not going to marry you, Travis," she said and shifted slightly from foot to foot. He glanced down. Her toes were turning blue. He frowned to himself. He didn't want her catching pneumonia before they had a chance to have a honeymoon.

"Go in the house before you freeze," he said and stepped around her.

"Travis! I said, I'm not going to marry you."

He glanced over his shoulder at her.

"You can't force me into this."

A chill wind kicked up out of nowhere and sent her loose, tangled red curls into a wild dance around her head. His heart staggered slightly with the full rush of love that swamped him. Four long years without her had taught him that once he had her back at his side, he'd never let her out of his sight again. All he wanted out of life for the next fifty or sixty years was to be able to look into her green eyes and hear her say his name.

But to have that dream, he had to connive, trick, and blackmail her into marrying him before she could go around town telling folks they were divorced.

"Me?" he asked, laying one hand on his chest in mock surprise. "Why, Katie Hunter, I'm surprised at you. I've never forced a woman to do anything in my life."

"Until now."

He grinned at her. "Don't think of it as force. Think of it as persuasion."

Her eyes narrowed. "You no-good, lying, rotten, disappearing . . ."

His grin got wider. Damn, but he'd missed her. "Think I'll go into town later today. Visit with a few old friends."

"Who?"

He shrugged. "Whoever I happen to meet." Then, leaving her shooting him a murderous stare, he headed for the barn.

Travis had a two-hour head start on her, damn it.

He'd said he was going into town later. How could she have known that he'd waltz into the barn, saddle a horse, and take off? Heaven only knew what he was doing . . . saying . . . She cringed slightly and wondered if the man she'd loved for so many years was really capable of ruining her.

Gritting her teeth, she slapped the reins over the horse's back, propped one foot up on the kickboard, and braced herself against the jarring, bumpy ride in a fast-moving buckboard. A saddled horse would have been faster, but if Travis hadn't said anything, she didn't want to stir suspicions herself. Today was shopping day and, by thunder, she'd take her buckboard and pick up supplies just like any other week.

As she rode into town, her gaze shifted from one side of Main Street to the other. Uneasy, she kept one eye peeled for Travis and the other on the lookout for any changes in her friends and neighbors.

It didn't take long.

Sylvia Butler stepped out of the dress shop and stopped dead on the boardwalk. Her gaze settled on Kate for a split second, then she ducked her head and hustled away.

Katie shifted uncomfortably. She wasn't the best of friends with Sylvia, but the woman usually at least waved.

Tom Decker saw Kate and immediately slipped into the blacksmith's. Well, for heaven's sake. Hester Sawyer sniffed, lifted her chin, and spun around.

A crawling sensation trickled down her spine and Katie felt as though dozens of eyes were locked on her. From down the street, a dog barked. A tinkle of piano music sifted through the half-open doors of the saloon. A door slammed and the plodding noise of her horse's hooves against the dirt seemed overly loud.

The farther she went down Main Street, the worse it got. Kate felt a slow rush of heat fill her cheeks. What had Travis done? What were all of her friends and neighbors thinking? Why were they staring and yet pretending to ignore her at the same time?

Hell. She knew why. She just couldn't believe that Travis Dean could be so . . . cruel.

"Blast him to China again," she muttered, regretting

now that she'd ever felt sorry for him. Shanghaied, indeed. Why couldn't he have just stayed away?

She eased her horse to one side of the street, hopped down and looped the reins over the hitching post in front of Maudie's store. Squaring her shoulders, she marched across the boardwalk and hurried inside, away from whispers and stares.

"There you are!" the older woman called out as the bell over the door announced Katie's presence.

Well, at least Maudie was speaking to her.

"Didn't expect to see you for a while after what Travis said."

"I'll bet," she muttered grimly and forced herself to cross the floor to the wide front counter. She ignored the jars of jelly beans and other assorted penny candies and set down her carefully made-out list of supplies.

Maudie smoothed one hand along the side of her hair, picked up the list, and nodded. "I can fill all this, but it'll take a while."

"No hurry," Kate said and meant it. When she'd finished her business, she'd have to go back onto the street and face all those prying eyes again.

"If you say so, honey," Maudie said. "But from what Travis was sayin', I don't think you got all that much time."

A spurt of anger surged through her. "You shouldn't believe everything you hear, you know."

Maudie leaned across the counter and gave Kate's hand a pat. "Now, honey, Travis is many things, but a liar ain't one of 'em."

Fine. Perfect. He'd been home a week and now even one of her best friends was ready to believe him over Kate.

"He's just busy as a bee today, too," Maudie was saying as she turned and began looking through the shelves for the items on Kate's list. "He's goin' from store to store, telling everyone his news."

Kate stuffed her hands into her coat pockets to hide the fact that they were fisted so tight, her knuckles were white. "Is that a fact?"

"Oh, and folks are so excited, you'd think nothin' like this had ever happened before."

Well, here in Tempest, it wasn't an everyday thing for a respectable woman to be called a harlot. Not surprising that folks were in an uproar.

"Although," Maudie said, with a quick glance at her, "I do think you could have told me yourself . . ."

Katie colored and cursed herself for being embarrassed. She'd done what any woman would have done in similar circumstances. For pity's sake, she'd had a child to protect.

"I . . . uh . . . didn't tell anyone, Maudie," she said and heard her voice crack.

"Well, I guess I'll forgive you, since I know now, thanks to Travis."

"Yes," Kate muttered thickly, seeing her old friend through a hazy mist of anger. "This is all thanks to Travis, isn't it?"

Maudie laughed shortly. "I just wish I could be there to watch that schoolteacher's face when Travis tells him."

Arthur. Katie waited for a stab of pain, but didn't feel it. Strangely enough, it didn't bother her to know that Arthur would think badly of her. What hurt was knowing that Travis was the one destroying her.

"Where is Travis, do you know?"

Maudie stopped, tilted her head to one side, and thought about it. "All I know is he promised to go by the icehouse for me before he headed back home. He hasn't delivered the ice yet, so he's still in town somewhere."

Ice. Katie nodded grimly. Turning, she started for the front door. Why wait until he came back to the ranch to kill him? Over her shoulder, she said, "I'll pick that order up later, Maudie."

Chapter Nine

She heard snatches of laughter as she stormed down the center of Main Street. One or two people actually had the nerve to look right at her and smile or wink. Kate inhaled sharply, muttered an under-the-breath curse directed at the gossips in general and Travis in particular.

Wait until she found him, she fumed. He might have ruined her good name, forcing her to move away from the only home she'd ever known . . . but before she was finished with him, he'd be sorry he ever survived being shanghaied.

Her bootsteps pounded against the hard-packed dirt. Her hands fisted and unfisted at her sides as she shot furious glances from one side of the street to the other. Where in hell was he, anyway?

With her concentration focused on finding Travis, she never saw Arthur until she plowed right into him. Between his slight weight and the power of her fury, he hadn't stood a chance. Knocked off his feet, the schoolteacher lay in the dirt, staring up at her as though she were a stranger to him.

Instantly contrite, Kate bent over him, reaching out one hand to help him up. He cringed away from her touch as though she were jabbing at him with a flaming torch. "For heaven's sake, Arthur," she said impatiently, "I only wanted to help you up again."

"No need," he said and rolled away from her before pushing his long, lanky body upright. He cast a wary glance around him, then looked at her briefly before ducking his head.

Apparently, Travis had already spoken to the man. Hell, Arthur couldn't even stand the sight of her.

It was for the best, she decided grimly as her gaze swept him up and down. How in heaven had she ever thought she could marry this poor little man? She had no interest in a husband she could terrify with a glance. She wanted a man to shout back at her. To stand beside her. To work and dream and build a future with. Someone like Travis? her mind prodded.

Like Travis, she assured herself silently. Not Travis himself.

"Have you seen—"

"Your . . . husband?" Arthur finished, swallowing heavily enough to cause his Adam's apple to swell to twice its size. "Yes, he, uh, came to, uh, see me and well, he, uh . . ."

For pity's sake, just spit it out! she wanted to scream.

"Where is he now?" she demanded, cutting him off rudely.

Arthur licked dry lips, pushed his spectacles higher on his long nose, and tossed a glance toward the edge of town. "The, uh, he was going to the—"

"Icehouse?" she finished. Really, why had she never noticed his infuriating habit of stuttering when he was nervous?

"Yes." He gulped, and as she turned away, he spoke up again quickly. "I'd like to say—"

"What, Arthur?" she asked, hoping it wouldn't take long. She needed to catch up to Travis while her temper was still hot enough to do some major damage.

"If I had, uh, known, I would uh naturally not have, uh, insinuated myself upon your, uh . . ."

A new flush of embarrassed anger enveloped her. She felt the high color flooding her cheeks and that fact only made her madder. Blast him, anyway. Blast him and Travis both!

Lifting her chin, she said tightly, "Believe me, Arthur, our time together is best forgotten. By both of us."

He looked so damned relieved, she wanted to throw something at him. Instead, she settled for stomping on toward the icehouse, leaving Arthur standing alone, covered with dust, in the middle of the street.

"Travis Dean!" she called out as she threw open the heavy door and stared down the stairs into the icy gloom.

"Kate?" A scrape of a match against a strike pad could be heard, and in an instant, a flashing flicker of light took hold in the darkness. Travis held the candle close to his face and looked up at her. "What are you doin' here?"

"I came to tell you what I think of you, you no-good, lying weasel of a man."

"That take care of it, then?" he asked dryly.

"Not by half!" she shouted and started down the stairs. Behind her, the heavy door swung shut, enveloping her in a shroud of blackness that only lifted the closer she came to Travis.

The still air felt frosty as it rushed in and out of her lungs. Blocks of lake ice stood in towers all around her. Every winter, when the waters froze, the townspeople chopped up the ice and then stored it here, belowground, where it generally kept right through to the following fall.

"Can this wait until we get out of here?" he asked and set the candle stand down on a nearby ice chunk.

"No, it can't." Kate shivered and flapped her arms across her chest in an effort to keep warm. It didn't help.

"Fine, go ahead, then," he said and dug the ice tongs into a small block.

While he hefted it onto his shoulder and blew out the candle, Katie started in. "You actually did it," she said, following him up the narrow staircase. "I didn't think you would, but you did."

"What'd I do now, Kate?" he asked, hitching the ice up higher onto his back.

"You told everyone in town that we were never married, you son of a bitch!"

He glanced behind him. "What makes you say that?"

"Because everyone in town is staring at me!"

"You're a beautiful woman, Katie. I stare at you all the time."

Cold. So bloody cold. She kept going, right behind him. "It's not that kind of stare."

He stopped on the top step and pushed the door handle. Nothing. He tried again, but the heavy door didn't budge.

"What's wrong?" she asked from behind him.

"The door's stuck," he said.

"What do you mean, stuck?"

"What do you mean, what do I mean?" Travis swung the block of ice down to the floor beside him and bent his shoulder to the door, giving it a shove. Still nothing.

Anger forgotten, Katie stepped around the ice and tried to help. As mad as she was, she didn't fancy staying in that icehouse any longer than she absolutely had to. But no matter how hard they tried, even the two of them together couldn't move the door an inch.

As they stood there in the darkness, the cold crept closer, reaching out with frozen fingers to pull them back down into the icy pit. Kate swallowed heavily, huffed out a breath, and watched it steam in front of her face. Her eyes accustomed to the darkness, she turned toward him.

"What do we do now?" she asked.

"Wait," Travis said. "Somebody's bound to notice when we don't turn up."

"We could freeze to death by then."

She thought she saw one of his eyebrows lift.

"We could keep each other warm," he suggested.

Good God.

"That ought to do it," Eli said and leaned back against the icehouse door. He looked at the ghost sitting beside him and grinned. "They can't get past us, so they'll have to work things out or freeze solid."

"And if they freeze?" Addie asked, settling in for however long she had to keep that door barred.

Eli shrugged. "They're stubborn, but not that stubborn."

"You care to make a wager on that?"

"I'll bet you my gold harp they'll work it out."

"You don't have a gold harp," Addie reminded him.
"I will have by nightfall, I'm thinkin'."

Hours must have passed, because that relit candle had done some serious melting. Travis looked from the tiny flame to the woman sitting nearby. Stubborn as all get out, she'd rather turn to a block of ice herself than cuddle up to him to stay warm. Hell, she hadn't even yelled at him since they'd discovered the door was locked.

Shaking his head, he silently reached out for her and dragged her up against him. Katie stiffened as a matter of principle, but then cold overcame her anger and she folded in close. One arm draped around her shoulders, he rubbed her upper arm.

"Why'd you do it, Travis?"

"It's not what you think, Kate."

"Do you hate me that much?"

"Hate you?" He drew his head back and stared down at her. In the flickering light of the candle, her green eyes looked magical. "Damn it, Katie, I *love* you."

Her gaze shifted. "You left me."

"You buried me," he countered, tugging her close when she tried to move away again.

She leaned her head against his shoulder and laughed shortly. "I gave you a nice headstone."

He grunted. "Yeah, but you planted me alongside Monster Morgan for all eternity."

She inched even closer and Travis felt pools of heat collect in the spots where their bodies touched.

"I wanted to hurt you somehow, Travis. Hurt you as much as you hurt me by leaving."

He sighed heavily. "I guess I knew that," he said softly, bending his head to plant a kiss in her hair.

"I missed you so much," she said, tipping her head back to look up at him. "At first, I thought I'd die from missing you."

"God, Katie," he whispered, letting the tips of his fingers dust along her jaw. "It was the thought of you that kept me alive. Kept me breathing when it would have been so much easier just to die.''

She shivered, as much from desire as from the cold, and Travis gathered her up against him. When she didn't resist, he laid her down atop the straw-covered floor and positioned himself alongside her.

''I want you, Katie. I *need* you.'' He paused, looked deeply into her eyes, and added. ''Without you, there's nothing.''

''I didn't want to need you anymore, Travis,'' she admitted. ''But I do. You're the missing part of me.'' Looking up at him, she reached for his face and cupped his cheeks in her palms. ''Love me now.''

He groaned and bent his head to claim her mouth. She went warm and liquid, at last giving him the welcome he'd dreamed of.

Chapter Ten

*T*he chill air settled over them, but neither of them noticed. Hands moved, breathing quickened, and in seconds, they were lying together, naked and heated, despite the cold.

He kissed first one nipple, then the other, rolling his tongue across the hardened tips, drawing a long, throaty moan from deep in Kate's throat. She reached for him, her hands dusting across his chest, his abdomen. Her short, neat nails raked his naked flesh, then smoothed gently over the whip scars on his back.

"Oh, Travis," she whispered, tears pooling in her eyes.

"It doesn't matter, Katie," he told her as he levered himself atop her. "Nothing matters but you and me."

And then he entered her, reclaiming her body, taking what was his, giving her all he was.

He moved within her and the sweet sensation crowded all other thoughts from her mind. Katie inhaled sharply, wrapped her arms around him, and pulled him closer, deeper. She'd longed for this moment and feared it would never come. Now that it had, she wanted to savor it all. To remember this coming together as their new beginning.

The rhythm of the dance increased and their breath steamed around them in filmy vapors. She stared up into his face. He met her gaze, dipped his head for a kiss, then reared up again. Their eyes locked, they rode the wave of completion together, and as satisfaction rolled through them, they clung to each other like survivors of a shipwreck.

And when it was over, they lay intertwined on the cold, stiff straw. Both arms around her, Travis closed his eyes and thanked whoever was responsible for bringing him home. Where he belonged. With Katie.

"Well . . ." she murmured, her breath puffing warm across his chest.

"Still want that divorce?" he whispered.

She tipped her head back to meet his gaze. "Don't need one now that you've already told everyone we were never married."

He frowned at her. "What?"

Kate shook her head. Strange, she wasn't even mad anymore. It didn't really matter if she had to move. She'd still have Jake. And maybe even Travis. "Everyone in town is whispering and laughing and staring at me, Travis. I know you told them. Hell, Maudie even said as much."

He propped himself up on one elbow and looked down at her. "I don't know what you're talking about."

"Don't lie to me, Travis," she said.

"So you thought I'd ruined you, but you slept with me anyway."

She scooted out from under him, but he pulled her right back. So much for not being mad. "I can't help loving you, Travis," she told him. "Lord knows, I've tried to stop."

He gave her that lopsided grin that had always been her undoing. "Glad to hear it," he said. "I love you, too."

"Then why'd you do it?"

"I didn't."

"You told them *something*!"

Bending his head, he aimed a kiss at her mouth, but when she turned her face aside, settled for skimming one across her ear. Then he laid one palm along her cheek and turned her back toward him until he was looking into those green eyes. "I told them that I was planning a big *second* wedding."

"A what?"

His smile widened as he let his hand slide down her throat, across her breasts, to the curve of her waist. "A second wedding. Told everybody that I felt real bad about sneaking you off for a secret marriage and that I wanted you to have the kind of party and celebration you deserved.''

A curl of pleasure unwound inside her. She bit her lip and swallowed back the tightness in her throat. ''You did?''

''Uh-huh.'' This time, when he bent to kiss her, she kissed him back. When he finally lifted his head again, he said, ''This way, we can be married and no one will ever have to know that it's our first time.''

''Travis Dean . . .''

''Yeah?''

''I think I love you.''

''Katie Hunter . . .''

''Yeah?''

''You keep right on thinkin' that.''

Then he was kissing her again and Katie couldn't have done any thinking if her life had depended on it. She didn't even stir when the icehouse door suddenly swung open and a shaft of sunlight shot down the steps to cover them in a golden ray of warmth.

''Well, good God Almighty!'' Maudie screeched from the doorway.

Instantly, Travis rolled the two of them behind a tower of ice. Katie buried her head in his chest and ignored the deep, rumbling chuckles shaking him.

''Go away, Maudie!'' he shouted when he caught his breath.

As the door swung closed again, Katie heard her friend call out, ''A steak, Kate. Just like I said, a good, thick steak.''

''Done!'' Eli crowed and took Addie's hand to lead her off to the Spirit Tree. ''I knew we could do it.''

Addie glanced back over her shoulder at the icehouse and sent a wish for luck and long life to her niece and the man she loved. Then she put her past behind her and concentrated on the hereafter.

''You figure we'll go right away?'' she asked, eager now to see what that Heavenly Reward the preachers were always talking about would be.

"I reckon so," Eli said, quickening his steps. In the distance, he spotted a soft, golden light caressing the gnarled branches of the Spirit Tree and shot Addie a smile. "See there? Somebody's waitin' for us."

The two souls hurried on, and stopped at the base of the old tree. Tilting their faces heavenward, they waited.

"You did well." A voice filtered down through the golden light and settled over them like a blessing.

"Then we can come on up?" Eli asked.

"Not quite yet," the voice said.

"What's that?" Addie demanded. "Why not?"

"This task was too easily accomplished."

"Easy?" Addie asked. "Weren't you watching?"

"Addie . . ."

"There are two more souls in need of guidance," the voice went on.

"This don't seem at all fair," Addie pointed out.

"We've been waitin' a long time," Eli argued.

"Your time will come soon enough," the voice said. "You must learn patience."

Eli shot his beloved a warning look. Addie never had been one for patience. As the golden light ebbed, leaving them alone at the Spirit Tree, she said, "I can't believe it. More waitin'."

"At least we have each other," he told her and she smiled, moving into his arms.

"True, and I reckon we could go to the weddin' now, too."

"Ought to be quite a party," he agreed.

"I love you," Addie said.

"And I you," Eli told her, "for always."

Redemption

DELIA PARR

Chapter One

JOHNSON COUNTY, NEW YORK, 1818

The snowstorm provided the perfect opportunity for Sarah to escape from Newtown Falls completely unnoticed.

Under the added cover of nightfall, she trudged down the middle of the deserted main street through bitter cold wind and blinding gusts of snow to return home to the isolated cabin she shared with her aunt on the far outskirts of town. Weighted down like a packhorse with sacks of food supplies and seamstress work harnessed to her back, she held tight to the canvas-covered lantern she carried to light her way once she cleared the town limits.

Fearful the cover that temporarily obscured the lantern's light would blow free, or worse, that she would lose her footing on the slippery roadbed, spill the lamp oil on her cape, and set herself afire, she made steady, but cautious headway past darkened storefronts and homes where she was no longer welcomed as a decent woman.

Even after four years.

Haunting memories of the scandal that still swept gossip through Newtown Falls penetrated her soul. Snow-laced wind stung her cheeks, whipped at her cape, and tested her determination. She was tempted to ask one of her few faithful friends for shelter overnight in town, but knew censure would be certain and swift. Left with no choice but to return home tonight, she yearned for the solitude she had found in the woods where no whispers of scandal could be heard.

Tears of frustration threatened to overflow and freeze on

her face, but she blinked hard to hold them at bay. She could not change the past any more than she could live in town and face down her accusers every day. But living in near seclusion had done little to change her position as a social outcast.

Chilled in both body and spirit, she turned at the corner to take the shortcut home on the footpath through the woods that surrounded the town. Her journey would have been easier had she thought to bring along her snowshoes. With her boots already crusted with ice, she slipped and the load on her back shifted. While she fought to keep her balance, she nearly dropped the lantern, and scarcely managed to avoid a disastrous fall. Breathing in hard gulps of moist, cold air, she paused to catch her breath and glanced down the narrower roadway that led away from the main street.

Muted by the falling snow, well-lit homes lined the roadway. With her pulse racing, she readjusted her shoulder harness and quickened her pace, hoping to reach the woods and disappear from view without being noticed.

Two houses left. Then only one.

She heaved a sigh of relief, but choked it back when the front door on the remaining house opened just as she reached it. Jenny Meyers, Mary Grace Horton, and Anna Clayton scrambled and giggled their way down the snow-covered walking path directly in front of Sarah. With her escape route blocked, she had no alternative now but to stop and brace herself for a confrontation she had tried so hard to avoid.

"Sarah Bailey? Whatever are you doing in town?"

She flinched, but held her head high. "I'm going home. I'm surprised you'd all venture out in this storm."

Jenny laughed. "Abigail's getting married next week, and we have to finish her wedding quilt."

"Who were you visiting in town this time?" Mary Grace asked, her question laced with the usual innuendo.

"She probably just came to pick up some work from Mrs. Dunlap," Anna suggested as she pointed to the twin sacks on Sarah's back. "Absolutely everyone ordered a new gown to wear to the welcoming party for Captain Hayes next month.''

Jenny sighed. "Imagine. A war hero is going to be living here in Newtown Falls. And he just happens to be a bachelor who's bound to need a wife once he settles onto his estate.''

"Maybe he'll bring a wife with him,'' Anna warned.

"He's not married. He's not even betrothed,'' Mary Grace quipped.

"I wonder if he's handsome—''

"Don't be silly, Jenny. He's famous, wealthy, and respectable, which is far more important.'' Mary Grace turned from her friends and stared down the length of her nose at Sarah. "Did Mrs. Dunlap give you the black velvet for my gown? You do work wonders with a needle, even if you're—''

"As a matter of fact, she did,'' Sarah responded, hoping the illustrious Captain Hayes was as well-prepared for the assault of the town's eligible young women as he had been during the war when he had battled British ships.

Jenny's face crinkled into a worried frown. "What about my gown? It's red and blue silk.''

Sarah nodded as visions of the gaudy gown Jenny had ordered flashed through her mind's eye. "It should be ready for a first fitting next week.'' She turned to face Anna. "And yours as well,'' she offered to the least mean-spirited of the three young women.

Anna shivered and pulled her cape tighter as she glanced up at the chalky sky. "I surely hope your aunt left for Danton before this storm started. This is my sister's first baby—''

"Aunt Martha left this morning.''

"Then you'll be all alone for well over a month,'' Mary Grace suggested.

Sarah shifted the load on her back. "I have lots of sewing to occupy my time. Aunt Martha is a midwife. She goes where she's needed.''

"How fortunate for the women she tends,'' Mary Grace retorted, "especially when they're close to home.''

Swallowing hard, Sarah refused to take the younger woman's bait. "I've a long walk ahead of me," she murmured. Without saying a word in her own defense, she stepped around them through snow that was now ankle-deep and made her way to the edge of the forest.

If anything, Sarah had been guilty only of using poor judgment by accepting Webster Chandler's proposal, yet the young women she left behind would have no reason to believe her any more than anyone else in town. After four years, it was pointless to argue against the common assumption that she had given herself to her betrothed, or that her aunt had used her midwifery skills to make sure Sarah's ruin would not result in the birth of a child—all thanks to Webster's shocking betrayal and subsequent chicanery.

When Webster broke their betrothal to marry Olive Boyce only weeks before Sarah's wedding, tongues wagged and singed Sarah's reputation with scandal, although she dared hope the notoriety would be short-lived. Like other women who had suffered a broken betrothal, Sarah had expected to find her friends and neighbors sympathetic. Eventually, she would have survived the social embarrassment and redeemed her reputation.

If only the scandal had ended there.

Unfortunately, Olive Boyce had named Webster the father of her newborn bastard child, and that had prompted their hasty marriage. In the eyes of society, Webster and Olive had redeemed themselves, but scurrilous rumors became solid accusations that Sarah had been just as weak as Olive and had taken Webster into her bed.

Victimized by her own naïveté as well as his charm, she had often been alone with him while her aunt was away. Left vulnerable and helpless when the charges against her expanded to forever brand her as a fallen angel, she had little hope of redemption.

Had Webster been a man of honor, he would have instantly squelched the rumors in town and defended her honor; instead, he had exacerbated the entire situation by adding licentious details that had guaranteed her social ostracism, and that he had used to his own demented advantage.

Thanks to Webster, few believed her virtue remained intact. No respectable man would even consider courting her, and Webster had proven his total lack of conscience by continuing to harass her to this day, hoping to get between her sheets and claim what she had long denied to him.

Troubled by her thoughts, she quickly reached the edge of the woods and turned around. The three young women had already disappeared from view, taking their disdain for Sarah and their dreams and expectations about Captain Hayes with them.

Sarah held no such illusions about the illustrious hero. His anticipated arrival and her exclusion from the town's planned celebration only reinforced her place at the fringes of polite society. Although disheartened, she nevertheless welcomed the windfall she would earn by sewing gowns for the young women who would compete for his favor.

With a heavy heart, she uncovered her lantern and eventually found the snow-draped footpath that led toward the empty cabin that awaited her. She paused and lifted her face to the sky to let the snow fall gently on her cheeks. The storm might have made for difficult traveling tonight, but she no longer had to worry about meeting up with anyone. Not even Webster would risk traveling in this storm, and for the first time in months, she had no fear he would follow her home or simply arrive on her doorstep while her aunt was away.

His body covered with a thin blanket of snow, Captain Thomas Hayes stirred to consciousness. Frozen to his bones, he lay very still and tried to unscramble the events swirling through his mind like the cold winds lashing at him with unrelenting fury. He dragged himself to his knees and saw the blurred vision of blood-drenched snow.

Momentarily troubled by nightmarish memories of sea battles and blood-washed decks, he tried to stand. With his forehead throbbing, he dropped back to his knees until his vision cleared and his memories receded. He vaguely recalled falling and striking his head after attempting to walk alongside his disabled horse after setting out from his new estate for New York, despite warnings about traveling in the storm.

He did not have the strength to return to his estate or to reach Newtown Falls, but he could not remain here on the roadway and wait for another foolish traveler to pass by, either. He had no idea how far his horse might have wandered or where the nearest homestead might be, but he knew he had to find shelter.

When he finally rose to his feet, his legs were shaky, but he managed to keep his balance. Howling winds, frigid air, and total darkness offered little hope he might survive. He was almost ready to concede defeat when he saw a muted flash of light out of the corner of his eye.

His pulse began to race, and he placed a gloved hand at his brow to protect his eyes from the wind as he searched for the light again.

Nothing but darkness.

His heart thudded against his chest. He stared into the dark, swirling mists of snow, again and again, desperate to find the source of the light and the promise of nearby shelter instead of facing the possibility the light had been nothing more than a figment of his desperate imagination.

There! The muted light appeared again, a bit farther to his left than he had thought at first, but it was real and unmistakable. Hope immediately consumed his despair, but he had taken only several shaky steps forward when the light disappeared again, only to reappear moments later. Confused, he worried his fall and the blow to his forehead had somehow distorted his vision until he realized the light was being blocked intermittently by stands of thick-trunked trees.

He stumbled toward the light. He made little progress in getting any closer and finally realized the light was moving, too. Someone else was caught in this storm. Someone who was traveling toward shelter.

He struggled to move faster and caught the fleeting glimpse of an angel carrying a lantern. He immediately dismissed the image as a distortion of reality, an indication he must have hit his head harder than he thought.

Until he saw the image again. With a flowing, hooded robe and snow-covered wings a bit thicker than he had ever seen painted by artists, this angel was quite unlike any he might have imagined. The idea there might be some counterpart in the woods to the sea nymphs who had lured sailors to their deaths was very real, but he had no other choice left to him but to follow the angel and her light.

He entered the woods and hoped he was not making the greatest mistake of his life.

Webster was following her home! In this storm!

Too frozen to tremble, Sarah could not control the anger that surged through her veins any more than she could keep her heart from thumping against the wall of her chest. Several miles back, she had dismissed the sound of a neighing horse as nothing more than howling wind, but she had not been able to get rid of the nagging feeling someone was following her.

Now footsteps. She heard the sound of heavy, trudging footsteps when the wind paused as if to catch a breath before starting again—a warning she did not ignore.

The footpath had long ago disappeared under banks of snow, and she still had more than a mile to go before she reached the safety of her cabin. She dared not extinguish her lantern for fear she would lose her way, but if she hurried, she might arrive home in time to prepare for his arrival.

With a burst of desperation, she hurried her pace. If he was determined enough to follow her home in this storm, it would be difficult to fend off his advances.

But not impossible.

This time when he came pounding at her door, he would meet quite a different woman than the one he expected.

Chapter Two

*I*f she had not been frozen stiff, Sarah would have leaped for joy the moment her cabin came into view. Expending her last ounce of strength, she charged awkwardly toward the cabin and stumbled inside. With her heart pounding, her breath clouded in front of her as she hastily dropped the door latch into place and collapsed back against the door.

She had precious little time to waste. She pushed away from the door and set the lantern down in front of the hearth. Without removing her cape or her wares, she knelt down and stoked the few remaining embers back to life before rebuilding the fire with wood she had stored inside. It would take at least an hour to chase the cold from the single-room cabin. Although it would take much longer for her body to thaw completely, she had to warm up a little before she could take steps to make sure Webster would never bother her again.

Shuddering uncontrollably, more from the fear that veiled her heart than the cold that had invaded her bones, she leaned away from the fire, removed her gloves, and set them alongside the lantern to dry before she opened her cape. The warmth that assaulted her body did little to ease her distress or the thought Webster might arrive within moments and attempt to take advantage of her isolation—with force, if necessary.

She might have discounted her fear as unfounded, save for the memory of his last visit when she had barely escaped with her virtue intact. Her aunt's unexpected arrival back home had thwarted him, but tonight she had only her determination and her wits to save herself.

She held her trembling hands closer to the fire and closed her eyes. This time, she vowed, would be different. No longer willing to spend the rest of her life as his victim, she settled her thoughts on a plan to convince him to leave her alone. Once and for all.

After falling several more times and reopening the gash on his forehead, Thomas finally stopped and leaned against the trunk of a tree for support. The light he had followed, seemingly for hours, had all but disappeared. He scanned the forest again, but saw no trace of light anywhere.

He sagged against the tree. With little sensation left in his body, he grudgingly surrendered and admitted defeat. Weakened from the blow to his head and dispirited by the sight of the blood that splattered the front of his coat, he filled his lungs with long breaths of cold air that numbed his throat.

No more angel. No more hope. Only a lethargic feeling that filled his body as well as his spirit and foretold his impending death. Instead of peace, however, anger filled his very soul and injected a rush of warmth that gave him the strength to push away from the tree to stand on his own.

He refused to die. Not here. Not now.

The sheer ignominy of freezing to death in the woods after surviving the war without suffering a single injury, and on the verge of winning the battle to contain the horrendous realities of war once and for all, fueled his very soul.

And the light returned.

Stronger than before. Brighter. And steadier, flowing through the window of a small cabin nestled in the middle of a clearing only a few hundred yards away.

Sheer relief sent him plowing through the snow toward the cabin. When he fell to his knees and could not stand up again, he crawled. With his strength disappearing with every beat of his heart, he dragged himself forward. Inch by frigid inch, even as the light began to disappear from the window.

He swallowed his pride, but his attempt to cry out for help emerged as nothing more than a strained whisper the wind easily consumed.

The chair Sarah used as a stool tottered, but she still managed to cover the single window in the cabin with the heavy drape she ordinarily used as a privacy curtain around her cot. She stepped down from the chair and carried it back to its place before storing away the hammer.

With visibility limited by the storm, and the indoor light that poured through the window now extinguished from view, Webster would find it more difficult to locate her cabin. At best, she had given herself enough time to prepare before he pounded on her door and tried to force his way inside. This time, she had to make sure he would not want to stay. Or ever come back.

She sat down at her sewing table, picked up the scissors, and put her desperate plan into motion. Battling tears, she had to stop several times because her hands were shaking, but she eventually completed her fateful task. After she cleaned the top of the table with a small hand broom she normally used to clear away bits of thread and fabric, she tossed all evidence of her work into the fire.

Pausing, she took a deep breath and watched the flames reduce her shorn braid, her one claim to beauty, to ashes. If she was right, Webster would now find her far too plain to warrant his interest; if she was wrong, she would have a very long time to regret what she had done.

The cabin was now cozy and warm, and she quickly changed into a dry gown and exchanged her boots for a pair of old leather slippers. Still chilled to her bones, however, she wrapped a shawl around her shoulders and tucked her curls beneath a mobcap before settling herself into the rocking chair in front of the hearth. Exhausted by her journey and apprehensive about the confrontation that loomed ahead, she tried to get a few moments of rest and gather her wits when a sudden pounding at her door announced his arrival.

With her heartbeat racing, she tried to ignore him, but

his repeated pounding at the door sent her heart lurching against the wall of her chest. Her throat tightened. Her breathing grew shallow.

"Go away!" She gripped the arms of her chair and prayed he would.

He pounded again. And again. Though growing weaker, the pounding continued until she nearly exploded with frustration. She knew better than to think he would leave. He would stay and try to break her will since he could not break down her door, a pattern that had become only too familiar over the past four years. Curious because he had yet to call out her name, she got up, pulled the curtain aside, and peeked out the window.

With the swirling snow distorting her view, she could not see him clearly, but he was there, huddled against her cabin with his body pressed against the door as though he barely had the strength left to stand.

Pity overwhelmed her fear and frustration. Although he certainly deserved a dire fate after literally destroying her life, she could scarcely condemn him to remain outside and freeze to death. And he knew it.

She dropped the drape back into place and braced herself for their final confrontation. Anxious to settle the issue of his unwanted advances once and for all, she pulled the shawl tighter across her shoulders as she made her way to the door. She tried not to think about how angry he would be that she had left him out in the storm for so long.

The moment she lifted the latch and opened the door, he lunged at her. With her arms caught beneath her shawl, she toppled backward, and they fell to the floor together.

Stunned by her fall and his violent attack, she gasped for air while pinned beneath his body. "G-get a-away from m-me," she stammered while shoving the length of her body against him. When he rolled aside, she inched away. Once she was safely out of his reach, she pulled herself up into a sitting position. Panting for breath, she leaned aside and closed the door before the cabin filled with snow and cold air eclipsed the warmth she had built inside.

Oddly, he remained motionless, face-down on the floor. Concern sent her pulse racing again, but the sight of smeared blood on her bodice nearly brought her heart to a standstill as she scurried to his side. Half hoping he was only playing yet another twisted, manipulative game, she turned him over onto his back and instinctively clapped her hand to her lips. The man who had been pounding at her door was truly injured, but he was not Webster Chandler!

Shockingly pale, although his cheeks had been chafed by the wind, he lay silent, and his weather-cracked lips were tinged with blue. An ugly gash on his forehead appeared to be the source of the blood that had splattered his coat and smeared her bodice. She carefully inspected the wound by lifting away a lock of his hair. Fresh blood oozed from the wound and ran down the side of his face. Apparently the gash was a recent injury, one he must have reopened when he fell against her.

Mortified that she had kept an innocent man out in the storm, she huddled over his unconscious form and knew she would never have mistaken this man for Webster Chandler if she had been able to see him clearly.

Although wet with melting snow, his garments suggested a man of substance. A traveler, perhaps, who had gotten lost and injured in the storm and sought only shelter in her cabin. When standing up straight, he would be at least a foot taller than Webster. His shoulders were broader, but they did share the same dark-colored hair. Unlike Webster, who was only commonly attractive, this man was unusually handsome. With chiseled features, wide cheeks, and a strong chin that hinted at a man of character, he had creases in the corners of his eyes that told her he was several years older than Webster.

He needed her help, not her curiosity, and she sprang into action. He groaned, but remained unconscious as she dragged him closer to the fire. She pushed the rocking chair out of the way and settled a bed pillow under his head before removing his coat. Rushing about the cabin, she pulled the blankets from both cots and covered him, set a kettle of water to heat, and gathered up her sewing notions and set them on the seat of the rocking chair.

Although she feared he might develop lung congestion or suffer from a very serious head injury, she was more immediately concerned about closing the gash on his forehead. After pouring the warm water into a basin, she used a fresh warm cloth to wipe the blood from his face and neck before cleaning his wound.

Once satisfied with her efforts, she waited for his skin to be completely warmed and pliant before she attempted to sew his wound closed. Her fingers shook as she threaded her needle, but by resting the side of her hand on his brow, she managed to make small, delicate stitches to close the wound.

When she finished, she wrapped a bandage around his head to cover it and washed the blood from her hands. There was little more she could do for him now, although she wished she were strong enough to carry him to the other side of the room and lift him into a bed where he would be more comfortable. Instead, she settled for making him as comfortable as she could on the floor in front of the hearth. She removed his boots and supposed she should have removed his damp trousers as well, but that would take her into territory she had to avoid at all costs.

After adding a fresh log to the hearth, she fixed the covers so his trousers were fully exposed to the heat of the fire and could dry while he slept. She changed her gown once again and curled up in the rocking chair, physically exhausted and emotionally spent. Tormented by regret, she straightened her mobcap, fully aware she had made yet another costly mistake as far as Webster was concerned. She did not relish explaining why she had cut her hair to Aunt Martha when she returned any more than she wanted to answer this stranger's questions when he woke up and demanded to know why she had left him outside in the storm for so long. She tried to think of a reasonable excuse she could offer to him and hoped he would be placated by her efforts to help him now.

She closed her eyes and sighed. The only thing worse than having Webster here was having a man, a virtual stranger, living at her cabin while he recuperated from his ordeal.

Especially one as handsome as this man. She kept her eyes closed and deliberately avoided looking at him for fear she might not be able to control her fascination with him. To no avail. Her mind's eye pictured the color of his eyes and settled on deep brown to match his hair. Imagining the way his lips would shape a smile as his deep voice murmured her name sent her pulse racing.

Stifling a groan of exasperation, she opened her eyes and stared at the herbs drying on the beams just below the ceiling.

For his sake, she hoped he would be well enough to leave in the morning when the storm had abated.

For her sake, he had better be long gone before anyone from town found out he was here. The shame she now carried would be branded anew, and the unfounded rumors about her questionable character might very well ring true.

And this time, the shame would be deserved.

Chapter Three

"*A*ngel."

Though raspy, his voice was deep, and Sarah rocked forward in her chair to find startling pale blue eyes staring back at her. Still half-asleep after only a few hours of rest, she caught her breath and held it for several long heartbeats. He gazed up at her from his sickbed on the floor with a beguiling smile that could snatch a woman's heart away, and dimples deep enough to hide it forever.

Battling physical attraction that covered every pore of her skin with gooseflesh, she left her chair and knelt beside him. "My name is Sarah," she murmured as she tugged his covers back into place. "You've been hurt. I'm here to help you."

"Angel," he repeated as he reached out and gripped her hand.

"Hardly," she muttered, unable to stem the wave of sensations trickling up her arm. His endearing name for her triggered memories of how often the townspeople had called her an angel of quite another sort—a fallen angel. She also knew he would change his opinion of her once he remembered how long he had pounded at her door before she let him into her cabin.

Guilt for prolonging his ordeal made her anxious to admit her mistake. When she tried to pull her hand free so she could think more clearly and fashion an appropriate apology, he tightened his hold and used his other hand to tug at the bandage on his head.

She clasped her free hand atop his to hold it still. "I've stitched your forehead, but if you disturb the bandage, you might rip the wound open. Then I'll have to close it again, and the scar will be worse. Hold still and rest a bit longer while I stoke the fire and heat something for you to drink,'' she urged.

He dropped his hand away and sighed.

Finding it hard not to be mesmerized, she stared into his eyes and saw no sign of fever. Only fatigue. And interest that made her heart skip a beat. For the first time in years, a man was looking at her with neither pity nor disdain, although she had never received such intense scrutiny. Her mind sounded alarm bells that gave her the strength to pull free from him and stand up.

Hopeful that his interest meant a night of rest was all he needed before he could leave, she added another log to the fire before heating a pan of cider. She filled earthen mugs with the steaming amber liquid and tried to think of a way to make sure he did not tell anyone who had helped him or where he had spent the night without revealing her reasons for wanting to keep those facts a secret.

If he had any sense of propriety at all, he would realize how damaging it would be to any unmarried woman's reputation if she spent time alone with a man, even an injured one, and she counted on his possessing some sort of conscience to aid her cause.

When she knelt down beside him and placed the mugs on the floor, he rolled to his side and bent his arm to brace his head as he held his upper body up in a half-sitting position. With his back to the fire, his face was shadowed, but his hand was steady when he took the mug and sipped the cider. ''Thank you,'' he murmured. ''I thought I'd never find shelter.''

''How are you feeling now?''

He drew a deep breath. ''Short of a blinding ache in my head and a chill deep in my bones, I'm fine.''

She turned the mug between her hands and studied the swirling cider as though it held the answer to the questions that gusted in her mind like the winds assaulting the cabin.

"I can't imagine anyone trying to travel through this storm. What happened?"

He responded with a soft chuckle and then finished the last of his cider. "Apparently, only fools and angels were out tonight. Since I'm ready to admit to being a total fool who got stranded in the storm, perhaps you'd like to tell me why you were out, unless that's your mission as an angel. Saving fools."

"I'm not an angel," she sputtered. "I'm a seamstress, and I was returning home after traveling into town to deliver some sewing and pick up orders for more."

He cocked a brow and winced. "You're a seamstress? Here? In the middle of nowhere? Why aren't you living in town?"

Her back stiffened. "I live here with my aunt."

He glanced around the cabin and frowned.

"Aunt Martha is a midwife. She left before the storm hit to travel to Danton. She'll be staying with Abigail Brown who's expecting her first baby very soon."

"So you're here alone. Is that why you were so reluctant to let me in?"

She swallowed her shame. "I apologize. I—I thought you were someone else."

"Really? And you were willing to let that someone freeze—"

"He knows he isn't welcome here," she quipped, disconcerted by how easily he had turned the conversation in her direction without revealing a single bit of information about himself. "Were you heading to Newtown Falls? What happened to your horse?"

He set his mug on the floor, lay back down, and closed his eyes. "I'm traveling to New York. My horse threw a shoe, so I had to walk. That's when I fell, hit my head, and lost consciousness. By the time I woke up, my horse was long gone, and I had little hope I'd survive the walk or into town. Luckily, that's when I first saw your light." He rolled toward the fire and presented her with his back.

"Sorry. Nothing but trouble," he managed between yawns as he struggled to get completely beneath the blankets. With an awkward burst of movement, he tossed the blankets aside and sat up. "No wonder I'm still cold. My trousers are still damp," he grumbled as he began to unbutton them.

Panic sent her scrambling to her feet, and she turned her back as he undressed. "I'm sorry. I couldn't. I mean, I'd hoped the fire would dry them."

His chuckles of amusement turned the warm flush on her cheeks into burning embarrassment when she heard him toss his trousers to the floor.

"I'm perfectly able to undress myself now," he offered, "although I must admit I prefer to have an attractive woman tend to that task for me when I'm not feeling out of sorts."

"Obviously, you're recovering rather quickly and will be able to leave in the morning," she snapped, and headed straight to her cot in the front corner of the cabin. Without any blankets to keep her warm, she settled for wrapping herself in her shawl and crawled into bed.

"You'd be warmer here closer to the fire."

"I'm fine," she insisted, determined he would not know that the interest smoldering in breathtaking blue eyes and a devilish smile was warmer and far more tempting than any fire in the hearth.

She still knew very little about the man who was lying only a few feet away from her, but oddly, she had no fear he would do her any harm, even if he had been in full health. Frustrated that she did not even know his name, she curled into a ball and fell asleep wondering if the devil had transformed himself into this handsome, blue-eyed stranger and had come to claim the fallen angel of Newtown Falls as one of his own.

Long after he heard Sarah's breathing fall into the gentle pattern of sleep, Thomas stared into the fire and watched the flames lick the thick logs into submission. While he could easily use exhaustion and the blow to his head as one reason for his abbreviated explanation of how he had become stranded, nothing could excuse his behavior with the angel-woman who had saved him from certain death.

He was not in port after weeks at sea, and he was not in the city where the women he had met expected him to flirt with them, if only to uphold his reputation as a daring sea captain who had become a national hero.

He muttered under his breath and cursed himself as no better than the social elites he scorned and hoped to leave behind. Perhaps he had been in their midst for so long it was too late to find himself again, but that did not deter his resolve. Or ease his conscience. Or soothe the incessant ache in his heart that drove him to search for a woman who would want him and love him as a man, not a hero to be captured and claimed like a war prize.

He glanced around the small cabin, amazed at how Sarah had transformed a rustic cabin into a comfortable abode. A number of hand-braided rugs decorated the wide-planked floor, and an array of herbs and flowers drying overhead added subtle fragrance as well as gentle beauty to her home. The patchwork cushions and table covers that softened the crudely made furniture and a collection of colorful dried gourds lining the mantel over the hearth testified to her many talents.

She was a gentle, country-bred woman who had earned his gratitude and respect, but he had returned her kindness by deliberately withholding his identity and making cavalier remarks no decent woman deserved. Perhaps he had been too intrigued to find that his angel was indeed human and twice as beautiful as he might have imagined as he followed her through the woods.

With alluring red curls peeking out from beneath her mobcap to frame her face, large, deep-set blue eyes, and a delicate, but well-developed figure, she was a vision he could only describe as exquisite.

Apparently, so did another man, one Sarah did not favor.

To find a woman like her living in this isolated setting where she would be particularly vulnerable to a man's unwanted attentions, even with her aunt present, was more troubling than surprising. Two women alone would make for easy prey, and apparently, someone had made Sarah his target.

Thomas had done little better, although he rather relished the idea of being with her a little longer before he revealed his identity. Instead of avoiding her questions, he should have told her his name and explained his unannounced visit to his estate. But spending time with a woman who had not set her cap to claim him just because of his wealth and his exploits during the war was a temptation he still found hard to resist.

Once she knew she had saved the life of Captain Thomas Hayes, she would probably be like all the others, but he had lost all right to find out if the open interest he saw flaring briefly in her eyes tonight was truly real or only a reflection of his own attraction to her.

After vowing to set things right before making a hasty retreat in the morning, he closed his eyes. For the first time in months, he fell asleep with a smile on his face as the red-haired angel of a woman joined him in his bed and his life . . . if only in his dreams.

Chapter Four

*T*he shrieking winds that had repeatedly battered the cabin and disturbed her sleep continued, even at first light. Sarah did not have to reach up and pull the curtain completely aside to know travel would be impossible anytime soon.

Her unexpected guest would not be leaving this morning as she had hoped last night. Or feared. Her attraction to him was too strong to be denied easily, and she ruefully admitted that the danger to her reputation did not lie with discovery, but within her own commitment to living a moral life. If she faltered, her cabin—her one refuge from scandal—could very well become her final undoing. Unless she extinguished her heated fascination for this stranger, her tattered reputation would soon be singed and reduced to ashes.

Facing the inevitable, she inched out of bed and tugged the drape down from the window. Blinking against the harsh, bright light, she restrung the drape as a privacy curtain, washed her face, and changed into a fresh gown before brushing her hair and plopping a new mobcap on her head. She managed to tuck in the curls that fanned her face without dissolving into tears, snatched an extra dose of courage, and stepped around the curtain into the room.

She found him kneeling at the edge of the hearthstone jabbing the poker into the fire. "I'll tend to that," she insisted as she rushed forward.

He looked up at her and smiled as he set the poker aside. "I've got the wayward log back into place now."

Her heart hammered in an erratic rhythm, and she braced to a halt. How could she possibly survive a full day in this man's presence? She lifted her gaze and studied the bandage wrapped around his forehead to avoid drowning in those captivating dimples. "You must be feeling better," she ventured as she changed direction and went to the far corner of the room to the pantry and set out half a dozen eggs.

He chuckled. "I'm more hungry than anything else."

He was half a room away, but she literally felt his presence as well as his gaze on her back as she cracked the eggs into a wooden bowl. Warm sensations tickled their way up her spine, and she whipped the eggs into a lather of pure froth. He moved toward her. Liquid heat melted her will and simmered in her bones. She whipped faster and drew in short gulps of air.

"Do you need some help?"

Mercy, he was close. Much too close.

"No." She muttered under her breath, took a deep breath, and turned to find him standing mere inches away. "You should be resting," she admonished, praying he would return to his place in front of the fire.

"Not until I've apologized for last night." He captured her gaze and held it with shimmering blue eyes. "I'm sorry I treated you disrespectfully last night, Angel. I intended to leave this morning, but obviously, that's impossible. Since you're going to be forced to endure my company, at least for today, I should introduce myself properly."

His eyes darkened, then flashed pale and clear. "I'm Thomas Hayes, and I'm truly grateful for everything you've done—"

"Thomas Hayes? *Captain* Thomas Hayes?" Her eyes widened, and she reached back to grab hold of the counter for support.

He nodded, and his gaze flickered briefly, even defensively.

"Captain Hayes isn't going to arrive until next month," she argued, as she arched away from him and locked her knees to keep them from shaking.

"Only officially. I've been in the area for the past two weeks inspecting my property, and I was returning to New

York to make the final arrangements for my move here when I got stranded in the storm.''

''Why didn't the townspeople know you were here?''

He clenched his jaw. ''Every man is entitled to privacy. Even a war hero.''

His words were cold and laced with sarcasm she found disconcerting. At best. ''Why didn't you tell me who you were last night?''

His gaze was steady but troubled as he squared his shoulders. ''I won't make any excuses for keeping my identity hidden, but I don't often get the opportunity to spend time with people, let alone a beautiful woman, without wondering if they're interested in me as a man or just fascinated by my reputation.''

She let her breath out slowly. If anyone could understand his motives, it was she. Truth be told, she was as anxious to hide the scandal that surrounded her name as he was to escape recognition. She did, however, have a decided advantage. While her social disgrace was quite local, he was a national war hero who could scarcely hope to find a town or village that would not know of him.

She dropped her gaze and relaxed her hold on the counter. She understood far better than he could imagine why he had decided to move to an isolated estate near a small town instead of remaining in the city. The war hero and the town outcast, both victims of society's whimsical fascination with notoriety of any kind, made for strange companions. But because she was reluctant to diminish herself in his eyes, she claimed the very same right of privacy, that had inspired him to try to keep his visit to Newtown Falls a secret, if only for today.

She moistened her lips and smiled. ''While I'm fixing breakfast, why don't you set two places at the table?''

Company or not, Sarah had work to do and commitments to meet. Jenny, Mary Grace, and Anna expected their gowns to be ready for a first fitting next week and that meant Sarah had little time to spend entertaining her guest. Or woolgathering, in spite of the most intriguing temptation he presented.

By mid-morning, she had a pot of lamb stew simmering over the fire in the hearth and gratefully accepted Thomas's offer to tend the fire while she sewed. She made only one alteration in her work routine. After storing her sewing cloth in a crate on the floor, she moved her worktable away from the outer wall to the middle of the room to avoid drafts of cold air coming through cracks in the logs. She was warmer, but being closer to Thomas only made it more difficult to concentrate or to control the gooseflesh that dimpled her skin when he spoke to her.

Luxurious black velvet draped the scarred wooden table. Accustomed to working with finery she could ill afford, she worked dispassionately and focused on the needed coins she would earn by completing her task. The work had the added benefit of helping her to avoid thinking about Thomas.

She stood to cut the fabric according to pattern under his ever-watchful gaze and answered his questions with no small measure of pride. She had learned to sew at her mother's knee, and she was more than good at her chosen calling. She only wished her parents had survived long enough to see her work, although their deaths when she had only been ten years old did spare them from sharing the scandal she endured as a young woman.

Ready to stitch the low-cut bodice together, she sat down in her chair so she faced the fire as she worked. She realized her mistake the moment she took her seat and looked at him. He sat in the rocking chair at the end of her worktable and she had a full, eye-level view of his face. She lowered her eyes and focused on the finely spaced stitches to avoid meeting his gaze.

Vanity kept her sewing spectacles hidden out of sight in her sewing basket, but until her eyes tired, her vision would be clear and her stitches perfectly made. "Tell me about your property," she suggested, hoping he would fill the lull in their conversation, which up to now had been directed solely at her work.

"A thousand acres of virgin woodland, miles from any-where," he murmured. His voice was relaxed, almost fan-ciful.

"Sounds like heaven . . . er, a haven," she corrected hastily lest he be inspired to call her Angel again.

"I hope so. I had the house built square in the middle of the property on a small rise overlooking the lake. It's serene . . . quiet . . ."

"And private," she offered with a smile, and she could not resist the urge to look up to judge his reaction.

"Very." The chair creaked as he sat forward and stared into the fire. "I'd hoped to live here in peace, undisturbed, but my reputation is proving to be more a curse than a bless-ing, I'm afraid. Even here."

She pricked her finger with the needle and yelped. "Curse? Do you know how many people admire you? We might have lost the war if you hadn't—"

"Their admiration gilds the brutal reality of war," he countered without letting her finish her thought.

She frowned and set her sewing aside. "People are hun-gry for heroes they can admire."

"Or devour," he snapped.

When she flinched, he raked one hand through his hair and sighed. "I'm sorry. I didn't mean to sound bitter or ungrateful. I've spent the better part of the past three years trying to put the war behind me, but everywhere I go, people flock around the man they see as a hero, glamorizing my exploits and the war itself, instead of seeing war as it really is—ugly and inhumane. They glorify death in the name of patriotism, turn ordinary men into idealized heroes, and use it all to their own advantage."

Sarah moistened her lips to keep from arguing against the cynicism that laced his words. The folks in Newtown Falls certainly met the description of the people he had ap-parently met before coming here. Ardeth Dunlap was not the only local shopkeeper benefiting from Captain Hayes's arrival, and Sarah herself had welcomed the opportunity to make extra coin by sewing the gowns for the women attending the reception in his honor. According to Aunt Martha, town officials also had a number of improvement projects under consideration and were counting on their illustrious new resident to influence potential investors to participate.

From her encounter last night on her way home, she also knew it would be hard to find an eligible young woman within forty miles who would not gleefully agree to marry Captain Hayes solely on the basis of his reputation as a hero. There were many others who were simply bursting with pride to have a man like him settle in their midst. "You can't make assumptions about everyone, especially the people who live here," she suggested half-heartedly.

He shook his head. "They'll prove no different from the others. The politicians are the worst, but the merchants aren't much better."

Surprised by his jaded view of people in general, she tucked her understanding of him next to the four years of disappointment she had stored deep in her heart. "So you just intend to turn your back on society and disappear into the wilderness?"

"Not disappear. Stake a claim on something the men who served under my command have been able to enjoy: some sort of normality."

She dismissed the very notion that she had done exactly the same thing by secluding herself here in this isolated cabin and avoiding her accusers. "Serving your country as heroically as you did is something that should make you proud."

"I am," he sputtered, "but I can't call my efforts during the war heroic. Men died at my hand and under my command. Late at night when I close my eyes, I can smell gunpowder and burning flesh. I can see the faces of men in my nightmares. I hear their cries of terror . . . and the whispers of their dying words." He paused and cleared his throat. "If people are so desperate for romanticized heroes, let them find some other poor soul. I've retired. From the sea. From public life. From society."

Stunned, she turned back to her sewing, but her fingers shook too hard to manage a single stitch. That he found his role as a war hero to be as unbearable as the scandal she endured shook the very foundation of her soul. While she sympathized with his frustrations and his disillusionment with society, she rejected the idea his status as a hero would ever be as stifling or as painful as the social ostracism she endured.

"People need you. As a friend and neighbor, as well as a hero," she ventured as she resumed her sewing. "When you attend the reception, you'll see I'm right." She offered him a smile. "You'll even see this gown I'm sewing. Nearly every woman has ordered a new gown or is making one for herself."

He scowled. "And are you making something new for yourself?"

Her hands stilled momentarily, and she felt the blood drain from her face. "I'm . . . I'm not going."

"At least you won't be disappointed."

She snapped her head up and stared at him. "Disappointed? Why would I be disappointed—"

"Because the guest of honor won't be there."

She dropped her sewing and flashed him a frown. "You can't be serious! Everyone is expecting you to be there. You can't change your mind now."

"Why can't I?" he argued.

"Because it wouldn't be fair. Or honorable. You gave your word you'd be there," she insisted.

He shook his head. "I received an invitation through my solicitor that was little more than an announcement of the reception. I don't accept commands for my appearance at any event. Not anymore."

"It sounds as if it's the way you were informed, not the event itself that you find objectionable. How can you be so mired in egoism instead of being grateful for the honors bestowed on you by the public?"

He squared his shoulders. "Obviously, you haven't listened to anything I've said thus far. Attending the reception

will only give townspeople an opportunity to glamorize the
war, again, while the town fathers form a cabal to convince
me to promote local investments that will line their pockets,
and every young woman in attendance will have her cap set
for a hero she's romanticized into her future husband. Tell
me I'm wrong, and I'll reconsider.''

Her gaze softened. ''You're not wrong. Not about a few.
But there are others. Some lost sons or husbands or brothers
during the war or were too old to fight for their country this
time. Others find life so difficult, even ugly at times, they
need an opportunity like this to take pause and celebrate
living. Perhaps you should, too. Meet them, Thomas. Help
them, and then you won't find it so hard to understand that
that's what heroes truly do. They use the courage and
strength forged in the heat of battle to help people face life
as well as death.''

Mesmerized, Thomas gazed at the woman who challenged him like none of the men under his command had
ever dared to do in all his years at sea. Battling his attraction
to her required more self-control than he had needed to out-
wit and outmaneuver the British, but her adamant single-
mindedness was more disconcerting than refreshing.
Touched, but unconvinced by her pleas, even though they
pricked hard at his conscience, he cocked his head. ''But
you're not going to the reception, are you? I'm curious to
know why you have no desire to 'celebrate living' by attending.''

She worried her bottom lip, and her eyes clouded with
misery. ''My reasons are my own, but I still think you
should reconsider and attend. For those who need to meet
a man of honor, to talk to someone who reminds them we
all have a bit of heroism in our spirits when life is hard. Or
unfair.''

He would have attended a thousand receptions to bring
a sparkle back into her dark blue eyes. ''Perhaps I will reconsider and attend . . . on one condition.''

She brightened immediately.

''Let me escort you to the reception. If you accept, I'll

make sure someone else fashions a very special gown for you to wear. White, perhaps. And fit for a very special, if not obstinate, angel."

Her lips trembled and tears added an unnatural shimmer to her eyes, but she struggled to keep them from over-flowing. "I'm afraid I have to decline," she whispered as she rose and disappeared behind her curtain before he could think of something to say to make her change her mind.

Disappointed, he sorted through images and snippets of their conversations to understand her rejection. A troubling thought niggled its way into his soul. She had talked about heroism in a wistful way, as though she needed a bit of courage in her own life. More than mildly curious about her, he was certain of one thing: he was prepared to do battle with whoever or whatever his rival might be to win her admiration, if not her affection. He could think of no better way than to follow the strategy he had used so successfully against opponents during the war: always do the unexpected.

Sarah pulled the covers over her head and burrowed her face into her pillows. Heavy sobs ripped through her body and sliced open the pain stored deep within her heart.

She had no right to challenge him about not attending the reception or isolating himself from society on his estate when she had chosen to live in virtual seclusion instead of fighting to reclaim her reputation. But meeting Thomas and learning he struggled with his renown had given her hope she might find a way to deal better with her soiled reputation. And she wanted others to have the chance to meet him and discover that heroes also struggled through life.

Declining his invitation to the reception had been necessary, but he was bound to find out he had invited a social pariah to be his companion for the event. Telling him the truth about her past now would only make him feel foolish and diminish her in his eyes even more.

As her sobbing eased into gentle weeping, she wrapped her arms around her waist. Whether he believed her shame to be undeserved or not was irrelevant. She could never allow him to risk tarnishing his name by accepting his invitation without telling him the truth, because Webster, among others, would be sure to take the opportunity to humiliate her publicly. Again. In front of the one man who had any chance of claiming her heart as well as her loyalty.

Loneliness, deep and heavy, filled her soul. Regret chilled her spirit. But the sound of footsteps approaching her cot sent her heart racing and thumping out of control.

Chapter Five

When Thomas sat down at the foot of her cot, Sarah gripped a handful of sheets and squeezed her eyes shut. He was not sitting on her cot. That was impossible. No, she must have fallen asleep, and this was nothing more than a dream that was quickly turning into a nightmare especially designed for her. Oh, why couldn't she just wake up?

"Angel? Are you awake? We need to talk."

"Go away. You . . . you shouldn't be sitting here with me. It isn't proper, even if this is a dream and you aren't real."

He chuckled. "I'm afraid I'm very real. And so are you, Sarah. Talk to me. Tell me what I did or said to upset you."

She snuggled deeper into her cocoon of blankets, but there was no escape. This was not a dream. He really was sitting on her cot, and she dared not admit how easy it would be for him to tempt her into his arms.

Her only hope lay in telling him the truth so he would leave, but she needed to apologize for her behavior first. "You didn't say or do anything wrong. I did," she whispered. "How or where you intend to live and whether or not you attend the reception isn't any of my concern. I don't have the right to make you explain—"

"Most people don't have the courage or the good sense to try, but that's not why you're crying, is it?"

"No. Not completely," she murmured. She held her mobcap in place as she emerged from beneath the blankets into darkness softened by argentine moonlight filtering through the window. He caught her gaze and held it. Facing her moment of truth, she tucked her dreams away and prayed she did, indeed, have a bit of courage in her soul. "Even if I wanted to go to the reception with you, I couldn't accept your invitation."

"Are you married? Or betrothed? Is that why you can't go with me?"

She dropped her gaze to avoid seeing the disappointment in his eyes when he learned about her past. "No."

"Then you must not find me suitable as your escort. Is it because I don't live up to your expectations as a hero? Are you so disillusioned with me you wouldn't want to be seen with me?"

She gasped. "No! I'd still be honored to go to the reception with you, but I can't. I'm not welcome there; I'm not considered fit to share polite society anywhere in Newtown Falls."

He cocked his head and reached out to pull a wayward curl completely out from beneath her mobcap and loop it around one of his fingers. "Why wouldn't you be welcome anywhere you'd like to be, Angel?"

Her heart began to race, but she could not back down from telling him the truth now. "I told you before I'm not an angel. If anything, I'm a fallen angel, at least that's what most of the townspeople believe. If they discover we've been here unchaperoned, they'll be certain they were right to condemn me."

"For saving my life?"

"For being alone with you. How that happened won't matter," she insisted. Shockingly distracted by his touch, she pulled back beyond his reach. "If you take me to the reception, they'll wrap your name in scandal, too. Respectable men, especially heroes, don't associate openly with loose women."

He snorted. "A loose woman? *My* angel? You've done nothing improper here with me, and I can't fathom how—"

"They won't believe you. Nothing can change their opinion of me."

He lifted her right hand and laced their fingers together. "Tell me what happened."

Although she was in a far more compromising situation with Thomas than she had ever been with Webster, nothing had ever felt so right. Or so wrong. But she could not move away from him.

Encouraged by the gentle pressure of his hand, she quickly recounted the events leading to the scandal, including her broken betrothal and her subsequent ostracism. He never once interrupted her. When she finished, she looked at him, studied his features, and saw nothing but disbelief.

"So what you're saying is that because the man you were going to marry betrayed you with another woman, a betrayal that resulted in the birth of a bastard child and a forced marriage, people just assumed you also had invited this scoundrel into your bed?"

She nodded.

"That's ludicrous! Did it ever occur to these people he strayed to another woman precisely because you would not give him liberties reserved for marriage?"

"I kept hoping they would, but Aunt Martha travels a great deal, and I was often unchaperoned when Webster came calling. That was my second mistake. I should never have accepted his offer of courtship and marriage in the first place."

He stiffened. "Is he the man you thought was following you back from town last night?"

"Yes."

"But I thought you said he was married now."

She swallowed hard. "He is, but he didn't want to marry Olive. Since no other man will ever ply his suit for my hand, he thinks I should . . ." She hesitated as a warm blush began to steal its way up her neck.

Thomas's eyes crackled with blue fire. "He still expects to share your bed?"

"I've tried to dissuade him, but he keeps sneaking out to the cabin—"

"Then move into town where he won't have the opportunity to seek you out without being noticed."

"It's not that easy," she argued. "I have my aunt to consider. And . . . and . . ."

"And what? I should think you would know moving to town is your only option if you expect to keep him away."

Her spine immediately stiffened. "I'm not a hero like you are. I'm just an ordinary woman. I don't have the courage or the will to face them all, day after day, getting glares every time I show my face and listening to them whisper as I pass by. I can't pretend I don't care when I'm excluded from gatherings, but I can soften the pain by staying here. I'm trying to live here quietly with my aunt until they change their minds about me. I should think you, of all people, might understand the pressures society can exert."

With her heart pounding, she waited for him to respond. To her great surprise, he did the most unexpected thing she could have imagined. He never said a word. He just tilted up her chin and kissed her.

Once. Then again. Gently and tenderly, offering only the promise of a great and glorious passion they might one day share together.

"Sweet, precious Angel," he whispered and rained soft kisses across her cheeks.

Her heart soared, but reality clipped the wings of her joy and sent her hopes and dreams plummeting back to earth. They had no future together, just this moment, and she desired him with her body as well as her soul in a way she had not experienced with Webster or any other man. She finally understood the inherent dangers of being unmarried and alone with a man she wanted beyond all reason.

Truly afraid she might dishonor her love for him by becoming the wanton woman others had judged her to be, she pressed one final kiss to his lips before she cradled his face with her hands. "Thomas, I can't . . . we can't . . ."

With passion-glazed eyes, he caressed her. "Sarah . . ."

"Please, Thomas. You have to go."

He traced her lips with his fingertips before he eased from the cot and tucked the covers tightly around her. "Sleep well, Sarah. We'll talk more about this tomorrow. In the meantime, I suppose there's firewood that needs to be brought inside.''

"F-firewood? Now? At this hour?''

He knelt down on one knee and kissed the tip of her nose. "Unless you have an indoor waterfall I can use, it's going to take at least an hour outside in the blizzard to cool the fire to claim you that's burning in my body. Go to sleep,'' he murmured and quickly left.

When the door to the cabin eventually opened and closed behind him, she was still awake. She was unable to find sleep and fretted because she knew once desire no longer clouded his judgment, he would realize they had no future together, only memories destined to remain forever bittersweet.

By the next morning, the blizzard outside finally showed signs of weakening, but the storm brewing inside the cabin threatened to be far more dangerous.

Sarah had to be creative to make the best use of her dwindling food supplies, but completely avoiding Thomas in a one-room cabin as he came to terms with her past required heavenly capabilities well beyond her means.

Reduced to wearing her sewing spectacles to accommodate her tear-strained eyes, she kept her hands busy stitching the rest of Mary Grace's skirt together and joining it to the bodice. Thomas made a virtual mission out of drying and rearranging the firewood he had hauled inside during the previous night. Judging by the sheer number of logs, she doubted there could be more than half a dozen left in the lean-to.

As she worked a million thoughts zigzagged through her mind. Every one of them centered on Thomas and the kisses she longed to taste once more.

When he picked up her broom and began to sweep the floor, she paused, glanced up over the rim of her spectacles, and shook her head. "What on earth are you doing now?''

"I'm thinking.''

"With a broom?"

He shrugged his shoulders. "Anything will do. You seem reluctant to continue our discussion, so I thought I'd try to clean up the mess I tracked in during the night."

"I'm sorry. I have commitments to meet. We . . . we can talk now if you like. I'll sweep the floor later," she suggested. Chagrined that he had seen through her efforts to appear thoroughly engrossed in her work, she hoped he might be gallant enough to reject her offer.

Without any hesitation, however, he leaned the broom against the outer wall. The devilish half-grin he wore as he approached her scattered her hopes as well as every decent thought in her head. Her heart skipped a beat, and when her hands began to tremble, she inadvertently jabbed her sewing needle into the palm of her hand. With a screeching yelp, she flinched. Her mother's thimble flew into the air and bounced back against the tabletop. With disbelieving eyes, she watched the thimble fall to the floor, ricochet against one of the table legs, and roll dangerously toward the hearth. As Thomas rushed toward her, she leaped up from her chair, scrambled beneath the table, and snatched the thimble scarcely in time to save it from reaching the fire. Heart pounding, she gripped the thimble in her fist as Thomas helped her to her feet.

"Are you all right?"

Flustered by the spectacle she had made of herself, she nodded and quickly rearranged her disheveled gown. "I pricked my hand, and my mother's thimble went flying and was rolling toward the fire," she gushed. She opened her fist to show him the thimble, but he was staring at her so intently she nearly forgot to breathe.

Without saying a word, he bent down as if to retrieve something from the floor and placed her mobcap into her hand.

"You knocked off your cap," he murmured.

Sarah stared at the mobcap. Dread churned in the pit of her stomach, bringing a warm blush to her cheeks. There was only one man she would ever want to find her beautiful, to see her as captivating, both in soul and body, and he was here, only inches away from her, gazing at her uncovered head. Alhough she had already ruined any chance of keeping his interest, now that he had seen how short she had cut her hair, he had another reason to turn away from her.

His gaze rendered her nearly immobile. Self-conscious beyond belief, she quickly donned her mobcap and tucked in her short curls. "Now you've seen with your own eyes what a foolish woman I am," she whispered.

"Foolish?"

"When I thought Webster had followed me home, I didn't know what else to do. He's so fascinated by my hair, I thought if I cut off my braid and burned it, he wouldn't . . . wouldn't want to . . ."

"He'd lose interest. Is that what you thought?"

She nodded and swallowed the lump in her throat. When Thomas came closer to her, she took a step away from him, and then another, until she had backed her way up against the worktable. With her legs turning to jelly and her heart skipping every other beat, she dropped her gaze and stared at the wall of his chest.

Thomas held perfectly still. He could not control the erratic pounding of his heart any more than he could deny his love for the angel-woman standing before him. She claimed his allegiance as well as his heart and stoked the fire of his passion as no other woman had ever done.

However much he disagreed with the tight boundaries society imposed in the name of propriety, he did not underestimate the level of social disapproval she had endured. He also carried burdens imposed by a society that claimed heroes as public institutions. While she had found some measure of peace in her isolation, she could not live here for the rest of her life.

Refusing to consider how he had set his own life on a similar course, he focused on her ability to persevere and hold steady to her chosen path to redemption, even after all these years. Admiration stirred the love in his heart and inspired an urge to protect her by using his status in society.

"You're right, Angel. Cutting your hair was foolish. Desperate and brave, but so very foolish," he admonished in a soft whisper. He removed her spectacles and laid them on the worktable before he gently lifted the mobcap from her head. Copper curls cascaded to the top of her shoulders and took his breath away. "I find you beautiful and totally fascinating just as you are. I need no braid of hair wrapped around your head to tempt me any more than I need society's approval to find you remarkable."

He gazed deep into her eyes and cradled the side of her face with his hand. "You are an angel with a golden heart. My angel," he murmured and captured her lips in a kiss.

Though unschooled, her lips were warm and yielding as he pressed her body closer. His kisses, at first gentle, grew hungry and more insistent, and his body demanded more than he had any right to claim.

Unwilling to take advantage of her innocence and dishonor her virtue, he needed no ordinary measure of self-control to set her away from him. "Let me repay your kindness by helping you restore your name," he suggested.

Her bottom lip trembled. "Help me? How?"

He shrugged his shoulders. "You said heroes should help people. That's what I'm offering to do. Accompany me to the reception. No one would dare speak out against you with me by your side."

She shook her head. "Even if I thought you were right, which you aren't, I couldn't let you take that chance. You don't know the townspeople here. They won't just forget everything that's happened and accept me just because you—"

"Yes they would," Thomas insisted. "They'll be so consumed by self-interest, they won't hesitate to do anything I ask or expect."

Surprise danced in her eyes. "Then you've reconsidered your plans to seclude yourself on your estate?"

"I didn't say that," he countered. "I said I would help you, not change my plans about how I intend to spend the rest of my life.'' When he reached out to pull her back into his embrace, she arched away from him.

''You'd use the townspeople to help me, then turn away? That's dishonorable. And it's beneath you.''

''It's expedient and necessary. I'm anxious to repay my debt to you for saving my life. Nothing more. I gave my country three years of my life during the war and all the years since then. Whatever my debt to society may have been, it's been paid in full.''

Sarah shook her head. ''Deliberately avoiding people is wrong. Our obligations to one another in this world never end.''

''How can you say that when you've hidden yourself away in this cabin for the past four years? What you've done with your life since the scandal is precisely what I intend to do on my estate: live far from the clutches of a society that is as demanding as it is judgmental.''

''That's not the same thing at all. I've stayed here hoping time would prove my detractors wrong.''

''Usually, it's only the guilty who hide from their detractors,'' he charged. ''The innocent fight for what is right. Don't let them control your life. If you attend the reception with me, I'll help you to prove them all wrong.''

Hurt flashed through her eyes like lightning ripping through a dark summer sky. ''No. I won't let you use me to get back at the society you seem to hold with such contempt,'' she whispered before she slipped away and disappeared behind her curtain. This time, he did not follow, even after he realized she had taken his heart with her.

Chapter Six

*B*y morning, gentle silence blanketed the snow-white landscape glistening under a bright sun nestled in a sky of clear blue. In stark contrast, the cacophony of Thomas's final words to her last night followed Sarah from her troubled dreams into the full nightmare of day.

While Thomas tested out her snowshoes one last time, she studied his features from her place at her worktable. Three days of stubble darkened his face. With his bandage now removed, a garish row of black stitches etched his forehead. He looked every bit the rakish privateer-turned-hero, but it was the stubborn set of his lips and the determination in his eyes that marked him as a man who rarely, if ever, changed course.

After he walked out her door today, they would part forever, and there was nothing she could do to change that painful reality. When he finally approached her, she braced herself for their final good-bye.

His expression was grim as he took a deep breath. "Once I return to my estate, I'll see that your pantry is restocked and you're compensated—"

"That won't be necessary," she insisted, silencing the whispers of her heart that cried out for love and understanding, and another chance to convince him he was making a mistake by retreating from the world that needed him as much as she did. "I only ask that you keep your stay here a secret. I have scandal enough without adding more."

He nodded. "Obviously, you'll have little opportunity to discuss my misadventure, but I would appreciate your discretion about my plans for the future."

His ice-blue gaze held steady, then cracked with anguish. Longing reached across the gulf of misunderstanding separating their hearts and joined them together for one brief but glorious moment. It carried her back to the first night they met, and completely mesmerized, she nearly forgot to breathe. But the magic of the moment lasted only a heartbeat—just long enough to etch his next words on her heart.

"Good-bye, Angel," he whispered. "Don't be disappointed. Perhaps not all fools were meant to be saved. Even from themselves."

He turned and slipped out the door, leaving behind a heavy ache in her heart and a lump in her throat. Her spirit cried out for him to turn back, to take her into his arms, but he did not.

Heart-weary, she eyed the sewing that awaited her. It held little appeal, but she had nothing else to distract her from the unbearable pain that crisscrossed her chest. She had scarcely run the thread through the eye of her needle when there was a knock at the door. Thomas! Her heart raced ahead of her feet as she rushed to the door, but heady joy turned to horror the instant she opened the door.

"Webster?"

He stared back at her, his features distorted by a mask of anger. "You expected someone else?" he snapped.

"No. I—I—"

"I saw that man leave, and if I'd been a few minutes sooner, I'd have seen more than just his back. Who is he, Sarah? Your lover, or just one of many men you entertain out here in the middle of nowhere while proclaiming your virtue?" he charged as he pushed his way into the cabin.

With her heart pounding, Sarah turned and faced him. "How dare you make unconscionable accusations against me!" She held the door open and pointed to his sleigh. "Get out. And don't ever come back."

"Is this how you repay my kindness? By consorting with another man when I'm the one who truly loves you?"

"Kindness? Love? You can't be serious. It wasn't kindness when you betrayed me with another woman and then refused to clear my name when others believed I had given you my virtue, and it isn't love that keeps you coming here. Now leave."

He glared at her. "Why should I? Obviously, you're more than willing to share your precious charms with at least one other man. Perhaps you expect coins for your favor. Is that what you want?" he spat, stalking toward her as she closed the door and backed away from him.

"I want you to leave."

"Not until you give me what I've been waiting for all these years."

When she felt her worktable at her back, she grabbed blindly for her sewing shears, but knocked them to the floor near the hearth. With her wits as her only defense, she squared her shoulders and held her head high. "What I do here in my cabin is none of your concern. Not now. Not ever again. The man who left was only a traveler stranded in the blizzard. I offered him shelter, nothing more."

His eyes widened. "You spent days with him here? Alone?"

"What would you have had me do? Let him freeze to death outside for the sake of propriety?"

"Being alone for days with a man is most unwise for any unmarried woman, as you well know, and you've finally proven your reputation is well-deserved."

Her chest heaving, she barely paused to take a deep breath of air. "As you've done with your own? I should think you'll find it awkward to explain why you came to my cabin today if you try to tell anyone what you saw."

He snorted. "I came here to make sure you survived your walk home in the blizzard. Mrs. Dunlap was most concerned about you, although I daresay she was not overjoyed when I offered to set her concerns to rest." The anger in his gaze changed to dark passion that turned her blood to ice. "Now take off your cap and unpin your hair for me as you used to do."

She hesitated for less than a heartbeat before she complied with his demand, and he reacted exactly as she had anticipated when she had cut her hair. His eyes opened wide, and his lips twitched. "W-what have you done?"

She shrugged her shoulders. "I should think that would be obvious."

"You cut off your hair? To spite me?" He raked a disdainful gaze over her face and form. "I suppose I could forgive you for ruining your looks if you take me to your bed," he suggested. "If not, I'll spread such sordid tales about you and your mystery guest that it will be impossible for you to show your face within a hundred miles."

"You hateful, spiteful—"

"Make up your mind, Sarah. Quickly, if you please."

"I please only myself," she spat. "And I will not take you to my bed. Not now. Not ever."

"So be it," he murmured. "So be it."

Thomas paused at the shore of the snow-covered lake and looked up at the house sitting atop the rise. As grand as his scheme to create a world of his own, the stone mansion stood stiff and immutable against a backdrop of endless sky. Only days ago when he had been stranded in the storm, he thought this house might remain as a testimony to his foolhardiness, but he had survived, only to find the vision of his future here shadowed and his heart burdened with doubt.

A wisp of smoke danced toward the heavens and drew his gaze upward to the land of angels, but his thoughts centered only on the red-haired woman who had saved his life. She had stolen her way into his dreams, replacing his nightmares with visions of wonder that tempted his very soul, and challenged his plans to reclaim his life. He should have known he was bound to be disappointed and ought to have left her cabin on that first day, storm or no storm.

"I should have done a lot of things," he grumbled. Shivering with cold, he dismissed his troubled thoughts and set off toward the house. Other than explaining his mishap, he would not have to reveal more than he cared to the small staff assembled inside. Like the crew that once served him, they respected his authority as their employer.

Unlike a certain strong-willed young lady, they dared not question his decisions, and he had worked too hard to build his dream estate to let her change his mind and alter the course he had set for himself. Especially a woman who spoke so eloquently of heroism and his responsibilities, yet hid herself away in the wilderness instead of fighting openly to reclaim her good name.

Anxious to get a new mount and return to New York to make the final arrangements for his move here, he trekked up the snow-covered rise. He was shadowed by the bittersweet realization that once upon a wintry day, he had met the angel of his dreams, only to discover she was merely a mortal woman like all the others. But this time was different. This time, he had lost far more than his pride or his dignity.

He had lost his heart.

During his long walk back to his estate, it was love that gave him a new perspective and allowed him to see her arguments for refusing his offer as naïve and idealistic rather than a ploy designed to force him to reconsider and alter his plans for the future. For a woman scorned by society, she was awfully stubborn and quick to defend her accusers, but the closer he got to his new home, the more optimistic he became. With luck, he might yet change her mind about attending the reception and accepting his help, and he dared to hope they might have a future together.

He had a lot to accomplish in the next month and quickly devised a plan to keep her occupied with thoughts only of him. Although she had refused any compensation for the help she had given to him, she would not turn down honest work. He had quite of list of things he would need her to stitch to turn the house into a home, and his housekeeper would be only too glad to relinquish those duties.

He grinned and took a deep breath of cold air. By the time he returned from New York, she would see he was right and change her mind. The very thought quickened his step and lifted his spirits as high as the heavens—the only place to keep safe the dreams of angels and fools.

Chapter Seven

*T*he three gowns were finally ready for a first fitting and packed together in the canvas bundle. Her harness for carrying the bundle lay ready next to her cape and boots. The winter sun was unusually brilliant and warm, melting away the last remnants of snow as efficiently as the flames licking the logs in the hearth, but the only thing keeping Sarah from delivering her work right now was her stubborn pride.

And fear, she admitted, as she plopped into the chair in front of the hearth and set herself rocking. Thomas had left nearly a week ago. With her aunt still away, Sarah had only herself and the ghosts of memories of her moments with Thomas and her encounter with Webster for companions.

With a spotlessly clean cabin and a completely bare pantry that precluded making anything for her midday meal, she had nothing to do now but wait for nightfall and battle the inner war that had been raging ever since Thomas uttered the words that challenged her very existence. Was he right about only the innocent having the courage to challenge detractors? In spite of her best intentions, had she fueled certainty about her guilt by secluding herself in this cabin?

Webster's threat only added to her inner turmoil. She had no doubt he had spread tales about her and the mystery man who had spent the blizzard in her cabin, making her his victim yet again.

With any hope for her social redemption now destroyed, resentment troubled her spirit. Thomas's offer to her to challenge society by attending the reception with him never seemed so tempting, or so wrong. She rocked in her chair as anger at her accusers flared, but her decision to refuse Thomas's proposal remained firm. She had lost her reputation on her own, and if she had any chance of reclaiming it as well as her self-respect, she must do it by herself.

She rocked harder and faster until she nearly became dizzy and braced to a halt. Breathing heavily, she stared into the fire, listened to the echo of her arguments with Thomas, and faced the bitter truth. She was angry and resentful, but not at others. Only herself.

She had no right to judge Thomas or to implore him to take his place in society, when she had refused to defend herself against the town gossips. Avoiding her tormentors for four years had done nothing to change their minds and persuade them she was a moral woman and perhaps had encouraged Webster to continue his pursuit. Instead of remaining in town and proving her innocence, each and every day, with courage, she *had* hidden herself away like a penitent sinner. She had waited for others to forgive her when she had yet to forgive herself for opening the door to social condemnation by allowing Webster to be alone with her during their betrothal.

She bowed her head, faced her mistakes, and accepted responsibility for her life as well as her future. It was far too late to hope she might one day share the love in her heart with Thomas, but she would not waste another day on self-pity or delusion, protected from her accusers both by distance and the shadows of night.

If she ever hoped to redeem her reputation, she must do so with her head held high in the bright light of day. Thomas would be her guide and inspiration. Her love for him would give her the strength to reach deep within to find the courage to go on, just as he had done during the war. She would face down her accusers now in hopes that justice, if not inner peace, would be her ultimate reward, and pray Thomas would one day do the same and rejoin the society he so scorned.

When shadows fell each night, she would shed private tears, but only for the love she had found and would never claim.

* * *

Conversation ceased the moment Sarah stepped into Ardeth's shop. Stares turned to glares, and the two women patrons stiffened their backs. She looked around the shop hoping Ardeth would give her a friendly greeting, but her friend was apparently in the back room securing finished work.

Sarah swallowed hard, and closed the door behind her. "I'll just leave these gowns in the back," she murmured and passed Eleanor Fenwick and Julia Meadows to reach the back room.

Eleanor sniffed. "I'm not surprised you survived the blizzard. According to all accounts, you had a splendid time entertaining your newest lover, but to show up here where respectable women shop is disgraceful and shocking."

Sarah paused and held her head high. "I have business here, and I did my Christian duty to help a stranded traveler, nothing more."

"You were alone for days with a man without a chaperone, yet you stroll in here as if you did nothing wrong." Julia shook her head. "I should think a woman with your scandalous reputation would already understand—"

"What I know now is that I can't control your thoughts or your opinions about what might have occurred during the blizzard any more than I can change your mind about what happened during my betrothal to Webster. In my heart, I know the truth, and you might ask yourselves why Webster was so quick to spread new tales about me. He wouldn't have done that if I had given in to his demands to take him to my bed. I refused him, just as I refused him any liberties when we were to be married."

"Webster is a fine man who did his duty and restored his name as well as Olive's. He went to your cabin to make sure you had returned home safely out of Christian concern. You've no right to tarnish his name or his intentions."

"You're right. Perhaps you should ask him why he's repeatedly come to my cabin these past four years to harass me when all I wanted was to live there in peace with my aunt."

"Webster is a married man now."

"That may be, but what I tell you is true. I don't expect you to give my aunt's words any credence, even though she's as honest a woman as you'll find in this town, but she would tell you I'm speaking the truth. Instead, just ask Webster," she repeated.

"Why have you suddenly become so bold and brazen? Are you trying to wreak vengeance on a man because he once betrayed you with another, when in truth you should be held accountable for your own licentious behavior?"

"I have no such motive. I've simply grown tired of being falsely accused. I've stayed away hoping you would all forgive me for making nothing more than a mistake in judgment where Webster was concerned, but I was wrong. As for the traveler, he knows the truth, which is all that matters to me."

"How convenient," Julia snapped. "I don't suppose you have the name of this . . . this traveler? It might be very interesting to listen to his side, although it would take a remarkable man to resist someone with your appetite for pleasures of the flesh."

The woman's angry words stung and Sarah blinked back tears. "On that account, you're right. He is a remarkable man, but he won't be returning to defend my honor or my reputation. I'll have to do that on my own. Now if you'll excuse me, I have work to deliver to Mrs. Dunlap, and a stop to make at the general store so I can return home before dark."

Relieved to have taken her first step back into society, she made her way to the back room to find Ardeth. Although the encounters she would have with other townspeople were bound to be just as unsettling, she had no other choice but to be true to herself, if only to bring honor to her love for Thomas. She prayed he would do the same and change his plans for the future—a future in which she would play no role other than loving him from afar.

*   *   *

Sarah followed the main road home and cut through the woods with only a quarter of a mile to go. The straps of the harness cut deep into her shoulders, but her steps were quick and light.

After her encounter with Eleanor and Julia, she had replenished her foodstuffs at the general store. She had left town without once lowering her gaze or sidestepping to avoid the townspeople who glared at her, an accomplishment she kept foremost in her mind.

As soon as the cabin came into view, she spied two trunks sitting in front of her door. Curious, yet half-afraid Thomas had sent her something to repay her for helping him, she hurried forward and managed to drag the heavy trunks inside without giving in to the urge to open them immediately.

She slipped out of her harness, knelt down to lift one trunk lid, and found a note resting atop a mound of brocaded fabric. Her fingers shook as she read the note once, and then again, as her heart sank into disappointment.

While I am in New York, I hope you will be able to turn this fabric into draperies according to the dimensions provided by my housekeeper, who is already overburdened by preparations for my move to Newtown Falls next month.

As you work, I hope you will reconsider your decision not to attend the reception. I pray you might yet change your mind.

Faithfully yours,
Thomas

Tears of disappointment welled, but she blinked them away. She had no way to return the trunks any more than she had a whisper of a hope left he would change his future plans.

She lifted the heavy fabric from the trunk and fingered the luxurious brocade. It was a stunning blend of colors that resembled a fractured rainbow caught forever in threads spun with gold.

Dismayed by his request that she would change her mind and attend the reception, she set the fabric aside and stored her foodstuffs in the pantry. It would be difficult to spend the next few weeks turning fabric into draperies for a home she would never get to share with him, but the work might help to deaden the pain as she contemplated spending the rest of her life without him.

Chapter Eight

Knowing his days as a public figure were numbered made it easier for Thomas to accept the pressures on his time in New York, and he met his previously scheduled obligations with a sense of excitement he found hard to contain.

On the eve of his scheduled departure for Newtown Falls, he attended one last soirée as the guest of honor. Starting tomorrow, he would be free. Unfortunately, he had yet to find a way to avoid looking at himself in the mirror when he shaved so that he would not see the scar across his forehead that reminded him of Sarah. Others, however, thought the scar was a battle wound. He was loath to tell them otherwise, even though he had little fear the gossip would travel as far as Newtown Falls. Experience had taught him to be cautious, especially about his private life.

The candlelit ballroom was a blur of muted colors mixed with myriad heavy scents that competed with the sound of the orchestra and the general gaiety for attention. But Thomas's thoughts were far away in a quiet little cabin in the woods with the woman who had claimed his heart. For a brief moment he wished she were here, dressed in a fine ballgown. He wished he held her tight in his arms, instead of the vapid creature whose father had proposed a matrimonial alliance that would make Thomas twice as wealthy as he already was.

He might have found the whole scenario bearable if he could share it with Sarah. Maybe then she would have understood how sorely he wanted to find a permanent haven far away from here. Once he settled onto his estate, his public days would be over, and there was only one woman he wanted to share his world—a woman he might never claim as his own.

Distracted, he remained completely oblivious to his surroundings until his companion alerted him to a disturbance at the far end of the ballroom.

"How dreary," she mumbled, her wide lips shaping a pout he found less than amusing, as he led her from the dance floor and delivered her back to her father. "Perhaps I should see what this is all about. You'll be safer here with your father. If you'll both excuse me."

He turned before they could offer an argument. Assuming the disturbance had little to do with him personally, he took his time to work his way through the crowd. But a fleeting glimpse of curly red hair sent him racing toward the entrance.

One full glimpse of a red-haired ragamuffin settled Thomas's pounding heartbeat, but when a brute started to drag the lad away Thomas rushed forward to intervene. When he broke the man's grip and pulled the young boy free, he got several quick kicks in the shin as a reward. "That's enough," he barked and pinned the boy against him. "Kick me again, and I'll throttle you myself."

"Let me go! I gotta find the captain. Where's Captain Hayes? He's the only one—"

"I'm Captain Hayes."

When the boy looked back up at him with a shocked, yet unrepentant expression that held no small measure of hero worship, Thomas held back a chuckle. "Speak your mind, son, before I change mine and turn you back over to this fellow."

The boy scowled at the man who had been dragging him out of the ballroom and attempted to straighten his puny shoulders. "Name's Paul Ratton, same as my pa. He said you wouldn't help, but I told him you would. You fought hard against the British. Didn't think you'd back away from a little fight like this one."

Recognizing the name of a man who had once served under his command, Thomas nodded, curious about the lad's

mission and his willingness to fight half the men in attendance to fulfill it. "Go on."

"It's private, sir, and none of anyone's concern," he
spat, glaring at the men who had surrounded them.

"The lad's a street urchin looking for a handout. I'll take
care of him for you, Captain."

"Don't trouble yourself, Captain. The boy's not worth
your time."

Thomas met the men's glares with one of his own.
"Since the lad went to all this trouble to find me, I think I
owe him a moment. Excuse us, gentlemen." With one hand
on the boy's shoulder, he led him past the sea of shocked
elites to a private, glass-enclosed balcony and closed the
door behind them.

Paul visibly trembled, but held his ground. "I didn't
mean no disrespect. Didn't know it was you I was kickin',
but I been outside for hours tryin' to slip inside to find you."

Thomas cocked his head. "Then this must be important."

Paul swiped at his tear-stained cheeks, smearing the dirt
that covered them. "The guard outside didn't seem to care,
but I knew you'd help if could find you."

"I didn't say I'd help. I said I'd listen."

And he did, paying close attention to every sad detail
that poured out of the boy's mouth.

"Pa said you wouldn't remember him, but I told him
heroes like you don't never forget a friend. And you weren't
too busy to help, neither. That's what heroes do. They help
people."

Thomas stared at the boy, wondering if Sarah had transformed herself yet again into a small boy whose words
tugged at his conscience and his decision to abandon the
society that looked to him as a hero.

"Heroes are just men. Ordinary men," he murmured,
humbled by the boy's admiration when he was mere hours
away from turning his back on what fate, not design, had
planned for his life. Sarah's words echoed through his mind,
but this time, they rang so true he almost trembled.

And he quickly formulated a plan to redeem himself in her eyes.

Hoping he still had time to alter the course of his life and still claim the woman of his dreams, he looked at the boy and smiled. "How far away did you say you and your pa lived?"

"A day's ride, but I walked. Took longer. We could ride back together this time," Paul suggested.

Thomas took a deep breath. Taking the time to help the lad's father make it difficult, but not impossible to journey back to Newtown Falls in time for the reception. But by the time he arrived, he would have very different plans for the rest of his life, not the least of which included winning the love and respect of one very special woman and using his position honorably to redeem her reputation and claim her, one day, as his own.

After successfully resolving Paul Ratton's financial difficulties by settling his debts and hiring him to work on the estate to pay off a promissory note, arranging for a surprise for Sarah, and then battling his way through another snowstorm, Thomas arrived in Newtown Falls only one day before the welcoming reception.

Although his fame always preceded him wherever he traveled, he was as yet unknown and able to stop in town without fear of being recognized.

He entered the general store, selected a pair of snowshoes, and paid in coin. Other than a few blank glances, he garnered little attention since the few other patrons were gathered at the front window. Curious, he joined the small crowd and froze the moment he saw Sarah walking down the planked sidewalk on the other side of the street in the full light of day with her head held high and her steps sure and steady.

"Common hussy," one of the women exclaimed. "The nerve! She's acting as if she were a moral woman when we all know the truth of the matter now. I don't believe what she told Eleanor about the so-called traveler she nursed back to health. Not for a minute. Webster has no good reason to lie. He discovered the truth and saw the man leave with his own eyes.''

Another woman also nearing the high side of sixty shook her head in dismay. ''Poor Martha. What a cross to bear. You'd think she'd keep that girl out to the cabin instead of letting her cavort through town with decent folks, but she's just not home enough, if you ask me. I may be old, but I know men. There isn't a one of them could keep his hands to himself for three days alone with that one. Might have been a traveler, though, like she said.''

''Or a saint. I'm surprised he didn't head straight for the tavern to brag about his luck being stranded with her.''

Thomas felt the hackles rise on his neck, but held silent as the third woman entered the conversation. ''Pity, isn't it? Such a sweet girl she was before—''

''Forbidden fruit is always the sweetest and the first to ripen and spoil. Martha should have married that young woman off long before Webster came along.''

''Well, she didn't, and you can't blame Martha. It's Sarah's lack of character that led to her downfall just as surely as it was Webster's that led him to do right and marry Olive.''

''Maybe the woman's innocent,'' he offered.

The three women spun around together like puppets set into motion. ''And you might be . . . ?'' one asked, her gaze flashing with indignation.

He tipped his hat. ''Just a stranger passing through town.''

''Then perhaps you'd best be leaving instead of meddling in affairs that don't concern you.''

''My intention, dear ladies, was not to meddle, but to offer a simple observation. It's usually the innocent who have the courage to face down their accusers, not the guilty. Forgive my intrusion,'' he murmured and hurried outside to find Sarah.

He looked up and down the street, but she had disappeared from view. Heartened by her demonstration of courage, his own hopes for tomorrow night's reception soared.

Chapter Nine

Sarah's trip to town yesterday had only deepened her disappointment. Since Thomas had not notified the town officials he would not be attending the reception, she was certain he had not changed his plans about retiring to seclusion on his estate. Aunt Martha had been detained in Danton indefinitely to help Anna's sister with the unexpected arrival of twins, so Sarah was still alone. She stirred the kettle of barley soup simmering on the hearth, before donning her cape and going outside to gather enough firewood to last the night.

She filled her arms and was halfway to the cabin door when a horse-drawn sleigh decorated with bells and ribbons and laden with packages entered the clearing in front of the cabin. Strangers occasionally appeared asking for Aunt Martha's help, and she assumed whoever needed a midwife was unaware Aunt Martha had not returned, although this could simply be a traveler who had lost his way.

The driver, an older gent with a crop of gray hair as long as the beard that trickled halfway down his chest, brought the horses to a halt and tipped his hat. "Might you be Miss Sarah Bailey?"

Stunned because he asked for her, and by name; instead of her aunt, she nodded.

"I've got a message for you, darlin', but first let me take that armload of firewood inside for you." He looped the reins around the brake, climbed down from his seat, and took the load of wood from her arms. He followed her inside and stacked the wood near the hearth before he pulled a folded paper from inside his coat pocket. "Name's Hawthorne. I have a message for you from the captain,'' he explained as he handed her a folded paper. "If you'll pardon me a moment, I'll be right back."

Her heart pounding, Sarah ran her fingers over the familiar scrawl on the outside of Thomas's note. Did he think he could use gifts instead of honest work to make her change her mind? What about the reception tonight? Didn't he have any concern for the townspeople who were preparing for a reception only hours away, and would be sorely disappointed when Thomas failed to appear?

"Where'd you like me to put this?"

When she glanced up, Hawthorne stood just inside the door with his arms filled with so many packages that his face was obscured. "What on earth are you doing?"

He chuckled. "Just followin' orders. Now where would you like me to stack these?"

"Put them back into the sleigh."

He poked his head around the packages and crinkled his brow. "Now I can't rightly do that, miss. The captain told me to make sure I delivered his gifts and didn't—"

"The captain has overstepped himself," she sniffed. "I'm afraid you'll have to take the gifts back, but you could do a favor for me." She pointed to the two trunks filled with draperies she had finished several days ago. "I've finished sewing the draperies for Captain Hayes. Could you put them in the sleigh and take them back to his estate with you?"

"I surely could if I had a bigger sleigh, but these packages take up just about all the room I've got."

Convinced that was exactly what Thomas had intended in order to make sure she accepted his gifts, she took the packages and set them on top of her sewing table. "We can leave these here. For now. I'm sure if you load the trunks in first, there'll be room enough. I'll help you—"

His dark eyes twinkled. "I'll take the trunks. I'll even take the gifts back. If you read his message first."

Sarah raised her brow. "Are you trying to get me to change my mind?"

He chuckled. "Now that's a foolish thought. A man my age knows better than to do that. Just want to know I tried my best 'fore the captain lops off my head and sets it on a spike. As a warnin' for the other staff, you see. Tough taskmaster, he is, but fair. Served with him at sea long enough to know he expects his orders to be followed to the letter. Now if I can tell him you at least read his note before you sent back his gifts, he might not—"

"Chop off your head. I see," she responded, returning his mock seriousness in kind. "I'll read his note while you load the trunks into the sleigh. I suppose I could even pen a reply begging for your reprieve."

"That'd be most generous of you, miss. Most generous," he murmured. While he hauled the first trunk to his shoulders and carried it outside, Sarah slipped out of her cape and sat down in the rocking chair. When she unfolded the note, a shadow of flames danced across his brief, but heart-rending message:

> *Attending the reception alone will be dismal, but life without you by my side in Newtown Falls will be unbearable. Marry me, Angel, and light my life. Tonight and forever.*
>
>   *Thomas*

Twines of joy and sorrow wrapped around her heart, and her love for him overflowed in tears that cascaded down her cheeks. He had battled his demons and won, but her presence in his life would only detract from his position here, unleashing notoriety that would only convince him he should have retired in seclusion as he had first planned.

Attending the reception would also require far more courage than she possessed. Traveling back and forth to town during daylight hours had been draining, but bearable.

Her downfall was too complete, her name ruined beyond repair now that Webster had spread new rumors about her, and she knew in her heart that redemption was still years away, if she ever found it at all, and she could not expect Thomas to wait for her forever.

Chance meetings with a limited number of people had given her time to refill her limited reservoir of courage before attempting another trip into town. If she accepted his invitation to attend the reception, Thomas would already be there when she arrived, alone and unescorted. When she faced all of the townspeople at the same time, they would have no idea she had been invited as Thomas's guest. She was bound to cause a stir that would make an earthquake seem mild in comparison.

Surrounded by few friends, she would have nowhere to run, nowhere to hide, if the townspeople collectively shunned her. She could not bring her shame to Thomas and expect him to shoulder her scandal and survive unscathed. He was only one man pitted against an entire town so convinced of her guilt they could not be expected to listen, even to a hero like him.

Unless . . . unless she found the wherewithal to attend and face her accusers on her own, matching the courage Thomas possessed to stand and fight for his place in the public world, reconciling the nightmare of his exploits during the war with his acclaim as a hero instead of simply escaping into a world of his own.

Dignity would be her only shield against gossip and injustice, but love would be her guide, and Thomas, her beloved inspiration, if she dared to reach out and claim his love.

By nine o'clock, Thomas had accepted defeat. Sarah was not coming. Despite his note. Despite his gifts. Despite his fervent belief that she had courage enough to challenge an entire town, accept his proposal, and forever light his world with her presence.

With his disappointment hidden beneath a practiced smile, he tolerated endless introductions, but declined to dance with the stream of young women who should have worn caps marked ''available'' instead of the frivolous lace concoctions plopped atop mounds of stiff curls and intricate braids. Even from a distance, he recognized the gowns Sarah had stitched during the blizzard, but he longed to see only one woman, his angel, dressed in the gown he had chosen for her to wear on this eventful occasion before leaving New York.

When the music stopped, an indication the customary speeches were about to begin, town officials began to assemble on the banner-draped dais. Thomas excused himself from a group of businessmen to join them, but immediately encountered two of the three women he had spoken to yesterday at the general store.

"You are a naughty one, Captain. Traveler, indeed. If I had known—"

"I should have introduced myself," he murmured, his words nearly obscured by a loud murmur of voices coming from the people crowded closest to the door. "If you'll excuse me now, ladies, I'm expected on the dais."

"Of course, but only if you promise we'll have an opportunity to continue our conversation from yesterday."

He nodded and continued on his way, but when the murmurs changed to heated discussion, he turned around. As the sea of well-wishers parted, he had a clear view of a woman standing just inside the door.

A woman dressed in a diaphanous white gown fit for an angel.

His angel.

Sarah.

His heart fairly hammered in his chest as he strode to claim her as his guest before battling the churning tide of public opinion to win redemption for the greatest love of his life.

Chapter Ten

Sarah kept her gaze on Thomas, but her heart still refused to stop pounding and her legs shook beneath her skirts. Confronted with harsh glares and a number of turned backs, she held her head high and her shoulders straight while making her way from the hall into the main reception room.

All thoughts of shame and scandal evaporated the moment she saw the love shining in his eyes, beckoning her to his side, inviting her into his life, and showering her with courage enough to take those difficult steps on her long journey to respectability.

Thomas had lined the path with added challenges, but they had been made easier because love paved the way. Even if she failed tonight, if she brought him shame instead of honor, she knew that in her heart of hearts, she had done everything in her power to earn his respect, if not his name.

Her first tenuous steps became steadier as she walked toward him, and her heart seemed to skip a beat when he took her hands and held her in place, only inches away from him.

"Angel of my heart," he murmured. "You are exquisite, as always."

Suddenly filled with doubt, she trembled. "Thomas, I'm not certain this is wise. What if—"

He silenced her with a kiss pressed to the back of her hand that sent tingles straight to her soul. "Trust me, love. I've not lost a battle yet."

"This isn't war," she whispered.

He smiled. "Ah, but it is. We shall soon both reap a

victory all the sweeter because we will be together," he promised.

Against a backdrop of startled and condemning looks that included no small measure of embarrassment at the social blunder the townspeople felt their guest was obviously making, Thomas took her arm and led her to the dais. The town officials immediately retreated, an ominous sign Thomas appeared to ignore.

He held her hand tightly and addressed the gossiping townspeople with a clear, firm voice. "Ladies and gentlemen, it appears you will be spared the customary speeches from your local officials, but I should like the opportunity to address you all. If you please."

Silence descended. A sense of expectancy kept Sarah's heart racing so fast she felt faint. Thomas's firm hold on her hand and his confidence, however, kept her steady on her feet and gave her the strength to look at the crowd without cringing.

"I am most honored to join you tonight as I begin life in my new home, but I would be remiss if I did not credit the woman responsible for my presence here tonight."

Surprise and skepticism etched the faces of every town official, but she focused instead on the encouragement she found staring back at her from her few friends.

"As you all know, it has taken months to prepare for my move to Newtown Falls. What you don't know is that I came here last month to inspect my property before finalizing my move here. To be honest, at the time I had little interest in attending this reception and hoped only to escape the demons fame entails to find peace and solitude on my estate.

"Several things happened to change my mind. The first was being fool enough to think I could battle my way through a blizzard to return to New York, only to wind up wounded and stranded far from my estate as well as the town. The second, and much more fortunate, was that Miss Sarah Bailey offered me shelter and quite literally saved my life."

A heated blush stole up her cheeks. Tears filled her eyes, and she tucked his public accolades into a heart already swollen with love and devotion for him. When she saw Webster leading Olive toward the front door, she took that as a sign Thomas had some chance to prevail against the others as the room began to buzz anew.

He held up his hand to silence the gathering once again. "Contrary to what you may have assumed about Miss Bailey, I can testify she was a model of virtue when she nursed me back to health. The scar I now carry on my forehead is not a battle wound, but testimony to her aid, and it is one I will wear for the rest of my life with pride, for there are few among us who have been touched and healed by an angel."

He paused, raked his gaze across the sea of disbelieving faces, and smiled. "Until recently, I have neither embraced recognition as a hero nor understood why success during a war that was brutally inhumane warranted admiration. People expect many things from the men they hold up as heroes. Honesty, integrity, decency, and honor. And they struggle to be people of character, too, fighting each and every day for a decent life for themselves and their families. They succeed as often as they fail. If they never give up the struggle to find peace in the midst of difficulty, then neither should I, which is something Miss Bailey kept reminding me during our brief time together. I will gladly use my influence to help any of you as Newtown Falls grows and prospers. I hope to build a good life for myself and the family I intend to raise here, with all of you as my neighbors and friends."

He turned and gazed at her with love shining in the depths of his eyes. "I could claim credit for my change of heart, but that belongs to Miss Bailey alone. She is a woman of courage and strong convictions, and she is my hero. It is to her, my future wife, that I pledge my everlasting troth, love, and respect."

Sarah caught her breath, watching and waiting for the crowd to respond to words forever etched in her heart, but

Thomas quite unexpectedly pulled her into his arms and literally kissed her breath away. Redemption of her own reputation was the very least of her thoughts. All she could think of was the remarkable man who held her crushed within his embrace. She would have followed him to the ends of the earth for the rest of her days, with or without society's approval.

Wild applause erupted. The tiny band began to play, and when Thomas finally broke their kiss and she looked out at the townspeople, she saw nothing but smiles and enthusiastic approval. "Thomas, they . . . they believe you," she sputtered.

He grinned. "Of course. I'm a hero, remember?"

"You are forever the hero of my heart," she whispered as she traced the scar on his forehead with her fingertips.

He kissed the tip of her nose and whispered into her ear. "Am I mistaken, or is the minister present tonight?"

She chuckled. "Reverend Blackwell is here. Of course."

"Lead me to him now, or I shan't be a man of honor for much longer."

"Now? Tonight?"

"Now. With the whole town here to celebrate our union before we slip away to the seclusion of our new home. I assume you have no objections if we don't see anyone for a few days."

"None," she whispered. "None at all."

TURN THE PAGE
FOR A SNEAK PREVIEW
OF BRENDA JOYCE'S
EXCITING NEW HARDCOVER,
THE THIRD HEIRESS . . .

PROLOGUE

*J*ill Gallagher could not remember a time when she wasn't alone. But eight months ago Harold Sheldon had entered her life, changing it forever. He had become her best friend and confidant as well as her lover. And now she was finally starting to forget and let go of the vague, shadowy fear and bewilderment that had been deeply imprinted upon an abandoned, lonely child so many years ago. A child whose parents were killed in a car accident when she was five. Her nights of insomnia, spent sleeplessly staring at dancing shadows upon the ceiling, filled with a fear she could not quite grasp, were finally a thing of the past.

As their rental car, a two-door Toyota, sped down the Northern State Parkway, Jill glanced at Hal sitting in the front passenger seat beside her. Her mood was more than light, it was exuberant, but her grip on the steering wheel tightened. Was something wrong? Hal was absorbed in studying the map he held, which was necessary—but he hadn't really said a word since they had left Manhattan, and that wasn't like him. Even though it was early April and unseasonably cool, they were headed for the North Shore. Jill was a professional dancer, and this would be their last chance to get away before the new show, where she was in the ensemble, opened. They had booked a room at a quaint bed-and-breakfast just steps away from the Peconic Bay. Jill was looking forward to a very quiet, intimate weekend before the grueling marathon of seven performances six days a week began. She was also looking forward to long conversations about the future they would share.

Of course, nothing could be wrong. Last week Hal had

asked her to marry him. Jill had not hesitated in accepting his proposal. And last night he had made love to her with even more passion than usual.

Jill smiled at the mere memory of his romantic proposal in a dark, closet-sized East Village restaurant. She thought about how amazing it was that a single chance encounter could change your life forever. A year ago, before meeting Hal, she had been resigned to the path of her life, to being alone.

The map rustled. The sound seemed intrusive, odd.

Jill glanced at him, her smile fading, because his expression was so set and hard to read. The Hal she knew and loved was the most amiable and carefree of people. He was always smiling. His good nature was one of the things she loved best about him—that and his passion for photography, which mirrored her passion for dance. "Hal? Is something wrong?" The tiniest inkling of dread rose up in her.

Immediately he flashed his very white smile. Although he was dark blond and British, he had a slight and perpetual tan. His family was wealthy. Upper-crust blue bloods or some such thing. His father, Jill had been told recently, was an earl. An honest-to-goodness earl. His older brother was a viscount who would one day inherit the title. Wealthy people, Jill knew, were always tanned. It was one of the facts of life.

She was going to marry an aristocrat. Her life had turned into a fairy tale. She had become Cinderella. Jill smiled to herself.

"Jill. Watch the road," Hal said tersely.

She obeyed, her smile and sense of well-being vanishing, confused because his tone was so harsh. As she concentrated on the traffic ahead, her pulse began a slow, distinct pounding. Hal said, "We need to talk."

Jill turned to stare at him in surprise. It was a moment before she could speak. "What is it?"

He looked away from her. Not meeting her eyes. "I don't want to hurt you," he said.

Jill almost swerved into the vehicle in the lane parallel

to hers. It was midafternoon and there was heavy traffic on the highway, but it was moving at a good clip, close to sixty-five miles an hour.

Her stomach flipped. Jill glanced at him, but he was staring straight ahead, out of the front window. His expression was so serious, so grim.

No, she thought, clenching the steering wheel so tightly her fingers began to cramp. He loves me and we're getting married next fall. This is not about us.

It couldn't be. She had already paid her dues. When her parents had died, Jill had been sent to an aunt in Columbus—an elderly widowed woman whose own children had long since grown up and had children of their own. Aunt Madeline had been distant, reserved, almost uncaring, and from a small child's point of view, unkind. Jill's childhood had been lonely. She'd had no real friends; ballet had been her refuge, her life. At the age of seventeen she had gone to New York City to become a dancer and she had never looked back once.

Hal's presence in her life now made her realize how lonely she had been.

Hal suddenly cleared his throat. As if he were about to deliver a prepared speech. Jill's head whipped around again, and this time she was acutely anxious. "What is it? Is someone sick in your family?" She managed a lopsided smile. "Oh, God, don't tell me. Harrelson refused your work!" Hal had been furiously showing his portfolio in the hopes of finding a gallery to hold an exhibition of his work. This particular SoHo dealer had been very enthusiastic upon their first meeting.

"No one is sick. Harrelson hasn't gotten back to me yet. Jill, I've been thinking. About what we discussed last week." This time he glanced at her briefly. His amber eyes were anguished. And he couldn't hold her gaze.

Jill gripped the wheel, focusing on the road with an effort. She was trying to recall what they had discussed last week, but it was impossible—her chestnut bangs were in her eyes and she was sweating. Her pulse interfered with her hearing—and her own thoughts. She did not like his tone—was he uneasy? There was only one subject she could remember them having discussed, but surely he was not referring to his wedding proposal now. *He was not.* "I'm not sure what we talked about—other than your asking me to marry you and my accepting." She flashed him a smile, but could not maintain it.

He leaned back against the seat, morosely. "I've had second thoughts."

Jill tried to stay calm but her pulse was rioting. She carefully slowed the car, glancing in her rearview mirror. She quickly began to get out of the left lane, a red sedan on her rear bumper. *This was not happening.* "You've had second thoughts?" She was in shock, thinking, I am not understanding him. "You don't mean about us marrying?" Her smile felt sickly.

"It's not about you," Hal said, his tone miserable. "My feelings for you haven't changed."

Oh, God. He was referring to their marriage. Jill remained in a state of disbelief, her mind seemed to be shutting down, refusing to function, refusing to assimilate what he was saying. She was staring at him. "I don't understand. You love me. I love you. It's that simple."

He seemed uncomfortable. He avoided looking at her directly. "My feelings for you haven't changed. But I keep thinking . . ."

"What?!" Jill's tone was harsh, a whiplash. *This could not be happening!*

But then, hadn't she expected this—on some deep, instinctive level? Because hadn't their love been too good to be true?

He faced her. "I don't want to live in New York for the rest of my life. I miss my family, I miss London. I miss the summer house in Yorkshire."

Jill could not believe her ears. Her hands were sweating as she clutched the wheel. Her white T-shirt stuck to her skin like wet glue. "Have we ever said we'd live in New York forever?" she asked hoarsely, trying to focus on the traffic ahead, but not really seeing anything. Her pulse had become deafening in her own ears.

"If this show is a hit, it could run on Broadway for years. Don't tell me you'd leave in the midst of a smashing success. You've never had this kind of opportunity before."

Jill wanted *The Mask* to be a huge success, and she believed it would be, and until recently, her career had been the mainstay of her life, but she thought, speechlessly, Yes, I would leave, if it meant losing you. She remained silent.

Hal was also silent.

"Are you telling me that you've changed your mind?" she finally managed.

"No. I'm not sure what to do. I think we need to slow down. I think I should go home for a while and think things through."

Jill inhaled, feeling as if he'd delivered a fatal blow. She was aware now of how her limbs trembled, of a terrible sickness inside her—as if she might throw up. She turned and stared at his perfect profile, aware now of an immense pain, a heavy, dread weight in her chest. And tears filled her eyes.

Good night, pumpkin. The voice was deep, a man's. Daddy. His lips touched her hair. His hand smoothed through her bangs. *Sleep tight. We'll be home soon. By the time you wake up.*

His smile was there, shadowy, loving.

Good night, darling. A woman's soft, loving voice, her mother's slender, graceful silhouette in the doorway of her pink and white bedroom.

The door closing.

Darkness.

Silence.

Terror. Being alone—forever.

Because they had never come back.

"Jill!" Hal shouted.

Jill jerked her gaze to the road. To her horror, a huge pine tree was looming toward them as their car hurled toward it. Jill wrenched at the steering wheel, already knowing that it was too late . . .

Nothing in her life could have prepared her for the moment of impact. Her heart stopped. Simultaneously, Jill's entire body was snapped against her seat harness and an air bag. The vehicle, a mass of steel and fiberglass, thundered and screamed and exploded in the head-on collision. Glass shattered everywhere. Pieces of it rained down on Jill's hair and bare arms, her thighs.

And then there was absolute stillness, absolute silence.

Except for the booming sound of Jill's heart.

Her mind came to, slowly, with dread. Her heart seemed to hurt her as it pulsed inside of her chest. Jill's body felt as if it had been snapped in half; it felt crushed. She could not move, she could not breathe. Her mind was blank with shock.

An accident . . .

And then she felt the trickle of liquid down the side of her face as her lungs took in air, as her lids slowly lifted. She did not have to see it or taste it to know that it was blood—that it was her blood.

She was breathing, she was alive, they had hit a tree— oh, God.

Jill opened her eyes and saw the shattered windshield. Her side of the car was quite literally wrapped around the tree; Hal's side of the car was folded in on itself like an accordion.

Hal.

Jill gasped, fumbling with her seat belt, which she could not see, the air bag in her way. She pushed at the bag, so she could see Hal. Blood and sweat and her too long bangs interfered with her vision. "Hal?"

She shoved at the bag and her bangs again. Jill froze. He, too, was crushed by an air bag. But his head lolled to one side, his eyes closed.

"Hal!" Jill screamed.

She turned and pushed at her door, almost beating on it until she somehow managed to wrench the handle open.

Her head now throbbing, unable to breathe, Jill stumbled from the car. She staggered around the back of the sedan, tripping on the rough ground, on rocks and sticks and dirt. At Hal's door, she froze again. Blood was gushing from his neck where glass from the windshield had apparently cut a jagged hole in his throat.

"No!" Jill wrenched at his door and it flew open. Frantically, she found and unbuckled his seat belt.

Jill put her arms around him and dragged him from the car. Blood continued to stream from his neck; the front of his shirt was turning crimson. When he was on the ground, she pressed both hands against the wound, desperately trying to staunch the flow of blood. It was warm and wet and sticky, seeping through her fingers. "Help!" she screamed at the top of her lungs. "Help! Help us, please!"

She sobbed, her gaze on his deathly white face. Then she saw his lashes flutter—he was alive!

"Don't die!" she cried, pushing at his wound, the blood spreading and spreading—endlessly. "Hal, help is coming, don't die—hang on!"

His eyes opened. When he spoke, his mouth filled with blood. "I love you," he said.

"No!" Jill shrieked.

And then he said, his eyes closing, "Kate."

PART ONE

THE LOVERS

ONE

Who was Kate?

Jill inhaled. Tears slipped from beneath her closed lids. Hal was dead and she was standing by the carousel at Baggage Claim in Heathrow Airport. It was almost impossible to believe where she was and, more importantly, why she was there. Jill was numb. Exhaustion, most of it emotional, some of it due to jet lag, did not help. Hal was dead, and she was bringing his body home to his family. The emptiness inside her, the pain, the grief, was astonishing in its intensity, and it was overwhelming.

Hal was dead. Gone, forever. She would never see him again.

And she had killed him.

It was the worst she could have imagined, a nightmare come true. She did not know if she could stand the pain and the confusion—and herself—much longer.

She did not know if she could stand the darkness much longer.

I love you . . . Kate.

Hal's voice, his dying words, pierced through her thoughts, her mind. It was a haunting litany she could not shake. Who was Kate?

Jill jerked. The baggage from the British Airways flight was beginning to come down the ramp, thumping onto the carousel, going round and round, like her own spinning thoughts. Hal's image as he died under the ministrations of a team of paramedics there on the side of the highway was engraved upon her mind. As were his last, haunting words, echoing cruelly, again and again. Words she never wanted to forget—words she never wanted to remember. "*I love you . . . Kate.*"

Jill hugged herself, cold and shivering. The luggage circling in front of her blurred. Jill knew, she absolutely knew, that he had been telling her, Jill, that he loved her as he died. He had loved her—the way she had loved him. Jill had not a doubt. And she knew she must seize on to and cherish this belief. But dear God, his death, and her hand in it, his speaking of this other woman, Kate, it was all horrible enough without their having had that last and final, irreversible, unforgettable exchange. If only he hadn't told her he had been having second thoughts about their future. He'd been having doubts about them, about her. Jill choked on a sob. She was in the throes of guilt and pain, grief and confusion.

Jill closed her eyes. She must not think about that conversation, it was unbearable. Everything was unbearable. Hal had been taken away from her. Just like her parents. Her love, her life, had been destroyed—a second time.

Suddenly Jill's world became too painful to bear. Blackness gathered before her eyes. Jill fought the urge to pass out, to faint. She must stop thinking, she told herself desperately, aware of tears streaming down her face, aware of the crowded terminal coming into and then out of focus. She fought for equilibrium as she swayed, her knees weak and buckling. She had to get her luggage. She had to get out of there—she had to get air. She must concentrate on the details of survival—and on meeting Hal's family, dear God. Hal's sister, Lauren, was picking her up at the airport.

And in that moment, Jill's mind went suddenly, frighteningly, blank.

For one instant, she was utterly confused. She was panic-stricken. She did not know where she was, or why. She did not know who she was. The crowd moving around her, the interior of the terminal, became more than a sea of shadows and faces. She could not identify anything or anyone. Even the letters on the signs became gibberish she could not read.

But everywhere there were pairs of eyes. Turning her way, wide and accusing, myriad hostile stares.

Why was everyone looking at her as if they wished she were dead? Jill was ready to turn and run, but run where?

Dead.

In the next moment, her mind snapped to, the shadows became walls and doorways, gates and railings, the shapes became people, the eyes, faces, and she knew everything and it was so much worse. People were staring at her, but she was crying helplessly, and she was at Heathrow, bringing Hal's body home to his family—tomorrow was the funeral. Did everyone present know that she had killed the man of her dreams? Jill wished she hadn't remembered anything. There had been bliss in the memory loss.

It had been like that ever since Hal had died—not knowing what to do, moments of terrible confusion, followed by other moments of sheer memory loss and then absolute, horrific recognition. Shock, a doctor had said. She would be in shock for the next few days, maybe even the next few weeks. He had encouraged her to rest at home and continue taking the medication he had prescribed.

Jill had thrown the antidepressants down the toilet after the first night. She had loved Hal so much and she would not sell her feelings short by trying to blunt or ignore them with Xanax. She would grieve for him the way that she had loved him, completely, irrevocably.

Jill removed her sunglasses to wipe her eyes with a tissue before replacing them. Her luggage. She had to find her single duffel bag and get out of there while she remained on her feet and in one piece. The one thing she must now do, Jill decided, was try not to think.

Her thoughts were her own worst enemy.

Jill glanced down at her feet, to find her carry-on and leopard-print vinyl tote there, along with her oversized black blazer. She turned her gaze to the carousel. To her surprise, most of the bags had been claimed. It seemed like only seconds ago she had been surrounded by the hundreds of passengers from her flight—now only a dozen people or so were waiting for their bags. Jill inhaled desperately. Had she blacked out? Somehow, she seemed to have lost time as well as her memory.

She wondered how she was going to survive, not just the next few days, but the next few weeks, months, years.

Don't think! Jill told herself frantically. She must not go where her thoughts would lead. Suddenly Jill saw her black nylon duffel bag. It was already moving past her. Jill ran after it with desperation, gripping the handle and swinging it off of the carousel. The effort cost her dearly, and she stood there for a moment, panting. She had never experienced this kind of monumental exhaustion before.

When she had regained her breath, she glanced around at the milling crowd. Now where did she go? Now what did she do? How would she find Lauren, whom she had only glimpsed in a photograph?

Jill was frozen, against her own admonitions helplessly thinking of the time Hal had so fondly and proudly showed her photos of his family. Hal had spoken often, not just of his sister, but also of his older brother, Thomas, his parents, and his American cousin. His family was, by his accounts, extremely close-knit. His love for them had been so obvious. He had glowed when he had told her tales of growing up as a child, most of them describing the summers in Staines-more at the old family estate in the north, where as children they fished and hunted and explored the nearby haunted manor. But there had been Christmas holidays at St. Moritz, Easter in St. Tropez, and those years at Eton, playing hooky and running wild in London's West End, chasing "birds" as he called the girls, and sneaking into clubs. Then there had been his football years at Cambridge. And always, since he was a small boy, there had been his first love, his true love, his photography.

Jill knew she was crying again. He had held her close on so many nights, telling her how his family would adore her—and that they would welcome her with open arms, as if she were one of them. He had been eager to bring her home, he could not wait for her to meet them. Until that unbelievable and final conversation of theirs in the car, when he had told her he wasn't sure he really wanted to get married after all, that he wanted to go home for a while, alone.

Jill knew she must not cry again, but the tears would not stop. Shaking and weak and afraid of blacking out another time, Jill picked up her bags and started walking slowly with the crowd. She must forget about their last conversation. It was the icing on the cake, incapacitating her with bewilderment and confusion. In time, they would have worked things out. Hal would not have walked out on her. Jill knew she had to believe that.

Jill followed the crowd through a barricade where Customs officials watched them go by, relieved at least that for the moment her tears had ceased. She was about to meet Lauren and the rest of Hal's family, and never in a million years would she have dreamed that it would be this way, with her bringing Hal's body home for the funeral. She wanted, desperately, to be in control of her physical functions. She did not want to black out in front of them.

She paused as she reached a circular area where a crowd was waiting for the arriving passengers, some of them drivers holding up signs with names written boldly upon them. And Jill's gaze immediately settled on a tawny-haired woman about her own age. Jill recognized the other woman instantly. Even if Jill had not seen photographs of Lauren, she would have recognized her because she looked so much like Hal. Her shoulder-length hair was the same dark blond, spiked with lighter strands of gold, and her features were also classic. Like Hal, she was tall and slim. Lauren had that very same look of casual elegance and worry-free wealth that had nothing to do with the designer pants suit she wore but everything to do with her actual heritage—it was an aura only those born to old money can have.

Jill faltered, unable to continue forward. Suddenly she was deathly afraid to meet the other woman.

Lauren had spotted her, too. She was also motionless,

and she was staring. Like Jill, she wore dark glasses. But hers were tortoiseshell and oversized, matching her beige Armani suit and Hermes scarf perfectly. She did not smile at Jill. Her face was stiff and set in an expression of . . . what? Self-control? Suffering? Distaste? Jill could not tell.

But she was taken aback and dismayed. Gripping both her canvas duffel bag and her carry-on, as well as her leopard-print vinyl tote, aware now of wearing faded Levi's and a white T-shirt, Jill walked slowly toward Hal's sister. "Lauren Sheldon?" She could not meet her gaze even through the dark glasses that they both wore.

Lauren nodded, a single jerk of her head, turning her face aside.

Jill swallowed the lump that was choking her. "I'm Jill Gallagher."

Lauren had folded her arms across her chest. Her shoulder bag seemed to be dark brown alligator. A gold and diamond Piaget watch glinted from beneath the cuff of her suit jacket. "I have a driver outside. We've already picked up the coffin. Because of the Easter holiday, we couldn't find you a decent room and you'll be staying at the house." She turned and began walking rapidly out of the airport.

For one moment Jill stared after her, trembling, in disbelief. The woman had not said hello, or asked her how her flight was. Hal had said that Lauren was kind and compassionate and more than friendly. This woman was cold and aloof, and not even civil.

But what did she expect? She had been at the wheel, and now Hal was dead. Lauren must hate her—the entire Sheldon family must hate her. She hated herself.

Far more ill than before, filled now with an accompanying dread, Jill followed Lauren out of the terminal, her mind going blank again.

Jill shifted so that she could see the highway behind her. She was in the backseat of a chauffeured Rolls-Royce, as was Lauren. Both women had taken to the farthest and opposite corners of the spacious sedan. The hearse was behind them. Jill watched it make a left turn. She continued to watch the long black sedan as it disappeared from sight. It was taking Hal's body to the funeral home, while she and Lauren were going to the Sheldons' house in London.

Jill did not want to be separated from the hearse. She almost felt like banging on the door, demanding to be let out. Her heart was thundering in her chest, and her sense of loss was, amazingly, worse. It was insane. Jill continued to stare after the disappearing hearse. She bit down hard on her lip, determined not to make a sound. She was shaking uncontrollably and afraid she might once again escape her grief by blacking out.

Jill forced herself to settle back in her seat and breathe deeply, her eyes closed, continuing to shake as she fought for equilibrium. She was not even going to make it through the next twenty-four hours if she did not somehow come to grips with herself and Hal's death. When she had regained a small amount of her composure, she glanced at Lauren. In the thirty minutes since they had left the airport, Hal's sister had not said a single word. She sat with her back toward Jill, her shoulders rigid, staring out of her driver's side window. She had not removed her sunglasses, but then, neither had Jill. They were like two hostile zombies, Jill thought grimly.

So much for kindness. They could comfort one another. After all, they had both loved Hal. But Jill did not feel up to making the first overture, not yet, and she was too aware of her role in his death. Tears burned her eyes. The funeral was tomorrow. She was booked to return home the following night. She hated the thought of leaving him behind, an entire ocean between them, yet on the other hand, if the Sheldons were all as compassionate as Lauren, it was for the best.

She opened her carry-on, a huge fake Louis Vuitton bag that she had bought for fifteen dollars from a street vendor, and searched for and found a Kleenex. She dabbed at her eyes. Lauren hated her. Jill was certain of it. She could actually feel the other woman's simmering resentment.

Jill did not blame her.

When Jill tucked the tissue back in her bag she looked up and found Lauren watching her, facing her directly for the first time.

Jill did not think. Impulsively she said, low, "I'm sorry."

Lauren said, "We're all sorry."

Jill bit her lip. "It was an accident."

Lauren continued to face her. Jill could not see her eyes through the opaque sunglasses she wore. "Why did you come?"

Jill was startled. "I had to bring him home. He spoke of you—all of you—so often." She could not continue.

Lauren looked away. Another silence fell.

"I loved him, too," Jill heard herself say.

Lauren turned to her. "He should be alive. A few days ago he was alive. I can't believe he's gone." Her words were angry and had she pointed her finger at Jill, the blame she felt could not have been more obvious.

"Neither can I," Jill whispered miserably. It was true. In the middle of the night she would wake up, expecting to find the solid warmth of Hal's body beside her. The coldness of her bed was a shock—as was the sudden recollection of his death. There was nothing worse, Jill had realized, than the oblivion of sleep followed by the absolute cognition of consciousness. "If only," Jill whispered, more to herself than to Lauren, "we hadn't gone away that weekend."

But they had. And she could not change the past few days, she could only have regrets. She would have regrets for the rest of her life—regrets and guilt.

Had he really been thinking of breaking up with her?

"Hal should have come home months ago," Lauren said tersely, interrupting Jill's thoughts. "He was scheduled to come home in February—for my birthday."

"He liked New York," Jill managed, avoiding her eyes.

Lauren removed her glasses, revealing red-rimmed eyes that were the exact same amber shade as Hal's. "He was homesick. The last few times we spoke, he told me so."

Jill was motionless. What else had he told his younger sister, whom he was so close to?

Jill thought she would die if Lauren knew about Hal's sudden change of heart about their future.

Then, angrily, she reminded herself that it had not been a change of heart. Nothing had been set in stone. Everything would have worked out, sooner rather than later.

Lauren also remained unmoving. Finally she said, "He mentioned you."

Jill jerked, eyes wide, staring now at Lauren as if she were a Martian. He had *mentioned* her? "What do you mean, he mentioned me?"

"Just that," Lauren said, putting her glasses back on. She glanced out of her window as the silver-gray Rolls sped along. "He mentioned that he was dating you."

Jill stared, stunned. They had not been dating. They had been discussing marriage—they had been on the verge of becoming engaged. She was speechless.

"How long were the two of you seeing one another?" Lauren asked bluntly.

Jill looked at her, the other woman becoming hazy and blurred. "Eight months. We met eight months ago." She was gripping the sensuous leather seat with desperation.

"That isn't a very long time," Lauren said after a pause.

"It was long enough to fall head over heels in love and to be thinking about . . ." Jill stopped herself short.

Lauren removed her eyeglasses again. "To be thinking about what?" she demanded.

Jill wet her lips. She hesitated. Everything raced through her mind—his ambivalence, her guilt, a woman named Kate. "The future," she whispered.

Lauren just stared—as if she had two heads. "He should have come home a long time ago," Lauren said finally. "He did not belong in New York."

Jill did not know how to respond. Hal had not told his sister about the extent of his relationship with her. Why? It hurt. God, it hurt, the way thinking about their last conversation hurt—the way he had hurt her by even having doubts about their future as man and wife. She lay back against the seat, severely exhausted. It hurt almost as much as his death hurt.

She needed to find a sanctuary and bury her head under a pillow and sleep. But then she would wake up and remember everything and it would be so awful . . .

The Rolls-Royce stopped.

Instantly Jill's tension increased. The Sheldon family home was now the last place she wished to be, because if Lauren's reception was any indication of the way Hal's family would greet her, then she was not ready to meet them, not now, not ever.

They were on a busy, two-way street in the midst of London, Jill realized. The driver was waiting to make a right-hand turn across the lane of oncoming traffic. Tall iron gates were open, but the road they wished to turn onto was barred by a mechanical barricade and a uniformed security guard. Jill wet her lips. Past the barricade, she glimpsed a shady, tree-lined street of huge stone mansions.

The Rolls crossed the road, the barrier was lifted without their even slowing, the officer on duty inside of a small security booth waving them on. Jill craned her neck as the Rolls rolled up the asphalt street, viewing palatial home after palatial home. A park seemed to be behind the homes on her right.

Jill wanted to ask where they were. She did not.

The Rolls turned into a circular driveway on one of the street's largest mansions and halted in the graveled drive before the house. Jill thought she could feel her blood pressure rocketing.

"We're here." Lauren stepped out of the car without waiting for the chauffeur to assist her. Jill could not move as quickly. The gentleman opened the door for her and Jill stumbled out. It had started to drizzle.

Jill did not move. The fine mist settling on her hair and shoulders, she stared at the house where Hal had been raised as Lauren hurried up the wide and imposing front steps. Two sitting lions, carved in stone, guarded those front steps.

For one moment, Jill was completely taken aback.

Hal had talked about his family's London home with pride. Hal had mentioned, oh-so-casually, that the house, built around the turn of the century, had about twenty-five rooms and one of London's most spectacular rose gardens. It was not the family's original London home, which had been built in Georgian times and was part of the National Trust. Jill had vaguely gathered that Uxbridge Hall, which was somewhere just outside of central London, was open to the public, although the family kept private apartments there as well.

Jill stared up at the city dwelling. She had expected opulence, yet she was taken aback now that she was actually confronted with the reality and the extent of it. The house was built of a medium-hued sand-colored stone and was three stories high—but the first two floors clearly had double ceilings. Thick columns supported a temple pediment over the oversized front door, and the numerous arched windows also boasted smaller pediments and intricate stone engravings. There were iron balconies on the second floor and the high, sloping roofs sported a jumble of chimneys. The stonework itself was amazing. Painstaking detail had gone into every cornice and molding. The house was surrounded by manicured lawns and blooming rose gardens; a wrought-iron fence circled the perimeter of the entire property, undoubtedly to keep the public out.

"God," Jill heard herself say. In spite of all the conversations she'd had with Hal, she could hardly believe that he had been raised in this house. And this was just their city home, not even their ancestral home, which Jill suspected was even larger and grander. She was suddenly aware of how small and shabby her own studio in the Village was. She suddenly wished she were not wearing her oldest, favorite, and most faded Levi's.

If Lauren heard her, she gave no sign, for she was already pushing open the heavy front door.

"I shall bring your bags, madam," the driver said behind her.

Jill hoped she smiled at him, thought she failed, and slowly followed in Lauren's wake. She found herself in a large entry hall with high ceilings and polished beige and white marble floors. Works of art hung on the walls, and the bench, marble-topped table, and mirror were all exquisitely gilded. Jill was grim. She was acutely aware of not belonging there.

Jill glanced down at her worn Levi's, and the black blazer she had put on in the air-conditioned car. The jacket was actually a man's sports jacket, but she had loved it upon sight and had bought it in a thrift store for herself. She was wearing Cole-Haan loafers, but they were very old, as soft as butter, and severely scuffed. Of course, she could only wear soft, broken-in shoes when she was not dancing because of the pain and damage her profession caused her feet.

She hesitated, afraid now to follow Lauren, feeling horribly out of place, wishing she had worn a suit like Lauren's. She didn't even remember dressing for the trip abroad. She had not a clue about what was in her duffel bag. If she was lucky, KC, her best friend and neighbor, had helped her pack, but Jill didn't remember even speaking to KC in the past few days. Suddenly she was worried about her cat, Ezekial. She would have to call KC immediately and make sure she was taking care of the tom.

Jill's gaze settled on a painting that took up an entire wall. It had to be a masterpiece, and it was depicting some kind of mythological scene that she was not familiar with. She swallowed, telling herself to take deep, steady breaths. She would meet his family, be polite. Surely they would be civil in return—unlike Lauren. In a few moments she would be shown to her room. It could not be too soon.

If only she were staying in a hotel.

Her anxiety had gotten to the point where she was ready to make a mad dash back out the front door. Jill glanced over her shoulder. The front door was solidly closed.

Her panic began mounting slowly, steadily.

Jill told herself that everything would be all right. To keep breathing deeply.

Hal's image, as he lay dying in her arms, his face starkly white, his mouth spouting blood, filled her mind.

Footsteps sounded. Jill tried to still her trembling hands and smile as Lauren reappeared. She had removed her jacket, revealing a beige silk T-shirt that probably cost more than all of the clothing upon Jill's body. "Come," she said.

Jill followed, filled with trepidation, Lauren led her into a large living room, far more lavish than the foyer. But Jill hardly glimpsed the faded but stunning Oriental rugs and the antique furnishings or the Matisse hanging on one wall. Three men were standing in the center of the room, one elderly and white-haired, the two other men younger, in their thirties, one golden and tanned, the other dark-haired and olive-skinned. Each man was holding a drink.

Lauren stopped, as did Jill. The three men turned. As one, they all stared at Jill.

Three pairs of penetrating eyes. Three pairs of accusing gazes.

This was Hal's family.

Jill knew she was facing William, Hal's elderly father, and his older brother, Thomas, and his cousin, Alex. She did not know who each of the younger men was, although she suspected Thomas was the blond. But at that moment, she could take it no more. For their stares did not relent. Their hostility was unmistakable. But then, she had been the one driving . . .

"Some time to think . . . I love you . . . Kate."

Jill tried to clear her head. She could not. Lauren was saying something, but her tone was as cold, as unfriendly, as the regards leveled at her. Those accusing, cold, hostile stares . . . Jill watched the figures before her begin to waver and blur. Hal's ghostly white face, the blood . . . She had been driving . . . The room had dimmed, and now it lightened, and then dimmed again. And then absolute darkness came.

It was a blessing.

GET $4 OFF BRENDA JOYCE'S NEW HARDCOVER!

Send in this coupon, along with your store receipt for the purchase of PERFECT SECRETS in paperback and Brenda Joyce's new hardcover THE THIRD HEIRESS, to receive a $4.00 rebate.

From the *New York Times* bestselling author comes a sizzling contemporary novel of romantic suspense and obsession you won't be able to put down.

To receive your $4.00 rebate, please send this form, along with your original dated cash register receipt(s) showing the price for purchase of both the paperback edition of PERFECT SECRETS and the hardcover edition of THE THIRD HEIRESS, to: St. Martin's Paperbacks, Dept. EM, Suite 1500, 175 Fifth Avenue, New York, NY 10010.

Name:
Address:
City:
State/Zip:

Coupon and receipt(s) must be received by October 31, 1999. Offer expires October 31, 1999. Purchases may be made separately. One rebate per person, address or family. U.S. residents only. Allow 6–8 weeks for delivery of your rebate. St. Martin's Paperbacks is not responsible for late, lost or misdirected mail. Void where prohibited.

St. Martin's Paperbacks

Survey

TELL US WHAT YOU THINK AND YOU COULD WIN

A YEAR OF ROMANCE!
(That's 12 books!)

Fill out the survey below, send it back to us, and you'll be eligible to win a year's worth of romance novels. That's one book a month for a year—from St. Martin's Paperbacks.

Name ___ANA M. PEREZ___
Street Address ___960 NW 132nd AVE W.___
City, State, Zip Code ___MIAMI, FL 33182___
Email address ~~AXP~~ ___JFERN@BellSouth.NET___

1. How many romance books have you bought in the last year?
   (Check one.)
   ___0-3
   ___4-7
   ___8-12
   ___13-20
   ✓20 or more

2. Where do you MOST often buy books? *(limit to two choices)*
   ___Independent bookstore
   ___Chain stores *(Please specify)*
      ✓Barnes and Noble
      ___B. Dalton
      ___Books-a-Million
      ___Borders
      ___Crown
      ___Lauriat's
      ___Media Play
      ___Waldenbooks
   ___Supermarket
   ___Department store *(Please specify)*
      ___Caldòr
      ___Target
      ✓Kmart
      ___Walmart
   ___Pharmacy/Drug store
   ___Warehouse Club
   ___Airport

3. Which of the following promotions would MOST influence your decision to purchase a ROMANCE paperback? *(Check one.)*
      ___Discount coupon

    ☑ Free preview of the first chapter
    __Second book at half price
    __Contribution to charity
    __Sweepstakes or contest

4. Which promotions would LEAST influence your decision to purchase a ROMANCE book? (Check one.)
    __Discount coupon
    __Free preview of the first chapter
    __Second book at half price
    ☑ Contribution to charity
    __Sweepstakes or contest

5. When a new ROMANCE paperback is released, what is MOST influential in your finding out about the book and in helping you to decide to buy the book? (Check one.)
    __TV advertisement
    __Radio advertisement
    __Print advertising in newspaper or magazine
    __Book review in newspaper or magazine
    __Author interview in newspaper or magazine
    __Author interview on radio
    __Author appearance on TV
    __Personal appearance by author at bookstore
    __In-store publicity (poster, flyer, floor display, etc.)
    __Online promotion (author feature, banner advertising, giveaway)
    __Word of Mouth
    ☑ Other (please specify) ON-LINE BOOK REVIEW

6. Have you ever purchased a book online?
    __Yes
    ☑ No

7. Have you visited our website?
    __Yes
    ☑ No

8. Would you visit our website in the future to find out about new releases or author interviews?
    ☑ Yes
    __No

9. What publication do you read most?
    __Newspapers (*check one*)
        __*USA Today*
        __*New York Times*
        __Your local newspaper
    __Magazines (*check one*)

__*People*
__*Entertainment Weekly*
✔Women's magazine *(Please specify:* VICTORIA _____)
__*Romantic Times*
__Romance newsletters

10. What type of TV program do you watch most? *(Check one.)*
    ✔Morning News Programs (ie. "Today Show")
      (Please specify: ABC - ~~~~) GMA
    __Afternoon Talk Shows (ie. "Oprah")
      (Please specify: _____)
    __All news (such as CNN)
    __Soap operas   *(Please specify:* _____)
    __Lifetime cable station
    __E! cable station
    __Evening magazine programs (ie. "Entertainment Tonight")
      (Please specify: _____)
    __Your local news

11. What radio stations do you listen to most? *(Check one.)*
    __Talk Radio
    ✔Easy Listening/Classical
    __Top 40
    __Country
    __Rock
    __Lite rock/Adult contemporary
    __CBS radio network
    __National Public Radio
    __WESTWOOD ONE radio network

12. What time of day do you listen to the radio MOST?
    ✔6am-10am
    ✔10am-noon
    ✔Noon-4pm
    ✔4pm-7pm
    __7pm-10pm
    __10pm-midnight
    __Midnight-6am

13. Would you like to receive email announcing new releases and special promotions?
    ✔Yes
    __No

14. Would you like to receive postcards announcing new releases and special promotions?
    ✔Yes
    __No

15. Who is your favorite romance author? _____

WIN A YEAR OF ROMANCE FROM SMP
(That's 12 Books!)
No Purchase Necessary

OFFICIAL RULES

1. To Enter: Complete the Official Entry Form and Survey and mail it to: Win a Year of Romance from SMP Sweepstakes, c/o St. Martin's Paperbacks, 175 Fifth Avenue, Suite 1615, New York, NY 10010-7848, Attention JP. For a copy of the Official Entry Form and Survey, send a self-addressed, stamped envelope to: Entry Form/Survey, c/o St. Martin's Paperbacks at the address stated above. Entries with the completed surveys must be received by February 1, 2000 (February 22, 2000 for entry forms requested by mail). Limit one entry per person. No mechanically reproduced or illegible entries accepted. Not responsible for lost, misdirected, mutilated or late entries.

2. Random Drawing. Winner will be determined in a random drawing to be held on or about March 1, 2000 from all eligible entries received. Odds of winning depend on the number of eligible entries received. Potential winner will be notified by mail on or about March 22, 2000 and will be asked to execute and return an Affidavit of Eligibility/Release/Prize Acceptance Form within fourteen (14) days of attempted notification. Non-compliance within this time may result in disqualification and the selection of an alternate winner. Return of any prize/prize notification as undeliverable will result in disqualification and an alternate winner will be selected.

3. Prize and approximate Retail Value: Winner will receive a copy of a different romance novel each month from April 2000 through March 2001. Approximate retail value $84.00 (U.S. dollars).

4. Eligibility. Open to U.S. and Canadian residents (excluding residents of the province of Quebec) who are 18 at the time of entry. Employees of St. Martin's and its parent, affiliates and subsidiaries, its and their directors, officers and agents, and their immediate families or those living in the same household, are ineligible to enter. Potential Canadian winners will be required to correctly answer a time-limited arithmetic skill question by mail. Void in Puerto Rico and wherever else prohibited by law.

5. General Conditions: Winner is responsible for all federal, state and local taxes. No substitution or cash redemption of prize permitted by winner. Prize is not transferable. Acceptance of prize constitutes permission to use the winner's name, photograph and likeness for purposes of advertising and promotion without additional compensation or permission, unless prohibited by law.

6. All entries become the property of sponsor, and will not be returned. By participating in this sweepstakes, entrants agree to be bound by these official rules and the decision of the judges, which are final in all respects.

7. For the name of the winner, available after March 22, 2000, send by May 1, 2000 a stamped, self-addressed envelope to Winner's List, Win a Year of Romance from SMP Sweepstakes, St. Martin's Paperbacks, 175 Fifth Avenue, Suite 1615, New York, NY 10010-7848, Attention JP.